M000101868

POWER

Arca Book 3

KAREN DIEM

Copyright

Copyright © 2018 by Karen Diem. All rights reserved. No part of this publication may be reproduced, distributed, or transmitted in any form or by any means, including photocopying, recording, or other electronic or mechanical methods, without the prior written permission from the author, except in the case of brief quotations included in critical reviews and certain other noncommercial uses permitted by copyright law.

This is a work of fiction. Names, characters, businesses, places, events, and incidents are either the products of the author's imagination or are used in a fictitious manner. Any resemblance to actual persons, living or dead, or actual events is purely coincidental.

Snausages is a trademark of Del Monte Corporation. Taser is a trademark of Axon Enterprise, Inc. Batman and Superman are registered trademarks of DC Comics. Spider-Man is a registered trademark of Marvel Characters, Inc. Crock-Pot is a trademark of Sunbeam Products, Inc. Kimber is a registered trademark of Kimber of America, Inc. These and any other trademarks appearing in the book are the property of their respective owners.

Cover art by Deranged Doctor Design.

★★★

eBook version 1.01, published May 22, 2018.

First Paperback Printing: May 30, 2018.

ISBN: 978-0-9975740-5-0

To contact Karen Diem or subscribe to her newsletter, go to http://www.karendiem.com.

Dedication

Dedicated to my family, my fearless and funny beta readers, and anyone who's ever wanted a pet T-Rex.

Table of Contents

Chapter One

In retrospect, perhaps ambushing your best friend was not the best way to start a conversation... especially in a cold, sullen drizzle that brought down the chilly October temperature several additional degrees and enhanced the scent of moldy leaves and wood smoke.

Rocking on her heels, Zita Garcia fought the urge to jog in place, or better yet, set up an obstacle course using the many Halloween decorations that littered the front lawn where she stood. *A nice free running session would make the waiting much easier.* As a trickle of water snuck inside her secondhand brown bomber jacket and dribbled down her muscular back, she glanced up at Wyn beside her. "I hope you know what we're doing."

Beneath an umbrella emblazoned with the logo of an environmental organization, her best friend smiled serenely and tossed an errant chestnut ringlet over her shoulder. As Wyn moved, creamy embroidery flashed at the wrists and waist of the close-fitted navy jacket the tall, sylph-like woman wore. She adjusted the dainty matching hat, her lashes drooping over hazel eyes. "Andy will be delighted to see us, and he needs this. We've allowed him plenty of privacy to grieve the failure of his romantic relationship. Now we should remind him he has friends."

"If you say so," Zita said, not bothering to keep the dubiousness from her voice. She studied the customer's house where her other best friend had yet to emerge. After quarantine for a mysterious coma had reunited her with two buddies from her teenage years in the cancer ward, she was still getting used to the idea of having close friends. Hiding their superpowers—and the enforced proximity of the quarantine—had only cemented the bond, so now they felt as much like siblings as her two actual brothers.

Of the three ubiquitous brick home models repeated ad nauseam in the older Maryland suburb, this was the single-story rancher with the requisite big living room window and miserly twin windows flanking it. The lawn clung grimly to life, though brown streaks and the litter of unraked leaves marred the green expanse visible between plastic interpretations of Halloween monsters. To offset the narrow lots that made conversations between houses possible without stepping outside, mature trees and shrubs delineated the properties and circled all the front lawns and yards. Despite the thick concrete sound barrier wall two houses to the south, noise from the nearby highway still leaked into the neighborhood. A tangle of overgrown bushes and the odd tree lined the barrier, filling the narrow strip between it and the closest home. Wyn's car waited several houses to the north, in front of a claustrophobic park that offered a fancy, oversized interpretation of a tree fort and a place for children to play if they didn't mind running a mere fifty feet in any direction.

Before they could say any more, Andy emerged from the kitchen door of the house carrying a black trash bag and wearing a rain poncho over wrinkled coveralls and a downtrodden expression. Little blue plastic booties on his feet squished and splashed as he approached and dropped the bag in the can. His mood and footwear did not change his normal smooth, balanced glide, the hallmark of an accomplished martial artist. He banged the lid on and trudged over where his dad's work van had been parked at the curb. Confusion crossed his face as he searched for the vehicle, and his eyes widened when he caught sight of the two women. "What are you two doing at a job site?"

"Remember, I invited you to eat with us?" Wyn said. She smiled sweeter than the tea she favored. "You never said no, so we came to take you to lunch. Shall we be on our way before Zita becomes an ice cube?"

"I am freezing my cute little brown culo off," Zita admitted, as icy rain dripped from the soaked hood of the fluorescent orange sweatshirt she had layered beneath her jacket. She glared overhead, and water spat in her face, proving the *clear and sunny* forecast a lie. *The eternal rain that has been plaguing Anne Arundel County this past month better not have spread to Prince George's County. I'm not ready to put my motorcycle away for the winter yet, and usually Maryland's okay for another month.*

Almost automatically, Andy shot back, "You can't freeze off what you don't have."

"Sure feels like I can, and if I pretend long enough, maybe I'll grow an ass someday," Zita said, cheering up at his response. *If he's feeling up to harassing me, he could be coming out of the funk he's been in since New York. It has been a whole month after all.*

"You keep telling yourself that," he grumbled, but the corner of Andy's mouth tilted up.

Her tone gentler than her words, Wyn took his side. "You'd need to remain still for more than a minute at a time, Zita, and I'm not certain you have that capacity."

With another shiver, Zita snorted. "Haters, both of you. Sitting around is boring. I'll remain awesomely fun and interesting, thanks. Can we go drip inside Wyn's new car now? Have you seen it? It's adorable and dry, though she needs to pump up the color, but I bet the heater works good."

Wyn giggled, raising a hand to her mouth. Her umbrella had kept the worst of the drizzle off. The few drops that escaped clung to her like tiny diamonds, accenting the face and form that could have stepped from the pages of a fashion magazine. "It would have to be some garish neon combination for you to approve of the paint."

Zita waved a hand in dismissal. "Not true. You could get something cool and discreet since you're not woman enough for neon. Oye, I know! You could do a red interior, a green exterior, and toss in some subtle stripes in a lighter green on the outside. Totally sweet."

Furrowing her brow, Wyn glanced down at her. "Are you describing a car or a watermelon? Andy, we should go. As usual, it's time to feed Zita."

"Lunch would be awesome," Zita admitted. Her stomach rumbled agreement.

Andy averted his eyes. "I have to work today," he said, his expression falling flat. "Maybe we can try to meet another day for lunch. You should take Zita and go before she turns into the half-drowned kitten she resembles."

"Kitten?" Zita said, her chin jutting out. "I'm at least a full-grown cat if you're going to say that sort of thing."

"While it's commendable that you're dedicated to assisting the growth of your father's business in between teaching classes, he said he could spare you on the next appointment, so you have plenty of time to eat with us." Wyn beamed at Andy.

Zita nodded. "Since it's the last appointment before he leaves on that big cruise he's all excited about, he scheduled an easy one and doesn't need you. He said so right before he took off in his work truck."

Andy continued to stare at the puddles on the ground.

If he's going to admit that he lost his university job, now would be his chance. Wyn just thinks he's been teaching nights, and I'm so not getting involved. When Andy didn't admit anything, Zita plastered on a smile and forged ahead. "Long lunches must be a perk to being the boss' kid, am I right? I can tell you being the boss' sister doesn't get you that kind of benny. Let's get going." Unable to stand still any longer, she bounded over to him and punched his arm. Even though his invulnerability would prevent her from hurting him, she kept the hit light.

If she had had any doubts before that he had been avoiding them, they were dispelled when Andy failed to raise his gaze and rubbed the back of his neck. "I... how did you guys find me, anyway?"

Zita shrugged. "Weirdly enough, your stepmom likes me. When we showed up at your dad's place and knocked on the door, she told us where to find you. Though really, mano, you need to get the whole idea that you and I got something going on out of her head. We both know that ain't happening." She shuddered and made a face, a gesture he mirrored.

Andy groaned. "That's certainly true. Don't worry, she just doesn't know you well enough to be grateful we have nothing between us. Give her time."

Before Zita could retort, Wyn strolled over and hooked Andy's arm with her own. His plastic poncho crinkled with the movement. "So, where shall we go?" She slanted a winsome smile at him.

He narrowed brown eyes at the taller woman, ignoring Zita. "Are you certain that interpreting statements to your own benefit isn't one of your powers?"

With the quirk of an elegant eyebrow, Wyn's smile grew. "Just the witchcraft and telepathy. Don't worry. I only use my powers for good."

Something crashed, once, twice, and then multiple tires squealed on the other side of the highway noise barrier. After another boom rattled Zita's teeth, a thin plume of smoke fought its way upward from the other side of the wall.

Glancing in the direction of the crash, Zita grimaced in sympathy for whomever had been involved in the accident. *That sounds bad, especially since we're not that close to the wall.* "Given the sounds of that, we should take back roads to get to lunch."

Andy said, "I appreciate the efforts you've made to come out here, but—"

Zita missed the rest of his excuse, as a man ascended in the air, his hands glowing. Light shot down once, twice, before he swooped out of view. "Save the ahoritas for people who don't recognize excuses when they hear them. Was that Pretorius?" she said.

She rose on her tiptoes, craning her neck to see better. Zita had gotten nothing more than a glimpse of a man's form and blond hair before he dived out of sight. "Is that murdering chingado asshole back in town? If he's kidnapping people again..." Her focus on the flying man, Zita sped off in a run past a startled Andy. *I'm not letting Pretorius get away with hurting anyone else. He assisted that psycho who tortured my brother, and even now, Quentin's still not the same.*

"Wait, Zita!" Wyn cried out.

Gunfire exploded on the other side of the wall in a series of rapid bursts.

Reaching the shelter of the bushes at the base of the pebbled sound barrier, Zita stripped off most of her layers of clothing down to a tank with its built-in bra and capris. Happily, she wore the Spandex-like sportswear—made from a fabric disappeared in her animal forms but kept her clothed in human ones—beneath her regular clothes. Others seemed to assume she was crazy if she tried to talk to them while naked. She barely acknowledged the warm touch of Wyn's telepathy tying her together with her friends in what they jokingly called "party line."

Zita, you need to calm down, Wyn sent as she ran toward the wall.

Calm down, my culo. Last time we saw him, he was supervising human trafficking, a meth lab, and a psychopath's sick games. I don't know what he's doing here, but it can't be good. He'll be even harder to catch now as he must've been practicing his flying. Before, he was slower, like he was riding an invisible escalator instead of zipping around like that. She shifted to the gray feathered form of a gavião-real harpy eagle and flew to the top of the wall. Perching there, her sharp vision let her take in the busy scene.

On the other side of the sound barrier where she perched, trees crowded close to the road, leaving only a narrow strip of grass before the asphalt began. The broad expanse of a multi-lane highway stretched wide before another slim bit of green, with the east- and westbound lanes split by a long low wall of cement traffic barricades. Another high wall on the other side separated the noisy road from whatever lay beyond it.

All lanes were shut down. To the west, two electrical poles had fallen in front of an overpass, one on either side of the highway, creating an impassable barrier of snarling, snapping live wires. At the far end, to the east, a cement truck and a sixteen-wheeler heavily laden with steel rods obstructed both directions. Armed men stood behind the shelter of the trucks, peering around them with an assortment of assault rifles. Farther down, past the thugs, a pair of police cruisers attempted to block the roadway. A seething mass of vehicles turned and escaped down the vacant lanes with only slightly more finesse than those near the electrical lines.

The source of most of the noise came from the west, beyond the poles, where a long line of cars had devolved into swirling chaos. Panicked drivers tried to turn around on the narrow shoulder or battled other cars to slip through a narrow gap in the cement barrier, showing little patience or care for anyone around them. Horns yowled, people shouted, and the occasional low-speed collision added screeching and crunching to the din.

At the edges of the west side, sparks arced and played in a wide aura around the snapped lines. One forlorn and unfortunate bucket truck sat on a broken power line, dark streaks blooming with each new incandescent discharge racing over it. The original wording on the sides of the vehicle was unreadable, and nothing moved within. Sorrow for the occupants tugged at Zita before the blond man from earlier caught her attention. He drifted in the air fifteen feet above the dangerous voltage. While she couldn't make out his words over the cacophony, he held a bullhorn to his lips, and the wind carried the occasional burst of derisive laughter.

Gray crest lifting, Zita shifted on her taloned feet. *Not Pretorius after all. I don't remember his name, but he's familiar and not in a good way.*

Just outside of the sparking area, a now-shattered tree and the curious angle of a vehicle straddling two empty lanes suggested a passenger van had been driven off the roadway. It had apparently spun upon impact with the wood and bounced partially back into the street. Now, a thin line of smoke drifted up from the wrecked vehicle's engine. Something moved inside.

In the area blocked off by the trucks and downed poles, two prison transport vehicles and a pair of police cars sat near the edge of the sparking area on the opposite side of the road from the crashed van. Tires on all four vehicles sagged, the rubber visibly peeling off one. The prison vehicles had been turned as if to make a run across a gap in the center barrier and down the westbound lane. One transport's windshield was missing, and the other had starbursts of broken glass where gunfire had pierced it, splattered with a lot of blood. Cops crouched behind the engine blocks and tires of their vehicles, weapons aimed at the truck blockade.

Incongruously, between the trucks and cruisers, a panel van with the logo of a major network news station was planted in the grass, all four tires flat. While no one stood outside, the driver's side window was down, and the black, inquisitive nose of a camera poked out at the scene.

Zita swore mentally. *Seriously? No way a news crew just happened to show up and be allowed that close. Whoever's doing this must've brought them or tipped them off. You guys need to see this. The mess of prison vehicles must be the target.*

Bracing herself, she was prepared when her vision doubled, and she had the sensation of someone breathing down her neck, a sure sign that Wyn was borrowing her sight. She fidgeted on her perch and focused on what she wanted her friends to see.

At least it's not rush hour, or the mess would be even worse, and traffic copters would be everywhere overhead, Zita thought. The double vision disappeared. When their party line's warm connection resumed, the first thing she heard was Andy swearing in resignation.

From behind the cement truck, another blond man—a more familiar and hated one—threw blobs of white light at those guarding the vans. His attacks forced the men to retreat behind the prisoner transport vehicles, the only solid cover left as the escort vehicles and ground around them became riddled with holes. Gigantic and hairy, a midnight-furred wolf stalked inexorably toward the prison vans, a large, feminine satchel slung across his giant withers. Zita wasn't a fan of him either. *Oye, that evil pendejo Pretorius is here, and he brought the deranged furball Garm with him.*

Oh, lucky us, Andy sent. *How many people do you think they're planning to murder today?*

The mass murder stuff was Tiffany, and she's in jail somewhere. Zita eyed the transports and the lumpy bag the wolf shapeshifter carried, suspicion whispering a nasty possibility. *I hope.*

Zita sailed down and landed on the ground by her friends. Once she changed to her disguise form, that of the woman known as Arca, she said, "So. It's totally a bad idea, but I'm going to interfere anyway. You guys in?" She shivered a little. Even though the rain was abating, the thigh-length hair that came with this shape was becoming a heavy, wet, and very cold weight. Her sportswear kept her clothed but offered no protection for her exposed limbs. Since she'd switch back to a bird again soon, she made no move to retrieve her other garments, even if it would have been warmer, especially for her bare feet.

Wyn groaned and opened her purse.

Though the witch had never said exactly what the limits were on the items she could store in the enchanted handbag, Zita suspected it was limited more by Wyn's willingness to carry an item than anything else. *Why else would she have room for everything but that leftover kimchi I wanted to bring as a snack?* Rubbing her arms to reduce the goosebumps, she turned her face—Arca's face, one of the few differences between this body and her natural one— toward her friends.

His long face dolorous, Andy sighed. "Yeah."

"People need us," Wyn admitted. She dug through the magic bag and removed a pair of masks, embroidered gloves, and a set of plum-colored sportswear. After slipping on the gloves, she offered Andy the clothing and a mask.

Accepting the items, he retreated to the bushes. Mournfulness filled Andy's voice. "I'm going as fast as I can, but I'm pretty certain I'm getting dressed while standing in a patch of poison ivy."

A flash of olive-bronze skin from his direction had Zita averting her eyes, well aware of Andy's issues with nudity. *Prude. A body's just a body, but if he's that uncomfortable, I'll ensure he knows I'm not peeking, though I have to ask...* "Does poison ivy still give you rashes? I mean, you're pretty much immune to everything."

"With my luck, it probably still does," he replied.

Grabbing the remaining mask from Wyn's hands and slipping it on over Arca's pointy ears, Zita said, "Do you have any of those enchanted zip ties, Wyn?"

"No, we used those all up in New York. By the way, I collected your clothing and put it in my bag." Wyn tapped an amethyst pentagram pendant hanging from her neck. At the touch, her favored illusion appeared in her stead... a slim, blond woman with the icy, forbidding perfection of a carved goddess, the glittery silver and green dress of a clubgoer, and the amethyst circlet of a princess. She blinked large, purple eyes and slung her purse diagonally across her body. The oversized brown handbag now appeared as a tiny, glittering one, the sort that held an ID, a lipstick, and nothing else of any real use. With a sigh, she tucked her umbrella inside too.

Rubbing her hands together, Zita thought out loud, rocking on her feet. "So, here's what we need to do. The cops are holding off the guys with guns pretty well, but they're losing ground to the metahumans. Andy, you jump over the wall carrying Wyn and set her down somewhere safe. Then you protect her—if you need to, step in to stop Pretorius or Garm from slaughtering anyone or bringing down more electrical lines. They've got a guy hanging out in the electrical zone, the one from the video in New York—"

Her perfect memory no doubt supplying the information, Wyn interrupted. "His name is Zeus."

"Sí, that guy. We can't do much while he's there, but you throw a tree at him if he acts up, Andy. Wyn, you hang back and take out the shooters by the trucks with that handy sleep spell. Once they're not outnumbered, the cops can handle dudes with guns better than us and clean up the rest. I've got the best chance of sneaking around unnoticed, so I'll see if I can get the people in the crashed van... and any other civilians stuck in that mess to safety. Once the shooters in the trucks are out or under control, Wyn, use your shield, and I'll bring whoever I'm rescuing to you so you can heal them. The cops will shoot everything without a badge that moves, so let's try not to attract attention or approach the prison vans if we can help it. You done yet, Andy?" While she hated every millisecond of delay, Andy's regular clothes always got shredded when he fought, and he had no way to disguise himself without a mask. Allowing him time to change was a necessity.

Wyn's hands fluttered, and a furrow appeared in her brow. "Actually, the shield only works against magic and magical creatures." The illusion pitched her warm tones higher, changing it to a silvery voice like a chorus of tiny bells.

That stopped Zita. "What? You mean in New York, you went up against all those people with guns knowing they could..."

Pale, Wyn nodded. "I had hoped to never repeat the experience."

Zita shook her head. "And I'm the one with a death wish?"

Andy growled from the bushes. "This'd be so much faster if I didn't have to handle my clothes like cobwebs to avoid tearing them. Super strength was much cooler when I didn't have it."

Another crunch sounded from the other side of the wall, and when Zita glanced that way, a flash of brilliant light caught her eye. "Momentito, what's that?" She teleported to the top of the wall and crouched there.

Sirens wailing, two more police cars squeezed up the shoulder from the east, one showing a damaged headlight where it must have clipped another vehicle on the way there.

A figure emerged from the morass of panicked cars and ran toward the mess. His speed belied by his muscular frame, a man with dark skin and the peculiar grace of a boxer sprinted toward the trucks. Large, wraparound aviator shades and a ball cap hid the upper part of his face, but she recognized his body and the way he moved. *Another old friend from quarantine and the cancer ward. We need to get down there.* "Jerome's here."

Still struggling in the shrubbery with his clothes, Andy gasped. "Oh, no, he's going to get killed!"

Wyn shook her head. "No, his body heals at a remarkable rate. It has to be useful as a private detective." Unlike Zita, the only indication of her impatience was in the frequent worried glances she gave the concrete structure separating them from the highway.

With a frown, Zita eyed Wyn. "His power wasn't our secret to hand out. He must have the same idea we do about helping that we do." With an impatient grumble, she shoved the long, black strands of Arca's hair away from her face.

Her pretty face flushing a rosy color, Wyn winced. "Sorry. I don't usually keep secrets from you two, and I forgot Andy didn't know. Why don't you come down and let me fix your hair for you? Andy's was braided for work so he won't need any help."

Zita shook her head. "Never mind my hair. Work on getting those shooters to sleep. The faster the bad guys go down, the sooner we can get out of here. Andy, can you stop Pretorius before he kills someone? Ideally, we can keep everyone here alive."

Andy's answer sounded as if it came through gritted teeth. "Doing my best to finish up."

From above, a fiery, androgynous figure flew from the direction of DC and hovered in the sky. "Who dares?"

The shape and belligerent tone were both familiar. *Aideen. It must be quarantine reunion week.* "This just got way more complicated," Zita said with a groan.

Chapter Two

Zita took a deep breath and considered Wyn, keeping her eyes averted from Andy, even if she was dying to know if he was dressed yet. She hung down from the sound barrier, then dropped the rest of the way, slapping the ground to absorb some of the force as she landed. After springing to her feet, she hurried to Wyn. "If we're lucky, Jerome and Aideen will tie up Pretorius, Garm, and Sparkypants enough so the cops can take over with just a little nudge from us. Let's stick to the plan. Andy, concentrate on protecting Wyn. I'll sneak around and help the crash victims, and we can figure out what to do after that." She felt someone—probably Wyn—grab her hair and consciously stopped herself from hitting them. "Hey!"

"Zeus, not Sparkypants. No one will take us seriously if you insist on such atrocious monikers," Wyn corrected, giving Zita's hair one last tug. "I put your hair in a ponytail."

When Zita opened her mouth to comment on playing hairdresser while people needed their help, a glance at her friend's drawn face, even illusory, revealed the gentle woman's distress. *Right. She needs reassurance. Messing with my hair is better than tromping through my mind. Well, if it soothes her, I can deal since we're still waiting on Andy. I promised I'd include them and ask for help when I needed it, and I can't handle that mess on my own.* She tried to moderate the words spilling from her mouth but suspected she sounded unenthused rather than cranky. "Thanks. It'll come out when I shift, though. If Freelance, Trixie, and the bear guy show up, see if you can get them to help too. Freelance can disarm bombs."

"Who?" Andy asked. "While a doctor like Trixie would be handy to have at something like this, why would she come? Then again, why are Jerome and Aideen here?"

"SWAT Ninja Man is Freelance," Wyn said. "She renamed the mercenary that only she has seen and swears he shows up at all our biggest fights. Her theory is that he's on a team with Trixie and a bear shapeshifter."

Zita bit her tongue and leashed her annoyance, knowing her friends were equally frustrated to move so slowly toward the fight. *I made a promise not to jump in by myself if there was an option*, she reminded herself.

Andy harrumphed. Sarcasm dripped from his tone when he spoke again. "Oh, right. I remember now. The gunshots definitely couldn't have been the police and SWAT teams doing their jobs. Can we skip pretend time and just get this done?"

"He's not imaginary, and they have a way of popping up and interfering with our..." Zita paused, unsure what to call their previous forays into crime-fighting.

"With our crazed suicidal schemes?" Andy said. He stepped out of his impromptu changing room. An inside-out gray T-shirt hung down over the pseudo-Spandex pants. He handed a pile of clothes and his shoes to Wyn. His mask was already in place.

Almost simultaneously, Wyn offered, "With our self-destructive and borderline inept antics?" She grabbed the rest of his things and stuffed them into her purse.

Zita sniffed, then became a gavião-real again and launched herself into the air. Her powerful wings beat hard to bring her above the wall and into stronger air currents. *I prefer to think of them as missions. We achieved all our goals except for having Garm and Pretorius arrested.*

Wyn grudgingly agreed. *Eventually, yes, but I'm fairly certain most of that was luck.*

What she said, with a plentiful helping of fail along the way, Andy sent. His sullen silence had disappeared, and now he frowned, rubbing his hands on the side of the tight exercise pants. The cold did not seem to bother him, but the highway situation definitely had.

Hating haters, both of you. Why don't we focus on getting the party started? Zita checked below as she glided well above the battle.

As they floated in midair, Aideen and Pretorius traded blasts of orange fire and white light, many of which came perilously close to the cops attempting to direct traffic away. Jerome appeared to be trying to take out some of the men shooting at the cops. The man floating above the live wires, Zeus, continued posturing and shouting into his bullhorn but did nothing directly. Whoever was in the crashed van still had not emerged.

As Zita drew closer, she could see the lettering on the door of the vehicle. *Dial-A-Ride. So probably at least two people inside. Dios, please don't let us be risking our lives to help corpses. You guys coming?*

Wind brushed her feathers as Andy jumped over the wall and past her, carrying Wyn curled in his arms. After setting her down behind the news van, he sprinted toward Pretorius and Aideen. "Hey! Watch where you're aiming! You're going to hurt someone!" he bellowed.

Zita scowled at his departing back as much as her beak allowed and glanced below. *You going to be okay without protection, Wyn? The shiny tinfoil dress makes you hard to miss.*

Wyn peeked around the rear corner of the vehicle, her face lifted toward Zita's bird form circling overhead. *I'll be fine. They're moving around a lot, which makes it difficult to target them with sleep spells, but I'll get as many as I can. Also, if I see a chance to help any of the injured cops, I'm going to take it. Fortunately, so much is going on that I doubt anyone will notice me behind here. Go on, help the accident victims.*

Biting back her protest that Andy should be protecting Wyn, Zita flew to the crash, hoping that whoever was inside still lived. She landed next to it, on the side that shielded her from the battle, and changed to Arca. The ponytail had disappeared with her shift to a bird, and her hair hung like a dark cape behind her. She slid on the mask that had been bouncing around her neck. *Even if my natural face resembles someone's cute mestizo babysitter and Arca's is more warrior princess, nobody needs any clues to my real identity.*

Inside the old vehicle with a number of dents likely predating this crash, a middle-aged man with a receding hairline stared blearily ahead in the driver's seat, blood running down one side of his face. Dogs barked their complaints from the depths of the van.

Poor puppies, Zita thought, setting to work.

It took a few minutes to retrieve the injured driver, the muscular wheelchair-bound passenger, and his two dogs from the vehicle. The larger dog, a bushy mess resembling seventy pounds of pit bull crossed with a demented wad of moldy cotton candy, turned out to be easier to handle than the dachshund puppy howling in a dented cat carrier.

As her small group scurried along the road, Zita checked on the others. *Wyn, be ready. I've got a semi-conscious guy, so I'm guessing he's real bad.*

Pretorius and Aideen circled each other by the prison transports. The cops and gunmen were in a standoff. Two men slumped by the wheels of the cement truck, though Zita could not tell if they were dead or asleep. Garm, Andy, and Jerome were not visible from her vantage point. Wyn still hid behind the news van, but the glimmer of her friend's pale hair was visible behind a corner.

Rancor absent from her tone, Wyn sent a mental impression of being frazzled. *Just once I'd like to investigate a loud noise and discover a raucous book club discussion rather than mass combat and bleeding people. I skimmed the minds of the men behind the trucks, and they're under orders to avoid shooting at or near the news van.*

Perfect place for you and these guys then. Now in gorilla form, Zita carried the injured driver and loped after the passenger and his dogs. With a comfortable ease that suggested long habit, the larger dog jogged alongside his master. The wheelchair-bound man rolled at a steady and impressive speed, despite the need to maneuver around chunks of debris.

Fire blasted into the pavement between them, so close Zita could feel the heat as it passed.

It must have upset the animals further because the dachshund launched into another high-pitched round of protests and the big dog raced around its owner in circles, wrapping the leash around the chair. The wheelchair-bound man tried to bring the chair to a stop and managed to keep it from toppling, but the carrier bounced out of his lap and spilled open.

Only one swear word escaped Zita's mouth in the form of a hoot before a tiny form bolted from the crate.

The dachshund puppy looked around, delicate ears and tail lifting, shaking with excitement. He went still as his focus passed over Zita and fixated on something beyond her. His bark grew even shriller as he charged across the highway, eyes plastered on his goal.

The massive, three-hundred-pound wolf.

No mames. Zita gaped.

"Pancho, no!" the man said. He turned his imploring gaze to Zita. "You can't let the wolf eat him! Here, put that guy in my lap and I'll move him." The big dog hid behind him, his ratty tail tucked between his fluffy legs.

Zita wanted to protest that the paraplegic wouldn't be able to make it to the van with the injured man but reconsidered. *His upper body development is really awesome. I bet his pecs can dance even if his legs don't anymore.* Changing back to Arca, she pulled the mask over her face and arranged the still-unconscious driver in the guy's lap. Without having to think about it, she slipped into a fake Mexican accent, a habit that was both comfort and camouflage. "Make for the news van. Don't lose the other dog." She raced after the puppy.

Somehow hearing the demented barking despite all the shooting, crunching, crackling, and screaming, Garm turned his huge, shaggy head toward the attacking puppy. His tongue fell from his mouth, and he snickered.

About twenty feet from the wolf, the dachshund skidded to a stop and stared, a growl reverberating through him, making his small form quake.

The laughter stopped. Garm's eyes narrowed, and he glared back.

In her best Cesar Millan voice, Zita said, "Pancho, come!"

Instead, the puppy did a remarkable imitation of an animal with rabies, all without letting his eyes stray from Garm or making any indication he had heard her.

"¿Neta? He's getting into a pissing match with a baby wiener dog? Once again, I have to ask what is wrong with you people?" Zita complained as she ran, keeping an eye on the ground to avoid injuring her bare feet. Years of climbing and aerial acrobatics had toughened them... but still. The hair on the back of her neck lifted, and her instincts wailed. She hurled herself to the side, rolling.

A massive crash sounded, and the air sizzled. Scorch marks marred the pavement where she had stood.

Zita tasted ozone and searched for the source. The lightning guy drifted in the air, his attention on her and the dog. *Andy, Zeus hates dogs and awesomely fun people. Can you get him off my back so I can rescue the stupid puppy?*

Seriously, Z, Superman and Batman never have to chase down dachshunds. How could it outrun you with those stumpy little legs, anyway? His tone was distracted.

Zita growled, but neither canine spared her a glance. *Hello, I'm trying not to be hit by lightning. Weren't you supposed to handle this guy?*

Exasperation sang over the party line as Andy replied. *I'm on my way. A double-length, completely full car carrier hit a cement barrier and blocked the turnaround everyone stuck in traffic was using. I had to lift it and the divider out of the way and set it down without hurting the driver or the stupid Mercedes that tried to squeeze by while I was doing so.*

"You have a job, Garm. Go do it," Zeus commanded, drifting back toward the live wires and lifting a hand snapping with lightning.

From the corner of her eyes, Zita saw the police still by the prison vans preparing to run toward the tree line, probably for the cover it offered as the only alternative was filled with electricity. *They need a distraction, and I can't let him kill that dog.* "Stop!" Zita yelled, bounding up and waving her arms. "Don't shoot the puppy. You can keep trying to kill me, but the animal's not involved. He's just... idiotic."

Garm snarled at the dachshund and lunged and snapped at it.

With a yelp, the young animal ran back to the other side of the highway.

The oversized wolf smirked.

Words popped out despite Zita's best intentions. "Ooh, you're big dogs now. You scared the puppy. What's next, stealing candy from babies?" She prepared to move, sensing she would pay for her comments soon. *Andy?*

Although he remained near the edge of the fallen wires, Zeus floated close enough to scowl at Zita. "Does she always talk this much?"

"Unfortunately," Garm said, his mouth curling into a snarl.

"Oye, I still kicked your behind at the museum, Garm," Zita shot back.

Andy's mental voice was stressed. *Can you hold them one more minute, Zita? Keep yourself safe, but Aideen's down, hurt, and Pretorius is gunning for the guards by the transport vans.*

Zeus snickered.

His ruff rising, Garm growled and took a step closer.

Zita waved a hand in dismissal, forcing her body to remain in a casual pose. "What? I'm just keeping it real. You had to be saved by your portal boy, Janus." *Yeah, I got this. Somehow.*

Light shot from the electrical zone and gathered in Zeus' hand. "Well, then, I'll have to put an end to this, won't I? This mouthy weakling isn't worth the time you're wasting on her, Garm. Shoo. Go do your job."

Zita backed up a few steps and prepared to shift. "And me without my lightning rod." With relief, she saw the police staging themselves behind trees at angles that would better let them fire on the attackers.

Garm growled. "Let me get farther away so you don't hit me too." Bottles clinked on his back. "Or Halja's things."

At that, Zeus glanced at the massive wolf and nodded. He might have drifted a few feet upward with the gesture.

While Zeus was distracted, Zita changed to a golden eagle and rocketed upward.

A crack sounded, and a purple and gray-clad form hurtled by, crashing into the overpass, then dropping right into the electrical field of the broken poles.

Andy! Zita shouted mentally, her heart stuttering with fear.

Descending to drift a few inches above the asphalt, Zeus smirked. "One down."

"Actually," Garm said and jerked his nose toward the sparking lines. "Look."

Andy had rolled to a stop and stood, tripping over one of the live wires. Chunks of cement tumbled from the overpass and bounced off his head. Electricity traced his form and hissed and fizzled around him. He stomped back the direction he had come, each step bringing with it another cavalcade of crackling sparks. His shirt hung in tatters. Mentally, he complained, though he remained silent out loud. *I really don't like that Pretorius. He cheats.*

Mano, I'm just glad you're okay. And yes, he's a real piece of work, Zita sent, winging higher.

Thank the Goddess you're uninjured, Wyn added.

Andy plucked a rock from his hair and dropped it. *Weirdly, the electricity feels kinda like a light massage. Kind of pleasant, except for the noise.*

Let's save massages for personal time and commence with the butt-kicking. Though you'll be happy to know your mask and pants survived this one, even if your shirt didn't. Zita circled, keeping a wary eye on Zeus and Garm below.

His expression unhappy, Andy patted his chest and tried to brush dust off the seat of his pants. *I liked that shirt.*

During the distraction, the dachshund had regained his courage and now charged Zeus, barking madly.

Zita dropped down, becoming a greyhound and hitting the ground at a run. After seizing the little dog by the scruff of his neck, she altered direction to aim herself at the news van.

The puppy yipped.

Zita had gotten up to speed within three strides and blasted by Garm, there and gone before he could even bite at her. She had crossed between the cement barriers when a flash of light and a prickling snap announced Zeus' failed attempt to strike her.

Despite the zig-zagging course necessary to avoid crossing the intermittent gunfire between the cops and the men behind the truck, she arrived at the news van unscathed. Zita checked over her shoulder for Garm as she spat out the wiener dog and shapeshifted to Arca. Before the puppy could run off again, she grabbed him and scanned the area for a safe place to corral him. His owner cheered from his chair. The other dog barked, and the driver squinted at her from where he sat next to Wyn.

"Somebody grab this," Zita said, holding out the squirming dog. She held it out toward the open window where a camera stared back. "Preventing them from killing the puppy is more important than filming us so put the microphone down and help."

Inside the news van, a pretty reporter squeezed into the front seat. "What are you doing? Why are you here?"

"Can't you just hold this chingado dog? Why am I here? We're here to fucking help. Duh." Zita shoved the puppy through the open window in the gap between the inquisitive nose of the camera and the reporter.

Chapter Three

Dogs and human civilians finally safe, Zita changed form to a golden eagle and flew up high enough to get a good vantage point. Andy and Zeus fought each other near the downed electrical poles, lightning crackling harmlessly over her friend as he jumped up, trying to punch the flying man. Still blazing, Aideen staggered, her arm across her ribs, and limped toward Jerome, who stood guard over the news van with a pair of gunmen at his feet. Wyn and the rescued men were not visible from her position though shrill barking issued from where she'd left them.

In front of the prison transports, Garm paced. Pretorius slowly descended as if riding an invisible elevator. As he approached the driver's door of one, he held out a hand, and the light of his laser—*plasma, Andy had said it was plasma*—filled it. He yanked the door open, glowing hand raised as if to shoot.

A body tumbled out, part of the head missing, covered in blood with globs of flesh that Zita's mind declined to examine any closer. Nausea swept through her, and she suppressed it. *No time for that.*

Pretorius kicked it aside and leaned in. Normally, Zita appreciated a fit man being active and bending over when she had a good view, but the mangled corpse and the knowledge that the big South African mercenary had been involved in her brother's kidnapping and torture ruined it.

Garm followed to stand at his back, scanning the area. His black ruff rose, and his nose lifted to where she circled above. Tilting his head at the van, he growled something.

When Pretorius emerged, a large key ring dangled from his fingers. He aimed a dongle hanging from it at the vehicle and pressed a button.

The prison van beeped, and the headlights flashed.

I guess that's one way to break into an armored transport, Zita thought, swooping closer.

Pretorius approached the rear of the prison vehicle and tugged at the doors.

Garm loped behind, his ears perked forward, tail up, and panting.

The van doors remained shut. Almost idly, Pretorius waved his glowing hand at a cluster of officers, sending a ball of light at them. Turning away, he began trying keys in the lock.

Zita couldn't tell if the blast had hit anyone or not, but it took down at least one tree, answering how they had managed to fell the electrical poles. *Too many and too well armed for me to fly down and fight directly, but they still outnumber the cops, so I have to do something. Hope cop reinforcements make it through that traffic soon.*

A key must have worked because Pretorius threw open both the outer and inner doors and stepped aside.

Someone fired from inside.

Garm bared his teeth, his ears flat against his head and his tail drawn down to stand straight out. He moved to attack whoever was in the van.

Zita dove, shifting to a giant armadillo in midair and curling into a tight ball.

Caught in mid-leap, Garm stumbled to the side when all eighty pounds of Zita hit him at speed.

She ricocheted off and rolled to her feet, protected by the armor-like scutes of her armadillo body. After swiping at the wolf with her huge, sickle-shaped front claws, she charged Pretorius' legs. *I don't have the power to take Garm and Pretorius in close quarters, especially at the same time, but I can at least give the guards inside a chance if I distract the bad guys.*

Pretorius danced aside and shot at her.

She rolled out of the way.

Garm yelped and skidded to a halt to avoid being hit. "Watch it," he growled, leaving his satchel on the ground behind a wheel.

Someone cried out from inside the transport, and a moment later, a handful of men straggled out, all big, burly, and wearing heavy-duty shackles. They grinned evilly as they greeted Pretorius.

"Anyone who wants employment, come with me. Otherwise, get lost," Pretorius said. "Bonus for the person who kills the shapeshifter."

The escapees started scouring the ground for weapons, hampered by their manacles.

Praying none of them had found guns yet, Zita became a hippo and lunged at the whole group, bellowing.

They scattered, except for Garm.

"Get the other van open!" The wolf charged her, snarling and showing his teeth.

Zita closed her mouth and took a couple steps toward him. When Garm reached her, she lowered her head and used it to throw him aside. As she turned around to give a warning snuffle to an escapee going after a gun, two more men emerged from the transport.

The first man reeled out as if he was on a multi-day drunken bender. His head hung low, his face hidden by disordered bushy brown hair. He only made it as far as the highway shoulder where he slumped down as if his strings had been cut. Oblivious to the surrounding chaos or his proximity to the firefight, he methodically removed his shoes and socks, discarding them next to him. His apparent apathy ended when a stray shot winged his arm. With a squeak, he raised his head and bared his teeth, chattering them rapidly.

Caramba. The last thing this fight needs is the Squirrel King ordering a million fat suburban squirrels to rip people to shreds. Zita was distracted from that discovery by the even more unpleasant recognition of the final man to exit, one she'd hoped to never see free again after his kidnapping and torture of her brother. *All this for that psychopath?* She indulged in a deluge of mental swearing. Externally, she made a series of lame snorting sounds.

A standard-issue jumpsuit stretched to cover Sobek's long, bulky torso, then fell, baggy and loose, making his stubby legs seem shorter, despite the fact that he stood almost as tall as his former employee, Pretorius. Dark hair shadowed his once-shaved head like a fallen and blackened halo. The stocky man had lost none of the homicidal swagger he'd exhibited when holding Quentin captive and gloating over his tortured victims. He held out both manacled hands, expectantly.

The big blond mercenary shrugged, murmured something, and headed toward the other transport.

His tone distracted, Andy asked, *Is there a reason for the flood of profanity, Zita? I'm trying to keep Zeus from throwing lightning at cops and traffic here.*

Zita reined herself in. *Sorry, didn't mean to leak that. They're releasing supers we caught previously. Sobek and Squirrel King are out, plus a bunch of other dudes.*

When Pretorius turned away, surprise flashed on Sobek's reptilian face. "Don't ignore me," he shrieked. "It's not my fault!" When he caught sight of Zita, he went white, then red. His fists clenched.

Zita flashed him a hippo smile even if she felt more like stomping on him. Her instincts screamed. Having learned the hard way not to ignore that warning, she shifted to a gavião-real again to take advantage of the eagle's maneuverability and spun away in time to avoid a bullet.

An escapee ran after her, shooting wildly.

Pretorius called over his shoulder as he withdrew a key ring. "Prove your worth, and maybe they'll reconsider, no matter how Gaia feels about you. Bring either a great deal of money or something valuable to them. I'd suggest both."

As she wove in and out of the area of the transports, Zita kept an eye out for a good spot to sneak up on her attacker from behind and disable him. The rest of her attention went to keeping up with other action in the area; she didn't need to escape one assailant only to be shot by another.

Most of the escapees, Sobek among them, had regrouped in the tight space between the two transport vans, peering around the edges to take potshots at the police with a variety of found weapons.

Garm's injuries had already healed, and he waited at the door of the second van, snapping at Zita once when she flew too close. He pawed at the closed vehicle. "Pretorius."

"One moment, Garm," Pretorius said. He continued trying keys in the lock.

Zita landed beside an abandoned police escort, changed to a feral pig, and waited.

Her stalker came around the corner of the car.

She charged him, sending the man skidding in one direction and his gun in another. Grunting, she shoved his weapon under the car with her nose.

After dropping to the ground, he fished under the vehicle for the firearm.

With an internal wince, she stepped on his arm and put weight on it until it gave way beneath her.

The guy curled up, screaming.

While she'd been distracted, Pretorius had opened the doors of the second van.

Trying not to think about the arm she'd just broken, Zita charged Garm and Pretorius, running over the wolf and sending the man flying into the side of the other transport.

Three women in prisoner's garb ran from the transport, blinking in the sunlight, seeming to all choose different directions.

"Bloody pest." Pretorius got back up, a light growing in his hand.

Garm lunged at Zita, but she darted to the side, shifting to a dachshund and skittering under the transport.

The scent of burnt fur filled the air as Garm tried to twist out of the way of the plasma and mostly succeeded, except for his tail. He yipped. "Mind the potions!"

Pretorius snarled. "Why is the shapeshifter still alive? Kill her."

A piercing shriek came from the edge of the road. "I come, my people!" The Squirrel King bent at the knees and gave a prodigious, wobbly jump away from the cops. Since he remained shackled, he stumbled when he landed but leapt again and again until he was lost from sight.

Breaking from the crowd behind the one transport, Sobek followed suit, using his own strength to propel him quickly down the gravel shoulder in the opposite direction.

Zita started to follow Sobek, the need to protect her family howling within her.

Before she could act, Tiffany careened out of the transport. Her jumpsuit overwhelmed her skeletal frame, though she more than had the height for it. Dark roots showed at the base of her bleached hair. Rubbing a hand over her face, she squinted, taking in the chaotic battle going on around them with dull eyes. The evil sorceress began to fall.

Garm limped over and inserted himself between Tiffany and the ground, so she collapsed onto his midnight fur instead.

Drugged, maybe? Zita thought. *I guess they can't keep her blindfolded, tied, and gagged constantly. She's a bigger threat than any of the others and probably why they're doing this. I can't let her get away too. Still, I don't want Sobek anywhere near my brother again.*

Garm half-carried Tiffany to a spot by the tires, using the bulk of the armored vehicle to protect her from the exchange of gunfire between the escaped prisoners and the police. He nuzzled her, leaving red smears on her clothing.

Tiffany stroked Garm's fur. "My love," she croaked.

"You. Guard her," Garm ordered an escapee, one with a shotgun. The wolf shapeshifter retrieved the leather satchel he'd dumped off earlier, dropped it beside Tiffany, and gave her hand a lick. He then tore off across the road toward Jerome, who was headed their direction cracking his knuckles.

Tiffany, wearing a dopey expression, snuggled her bag.

Light glowing in one hand, Pretorius bent down to check under the van.

A shrill shriek echoed over the highway, and a fireball exploded nearby, so close that heat washed over Zita's fur and the stench of blistering rubber filled the air. Although Pretorius dodged, his clothing got scorched. Backing up, he abandoned Zita to lob his next attack at Aideen. The big man pointed to the escapee guarding Tiffany and said, "Shoot the pest before she goes down another rathole."

If her bag has that magic napalm she used before, I can't let her start throwing it around. This place has no way to smother that awful stuff. Dios, keep my brother safe. Please let Sobek have forgotten his grudge against my family; I can't go after him right now. Zita growled.

Tiffany's guard bent down to aim his shotgun under the van at her.

Since he was by the front passenger side, Zita scurried out the rear and hid behind the tire.

He swore and moved to follow her.

Tracking his feet under the van, she ran back under the vehicle as soon as he got close. She snuck up behind him and bit his ankle.

Her opponent, surprisingly smart enough not to shoot himself trying to get her, shouted and lifted a foot to stomp on her dachshund form.

Zita became Arca and spun in a modified rasteira de costa. Her spinning back-kick hit his injured leg and sent him tumbling down. She propelled his gun under the transport with one foot and ran to get the bag from Tiffany.

While she had been fighting, Tiffany had recovered enough to stop cuddling her satchel and withdraw a glass vial, rolling it between her fingers as she eyed the battlefield.

Zita stilled, recognizing the ebony sludge roiling in the bottle. Her eyes darted around as she tried to guess where the woman would throw it. Tiffany had only two viable targets: Zita or Aideen, who floated in midair by an abandoned escort cruiser, scanning the area. The fiery woman drifted higher, revealing Wyn crouched below, a soft, verdant glow outlining her hand and a man with hideous burns lying at her feet. Zita's stomach clenched. *Wyn! Move before Tiffany gets you!*

As if in slow motion, Zita saw her friend look up, the healing spell fading from her hand.

Tiffany smirked and wound up for a sloppy overhand pitch.

Wyn flinched. She tugged at her patient, clearly trying to get him to safety.

"Napalm!" Zita shouted, pointing at Tiffany and hoping to distract her.

Aideen's head turned at the shout, then she focused on Tiffany.

Tiffany smirked at Wyn and threw. "Pretender," she slurred.

"No." Aideen flicked a speck of fire at the bottle almost immediately after it left the hand of the evil sorceress.

Acting on instincts, Zita dove away.

The bottle exploded into iridescent ebony and orange flames in midair. Most of it splattered the ground around Tiffany, who screamed, a high, shrill sound, as napalm hit her left side, arm, and face. She collapsed, twisting and screeching.

Aideen rose higher in the air, more fire swirling between her fingers as she drifted away. Her previous injuries were gone.

Horrified, Zita called out, "Muse, be ready to heal Tiffany." She sprinted after Aideen. "Oye, Fireball! Put out the flames on that woman!"

Wyn nodded, ending her spell on her current patient. She murmured something to him and ran to Tiffany's side.

"Why? She attempted to kill me," Aideen said, floating and scanning the area. "Where'd that blond asshole go?"

"Because a woman is burning to death and nobody deserves that?" Zita growled. *You stubborn, self-righteous bitch*, she thought. Squinting at Aideen, she remembered the trick that had worked before. *No one else is close to me, so at least nobody else is in danger if I piss her off too much.* "Oh, I see. It's beyond your powers to put out the weird fire, then."

Crouching by the writhing woman, Wyn sent, *I can't extinguish it on my own. If I can get close enough, I can remove the magic.*

Aideen narrowed the dark caverns that passed for her eyes and casually rolled flames over her knuckles. "No fire is beyond me."

Zita pointed at Tiffany. "Prove it, then." She put as much mockery into her voice as she could.

Aideen whirled to face Tiffany's form, which had stopped making noise and now merely convulsed. Raising her arms, Aideen spread her fingers wide.

The sickening flames reduced, but still lined half of the sorceress' body.

Doubt trickled in. Tiffany stopped screaming and went limp. The heat coming off Aideen increased until Zita was forced to back up. *Oye, what if she really can't stop it? Even if I could apply mud as fast as Remus, pouring highway roadside dirt on open burns would kill her anyway.*

As her fingers danced in a complicated pattern, Wyn stayed a few feet away from Tiffany, whispering something.

The flames went out, though whether that was from the magic or Aideen's efforts was uncertain. Nothing of Tiffany's face was recognizable. The portion of arm Zita could see was horrifically burnt, and glimpses of charred bone below it seemed even worse.

Aideen turned and drifted away. "Told you."

I'm afraid to touch the poor woman, but I don't think I have a choice. Wyn rushed over, and set her hand on Tiffany's ankle, the uninjured one, murmuring the words of her healing spell. A familiar green glow, like the first buds of spring, sprang up. *She's dying. You'd think Aideen would have more sympathy given I just healed her from some nasty wounds a few minutes ago.*

Zita rubbed her own arms. *Tiffany's a horrible person, but nobody deserves to go like that. Also, we're so not having barbecue for lunch.*

A hum of acknowledgment came from Wyn, who bent over the sorceress, her healing spell bright against the charred, black, and oozing mess.

Tiffany's form began to lose some of its tenseness.

A howl from across the battlefield preceded Garm's attack. He charged at Wyn. "Halja!" he shouted, calling Tiffany's chosen name.

Shifting to a feral pig, Zita blocked him.

He backed off, his eyes wild. "Call off your friend."

I wish I could talk in animal form, Zita grumped. *I don't dare change shape though for fear he'll get Wyn.*

Give me just a few more, her friend sent. *Healing takes time, and I haven't even finished with the worst of it.*

The wolf lunged, all rationality gone from his eyes.

Zita intercepted and blocked again, tossing him against a nearby vehicle. *Doing what I can.* She returned to her Arca form. "She's trying to save Tiffany, not hurt her. Back off!"

He staggered to his feet and howled again.

When the hair on the back of her neck rose, and her instincts screamed, Zita ducked and rolled. Lightning crashed where she had been, close enough to taste the ozone and feel her hair prickle from the static. *They're too many and too powerful. I really want to punch them all in the nose.*

Garm lunged for Wyn, the great wolf still limping from Zita's last hit.

Her ears rang from the closeness of the lightning. Zita shifted to a rhino. Intercepting Garm's charge, she angled her big body so he bounced off. While he was stunned, she charged and tossed him aside. Her stomach curled into a hard lump at the blood oozing down her horn and the crack of bone from the wolf when he'd impacted against the side of the other prison van. *Andy, I can't fight Zeus and Garm both at once and protect Wyn. Speaking of which, is the healing almost done?*

Words tumbled out from Wyn's end of the telepathic link, sounding both panicked and distracted. *I'm hurrying. The spell can only go so fast, and it's fixing the big stuff first, but there's so much damage it'll take a while to get it all.*

"Pretorius! Come fetch Halja. The stupid bitch is injured, and her lapdog is useless," Zeus shouted.

To protect her friend, Zita thundered closer. *Oye, Andy, we need you. It's three on one here. I'm outmatched and Wyn's exposed.*

Sorry, Zeus threw something at some cops, and I had to help. Pavement crunched as Andy did one of his preternaturally long jumps to join them.

Zita shifted to Arca, splitting her attention between their enemies. "Take as many of them as you want."

Andy cracked his knuckles. "It'd help if they'd land," he grumbled. Bending his knees, he jumped into the air and swung at Zeus. When he landed, he backhanded Garm, who had recovered enough to creep toward Wyn again. The casual blow sent the wolf flying back into the other police transport again, making it rock and the men hiding behind it swear.

Heat and light exploded overhead. "Hey! I'm not done with you!" Aideen shouted, lobbing a ball of fire at Pretorius, forcing him to dodge and halt his slow flight.

As Zita stood guard, she heard a gurgling sound from inside the truck. A quick check revealed a pair of female guards, both of whom were well beyond help, and a man in a blood-spattered lab coat, who twitched and held out a hand, imploring without words. *Carajo*, she swore. *Garm's still healing, and Andy seems to have Zeus under control. Aideen and Pretorius are keeping each other busy.*

"One injured in the truck!" Running to the medic, Zita stripped off the man's lab coat and examined him to figure out the source of all the blood, hoping to slow the bleeding long enough to get him to her friend. To her horror, she saw a long, thin piece of metal buried in the medic's chest, the end just poking out. *That's not in his heart, but it's awfully close. I don't dare move him, and his breathing sounds awful wet. This is so far beyond my first aid certification.*

"Dying... don't... alone," the man coughed, his brown eyes pained and frightened.

Zita winced. "We'll see about that." Afraid any other movement would bump the shard into an even worse position, she kneeled and took his bloody hand. "Muse! If you've got Halja stable, this guy won't make it without your spell." She repeated herself mentally, in case her friend hadn't heard her.

Eyes sliding shut, the man's fingers twitched in Zita's. "Not... alone."

"Hey now, no dying on me. You hang on, hombre." Zita squeezed his hand and checked over her shoulder on her friend's progress. Guilt pulled at her; she should have been able to figure out a way to stop the bad guys from getting into the vans.

Aideen appeared to be exchanging blows with Pretorius again, while Andy fought Zeus, or at least tried to as much as was possible. His quarry could fly and seemed disinclined to stand still and let Andy punch him. From behind trees, and any other cover they could find, the police appeared to be adopting a slow, orderly forward movement to end the standoff with the gunmen.

It felt as if Zita had been watching the others fight for centuries when Wyn finally joined her and the fading patient.

"Halja still needs help but... Oh, Goddess help us all. Right." Brow furrowing, Wyn said, "Would you please remove that without making the injury any worse than necessary? My spell can't heal with the metal there, and he won't survive much longer. Once it's out, press the lab coat to keep him from bleeding out. I don't know if I can do this, Z... Arca." Despite her words, and the way she gnawed on her lower lip, her gestures were precise. Her hands ignited with the verdant light of the healing spell as she set them on the injured man.

"We both know you're a badass witch. You got this." Zita prayed silently as she released his hand, trying hard not to leak the mental plea on the party line. *Dios, I hope she's got this. And that she didn't just hear me doubt her.*

The semi-conscious man made a protesting sound, and his fingers grabbed weakly at the air.

"Be strong, dude. This'll hurt a lot, but my friend's awesome and is going to save you," Zita said, nearly choking on her own fake Mexican accent, her nerves drawn taut. She eyed the injury and the offending metal, and took a grip, mentally calculating where the bones and organs likely were.

Wyn inhaled, squeezed her eyes shut, then nodded at Zita.

After another prayer, Zita pulled out the shard. Blood fountained from the injury, and she pressed the wadded lab coat over it as fast as possible to lessen the flow, discarding the metal on the floor. "Now!"

Their patient made a gurgling moan.

Wyn's lips moved, and her chanting took on an almost frantic tone.

Although she knew it wouldn't help the spell, Zita crossed herself and muttered a quick Hail Mary under her breath, her other hand holding the makeshift pad to the wound. She averted her eyes from the dead guards staring accusingly at her from the floor of the vehicle. *It's much easier when I can just kick a thug or fly away.*

A discordant noise, like someone bellowing, belching, and gargling all at once, rose above the scattered gunshots and shouting. It startled Zita out of her self-recrimination. *Was that a howler monkey? In Maryland?*

As she craned her neck to see outside the vehicle, she caught the glimmer of a large hole, the edges lit by an incandescent glow. As she watched, Pretorius, carrying Tiffany, disappeared through it, followed closely by Garm's furry tail. A few surviving escapees followed.

At the edge of the portal he had generated, Janus braced himself, pale and unhappy in the bland beige polo shirt and khaki pants more suitable for summer resort staff than a Maryland jailbreak in October. If possible, the teenage boy seemed even more malnourished than their prior encounter. Constant shivers wracked his gangly frame.

Raising the bullhorn to his lips, Zeus paused by the portal. "You can't stop or hold us unless we let you. Give up and just surrender before our power!" He smirked and tossed lightning at the truck where Zita and Wyn worked.

Andy threw himself between them, and the bolt dissipated around him. A moment later, he moved out of the way. "Guys? He's gone."

Wyn glanced up and smiled. "But this man's not. I think he'll survive. Thank you both for helping."

As Zita sat back on her heels, relief flooded her. She released the makeshift pad she'd been holding and retreated to the edge of the vehicle where she could see more of the action outside. "And you were worried. I knew you had it."

Although Wyn quirked an eyebrow, her smile faded as she gestured at something behind Andy.

He turned, and they all watched as the portal closed, leaving the boy behind.

"Janus! Now's your chance! If you run, they won't know for a while!" Zita shouted.

The teenager turned and stared at her for a long moment before he flexed his shoulders and shook his head. He flinched at a burst of gunfire.

"Come on, Janus, you know you don't want to help them!" Zita willed him to run for it.

He gestured, and another, smaller portal opened. He jumped through it and disappeared. The glowing hole closed behind him.

Light flashed like a grenade as a new portal dumped out Janus by the cement truck. When it closed a second later, he ripped open yet another, pulling on the edges of it until a giant rectangle appeared in front of the vehicle. The engines started up, and the truck drove through, followed by the sixteen-wheeler loaded with the metal rods. A thug toting an AR-15 and the teen leapt through it. The portal disappeared behind them.

Chapter Four

After an instant, Zita realized she hadn't heard any gunfire for a while, but a persistent knocking sound in a short, sharp pattern came from somewhere. Wyn and the newly healed medic peeked out from the transport next to her.

"I'm getting a better view," she said, shifting to a gavião-real and launching herself.

Beside the road, the cops slowly emerged, guns down but still out. Zeus' people had disappeared, leaving behind only their injured, their dead, and their smoldering dead.

Aideen hovered by the news van, hands on her hips.

Jerome set down a bloody police officer by an ambulance and sauntered back toward the highway, his head turning side-to-side as he scanned the area.

Andy and Wyn escorted the medic from the prison van to the line of ambulances, with Wyn peeling off to kneel by someone on the ground.

Zita tilted her head and adjusted her wing angle. *Knocking? Why do I hear knocking? It's loudest near those downed poles, but you couldn't pay me to go in there.*

The pounding throb of approaching helicopters drowned out the sound, and she swooped lower.

No one lingered by the snapping electrical lines, but motion in the blackened bucket truck caught her eye, and Zita stared that direction. She landed nearby, not so close that her feathers rose with the proximity of the dangerous voltage, but near enough to allow her avian eyes to determine what was inside.

Zita changed to her Arca shape. "Carajo, someone's alive in there," she said, staring at the pitted truck trapped in the middle of the live wires. As she watched, an eye-searing bolt shot out and raced over the vehicle, sinking into the surrounding ground.

Another series of thunks sounded, and a dark shape moved in the front seat.

She winced and steeled herself. *Maybe it's not as bad as it seems.* Her instincts screaming against every step, she approached the zone of broken poles and tangled, sparking wires. When the fine hairs on her arms stood on end, she stopped. *It's obvious I'm not the right woman for the job. Fortunately, I know who is. Hey, Andy! I need you over here. Someone's alive in the bucket truck between the broken electric poles.*

His tone dry and long-suffering, Andy responded quickly. *Did you call me a girl, then ask for my help? Why are we friends again? I'm helping Wyn with the wounded.*

Zita shrugged, unwilling to admit she had not meant to share all of her thoughts. *Because we're smart enough to know the difference between friends ribbing each other and actual insults? Seriously, dude, someone needs you.*

A moment later, the sharp snap of breaking asphalt sounded behind her, and she heard familiar running footsteps. "Where? There? You've got to be kidding. Nobody's alive in that."

Zita blew out air in a huff. "You survived it earlier, and I heard them. If they stay in the truck, it's eventually going to burst into flames, explode, or melt around them. On the bright side—you'd get a free massage out of it."

Andy opened his mouth to protest, but whoever was in the vehicle lifted their arms and hit the door. "Weirdly enough, you're right. Someone is there. I'm on it." He rubbed his arms, then the back of his neck, and took a few deep breaths. As he raced into the area, he flinched whenever a bolt came near him but didn't seem to notice when they struck him from behind.

"Oye, it is not weird that I'm right!" she called after him, backing away from the electricity. She glanced over to check on Wyn, who still knelt by the same person, her illusory face intent and the familiar glow of her healing magic emanating from her hands.

Andy walked by, carrying the truck overhead. "Do I need to tell you how many laws of physics it breaks that I can do this without ripping it apart?"

"Please don't. We've already heard it," Zita said.

Wyn concurred. *Indeed. I can recite the last several diatribes where you protested that our powers, and those of people like us, are sometimes more convenient than science would seem to allow.*

Please don't start the magic versus science debate again. We need to go before the cops arrest us and I miss lunch. Zita frowned at Wyn.

Your priorities are at least consistent, Zita. Wyn's words carried a laugh as she ended her spell and eased away from the person on the ground.

Andy set the vehicle down and ripped off the door. *Yay for freakish strength*, he sent with no real cheer in his mental voice. He made a gagging sound and took an involuntary step back after peeking in the window. *One guy got fried, but a woman with a head wound is alive in there. Wyn, when you have a minute, can you help her? She seems banged up, but she's not charred and grisly like her poor friend.*

Wyn rose and scurried toward the scorched bucket truck. She picked her way around the detritus littering the highway: sparkling glass, stinking scorched plastic, and endless unidentifiable pieces of metal trash. *Coming, but I'd like to finish working on that other gentleman if I can. He'll survive at this point, but I want to get him home to his family tonight.*

With a deep breath, Andy trudged to the other door and tore it off. He reached into the vehicle, his distaste at the proximity to the dead man transmitting over the party line. Lifting the injured woman, he carried her to the closest grass and set her down.

Since Zita wasn't certain he had meant to let them know how much the body disturbed him, she said nothing, focusing on calming her own queasiness and not staring. As the rush from the battle faded, she became conscious of how cold, tired, and outright filthy she felt. A gust of wind brought the scents of offal and cooked meat to her overworked nose, and she almost gagged at the reminder of the death surrounding them. Her mind refused to process the entire scene, instead focusing on pieces here and there. Small, bloody, frequently scorched pieces. *This blows.*

For all her squeamishness about fighting, Wyn did not hesitate to go to the injured woman and kneel beside her.

Andy backed away from the two women and scanned the area, his breath hissing, shallow and fast through clenched teeth. His muscles tensed, and his gaze went everywhere other than to the dead, even scanning the sky.

Zita slapped his shoulder. "They're gone, mano. After this, she'll be able to do that healing spell in her sleep."

He nodded and punched her back, the sort of sissy tap that would have had her growling at him at any other time.

In the midst of the prison escape, however, it was comforting to know normalcy still existed, and Zita seized on it. "Listen, the cold is killing me, so I'll change shape and keep watch from overhead. If I see trouble, I'll let you guys know. You stick with Wyn and her patients and get her to safety if someone comes after her, okay? I'll come back down when she finishes healing whoever you pulled out of the truck."

He grumbled something unintelligible.

She took that as agreement. Remembering his preference for golden eagles, Zita became one and threw herself eagerly into the waiting sky.

***

When Wyn's spell ended, Zita dove and landed, returning to Arca's form. "We good now?"

Wyn rose, touched the rescued electrician's shoulder, and offered her a serene smile. "That should help, Rani, but I'd still suggest being seen by someone with actual medical knowledge. I need to finish up with that cop, Arca. Then we can go." Wyn drifted back to the injured man who struggled to half-sit up, confusion and blood smeared in equal measure on his face as he stroked the scorched holes in the Kevlar vest over his heart.

Andy trailed behind Wyn.

"Here, I'll give you a hand up," Zita said, hauling the electrician to her feet. Almost absently, she considered the other woman's fitness. *Not a gym rat,* she decided, *but plays tennis or basketball and doesn't know martial arts or she would have gotten up better from a prone position. With all that height, she probably got invited to a lot of teams. Good confidence in her motions, though.*

The electrician blinked and released Zita's hand. "Call me Rani. You're quite... muscular, aren't you?" She tucked black mink hair, styled in one of those pointy modern cuts, behind her ears.

"Sí." Zita grinned. Sobering, she said, "So, the cops and the EMS people will take care of getting you home and all. I'm sorry your friend didn't make it."

"Thanks. None of it has hit yet, but Harvey was a good guy," she said, glancing at the wrecked bucket truck, then away with a shudder.

Hoping to lift the other woman's spirits, Zita offered, "Bet being immune to electricity is handy for an electrician."

Bemusement on her face, Rani blinked at her. "I hadn't realized I was... until now, that is. But I guess."

"It's the only thing that makes sense. Let's get you going, so somebody professional can check you out." Zita took a few steps toward the ambulances.

Rani licked her lips and said, "I know it's a bad time, and I can't believe I'm saying this, but I may never get another chance... Can I ask you a few questions?" She slowly approached Zita.

"Depends what you want to know." Zita's eyes narrowed.

"Your blond friend over there... are you two together?"

Zita snorted, and tension seeped away from her shoulders. "Never happening. I'm into dudes."

Rani hastened to keep up. "So, is she seeing anyone?"

With a glance at Wyn, Zita saw the cop had revived and was gaping up at her friend with a dopey, incredulous expression. His mouth hung open, and he blushed beet red. *Wyn goes for men with pretty faces, impeccable clothing, and self-confidence.* "Not as far as I know, but that guy there doesn't have a chance. He's not her type."

Rani gave a slight, pleased smile, the long lashes lowering over her eyes in a move Zita had seen Wyn make millions of times. "I see. Would you walk me over? I know I'm okay, but I can't seem to keep from feeling like I'm going to wake up and be trapped with poor Harvey again."

Zita shrugged, remembering Wyn's moniker an instant before her mouth kicked in. "Sure thing. Muse said she's sending everyone over to the EMTs to check out, so how about I take you to the cop she's healing now, and you can go with him to the ambulance?

Don't mean to abandon you, but the cops will want to talk to us helpful citizen types now, and you know how they can be."

Rani nodded and followed.

Wyn disengaged from the cop, glow disappearing, and she pointed at the closest ambulance. As she crossed paths with Zita and Rani, she waved and headed to Andy.

With heavy-lidded eyes, Rani smiled as she watched Zita's friends. "Thanks for the company on the walk over. And, you know... the rescue." Turning to the still-blushing cop, she offered him her hand and murmured something.

"No hay bronca. Sorry again about your friend. Take care," Zita said. She headed toward her friends, turning when she heard the rapid patter of steps behind her, falling into a defensive position for a moment before she recognized the electrician.

Rani ran up to Zita, her cheeks flushed under the rich topaz of her skin. "Listen, would you give your friend this? She can call if she wants when this is all over. Tell her to use the cell number." She pressed a business card into Zita's hand.

Zita pocketed the card without reading it. "Whatever, but no promises."

"The first child will be named after you if it works out," Rani said, scurrying back to the cop with one last glance over her shoulder.

With a laugh, Zita joined her friends. She nudged Wyn. "Hey, the lady over there gave me this and told me you could call the cell if you wanted. Made a joke about naming the first kid after me and all, but I'd rather the niño had a cool name, like Bruce Jet Bimba or Michelle Cheng Maria."

"Did you just name off a bunch of martial artists at random?" Andy asked. "And whoever Bimba is, I doubt Muse'd pick that name."

Wyn glanced over her shoulder. "Really?" She took the card, and added, "I would also never choose Bruce as a moniker after knowing about your, ah, personal appliance." After scrutinizing the card, she put it in her bag. With a small smile, Wyn nodded at Rani and wiggled her fingers.

"You're going to call the cop?" Zita said. She eyed him from the top of his close-cropped hair to his clown-sized feet. "I guess he's in decent shape, but I thought you liked the polished type." *I prefer long, yummy, streamlined muscles, myself.*

"Not him. Her," Wyn said, roses blooming in her cheeks. She seemed a little uncertain, and her shoulders tightened.

Realization hit Zita like a pillow to the face. "Oh." She blinked, then shrugged. "So, I should stop pointing out the hot guys to you? Sorry, didn't know they weren't your thing."

Wyn shook her head. "It's fine. Gender's not a huge consideration in a romantic partner for me. I don't advertise because my boss is conservative that way, but it's not really a secret. It just hasn't come up—before now."

"Huh. Okay." Zita shrugged. Studying the electrician, she tried to evaluate her as a date for Wyn. After a moment, she grunted. *I guess she's gorgeous, like a living statue in warm wood tones, all cheekbone, big eyes, and queenly posture. She makes sense if I use the same criteria for her that I do picking guys for Wyn.*

Her face nervous, Wyn nibbled her lower lip and studied Zita and Andy. "You're both not too upset by this, I hope?"

Zita waved a dismissive hand. "Por supuesto. What do I care who you sleep with provided they treat you right and are good for you? I'm all about the dick, so I wasn't interested in you, anyway. Actually, I'm happy for you because it opens up your options. It'd be nice if one of the three of us could find someone."

"Same," Andy said.

Zita snickered. "Well, I'll point out the hot dudes to you too, mano."

He turned red. "I didn't mean that part. I'm straight. I meant... her preferences don't bother me."

Wyn swept both of them up in a hug, her eyes shiny.

"Did I miss something? Why are we hugging?" Zita gave her a squeeze and patted her back.

"So, what're you guys talking about?" Jerome asked as he sauntered up, Aideen drifting behind him.

Releasing the others, Wyn glanced toward the electrician and back. "Oh, nothing much. We were preparing to leave."

Unable to resist the gathering of vigilantes, the reporter over scurried to join them. Her cameraman followed close behind.

With a smile whose wattage was undimmed by his sunglasses and cap, Jerome angled his face down to shadow his face better and held his hand out to the woman. "You can come closer if you want. I hope nobody hurt you?"

Caution warred with gleefulness in every line of her body as the reporter stepped nearer, her gaze locked on his. "Thank you. No, we're all fine. When we got a call something would happen, the tip was specific that we had to stay in our van or die, so we did. Who are you?" she breathed, leaning toward him and running her hand with the microphone up his arm.

The pause was almost imperceptible. Jerome glanced down, tapped his sunglasses and the bill of his hat down more, and said, "You can call me Chevalier, baby."

Player and cub reporter. She seems so young. Wonder if she hates hearing that as much as I do? Probably not, given her profession. In unspoken agreement, Zita and Andy withdrew to the tree line, well away from the microphones and cameras.

Still blazing, Aideen stepped in front of the reporter. Her words boomed out with an undertone of hissing as she spread her arms wide and rose a few feet from the ground. "Know that I am The Living Flame, mistress of fire."

"Oye, she's selling herself short. Don't you hate it when people do that? I bet she could be so much more than fire's side piece," Zita commented sotto voce to Andy.

He didn't move or smile at the joke.

Half-hiding behind Jerome, the reporter nodded at Aideen, wide-eyed. She inched away from the fiery woman, undoubtedly having realized that the same hair products keeping her hair motionless and television-ready would ignite with any stray spark.

"Is it just me or has Aideen forgotten that most people aren't fans of burning alive now that she's a walking human-shaped inferno?" Zita said, hoping to lure a reaction from Andy.

Wyn gave a sweet chortle, the sound carrying like laughing bells and trouble. She announced in ringing tones, "Then you can call me Muse, Queen of Wyrd and Spell." She spread her arms wide, then brought them down, hair floating around her face and shoulders in a breeze that had been nonexistent a moment ago. With her halo of hair and almost luminous skin, she was unearthly and beautiful and wild.

The camera swung to her and stayed.

Aideen glowered.

Wyn giggled and winked at the camera. "Or just Muse." Anything she said after that was lost.

Andy stared at the newspeople busy filming Wyn, Jerome, and Aideen. He inched closer to where Zita leaned against a tree. "I'm totally going to lose my geek card. It'll spontaneously combust. I still haven't thought of a good superhero name."

"Birdbrains?" Zita suggested, keeping her own voice low and grinning. *If he's talking to me, he's not wallowing in self-pity, and that's a huge improvement.* "Birdseed Pervert might still be available. That totally would work for you."

He snorted. "No. You suck at names. I wish I had my phone so I could check and see which ones are trademarked. J—Chevalier is awesome. *He* had his name all ready."

Zita shook her head and turned away, scanning the highway. The mass of cops must've felt confident they had the situation in hand, as they were allowing EMTs to tend to the wounded. "You just got a massage from a live electrical wire and broke an overpass with your butt. Are you seriously worried about trademarks?"

"What? Lawyers cost money, especially the sharks I'd need if one of the big comic companies came after me for infringement."

She rolled her eyes. "Pick something easy, then. How about Thunderbird? Your big form resembles one, and it references a muscle car. That's all macho and might fool someone."

Andy grimaced. "I'm really feeling the love here. No. Almost every Native American superhero in comics has a name like Thunderbird or Chief Something-to-do-with-animals, even if it's somewhat... sacrilegious. Not to mention, it feels wrong to pick my own name. You don't give yourself names. Others gift you with them."

She rubbed the back of her neck and watched the other three goofing for the cameras. "You may be stuck with Mano then. Arca's okay. It's short and easy to spell."

"I don't like Mano. I mean, maybe Dreadnought—no, that one's taken—or something cool. Dr. Dreadnought?"

"Doctor Birdseed Pervert?" Zita poked his side, her smile conspiratorial.

Andy rolled his eyes.

"More seriously, mano, I'll help you think of something. Though I still think you should run with Birdseed Pervert while you got the chance. That name could be big."

In the distance, Aideen visibly huffed at something one of the others said, folded her arms across her chest, and turned away. She rose into the sky in a burst of heat and a flare of her fiery aura. When the reporter and a few of those hurrying by fell back, her derisive laugh echoed and crackled, then she sped from sight, trailing sparks like the tail of a comet.

Jerome and Wyn shook their heads, conferred in low voices, and turned the full force of their joint charisma on the reporter.

Andy muttered, "I don't know why I didn't expect them to break out of custody sooner. In the comics, they never stay locked up long. Most of the comic book prisons have revolving doors."

"What?" Zita whirled to face Andy.

"Never mind, Z, never mind." He stared out at the highway.

Following his gaze, Zita tried to change the subject. "Cleanup on this will take forever. They'll need to use those industrial jetpacks to fix the overpass unless they want traffic sucking here for months. It's not the Beltway, but it's still a big road."

Andy's attention cut to her. "I'm surprised you know about those. Most gyms don't have construction equipment, and jetpacks are still rare."

"They look like fun, but they're meant to lift heavy machinery, like cement pourers with massive hoses. That means they're too hefty to pick up unaided, plus they're not balanced for a human body." She caught him rolling his eyes. "What? You can't blame a girl for considering taking one for a spin. I would've given it back."

He snorted. "That explains your interest. I can just see you telling us to hold your beer and watch this."

Zita frowned. "I don't drink."

"It's a bad joke. Forget about it." As if his brief moment of levity never existed, Andy scowled at the ground and shoved both hands into his pockets.

He hasn't even tried making a pun lately. I didn't think I'd miss that. Zita put her hands on her hips as Wyn and Jerome laughed and spoke with the reporter. A pair of young uniforms hovered at the edge of the group, apparently unwilling to interrupt the impromptu interview.

Andy nodded to himself, his gaze distant behind his mask. His mouth turned down, and he plucked at the scraps of his shirt. "I should go soon so I can get back before Dad wonders where I am."

"After new clothes and lunch, I hope. No shirt, no shoes, no service after all," she teased. When he made no response, Zita frowned and stopped talking.

The silence lasted all of a minute.

"Cops," he said, jerking his chin toward several uniforms who appeared to be heading toward them. A grizzled veteran led the charge, one who didn't seem to care about the reporter. Not all the police had holstered their weapons.

"Guys, if you're all done with the showboating, we should go," Zita urged, raising her voice to be heard and walking closer.

Clouds gathered overhead, darkening the day.

Dragging her attention away from Jerome and Wyn, the reporter's wide brown eyes settled on Zita. She blinked once or twice as if she had not realized Zita and Andy were there.

Yes, lots of bystanders hang out in purple Spandex and masks at crime scenes. It's a fad these days. Zita glanced at the approaching police officers and fidgeted.

Wyn laughed over the party line.

With her microphone raised like a shield, the reporter stepped toward Zita and Andy, most of her attention on Andy. "And you are? What can you two do?"

Zita raked a hand through her hair, mind racing. "They call me Arca, and this is... well, if you think the size of that wolf was impressive, you should see the wingspan there." She nodded toward Andy.

He said nothing aloud. *I really need to think of a good name. We need to get out of here.*

Sure, if you use your bird form, they won't see where we go, since you always like to detour past Arizona. Zita nodded at the approaching police. "Incoming cops. Vámonos, amigos. Anyone who needs a lift, come with us."

Folding his arms across his chest, Andy said, "I'm not shifting. If you want me to carry you when I jump, let me know." His voice was unexpectedly lower and raspier than normal.

Did you suddenly come down with a head cold? Zita wondered.

The tips of Andy's ears burned red. *It's a standard way to disguise your voice. Classic superhero move.*

Zita tried to keep the dubious tone out of her mental voice, but some leaked through. *If you say so.*

Jerome laughed, sprinted south across the highway to the sound barrier wall, and did an impressive leap, even if it wasn't as high or far as the ones Andy could do. He caught the top of the wall and pulled himself up with one arm. Once there, Jerome raised his hands, folded them into finger guns, and pretended to shoot them at Andy, Wyn, and Zita. Despite the distance, his grin was visible before he dropped on the other side.

The incoming police sped up.

Wyn pursed her lips. "I could use a ride."

Andy gave a brusque nod. "I'll assume you're good, Arca. Hang on, uh, Muse." He grabbed Wyn around the waist, bent his legs, and leapt away to the south, though at a different angle from where Jerome had gone.

The remaining cops barreled toward Zita.

Shaking her head, she stared at her retreating friends. "Sure, leave the shapeshifter behind." She switched to a golden eagle and jumped up as far as possible, flapping hard to gain altitude.

Irate shouting from the ground followed her as she circled higher and surveyed below, not all of the voices directed at her. The older cop had plenty to say, his body language screaming annoyance, to the two young policemen who had let Wyn and Jerome talk to the reporter uninterrupted.

New vehicles arrived every second, releasing angry, focused crews of cops, forensic technicians, and medical personnel. The cops swarmed everywhere like an agitated hive of bees, guns in ready positions, with what Zita assumed were technicians following more meekly behind and wielding weapons of science. Uniforms directed the traffic with tidy and brutal efficiency. The men that Zeus had abandoned were all being loaded into police vans or ambulances, save for those who had the creepy boneless sprawl of the truly dead.

She tried not to scrutinize those closely as her stomach lurched.

With an unhappy expression on her face, the young reporter spoke to a policeman. When Zita spotted the cameraman—sans his equipment—being questioned to the side, she knew why the newswoman was upset. EMTs scurried from one victim to another, barking out commands, though she suspected her friends had already healed the worst injuries of the survivors. The man with his dogs and Wyn's electrician admirer must have been hustled into a vehicle and taken elsewhere.

A mile away, Zita spotted Andy's form leap over the highway, heading north and toward Wyn's car. *I'll give them a few minutes to walk there. It's warmer as a bird than as a human, so I'll just keep an eye on things up here. The cops don't appear to be able to follow him fast enough.*

Another few loops over the area revealed little else. The police continued bringing everything into order, only to have it descend into chaos again when a fleet of unmarked American cars and vans arrived and disgorged men in suits, doubtless waving a mess of acronyms and badges. Two electric company trucks sidled past the fried one and parked by a standing pole, well out of reach of the snapping, snarling electricity by the live wires.

Zita? Are you coming? We're hiding in the children's jungle gym in that little park. Wyn's mental voice broke into her thoughts.

She blinked. *Isn't your car right there?*

Andy sent, *Just hurry.*

Are you both okay? Zita angled her wings to approach obliquely, hoping she was not being tracked.

Wyn's mental voice held soothing tones. *We're fine. A police cruiser passed by and we hid. Would you mind scouting to ensure the authorities have left the immediate area? And to ensure we do not have witnesses for our run to the car? Visibility is limited in here.*

So is the space. Andy seemed grim.

If her current form had possessed eyebrows, Zita would have raised them. *No hay bronca, I'll check.*

The constant snap and crackle of the sparking electrical lines below suddenly stopped, and after a second of stunned silence, a small cheer sounded from those assembled.

Gliding up into the clouds, Zita shifted to a grackle. Once she'd circled around to the right block, she zoomed at top speed through it from a lower elevation. If some part of her gloried in the flight while she checked for surveillance, she did her best not to let it leak into the shared telepathic link. *Who would be watching? It's the middle of the day. Stay-at-home moms will be feeding their kids, and retired folks should be watching their telenovelas, so maybe just people working from home or hired to be outside?*

She landed in a trio of shrubs to return to her own form. As she emerged, she brushed twigs and drops of water off her exercise wear. *The fight seemed so much longer.* "Clear," she said. "No cops, dog walkers, or landscapers that I could see."

Andy shot out from the children's fort as if fired from a cannon. Wyn unfolded herself more gracefully. "Not the best hiding place I've ever used," she mused.

Zita scanned them both and saw no obvious injuries. Her shoulders loosened as tension dissipated. "Better than nothing."

After a few steps, Andy paused and blinked at Zita. "Wow. I didn't see that under your hood earlier. You dyed your hair but didn't get it cut at the same time?"

Wyn rolled her eyes. "It's Zita."

Zita frowned at them. "Why pay to get it cut when I've got perfectly good scissors at home?" She ran her fingers through her short hair. It no longer felt like hamster fur but was too short to tangle much and rarely required more than a finger combing. She brightened as she continued. "It doesn't need cutting since it's not in my eyes yet, and I didn't dye it. I'm using it to practice shifting just one part of my body since changing my fingerprints is boring, though I got that one down. It's fun, isn't it? I can also give myself temporary tattoos, but I still have to use a mirror for those."

Andy grimaced. "I don't know why I asked. Really, I should know better by now. It's... ah... bright, and I like how you put all the colors in correct rainbow order."

"That was the goal," Zita said.

Wyn shrugged and repeated herself. "It's Zita."

As he reclaimed his poncho and slipped it on over his shoulders, Andy nodded to Wyn. The transparent plastic did not hide the tattered remains of his shirt or the smooth expanse of skin and lean muscles beneath. "Definitely."

"You say that like it's a bad thing," Zita said, rolling her eyes.

Andy studied the ground, his face closing, and his hands diving into his pockets. "It's very you, Z. I need to get going..."

Zita took a deep breath. She'd seen that expression on Quentin's face right before he said something stupid. *Wyn's been pushing me to speak to Andy. What did she say I should do? Subtly encourage him to talk to us and remind him that we care.* Words tumbled out of her mouth, and she had a sinking feeling, even before she finished speaking, that they were the wrong ones. "Come on, Andy, put on your big boy panties and cheer up. Have lunch with us. We're all worried about you. Pues, if you had any other friends, they'd be worried too."

"I have plenty of friends! Lots of friends! I'm like the social butterfly of physics!" His hands sailed from his pockets and settled on his hips.

Wyn buried her face in her hands. "And here I thought you were doing so well at learning diplomacy, Zita."

"If you had any other real friends, they'd be here trying to cheer you up too. Or get Wyn's phone number. When we hang out, a lot of guys approach me to try to do that. I don't mind too much. At least it weeds them out early on because anyone who's interested in her won't be happy with me," Zita said.

Andy winced. "Harsh, Z."

Rubbing the top of her head, Zita tried to fix the damage. "Oye, did I hurt your feelings? I didn't mean to be sensitive."

He stared at her, tilting his head. "Clearly not."

Wyn's mouth gaped open.

Zita realized what she said. "Insensitive, not sensitive. Sorry. Wyn said you were having a rough time, and I should be helpful and uplifting and supportive and all. Is it working?"

With a sidelong glance at the woman in question, Andy replied, "Wyn talks too much."

"Exactly. Not like me. I'm silent. Except when I have something to say. Like when there's free food or you should feel better. Seriously, mano, didn't mean to hurt your tender man-feelings." Zita gestured to underscore her words as if that would stop her from making a greater mess than she already had.

Andy sighed. "Fine. Lame apology accepted. Please help me less."

Wyn closed her eyes and shook her head. "Zita, you need to hush up now. I am a terrible teacher. Sorry, Andy."

He shook his head. "It probably has a lot to do with your student, Wyn." Switching his attention back to Zita, Andy touched her shoulder. "Can you get her to her car from here?"

She gestured toward the little blue hybrid vehicle parked at the curb. "Yes, it's right there, but—"

Before she could finish speaking, Andy crouched and jumped away, his prodigious strength carrying him well over the rooftops of the nearest homes.

Gesturing after him, Zita glared in the direction he had gone. "Did he just ditch us again? That's totally cheating." From somewhere in the distance, she heard a thunderclap, resembling a sudden storm or a certain giant bird's wings.

Wyn pursed her lips. "Yes, yes, he did."

"He's a cheating cheater." As the remaining dregs of Zita's adrenaline faded, weariness set in, and she became suddenly conscious of wearing a tank top and exercise shorts in the cold. *At least the rain's stopped.* She shivered. "Fine, you were right. It's time to intervene, and we can do it your way."

With a triumphant smile, Wyn pressed the key to unlock her car and the blessed warmth within.

Chapter Five

Teleporting home after a subdued lunch at Wyn's house, Zita turned on her phone and tossed it on her bed with her clothes. It began a mad cacophony of buzzing and vibrating. She stared at the usually silent device. When she flipped it open and checked the missed list, she noted all the calls (and texts and voicemails) were from the same three people: her mother and her two brothers. Her stomach clenched. *Which one of them is hurt?*

As she picked it up to dial her mother, it rang again. *Miguel.* "¿Qué pedo?" she said.

"Zita! Where have you been? Why haven't you been answering your phone? You should have it with you at all times!" Her oldest brother almost shouted.

Ordinarily, I have to do more than answer the phone to get him upset. After kicking off her shoes, she sat. "I see your point. Why would I ever delay you yelling at me when I learn so much from these talks? Not that it's any of your business, but I was at lunch with friends. Why is everyone lighting up my phone? Is someone hurt?"

Miguel inhaled, and when he spoke again, his voice was tight and controlled. "Everyone's fine. We got some very interesting news we really need to talk to you about."

A lump formed in her throat, and she stared at her sneakers. *Do they know? Did they guess I'm Arca despite my precautions? Should I grab my go bag and disappear? Will that be enough to keep them safe? My powers are awesome, but I can't protect my family all the time, so if my secret's out...* Janus' miserable face swam to the forefront of her mind, and she shuddered. Trying to keep her tone light, she said, "Oh? What's that? My brothers are gonna stop setting me up on blind dates so I can run my own love life?" Belatedly, she realized she had slipped into the Spanglish of their childhood.

Miguel switched over to the same language without comment. "Don't be ridiculous. In fact, I had someone lined up for you, but I'll put that on hold. No, this is serious."

Zita swore internally and reached for her shoes. *They know.* "So, you going to keep me in suspense or what? Did they nominate Mamá for sainthood despite her still being alive?"

"They should, if only for all those years dealing with you." Miguel's tone was dry.

"I know, right?" After a second, she caught the insult. "Wait, you mean all those years handling Quentin. That man is trouble. I am an angel, an angel of awesomeness." Papers rustled wherever Miguel was. *Probably at work. I swear he loves his job the way I love exercise.*

He switched to English as if the formality would make her take him more seriously. "Our brother makes terrible life choices, but he has nothing on you. Listen, don't be frightened, but Tracy Jones, or Sobek as he calls himself, has escaped. You need to get to safety. I want you to lock all your doors and windows, get that Taser I gave you last year for your birthday, and wait for Quentin to get there."

Her body relaxed, and she flexed her shoulders as relief ran riot through her. She let her shoe drop to the floor. "Oh, is that all?"

"A serial killer with a vendetta against our family escapes and you're all no hay bronca... I need a minute." Over the line, she heard Miguel's breath evening out, falling into a regular pattern.

She waited, wondering if he still counted backward in English to calm himself.

The phone clicked when he picked it back up. "I've almost finished up work for the day. Quentin will stay with you until I can get there. After that, we'll move you to Mamá's so you can be safe. Expect me in about four or five hours."

She switched to English as well. "Oye, no way. Are you forgetting who got away last time?" *And escaped from your men when you tried to pen me up in your office?*

The tone of his voice brooked no argument, not that that had ever stopped her before. "You were very lucky, Zita. You know what Mamá says. Luck runs out, so you always have to be prepared." Paper rustled louder as if he could not stop himself from shaking his files at the phone.

"Sí, and she also didn't raise no shrinking violins. At least, I'm not one. Jury's still out on you and Quentin, though. There's got to be a reason neither of you have given her those grandkids she's been wanting yet." Zita sometimes had the sacrilegious thought that she'd be able to bring him back from death someday simply by saying something wrong in the vicinity of his dead body. Knowing her brother had never been able to resist correcting her, she grinned and waited.

He huffed and fell for it. "Violets, not violins. Be serious for once in your life. Just let us hide you. It's not like you have anything else planned."

Zita made a rude noise. "If I had plans, I certainly wouldn't tell you now. Is Quentin going to hide?"

Miguel cleared his throat. "He said he can't, yet. Apparently, two of his men are expectant fathers, and he doesn't want to leave them in the lurch."

Given the way Quentin's been neglecting his bookkeeping the past few months, that excuse will hold him forever. Then again, I've been going in weekly to keep his books up-to-date, so maybe not that long. She fluffed a pillow and squared the corner of the bedspread. "Really? I'll find out which two and when they're due. I can freeze them some enfrijoladas, and maybe find the babies some sneakers at the thrift shop, too." *It's never too early for athletic shoes, right?*

"That sounds good. You think a red sauce or..." His voice hardened. "Enough. The babies won't be around for a while yet, and we have to keep you safe. Jones may be on the run, but I suspect he has accounts we—the government, that is—never found from his various criminal enterprises. Between that and his contacts, he'll have resources. We should move you to Mamá's for safety. If you won't go there, don't you have some menial job in Brazil or South America where you could hide and squander your talents for a while?"

Neither one of them had to say what would happen if someone attacked her while she was with their mother. Nothing fazed Mamá, and nobody threatened her babies. Nobody. In fact, Zita suspected she had survived cancer due to the sacred trinity of her mother's prayers, her mother's enchiladas, and sheer combined Garcia willpower. "I like how you slipped in that criticism of my lifestyle there. Totally smooth and supportive, mano. Look, I have things I have to get done, like getting a paycheck before I lose my home. You already floated me a month or two on rent, but you still need the mortgage paid on this place. Being stuck in quarantine for all those months did a number on my bank account. I didn't even get any cool powers like others that got the sleeping sickness. Did they ever figure out what was up with that?" Her throat burned with acid at the lie, but it was for his own good. *What he doesn't know can't hurt his career or our relationship.*

"I'm an investigator, not a scientist, so how would I know? Life is much easier for all of us that you don't have any powers," Miguel said. "Don't try to distract me. You need to get somewhere more secure."

Quentin's staying here. He's much safer if I'm around. Zita paced back and forth in the small space of her bedroom. "Tell you what, if we see any signs of him sniffing around, I'll go underground like I did before. I got a job offer in Brazil I could take, but I was planning to stay up here this winter and earn better money. You hurry and catch him."

"I'm off his case, remember?"

She padded down the hall to her exercise room and contemplated the equipment, mentally working out what routine she'd follow after this call. Wrinkling her nose at her own smell, she corrected that to after the call and a shower to sluice off the worst of the battle debris. During lunch, Wyn had made her sit on towels like a toddler with spotty toilet training. "Like you'll keep your nose out of it. You know you ask about the progress every time you walk by whoever's got the case."

"Actually..." Miguel cut himself off, sighing. "I'm not going to convince you, am I?"

Sensing his capitulation, she pressed her advantage. "Not a chance. I'll stay alert and go into hiding if there's any sign of that psycho nearby, provided that Quentin gets to safety too. He's been chingado off since he was kidnapped and tortured the first time. Going through it again would not help." Zita flexed her shoulders and adjusted a weight on one machine.

"Quentin's been off?" Miguel asked.

She ran a hand over her head, forward and back, debating how to answer. Finally, loyalty to Quentin had her downplaying it. *For now. If he doesn't shape up, I will have to call in the big guns and tell Mamá.* "Yeah, but don't worry about it right now. He probably just needs time."

***

One week later, Zita tugged her boring jacket again, a halfhearted attempt to force the too-small garment to close in front while she paced in the small hallway outside her manager's office. She had always hated that black suit, not just because it was dreary and purchased for a funeral, but also because she feared the coat would rip at any moment. It was meant to be worn by a teenager, not an adult with a woman's curves and serious shoulder muscles, however petite she might be. Wyn had assured her the outfit was as professional as her closet would get, whatever that meant. Earlier that morning, she had caught and returned a neighbor's errant Chihuahuas, dogs that escaped the elderly woman at least once daily. She heard an ominous series of tearing sounds and prayed the jacket would last long enough to get through this meeting. *At least the blouse is a nice, vibrant blue that matches some of the sequins in my good work sneakers.* Trying to soothe the growing ache from holding her shoulders in an unnatural position required to avoid further damaging the strained fabric, she leaned against her supervisor's door.

Her boss finally returned, the scent of spaghetti and wine on her breath. The woman stopped, then took an involuntary step back, seeing Zita blocking her path.

"Hi, Emilia," Zita said. "We need to talk."

"Were you scheduled to be in today?" Emilia's eyes darted left and right before returning to Zita.

As she straightened, Zita shook her head and tugged at the stupid jacket again. "No, and that's the problem. I've tried to talk to you through emails, but you just say you'll let me know and never give me more hours."

One of her boss' hands dove into her purse and emerged with a small bottle of antiseptic gel. She rubbed it over her dusky palms. "Yes, and I will get back to you on that. We don't have much extra—"

Another employee slipped by, headed for the bathroom, then stopped. "Zita? Are you back from your trip? Thank goodness! It hasn't been bad for this time of year, but we've all been pulling long shifts and telling Emilia that she needs to schedule another person into the rotation to take off some of the pressure!"

"I hope so. Munchkins doing good?" Zita said, straightening and putting her hands on her hips. She raised her eyebrows while watching Emilia's reddening face.

Oblivious to their silent byplay, the other tax preparer chuckled. "You know kids. Always up to something but otherwise good. Anyway, I need to take my break before someone else comes in..."

"Not a problem," Zita assured her coworker as she passed.

Turning toward her boss, she caught the older woman eying her and the door as if one or the other would bite. Zita thumbed toward Emilia's office. "Did you want to chat in there?"

Her boss sidled a step away. "No, no need for that."

"We could use the lounge then."

"Why don't we... just take a walk and chat? I'll see you by the benches in a few minutes."

Finding herself ushered out the door, Zita stalked across the road. Since Emilia did not immediately appear and the Cuban-Chinese fusion food truck was there, she moseyed up to it. Her stomach rumbled in agreement with the decision.

"Zita! So good to see you back again. I was getting worried," the middle-aged woman in the truck said, loading up a plate without being asked. "Business hasn't been the same without you." She beamed and added a tiny container of tamarind ketchup to the order.

Passing over a few dollars, Zita accepted her food with a fond smile. *At least someone's happy to see me.* "Hola, Rosita! How's my favorite food truck doing?"

The cook shrugged her narrow shoulders. "Ah, you think I don't know you say that to all the trucks? We talk, you know. Business has been down since that company closed a few doors down and you've been out of town or wherever. All my other regulars must be dieting. I've hardly seen anyone and may have to move to another corner soon. The only customers I'm getting is when Chinese speakers stop by to ask why nobody at your office speaks a civilized language anymore. They wouldn't even do that if they didn't see my signs." She waved at her menus, prominently displayed in all three of Rosita's languages, English, Spanish, and Chinese.

The smile dropped from Zita's face. "They've been turning people away? I made that big sign in Chinese with instructions on how to make appointments even if I'm not there." She turned and scanned the front window of the office, frowning when she didn't see the splash of crimson where it had been before.

Nodding, the vendor said, "It's gone. Far as I can tell, the only Chinese getting service in there these days are the ones who speak enough English to brave one of the others. My mother will be worried if you're not available come tax season. She doesn't want to step on any toes by picking the wrong person in Chinatown. Did you finally decide to hold out for a raise?"

Zita shook her head. "No, she just hasn't been giving me any hours, and almost all of those are loaning me to other offices."

"You should find a new boss, one who pays better. I'd hire you, but you'd eat all my inventory." The twinkle and sympathy in Rosita's eyes softened the sting out of her words.

Her smile rueful, Zita nodded. "True, that. Nobody makes Peking chicken and yucca fries like you though, so can you blame me?"

They chatted amicably for a few more minutes while Zita waited for her food to cool after a quick bite of a fry seared her mouth. Finally, however, Rosita had to handle other customers, and Zita gave up waiting to eat. Commandeering a nearby bench, she sprawled on it and dug into her food.

Several minutes later, Zita had finished her chicken and had started on the fries when she caught sight of her boss scurrying across the street. She called out a greeting and gave a restrained wave, licking salt and ketchup off her fingers before she did so.

Stopping six feet away from Zita's bench, Emilia took a deep breath as she approached and smoothed her asymmetrical jacket down over broad hips. Her eyes darted around the street as if afraid of being seen. When he spoke, her words were as rapid as an assault from a machine gun. "Zita, it's a pleasant surprise to see you, but you really shouldn't have come all this way without letting me know first. As it is, I have only a few minutes to spare, and it's only luck that you caught me in at all."

Probably because you were at lunch for two hours. This doesn't sound promising. Drying her fingers on a napkin, Zita held out the cup of fries, knowing her boss' partiality to the treat. "Want some? I've got plenty."

Emilia took a step back before she caught herself with a visible effort and plastered on the smile she used with difficult customers. "How sweet of you to offer, but I just ate. Thank you for your consideration. How are you doing? Any relapses?"

"Relapses?" Zita echoed, trying to recall if she'd ever mentioned that her cancer had been in remission for over a decade. "I'm fine. My health has been great. Never felt better."

"You sure? Not feeling odd at all?"

After a second, Zita realized what her boss was actually asking. "Are you talking about the coma sickness? I haven't been sleeping more or less than I did before that, and my doctor cleared me." *Or at least the local witch and her handy healing spell. I'm not going through any testing until I know if having powers shows up in the bloodstream.*

Another smile greeted her words, but Emilia's eyes did not match. "Good, that's good." She gripped her handbag close over her stomach, her knuckles turning white.

Zita withdrew the cup and plucked out a fry while she considered her boss. *Is she frightened or is it just the way she drew on her eyebrows this morning? Her body says flight, but her face says business.* She went straight to the point. "No problem. So, listen, about my hours—"

"Zita, I can't give you more hours, not now and probably not anytime soon." Emilia raised both hands in the air and retreated a step. "Don't come in unless I call you. What with the budget cuts and all and the new district head cracking down, I just can't do more for you."

Feeling her own, entirely natural, eyebrows climb toward her hairline, Zita said, "Wait, isn't that the job you wanted? I'm sorry you didn't get it." *So someone else would be in charge here to give me more hours.*

Emilia shuffled pointy-toed heels and frowned. "Yes, but I'm certain everything will work out for the best. The truth is, we don't have the hours to give you because we lack the clients."

Zita waved a hand toward the window. "What happened to the sign? You'd get more clients if that was back up since people have to commute past here to get to the Chinese grocery store. You need me to do another one?"

Emilia's eyes darted away. "Oh. It fell when the floors were being cleaned and got ruined." She fumbled in her purse, withdrawing her ever-present bottle of hand sanitizer.

Feeling as if she was missing something, Zita tilted her head and stared at the woman. "I laminated it to prevent that from happening."

The bottle squirted from her boss' hands and went flying.

Zita jumped up and caught it before it could hit the sidewalk, offering it to Emilia. "You want me to make a new sign?"

Emilia could not wave in negation fast enough. "You know what? You can keep that. You'll need it to cleanse your hands after eating, anyway. The sign... we need to make our window conform to corporate standards, so we can't have it there any longer. Listen, Zita, I understand if you want to hand in your notice, but I can't give you any more hours." She babbled a few other things, but Zita stopped listening.

Well. That clears up what she wants; she wants me to quit to avoid a discrimination lawsuit for firing me because of the time I spent in quarantine. She needs to woman up and say the words if she wants me gone. I'll keep even the few hours she'll give me until I can get something new. Zita shoved her new bottle of hand sanitizer into her jacket pocket with more force than necessary. Her throat had an unexpected lump in it, and she realized Emilia had fallen silent. "I see. Well, if you don't have the hours for me now, I understand. I'll see you when the classes for the spring tax season start next week?"

Emotion flickered on her boss' face, none of it happy. "Ah, yes, the training."

Zita forced out what she hoped was a pleasant expression and tugged her jacket, ignoring the tearing sound from one shoulder. "Right, the mandatory training. Is it here or at the main office?"

A smile so bright that it seemed radioactive suddenly appeared on Emilia's face. "Guess what? Remember what you wanted last year? You can take all of those courses online. I got special dispensation."

From who, the Pope? Pain seared Zita's tongue as she bit herself to keep from saying the words aloud. "Cool, then. Will you send the link, or should I check corporate?"

"No need to disturb anyone at corporate," Emilia said, still wearing a sickly expression. "I'll send you the link. Now, I really must be going."

"Great, then I'll email to remind you if I don't see it soon," Zita said, plopping back down on her bench and picking up the discarded fries. *At least she has to pay me for the training classes. That should cover rent for this month if I eat a lot of rice and beans. Plus, I got a quick nap while waiting for her, and that irritating woman didn't show up in my dreams. It's bad enough she uses some power to nag me while I'm sleeping, but she won't even be specific about what she wants me to do.*

Without even a glance back at Zita, Emilia skittered across the street and disappeared into the office.

"Hey, Zita. What'd you do to her?" Rosita called out.

She bit into a fry. *Set off every germophobic bone in her body, apparently, so now she's trying to get me to quit.* Aloud, she pretended ignorance. For some reason, everyone always believed her when she did that. "I think something disagreed with her stomach."

Rosita sniffed. "Should have bought her lunch from me instead."

Chapter Six

As she drove her brother's van toward the office the next day, the setting sun was in her eyes. Zita grumbled to herself and tapped her fingers on the steering wheel as she passed through Jessup, a little Maryland suburb. While the road was pretty—lined with trees, random strip malls, and cramped houses, many of which had been converted to businesses—she ignored it all in favor of calling her brother.

He didn't pick up, so she fumed into his voicemail. "Look, Quentin, I don't mind getting a few extra hours, but I'd rather not get them because you're blowing off work to get laid. I especially prefer to avoid any more jobs where a horny slut in lingerie and a martini-soaked smile is waiting to be serviced. She ordered me to send out a male with a big dick, as if I'm a pimp! Then she tried to skip paying me even after I let her in her stupid house. Now I know why your crew asked me to cover this one. Neta, a vice squad will bust you if you're doing clients like that. Mano, you're out of control. I can't believe I missed dinner for this and covered for you with Miguel. Call me." She slammed her phone shut and tossed it on the passenger seat.

In her irritation, Zita almost missed the small, hand-lettered sign advertising One Dollar Tacos on Tuesdays, prominently placed under a street light. *I should come back on Tuesday. Wait. That's today!*

The van tires screeched as she cut across to the right lane, the rear of the vehicle fishtailing some as she searched for a safe place to pull over. A giant picture of tacos taunted her from the front window of a tiny taqueria that took up half of a house. The parking lot was full, and the one next to it was a weedy mass of red and orange-tinged forest. About a block away, she spotted a narrow turnoff where someone had widened a section of driveway to better access their mailbox, and she pulled in there. Another car honked as they sped past, but she barely noticed the sound over her stomach grumbling.

Whoever lives here should be able to squeeze past me to their place. I'll just grab food to go, and hopefully, nobody will notice me here behind this overgrown boxwood. If I keep moving, it's warm enough to just wear my exercise gear and not get my work clothes dirty. As she hopped down from the driver's seat, she paused, then stripped off her jacket and work coveralls, stuffing the wallet in a pocket of her capris, sealing the hook and loop fastener. Moving fast, she pulled down the magnet signs advertising Quentin's business from the sides of the van and locked them inside.

The last thing Quentin needs is a nasty online review because I needed to eat, even if it is his fault I'm starving. After tucking the keys inside her other pocket, she took off into the brushy tangle of the woods toward the promised taco land.

As she cut through the vacant lot, a brief flash of unnatural light, shaped like a rectangle, caught her eye from deeper within the forested area. Wariness ran electric in her, and she shifted to a jaguar, slinking through the brush without a sound and leaving her shoes behind. When she heard voices, she slowed, stopping beneath an untamed red chokeberry bush and crouching low.

To her dismay, she recognized Pretorius and Janus, standing close together. The big mercenary loomed over the scrawny teenager and was saying something too softly for even feline ears. Two beefy men in camouflage gear with Uzis waited nearby, whispering to each other.

"Stay with the boy while I see what I can get," Pretorius ordered. He rose in the air, slow and gradual, drifting by the men.

His guards saluted. "Yes, sir." One shot the kid a smirk as he brought the gun around to hold in a ready position.

Janus folded his arms over his chest and stared at his feet. Resistance sang in every tense line of his underfed body, and his shoulders slumped. As she watched, he brought a hand to his mouth and gnawed on his fingernails. He kicked at an abandoned square of metal stuck in the ground.

The man next to him had no patience for the teen and freed a hand from his gun to slap the kid in the back of his head. "You're not allowed to hurt yourself. Just wait for Pretorius to return, then you do your thing, and we all go back to the compound. You don't want me to tell anyone you weren't cooperative, do you?" His words held the flat accent of the American Midwest.

Zita fought the urge to smack the guard, though a low rumble escaped.

The other sentry came alert at her sound but didn't seem to notice the jaguar hidden under the bush.

His hand dropping from his mouth, the teenager glared. "No, no need for that." His voice held sullen despair.

I don't know what I want more, Zita thought, *to punch his captors, or to give Janus a sandwich and take him home to his family. The poor kid's a living example of why I won't let anyone know about my teleportation other than Wyn and Andy.*

The more watchful of the two guards continued to scan the area. "Did either of you hear something?"

Her eyes narrowed. *His English is fine, but his accent is Brazilian? Interesting.*

Janus grunted. "Cars. The food place." He sniffed the air and licked his lips reflexively.

His guards inhaled as well, and the one relaxed. "Probably was nothing," he said.

The scent of cilantro and seasoned meat was perfume to Zita, though she resisted the siren call for now. *I don't know what they're doing here. I haven't seen much worth portaling here to rob unless someone's got a vendetta. Pretorius didn't seem to be heading to the strip mall. Do I follow him or help the kid?* She checked the sky.

Pretorius disappeared behind the screen of the autumn treetops, thinned but not yet barren of leaves.

She swore mentally. *Pretorius could do the most damage... I'll turn into an owl and see what he's doing. These guys are just sitting here. The shopping center is close, so I can't take two at once as they could fire their guns and accidentally hit someone. Maybe I can help the kid get away and weaken Zeus' merry band of thugs,* Zita thought, her mind churning through plans.

The Brazilian guard abruptly lowered his weapon. "I'm going to grab some food. Both of us don't need to watch him, so I'll bring you something. Smells better than the slop at the compound," he told his friend.

His American buddy nodded. "Make sure mine has cheese. The last time we hit a place like that, the grub had pickles and cabbage and green stuff on it. I'll keep an eye on the boss' pet. He's going to be a good little boy and stay here." He cuffed Janus.

"You don't appreciate tacos done right, but sure, I'll get a few americano style." With a harsh laugh, the Brazilian walked away toward the taqueria. His stride was all strength and swagger, with no grace.

Probably lifts and does hodgepodge street fighting, but he's comfortable with a gun. If American Taco Thug is similar, I might be able to take him if I'm fast enough. Once he's down, I can set Janus free and knock out Brazilian Taco Thug when he comes back with his hands full. Maybe I can take out Pretorius too while he's searching for his pets. Zita slunk around to get behind the guard and the boy, and crept closer, so low that grass and twigs brushed against her furred chest. Changing shape to a gorilla, she picked up a pebble and threw it at the sleeve of the guard, on the arm farthest from the boy.

He turned, changing to a one-handed grip on the gun and slapping at where her projectile had hit.

Zita bounded the couple steps that separated them and seized his gun, one hairy arm on either side of his head. She curled one hand around the trigger guard to prevent him from firing. With a sharp yank, she smashed the Uzi against his face, though she held back to avoid killing him.

With a curse, American Taco Thug tried to punch her and pull his weapon away. The pain accompanying his hit was greater than she had expected, given his poor angle and leverage.

Super strength? Their thugs at the museum a month ago were extra tough and strong too. Zita smashed the gun in the guard's face again, this time eliciting a scream and a crunch that had her wincing.

When he released the Uzi, she tossed it aside and wrapped her arms around his throat in a chokehold. Even with the increased size of a gorilla, the guard was still taller, but the extra few inches afforded her the leverage she needed to keep the hold, despite the pain of him clawing at her arms. She held on until his struggles ceased, counting the seconds mentally.

Janus stared at her, wide-eyed and backing away.

Not for the first time, Zita wished she could speak in animal form. After easing the unconscious American Taco Thug to the ground, she shifted to Arca and checked his pulse. *Still alive, good. Now I can try to convince the kid to escape.*

"Stay back," Janus warned her. A large rectangle opened to someplace sunny and green, too green for autumn, accompanied by the distant screeches of howler monkeys and macaws.

That's the second time I've heard howlers. Since those are only in Central or South America, I wonder if his range is the whole world like mine. She held out empty hands, palm up, and said, "This is your chance, Janus. Go be free. You don't need to work for them anymore."

His face wild and desperate, Janus laughed. "Shows what you know." He shuffled his feet.

Keeping her voice low and soothing, she made no move to approach. "You're in lousy shape, and you're more miserable every time I see you. Based on today and at the museum, they've got you handling transportation for their crimes. Go, go somewhere they can't find you. If you're worried about it, you can try going to the cops. They'd love to have you tell them everything about the bad guys, but I wouldn't suggest staying there for long."

He squared his shoulders, his face revealing hopelessness he should be too young to know. "No, I really can't." His portal flickered.

The sharp report of a gun echoed from the direction of the restaurant, following by people screaming.

Zita swore. "It's Taco Tuesday. Is nothing sacred? They can't even order food like a normal person? Everything has to be a crime." She eyed Janus and his portal, then turned and ran toward the sound.

As she approached, people in both street clothes and cooking whites stampeded from the brightly lit back entrance, spilling out past the dumpster and a collection of dented metal trash cans. A wave of scent, cooking food heavy with cilantro and familiar spices, poured out of the kitchen as the door slammed closed. When she got closer, a car peeled out of the parking lot.

"Go, go, go! And someone call the cops!" she urged the fleeing staff as she slowed. Pushing herself up against the dingy white siding of the converted house, she inched toward the window until she could see in the gap between two beer posters.

With his back to her, Brazilian Taco Thug stood in the middle of a cramped dining area. His Uzi was in one hand, and the other clenched the tangled, bleached hair of a pretty woman in a short skirt and puffy jacket. Neon from a tequila sign threw red and blue shadows across the faces only visible in the long mirror lining the scratched bar.

Must've been a warning shot. He's taking cash and tacos. Rude and stupid. As much as I want to know what Pretorius is doing, I can't run off and leave these people in danger. Zita exhaled and forced her racing thoughts to calm. *He can't carry his loot, the woman, and his gun out of there. I'll jump him when he leaves with his hands full, and if he's still got the woman, that gives me a chance to free her.*

As she crept along the wall, Zita kept checking inside to keep track of the gunman and to assess the location. Half the dining room was a bar with wicker stools. The ones in front of Brazilian Taco Thug had been knocked akimbo, and the other half held tiny tables crammed tight together and decorated with yellow vinyl tablecloths and drooping fake flowers. With relief, she noted the white popcorn ceiling had a hole in it, and no one seemed to be bleeding yet. Behind the bar, a chunky waitress in a too-small polo shirt that matched the tablecloths shoveled cash into a bag. A short, stocky man with angry eyes and a staff shirt stuffed a stack of foam containers into a bag beside her. All the other customers must have fled. Abandoned coats and half-eaten food remained at the tables, nestled next to decimated baskets of chips and tiny bowls of salsa and guacamole. Steam still rose from a pan of fajitas near the door, tilted as if jarred in a hasty departure. Snippets of a ranchera song, heavy on the accordion and El Rey, escaped through the peeling window frame, but none of the conversation inside was intelligible.

I need to wait. I hate waiting. The guy in the woods is probably awake by now, and Dios knows when Pretorius is coming back. Hurry up, loser. Pursing her lips, Zita ghosted along the wall until she stood just outside the entrance. She peeked in again.

The captive woman held the food and the sack of money and stumbled as they moved. Brazilian Taco Thug still gripped her hair, hauling her body left and right like a large toy. Backing toward the exit, he stopped next to the doors. He lifted his gun, aiming at the staff members behind the bar.

Zita bolted into action, afraid he meant to fire. When she pulled open the door, a wave of richly scented air and a flourish of musical trumpets washed over her as she dashed in and knocked his arm upward, aiming for the pressure point on his wrist.

A burst of gunfire peppered more holes in the ceiling and made her ears ring, so her voice was louder than necessary when she taunted him, "Shot too soon? I've heard a lot of guys have that problem." She whirled, kicking his already-weakened hand hard enough to make him release his weapon, and then spinning to send the Uzi flying with another strike.

Brazilian Taco Thug turned toward her, tossing his captive aside. He wasted time swearing and then grabbed for Zita.

Dancing backward, she seized the fajita pan from a nearby table, heat from it burning through the frayed red handle cover and threw the food at him.

As he howled, he swiped at his face with one arm, trying to clean it.

Zita pushed the blond woman out of the way and threw her weight behind a hit on his dominant arm with the cast-iron fajita pan, then reversed her strike to hit him in the face again. "Run!" she shouted to the others in the restaurant.

Brazilian Taco Thug yelped and swung at her, an uncoordinated haymaker.

Zita held the pan in front of her face, and his fist landed on the iron skillet with a painful-sounding thud. The force of his hit drove Zita back against the door and actually dented the pan. *Another super strong one, great.*

The gunman roared, shaking his injured limb. He struck out at her again, this time clumsily with his off hand, his other one cradled close to his chest.

Letting herself drop, Zita dove between his legs to dodge. She spun around and kicked him with both feet.

Brazilian Taco Thug collided with the door, cracking the glass and leaving a red smear behind. Staggering forward, he swiped at her again, blood running down his forehead and trickling onto his shirt.

After leaping onto a table, she kicked the tiny bowls of food at him, jumping up to evade his increasingly wild swings. *Gun. I should move it before he remembers he brought one.* Zita scanned the room.

The enraged man wiped salsa and guacamole from himself and lunged for her again.

Need to get him out of here. Spotting his Uzi, she hopped along the tables until she reached it, then rolled off (to avoid another attack) and picked it up from the floor. "Catch me if you can!" she said. Gun in hand, she shoved the door open and darted outside.

He chased after her, blood dripping with every step.

Picking up speed as she rounded the corner, she ran toward the back of the restaurant. When she had almost reached it, she did a wall run for four steps, getting high enough to dump the gun into the dumpster, leap off the springy siding of the building, and roll to her feet. She whirled around and fell into a ginga.

Her pursuer thundered up. "I thought you'd be taller. Well, I'll crush you underfoot, little girl." He sneered.

"Promises, promises, but not likely with that crappy footwork," she said, feinting at him.

He lunged, his whole body behind a powerful uppercut.

Too bad she had done an esquiva, dropping low to dodge him, and then used her position to hook his ankle. She pulled.

Brazilian Taco Thug fell on his back and rolled to one side.

She kicked him in the chest.

Gasping, he curled up.

Faint sirens sounded.

Keeping herself ready for an attack, she flicked her gaze to the street. *No cops yet, but I hope that means they're on their way.* Her skin prickled as if she were being watched, and she threw herself to the ground.

An eye-searing blast of heat and force wailed overhead and into the building behind her. Splinters went flying, and a strange liquid sound began.

"Retreat!" Pretorius shouted.

Zita rolled under a bush.

As she lifted her head, she could see through a blackened, scorched hole in the siding. Water gushed from the now cracked and broken toilet, the source of the odd noise. Someone screamed from inside the restaurant.

She swore and hesitated.

Brazilian Taco Thug scrambled to his feet and disappeared into the woods, but the screaming from the taqueria drew her attention.

Abandoning her pursuit, she ran back into the building to ensure the people were safe. As she entered, she dropped to the floor in an instinctive move.

A shotgun blasted over her head, and a nearby table toppled, pouring food on her.

"I came to help! Don't shoot me!" she shouted in English, repeating herself in Spanish and rolling to her feet.

From behind the bar, a man said, "Get up slow." His words were even more heavily accented than her own had been.

Zita stood and brushed as much food and debris off herself as she could manage. Chips and chunks of tomato rained down, and the scent of guacamole rose from her hair. "Sorry about the mess. I did try to take it outside," she said.

The man behind the bar lowered his gun. "Where is the robber?"

"He got away. I heard screaming from in here and came to help," she said.

The waitress emerged, a baseball bat in her hands. "Our guest got overexcited."

Beside her, the former hostage peeked over the bar and offered a sheepish smile. "I thought he was returning to kill us."

Zita eyed their weapons. "I see. I'll just be on my way, then."

The man lowered his weapon. "Yes, you do that. You've done enough damage."

She held up her hands in protest. "Hey, I just spilled some food. The dude who broke your place throws hot goop balls. Plasma, I think. Tell the cops the robber's gun is in your dumpster, and you might want to turn off water to the toilet."

Flashing light poured in through the front door, and she glanced that direction. "Really sorry. The food smelled great. Bye." She ran through the restaurant and out the back door even as tires screeched and police pulled up, sirens roaring. The woods beckoned her, and she fled, scooping up her abandoned shoes as she passed them.

***

Four days later, Zita strode through the grassy commons toward her apartment, eager to get home and start dinner. The chilly air bore the strong sting of exhaust from the road nearby, mingled with the spicy autumn scent of the trees and a hint of... carrion?

She stopped and sniffed, wrinkled her nose, then resumed her walk. *Poor creature must've just been hit to smell this awful in the cold weather. Hope that's a squirrel and not someone's pet.* For a second, she considered a place farther away from the city, but then laughed at herself. In addition to being within a few miles of the metro trains, an easy walking distance, her complex was quiet and affordable. Since her brother actually owned the apartment, her landlord was also good if her rent was late. Not to mention, the condo association let her trade work for a space in an equipment shed to store her beloved motorcycle during the winter. Most places wouldn't allow her that luxury.

A scream split the air, followed by a string of old-fashioned profanity in Spanish and English and loud sobbing.

Zita ran toward the sound, her heart pounding and her eyes squinting. As usual, the visitor parking areas were unlit, save for a single light here and there. Up close to the buildings, though, overhead lamps burned as bright, cheap, incandescent suns. Since she and Quentin had installed them, she knew the lights had two purposes. They allowed the low-end security cameras to work, and they reduced slip and fall lawsuits by the apartment residents, most of whom had passed sixty a long time ago. As the odors of metallic blood and stomach-churning death grew stronger, she skidded to a stop on the sidewalk by an elderly couple from her building. She held out her hands. "Are you okay? Is someone hurt?"

One of the two men there nodded toward resident parking. The guy's arms were tight around his weeping partner, and his eyes were misty. "Miss Gloria must've let her little yappers outside alone again," he said.

Zita followed his gaze, realizing the issue was in her assigned spot. Two very dead small dogs in matching collars, one pink, one blue, festooned the metal panniers of her bike, gray-brown leashes trailing down to rest by four large, shriveled leaves. She stared at it for a minute before her mind made sense of what she was seeing. *Those aren't leashes and leaves. Those are entrails and ears.* Acid burned in her throat as her empty stomach revolted, and a hand rose to her mouth.

A blood-smeared paper heart was taped to each of them. The first held a phrase, painted in ink she suspected the dogs had supplied, and the other had a horrid smiley face on it, one with the jagged teeth of a shark... or a crocodile.

Gagging, Zita pulled her shirt up over her nose to blunt the stench and forced herself to move toward the horrible scene. She swallowed the bile in her throat, stepping just close enough to read the five words printed on the paper. '*Sorry to have missed you?*' *Sobek must not be too busy as an escaped felon to have time to harass us. Quentin! I need to check on my brother. What if it's too late? I wouldn't have even seen this until morning since I was coming through the commons instead of the parking lot.* After a hasty retreat to the sidewalk, Zita patted her pockets for her phone.

"Will you be all right, Miss Zita? Why don't you come with us while I get Hector to his chair, and we'll call the police together," one of the men said.

She shook her head, turning her back on the gory remains. "I got the cops. Do you have Miss Gloria's number? Can you call her and see if she's okay?" *Please don't let Sobek have butchered her too.*

He nodded. "I'll do that, but I can see her television through her patio curtains, so she probably just let the dogs out and assumed someone would bring them home."

His companion sniffled, a trembling hand over his mouth. "Last night, I complained about having to bring them to her again. This will break her heart."

Zita exhaled. "I know what you mean. I've dropped them off every morning this week and last." She patted his back, two quick taps.

"Take care of each other and shout out your door if Miss Gloria doesn't answer so I can tell the cops." Pressing Quentin's number, she said a quick prayer. Her right foot quivered with suppressed energy, and she forced it to stop tapping.

"You know where we are if you want company." Supporting each other, the men scurried into the apartment building with enviable speed given their ages.

When her brother answered, she took a deep, relieved breath. "¡Gracias a Dios!"

"Zita? This better be good. I have a hot date to get ready for," Quentin said.

She inhaled. "Cancel it. Sobek just left dead animals all over my bike, so he's after us again. You call Miguel. I'll call the cops and Mamá when I get a chance."

He took a ragged breath and then exhaled. "Right. Why do I have to be the one to contact Miguel?"

"Because I don't got time to calm him down from his inevitable hissy fit. Watch your back and let him know, and I'll call you when I'm done with the cops. Love you. Keep your gun on you." She hung up and dialed the police.

As she waited, Zita snuck another glance over her shoulder at the remains. She shuddered, anger rising. "Great. Now I'm going to have my bike impounded again, and those poor little things had to suffer because that pendejo can't keep his steaming pile of psychosis under control."

***

Two hours later, Zita had just picked up a weight when she heard the series of clicks that heralded her front door being unlocked. Holding the twenty-pound barbell like a sap, she padded silently toward the front door. *If that's Sobek, he's in for a surprise and headed back to jail once his concussion heals.*

Quentin's face, strained and tired, burst into a smile. "Zita! You're okay." His shoulders lost some of their tension. At the sight of him, she felt a rush of concern. He'd been avoiding her, so she hadn't known he'd dropped fifteen pounds, a loss he couldn't afford as he normally kept himself toned enough to please the ladies without devoting a second more to working out than necessary. Dark eyes held shadows beneath them like bruises, and his long, soulful Quechua features were haggard.

She lowered her makeshift weapon and set it aside. "Por supuesto. I'm a lot harder to catch than you or Miguel give me credit for."

He snorted. "I give you a lot of credit. Miguel hasn't ever recovered from when you went out on the window ledge to make friends with the pigeons. You had on your nightgown, and your hands were covered in peanut butter and bits of tortilla because you thought a sandwich would lure them to you, but you got hungry and ate most of it." Despite his words, he moved in and hugged her.

Pain shot through her ribs at the strength of his embrace. She rolled her eyes and made a rude noise as she pushed him away, fighting the urge to gag at the strong perfume that clung to him like a cheap and jealous lover. "For the last chingado time, I was five.

I'm certain it seemed like a great idea at that age. Can we let it go already?"

"No, because if we didn't remind you of that sort of thing frequently, it might break our sacred family bond," he said. He bumped his fist on his chest twice, the edges of a grin tugging his lips upward. "So, this is probably a stupid question, but why aren't you packing? Miguel said you'd agreed to go away for a while." As he scanned the room for her bag, his smile faded.

She picked up the barbell and did a few distracted lifts before setting it down. "I needed to work out more than I needed to pack. I've got a go bag ready that'll do for now. You're going too, right? Miguel said you'll go visit Mamá?"

Quentin hugged her. "I'll be taking time off, yes. I could use a vacation, anyway," he said. "You take care of yourself, okay?"

"Nobody's heard of where I'm going," Zita started the story while hauling her oversized duffel out of the closet. "It's just opening, so there's no Web presence, no tour guide lists. The name of the place is—"

"Don't tell Miguel or me," he said, holding up a hand to forestall her.

She quirked an eyebrow, some part of her relieved she didn't have to lie. *Well, lie more. Not telling them makes this easier.* "Why?"

"If he manages to catch Miguel or me, that way we can't reveal where you're at, other than out of the country." Quentin wouldn't meet her eyes, but something dark and painful shadowed his face, and for a moment, he seemed all of his years and then some.

Sobek will not lay a finger on you again if I can help it, she swore silently. Forcing her voice to be casual, she gave his arm a light punch and grinned. "You never could keep a secret. Fine. I'll leave here for a bit. Hopefully, Miguel will find him before too long." *Or my friends and I will.*

Quentin shook his head. "Miguel's off the case. Too many personal ties, conflict of interest and all that."

She snorted. "Like that's ever stopped him when it comes to family?"

A smile found its way to Quentin's face, chasing away the somber expression that seemed so strange on her normally cheerful brother. "Verdad."

She relaxed, then remembered his behavior over the past few months. "Your books are set up, so all you should have to do is designate one of the guys to access the bank account. Tyrese maybe for that? Carlito'd be good to do estimates since he's usually pretty close on the numbers."

Her brother raised his eyebrows. "Tell me my business, why don't you?"

Zita lifted her hands in the air. "What can I say? It seemed like a good idea since you've been neglecting work lately in favor of getting laid. I thought you might need a refresher course."

Quentin's voice held an edge. "That is none of your business, Zita."

She ignored it, other than to make a mental note to be gentle. "It is when your company suffers, you look like shit, and you're almost begging for STDs. If you don't care about your own health, you have employees to think about, not just me but your crew too. They've got families to feed and babies coming up. Diapers ain't cheap."

He folded his arms across his chest. "Butt out, Zita. I'm doing fine. A man has needs."

She fisted both hands on her hips. "I've survived years without getting any. You can keep it zipped until Sobek's caught. How long did you go between women this last time? A week?"

He evaded her eyes.

"Days?"

"That's not the point."

Zita gaped at him, and words spilled out, regardless of her original intentions to handle the subject delicately. "Carajo, hours? You have to cut back on the women. What if Sobek goes after them the way he did Jen because you were on a date with her? It's not like you to endanger anybody."

Quentin's mouth firmed into a straight line, an expression she'd never seen on his face before. "Cállate. You don't get to judge me."

"Mano, I'm not judging—okay, I am, because you're being a total man-whore—but you can't keep going like this, putting people and their livelihoods in danger. Pues, if you get the itch and need to scratch it, just tell the skanky ladies no and go take care of business yourself. Use your fist or a blowup doll or something."

He opened his mouth, then closed it, his expression thoughtful. "I'll handle my problem."

Even though she'd won, trepidation ran through her. *Something's not right.* "Good? You'll head to Mamá's?"

"No worries, Zita. I'll hand off some responsibilities to Tyrese and Carlito, and then I'll go. We need to keep you safe though, so I can go do stuff. Now get your bag and let's get you out of here. Make sure you check in with Miguel periodically so he knows you're safe."

She narrowed her eyes but put away the barbell and grabbed her bags.

Chapter Seven

Tonight, Zita would beard the monster in his den, armed only with her courage, cast-iron stomach, and dubious diplomatic skills. She prayed that her excess of the first two would make up for her horrible deficit in the last. Or that she could at least hush the part of her brain that doubted the wisdom of her cunning plan. *Well, it's a plan, anyway. Hopefully, this will go better than my talk with Quentin. It'd be hard to go worse,* she thought. The cold slap of steady drizzle reminded her that she'd prefer anywhere else in Maryland, places that weren't experiencing near-constant rains, even while the rest of the state suffered under a drought.

Zita knocked on Andy's door.

She knocked again harder.

When that brought no response, she resorted to slow kicks at the door and bellowing. "You know I can keep this up all night. Sooner or later, your neighbors will notice." *I need to practice my form, so at least I'm doing something useful while I wait patiently. He's so jumpy about nudity that he'll have a heart attack if he's not dressed and I pick the lock and let myself in.*

Andy yanked the door open after the fifth kick. A wave of unpleasant odor and stale air swept over her as he gave Zita a sullen glare. Baggy sweats, stained with food, hung from his leanly muscled frame. His hair tumbled in a long, tangled snarl down his back and his eyes were bleary and red. Despite his dishevelment, his body tensed into what she recognized as a judo defensive stance. Had he not appeared so unkempt, she might have been more disappointed at not getting to continue practicing her kicks.

She stared at her friend, lowering her leg. *Caramba, he's defending against me when we're not sparring? We're practically like siblings, if siblings had no blood relationship and had bonded over excessive puking during chemotherapy. Actually, given my relationships with my brothers, I guess it's not that surprising.*

"What? Why are you here?" he growled.

Zita realized she had turned sideways to better evade an attack and forced herself to relax into a more comfortable position. *I should've tried this sooner. His dad only left for the cruise a week and a half ago, but Andy is nasty. He needs a bath and a shave. Well, maybe not the shave. He never has enough beard for me to tell one way or the other if he ever shaves. Probably better if he doesn't need to since his hair might wreck anything he tries to cut it with given his near-invulnerability.* "Right. You've turned into Andy the hermit. Make that Andy the stinky hermit." In case he missed her subtle hint, she waved a hand by her nose. "Don't worry, I didn't forget the way you've been ignoring my calls and texts, but I had to come here."

"Take a hint and go away, Z. We can hang another time." He closed the door.

When the lock clicked, she knocked again and again and again.

He yanked it open. "What?"

"I can't go home. Sobek visited my place, so now one of my neighbors no longer has dogs, and I have to clean blood off my bike," she said, shifting from foot to foot. "I'm fine, but my family is freaked. I had to promise them that I would drop off the grid for a while and make it hard for him to find me. Can I crash here? The alternative is hiding at Mamá's house with Quentin." *Once he's safe with my mother, she'll figure out why he's been acting so stupid and fix him. It's better if I'm not there to mess that up further or to distract her.*

Andy snorted. "Miguel's idea, I bet."

The Andy Zita had known before would not have hesitated to offer her an invitation to stay, but the way he was acting... "Pues, we all know hiding at Mamá's ain't happening, and yes, it was his idea. I don't think we can afford to ignore whatever Zeus, Tiffany, and their thugs are planning, and my mom would notice if Arca appeared somewhere just when I've gone missing. Anyway, your dad and stepmom are on that big twentieth-anniversary cruise, and since you've been antisocial as heck, you won't have anyone else around here soon to risk—"

"Gee, Zita, thanks for the reminder that I have no social life and what I do have sucks," Andy murmured. He paused. "Of course, you can be my temporary roomie. I'm surprised you're not staying at Wyn's? You've been sticking together since you patched things up."

Zita rocked on her feet. "She left for a librarian conference in New York and has her phone turned off. While I could easily let myself in, that would be rude, plus you're better equipped to defend yourself against a psycho than she is. I'd like to see him try his knife on you. Garm and his gang breaking into her house in August rattled her pretty hard too, and I don't want to do that to her."

Andy rubbed the back of his neck and sighed. "And inviting yourself to stay here is polite?"

Her shoulders slumped, and she scrubbed a hand over her hair. "Seriously, mano? I'll just go. I've got plenty of friends with sofas." *Somewhere. Maybe coming here was a mistake.*

He was gruff. "Don't be silly. You're staying here."

Zita grinned and gave him a quick hug, wrinkling her nose at his stench. "Thanks! The food's good here, and your parents are away, so there's no one else to hurt. You're also the only friend I have whose sofa doesn't smell like somebody had sex on it lately."

Andy reddened, then grimaced. "Way to rub salt in the wound. I'm already regretting the invitation—so clearly all that time you've been spending with Wyn has really helped your diplomacy skills."

"Work in progress, mano, work in progress. I think I'm getting smoother though."

Giving himself a shake, Andy said, "So, Sobek came after you instead of running off like a regular escapee? Will your brothers be safe?"

"Miguel has been transferred to New York and is staying with another agent until he finds a place. Quentin was going to tie up some loose ends out here, then stay with Mamá. Theoretically, he'll keep her safe, though my mother isn't any kind of victim. The Feds think us being somewhere other than our homes should work because Sobek no longer has the resources to search for us. Since he's an escaped prisoner on the run, they're assuming he's busy hiding most of the time and only coming up for short gulps of psychosis." Zita scooted down the two steps to the driveway, grabbed her bag, and hopped back up. *Por favor, Dios, let the time with Mamá help Quentin get his head on straight. He's jumpy and has been sleeping with everything that moves, not a good combination for a Marine with a gun.*

Unaware of her continuing inner monologue, he continued. "Fine. You can have my room. I'd offer you the run of Dad's house upstairs, but I want to be able to protect you without kicking down doors."

"Nope," she said. "I'll take the couch. You're too tall to lie down on it and stretch out, while I, on the other hand, am fun-sized and will fit fine. Bet you're regretting those late-night growth spurts now, sí?" She poked his stomach, regretting it when it felt as if she had jammed her finger into concrete.

He shoved his hands in his pockets. "It doesn't seem right," he said but did not contradict her reasoning.

Flexing her fingers, she waved them in the air. "Don't worry about it, mano. I slept on Quentin's couch during college. His social life was slower then, but not by much. I'll spend most of my time sleeping in animal form, anyway. The lady in the Sunday hat who nagged us in our dreams during the knife thing is at it again, but she tends to leave me alone when I sleep as an animal. Plus, if Sobek or his goons break in here, it's easier to wake up as a cat, and I don't want to miss that fight."

Andy made a face and nodded at the mention of the dreams. He studied the floor for a moment. "Fine. I'll get you a clean pillow and blanket."

"In case she's been bugging you too, I brought the enchanted dream catcher Wyn made. I figured if you hang mine with yours, you might sleep better too."

He finally stepped aside to allow her entry. "Thanks."

Zita tromped inside, dropped her duffel bag on the sofa, and surveyed where she'd be staying. *Dios save him, I understand why he didn't want to let me in. This place is a wreck.*

Before, at worst, it had shown the benign neglect common in homes where the owners had lives outside of cleaning; it had been untidy and a little dusty. Now, it was a morass of unwashed clothing, discarded wrappers, and scattered papers, with the faint scent of spoiled food beneath the layer of Andy-sweat that coated everything. Random bits of modern electronics still broke the monotony of old, worn furniture, and crooked bookcases stuffed to the brink of collapse. While the desk remained where it had been, the ancient exercise equipment had been shoved into a corner and half-buried under dust, boxes, and stacks of paper. His giant television with its strange consoles and alien remote controls was still the room's centerpiece, but now it sat dark, surrounded by a corona of crumpled jerky and chip bags. Adorning the walls, his "cosplay" (whatever that was) costumes hung untouched by the mess, every impractical weapon and needless ornamentation in place, including the Batman mask with the purple paracord she had used to replace a snapped string peeking out from behind it. *Wait, is that a soda bottle embedded in the dark wood paneling next to the giant plastic sword?* Every door was closed so she could not evaluate any of the other rooms or the staircase leading up to his father's kitchen, but she hoped the rest of the basement was in better shape.

After closing the door behind her and locking it, Andy walked into the laundry room for the promised bedding. "I know you're up at or before sunrise and in bed by ten most nights, but I'm keeping odd hours lately and doing a lot of raids, so..."

When he returned, Zita held up a hand to forestall whatever he was going to say, then took the pillow and blanket from him. "You know, we can work all that out after you wash up. Seriously, dude, I'll wait. Get a shower, some clean clothes, and brush that hair." She made a face and pinched her nose shut.

He glanced down at himself, realization dawning as if he had not noticed his state before. "Subtle, Z."

"What're friends for? No worries, I'll wait out here." She searched for a clear spot to put her armful down. "Somewhere." *While I'm aware that living for years in crappy places with bugs and rats are why my brothers and I prefer things clean, this is disgusting.*

Andy spun on his heel and retreated to his bedroom, closing the door behind himself.

Her fingers itched for cleaning supplies. Zita swept a heap of clothing and crumpled papers off one couch cushion so she could put down the bedding. Almost without thinking, she opened windows to let in the sweet, rain-washed scent of the autumn outside and began tidying, piling dirty clothing into an overturned basket. Absently, she cracked her knuckles. *I'll just clean a little, as a favor. Good thing I know where everything is from helping paint the dining room.*

***

An hour later, when he returned, Andy almost seemed like himself in clean jeans, a T-shirt with an incomprehensible equation on it, and sneakers. His raven hair hung down his back in a tidy braid. The odor of soap lingered around him, blending with his natural scent. The surly expression on his face was new, though. He blinked and did a double-take. "Did you... clean my living room?"

Zita lowered the rag and the cleanser in her hands. "You're welcome, but you're on your own with the bedroom and fixing the hole where the soda bottle was. So, dude, about Brandi..."

Andy groaned. "Et tu, Brute? You're the last person I thought would want to dissect the crash and burn of my relationship with her. Even my stepdad was higher on the list of people wanting to 'help,' and he hardly talks at all."

"I don't want to," Zita said.

"Good, because people need to stop asking me about it. Our breakup was for the best. She's safer, and I don't have to worry about hurting her with my cursed strength anymore."

Zita blinked. "Uh..."

"I'm doing fine. I don't need a relationship. It's better—I'm better—without one, and I'm plenty busy."

She tried again, curling her fingers into the cleaning cloth in her frustration. "Mano—"

He interrupted. "So, you go tell Wyn you tried, and we can go back to not talking, understand?"

Zita threw the rag at him. "Will you let me finish? All I was going to say about Brandi was that she's real happy we kept our promise to give out the experimental sportswear. She sent a whole new batch via Remus, with a few extras for us, including masks in the special material so we don't keep losing them. Plus a bunch more to hand out, of course. Wyn and I got the distribution covered, but we need to know if you want the shirt to match the pants you wore home the other day."

Andy deflated. "Oh. I suppose so."

She huffed. "Fine. We'll get it from Wyn when we see her next. She's keeping the spares in her magic purse because it's easier to hand it all out that way." Pausing, she decided a good friend would probably say something sympathetic and struggled to find the right words. "I'm sorry about your breakup. If you want to go spar or something, I'm here for you even though you've been blowing me off for the past month and a half. Given all that other stuff you just said, I guess you're still all chingado about the whole thing."

He sighed and turned his face away. "I don't need a pep talk, Zita. Or whatever this is supposed to be."

She snorted. "Like I'm the person to give one of those about relationships? Brandi might make a sweet set of gear that works with our powers, but she's an idiot to dump your ass... unless you mentioned your plans to stop showering and hanging with your friends. 'Cause seriously, mano, going without bathing is not one of your superpowers." Zita made a face and pretended to gag in case he missed her meaning.

Her friend turned back around to scowl at her.

"Don't make a face at me. I'm just telling it like it is. You ditched us after the Water Balloon Death Run 3000 when we had all agreed to go to that buffet near the obstacle course. Who does that? It was all-you-can-eat, and they had the giant snow crab legs and a sundae bar! It's inconceivable you would skip it! Just inconceivable!"

"I don't think that word means what you think... Never mind. You wouldn't get it." He fidgeted. "Wasn't hungry, and not all of us are slaves to our stomachs. Look, I'm not good company right now anyway—"

Zita waved a hand dismissively. "You've made some dick moves lately, but you're still our friend. Wyn and I don't give a shit about you amusing us. After all, we know you, or did before you stopped sparring or responding to texts or anything, even when Wyn emailed that really funny cat picture."

"If you're working through a script of some sort, you can skip to the sympathy part," he said.

With a mirthless laugh, Zita hefted a barbell and carried it over to the newly dusted set in the corner. She placed it next to its mate after a couple quick bicep curls. "No script here. You want sympathy, talk to Wyn. She's dying to pat your hand and give you ice cream. Me? I think you're doing just fine with your own sorry little pity party, but it's time to end it."

"Wow. Can you be less sympathetic?"

She rolled her eyes. "If I didn't feel bad for you, I wouldn't have given you more than a month to put on your big girl panties... or Spider-Man boxers, whatever."

Andy frowned. "The fact that you know anything about my underwear is frightening, but at least you recognized Spider-Man."

Waving a hand at the overflowing basket in the corner, Zita said, "His name is on the butt of that pair right there. My point is, if you can't handle it yourself, you need to talk to somebody."

His face flushed with color. Andy edged over, picked up a shirt that had fallen from the basket, and draped it over the top of his boxers. "Yes, why give me any hope you could recognize a hero? Who could I talk to, anyway? Don't say yourself. I can't take much more tough love."

Zita waved her hands in frustration and paced, now that she'd cleared enough space to do so. "It doesn't have to be me. Wyn'd be a good choice, but I know you haven't spoken to her about anything. She's made it clear, and so did your office." *I'm probably the third-worst choice in the world to be his confidante, coming in only after Miguel, who has to remove the stick lodged in his ass first, and the Squirrel King, who badly needs medication and a serious vacation from the rodents. Still, I have to try.*

He stopped and glanced at his computer. "My office?"

"The one you used to have. About a week after we got back from New York, I went by your office at the university to see if you wanted to hit this street picnic with free food samples. Imagine my surprise when they told me they let you go at the start of the semester."

Andy looked away. "Oh, that."

"What happened?"

"A post-doctoral student works cheap, but a graduate student is cheaper," he said, his mouth a tight line.

She winced. "Did you tell anyone?"

He folded his arms over his chest. "Other than you, my dad's the only one who knows. I had to explain why my rent would be late. He's got me doing apprentice stuff for Cristovano Heating, Ventilation, and Air Conditioning, and has even been talking about adding an 'And Son' for me. So?"

Zita winced. "First off, that sucks. I know you don't mind doing HVAC to help your dad's company, but it's not what you want to do. Second, Wyn will notice eventually since she still works on campus. You should tell her before that, or you'll be the one in trouble with her this time."

"We don't need to mention it to her."

Zita ran a hand over her short, uneven hair. *How long does he think he can keep a secret from a mind reader?* She snorted. "I'm not lying about it. I just got out of the doghouse with her, and I'm not going back, even if you add air conditioning."

His mouth twisted. "Sure, side with her."

Knowing how much he hated it when people pointed, especially at him, Zita put her hands on her hips. "Oye, it's not a war. I won't say anything unless she asks me direct. If that happens, I'm busting out the truth. I have enough trouble lying to my family about my powers and where we go sometimes. Wyn is going loca wanting to cheer you up. Helping you find a job will distract her from finding you a date. Plus, she needs something to do other than obsessing over the lawsuit mess with her parents and her sick aunt and when's the right time to tell her new girlfriend her real identity behind the illusion." *Did I just play the guilt card like a pro? I think I did. And Miguel thinks I never learned anything from him.*

Emotion flickered on his face. "How is she?" he asked, his voice gruff, even if he wouldn't meet her eyes.

Zita shrugged. "Hanging in there. Her lawyer says the lawsuit is meant as a nuisance suit, and that her parents are hoping for a payout to make it go away. Apparently, they've got a history of such cases behind them and are doing the minimal effort thing. It's a lawsuit, so it's slow. She visits her aunt regular to keep her from getting worse. For the dating stuff, ask her, but I get the impression it's going well. She gets that goofy smile thing when she talks about it."

He grunted.

Touching his arm, she leaned closer. "Andy, you should tell her. She might know somebody who can get you a job that doesn't involve possible gas furnace explosions."

"Hadn't thought of that for a while. Thanks for reminding me of a truly stellar day in the world of HVAC." Andy rolled his eyes before his face lost even that animation. "No physics jobs are available unless I want to move out by my mom and teach high school science on the Diné reservation. When I was little, it wasn't so bad. Now, after living in this world for so long and never really being part of the tribe, I'd be politely treated as an outsider the rest of my life."

She huffed, annoyed. "We'll find you something, and once we get the job thing fixed, we'll get you a woman who will work out better." A thought struck her, and she bounced to her feet. "Pues, we should hook you up with an athlete. Maybe a chick who owns her own dojo! That'd rock. That way, we could all work out and tag team spar if I find a dude who likes sparring and sticks around for more than one or two dates."

"The likelihood of you finding a guy who lasts that long is... wait, is this about you or me?" Andy said, blinking.

Zita grinned. "What? Is it wrong to hope you find someone fun so we can skip the whole my-girlfriend-thinks-you're-a-bad-influence thing? I hate that speech even more than the it's-not-you-it's-me one, though at least with that one, it usually is me."

"Voice of experience, then," he said, a corner of his mouth quirking upward. "Don't worry, Z, you're family, and any girlfriend would have to deal with you. Every family has a black sheep, so she'd have to understand."

She wrinkled her nose, scooped up her dust rag, and headed for the treadmill. "Whatever, hater. Listen..."

His smile faded, and his gaze dropped to the floor. "I don't think another girl's in the cards anyway, so it's all a moot point."

Zita rolled her eyes while dusting the treadmill. "Wallowing, much? Is this about your strength and sex? If it is, we need serious snacks, maybe more brownies or brigadeiros, before we talk about that again."

"You don't understand," Andy said. He frowned at the rug. "I have no job. I have no people—"

She poked him in the stomach gently to avoid hurting herself. "You've got us. I'm totally a person, except when I'm not, and Wyn's always herself, unless she's an illusion."

Andy didn't even smile. "No tribe, then, as I know little about my birth one and don't have any Diné blood. I probably can never have a romantic relationship again, and pretty much I'm coasting, living off my dad and the spare five hundred bucks I get every month for maintaining a fan site devoted to a far more brilliant physicist than I'll ever be. So, I figured if I'm a failure as a regular human, I could at least do some good as..." His ears tinged with red, and he mumbled something, but she couldn't make out the words.

That's not bad money. I wonder if maintaining a fan site is hard? Bringing herself to a stop by him, she said, "Mano, it's not that I'm not listening, but I missed that last bit."

He sighed. "I figured if I couldn't live a normal life, I could try to be a superhero. That's the deal. You get superpowers. Your normal life goes to crap, and you spend all your time fighting crime and helping others. In all the comic books, the hero patrols the city and ends up somewhere high and broods while he watches over the city. Not only did I not stop anything, I didn't even manage to get on top of anything. All I did was break a building façade. Once or twice, I thought I saw Pretorius and Janus by this office building, but when I went over, nobody was there. I staked it out for a couple nights and saw nothing."

Zita waved her cleaning rag in his direction. "See? I told you climbing is a useful skill. If you took lessons from me, you'd know how to do it without damaging surfaces as much. We should go practice that. And sitting in a high place and brooding doesn't sound useful. You at least need something to do up there."

"That's your take away from this? I just revealed that I'm a failed vigilante. Zeus' gang robbed electronics warehouses on one of my patrol nights, but I didn't notice, even when it was in the same area as me. I can't even do that right."

She pursed her lips. "Why exactly did it make sense to roam around in a mask looking for... I don't even know what you wanted to find. Just because your life has been crappy is no reason to go searching for trouble. You're a physicist who happens to have superpowers, not a cop or military person trained to handle combat and criminals."

"Of course not," he said, "you're not genre-savvy. It makes total sense if you've read as many comic books and played as many video games as I have. Not that it matters, because even though you have no clue what you should be doing with your powers and waste them playing, you still end up being all heroic."

Zita froze, then whirled to face him. "Waste them? Why would you think that? Por supuesto, something goes down in my neighborhood, I'll pitch in and help. Contrary to Miguel's opinion, though, I don't wander around searching for trouble, and I only interfere if the cops or somebody else don't got it under control. I just live my life, have some good times, and try not to piss off God too much."

Folding his arms over his chest, he continued staring at the ancient avocado shag rug. "Stuff happens to you, like the Squirrel King bomb incident, the guys at the zoo, the taqueria, and whatever the food truck thing was. You got to fight Sobek, Pretorius, Garm... Z, you've almost got a full-fledged rogues' gallery going on. Either you're super lucky or super unlucky or wearing supervillain-attracting perfume—"

She seized on the part of that she understood best. "I don't wear perfume."

He exhaled loudly "Not a surprise or my point. Stuff happens to you. It doesn't happen to me like that."

Zita sat down on the sofa next to him and placed a gentle hand on his arm. "Andy, mano, I have no idea why all the crazies are popping up. If what you really want is to run across that more..." She shook her head and withdrew her hand. "Pues, you got problems. Have you not noticed that the bad guys keep trying to kill me? Not fun. Second, this isn't a comic book or video game. Real life don't work like fiction."

"Are you certain about that?"

She continued on. "Third, you won't run into anything if you're busy hiding in your dad's basement. You need to get your culo out there and do something. Stuff never happens when you're ready for it. It just happens. Trust me on that one. Wyn's run into a few situations on her own as well, but she's better at defusing them without violence."

His shoulders slumped, and Andy said, "Wyn too?"

"Well, sure. The last one was when she was on a date with Rani, the electrician you rescued. They saw Janus and some strange men loitering. Wyn used illusions of you and I and cops to scare them off. Probably impressed Rani, too." She beamed at him. "In the meantime, I'll give you some tips on spidering up a building."

He replied with a short shake of his head and rubbed his arms. "The one time I got on a roof, I just wanted to fly."

Zita hopped to her feet, unable to stay still. "Can't blame you. Flying rocks. I could hook you up with a No-Fly Zone map so you can avoid trouble if that's what you're worried about."

Andy rose and paced. "I'm not trustworthy as the bird. It's all fuzzy, and I'm not in control."

"Oye, you worry too much. Go for a flight. Your control won't improve if you never use your bird shape, which, by the way, is feathered, not fuzzy."

"No." He stopped in front of the hole in the wall and touched it with one finger.

She grinned. "If you're holding out for someone to create a humongous birdcage and keep you in it, it's probably not going to happen. I can just see it now... giant perch, a huge rope to gnaw on, an Olympic-sized pool to bathe your feathery butt in, and a big-ass mirror to stare at. Can you talk in your other form? Have you tried? Every shapeshifter but me seems to be able to do so."

"Please stop."

Snickering, Zita gestured as she spoke, her movements growing wider as she got caught up in her enthusiasm. "Too late. In my head, you're asking yourself who is a pretty boy in front of the mirror. Can't forget the pile of birdseed the size of a small hill."

Andy stared at her, eyebrows lifted. "That's really disturbing, except for the bird seed."

She chortled, still amused with her mental images of Andy-the-bird. "Fine, but I'm not hunting down any elephants for your other shape to eat or anything. Go flying, seriously though. If nothing else, you need the exercise. You've been sitting in here, skipping our sparring sessions and likely everything else. I'd be loca by now, so it's no wonder you're down."

He snorted, got to his feet, and hefted his laundry basket. "You'd be crazy after a few hours without a workout. Stop pushing me to fly. I'm going to wash these clothes, and then we can go upstairs to eat some of the frozen food my stepmom left me. You can set up the couch and get comfortable."

Zita tried to resist, but the siren call of dinner was too strong. "Ooh, leftovers from your parents? Sweet. Can I stash my motorcycle in your shed? My complex doesn't let me store it until they're done with the lawn mowers for the season. I'll clean off the dog blood first."

He shuddered. "Sure, Z."

Chapter Eight

Later that week, Wyn pushed aside the curtain and spun in front of a mirror, allowing the very short skirt of her dress to flare out around her slender thighs. Golden flecks in the fabric sparkled in the shop lights. "Andy's crankiness is our good luck today."

Zita awakened from her half-doze with a snort, sitting up from her sprawl in a fancy velvet chair. Plastic shopping bags escaped her lap to tumble toward the floor, but she caught them before they hit. This wasn't the first dress Wyn had tried in the tiny little New York boutique, but she'd been happily absorbed long enough for Zita to get comfortable. The plush Oriental carpet muffled any sounds of movement, and the saleslady's voice was a low, constant murmur as she assisted another pair of shoppers. The manager had long ago retreated to the employee area, probably to watch them through the security cameras discreetly placed throughout the store. Zita's eyes had naturally drooped. "What?"

Wyn fluffed her chestnut curls and smiled. She turned sideways to view herself from another angle. "If he hadn't blown us off again, we wouldn't have gotten to go dress shopping!"

"So, he's the one to blame for why we're dress-shopping instead of buying hiking boots like we had planned?" Zita blurted out the first response that came to mind and resolved to feel less guilty about crashing at his place. Situating the bags again on her lap, she flexed her back; flying in bird form to New York against strong winds had been a fun challenge, but her shoulders still bore the faint burn of a serious workout. It didn't help that Andy had played video games half the night—and forgotten she was there, twice tossing something on top of her snoozing form and shouting incoherently about owning things. Even though he had worn headphones, she slept lightly enough that the flashing lights and murmurs when he forgot himself had woken her several times.

Wyn shook her head, laughing. "We'll look at boots after this. Have you made any progress getting him to emerge from his basement?"

Blinking sleep from her eyes, Zita exhaled. "No, but I got him eating the meals his parents froze for him, plus rice and beans from my Crock-Pots. That's far healthier than the crap he was eating before, plus I got him to shower a few times."

With an assessing side glance into the mirror, Wyn frowned. "I'm worried that his recent hermit-like behavior might become a habit, so keep at it. I've tried talking to him, but he makes excuses and escapes. Strangely enough, I suspect you'll have more luck with him. Do you think this dress or the red one?"

Zita had learned to hate that dress question. Really, really hate it. She took a deep breath; she had promised to try harder to be a friend. *Who knew being a good friend meant spending so long shopping? New York's made for rooftop parkour and urban climbing, but here I am instead.* She tried for a neutral answer. "I like them both. The red is bright, but this one is like a disco ball, only sunnier."

The velvet curtain separating the fitting room from the rest of the shop whipped shut so fast that the whirling fabric almost slapped Zita. Wyn's voice came from inside. "Not that one, then. Let's see the red one again." When she emerged, she had poured herself back into the other one. She examined herself in the mirror, rising onto her toes and turning sideways. Smoothing her hands down her sides, she eyed herself. "Does it make me seem fat?"

With a long-suffering sigh, Zita eyed the dress and faked enthusiasm as if it weren't the third time her friend had tried on the dress. *Perhaps if I mention the best things about it, she'll buy it, and we can stop shopping? Por favor, Dios, let the shopping end.* "Not fat. It's a nice color, and it makes your butt seem big and round. Dudes or Rani will love it. Can we go now?"

With a distressed squeak, Wyn slammed the curtain shut. The red dress dropped unceremoniously outside the stall. "Neither one then. Ah, we'll have to keep shopping. At least there are plenty of boutiques along this row."

Zita buried her face in her arms and fought against moaning audibly. *Ay, I'm doomed.* Getting to her feet and shuffling Wyn's previous purchases under one arm, she picked up the discarded dress and hung it up. "I should probably get back to Andy's and make sure he's out of bed." Her stomach gurgled. Loudly. So loudly that the women in the front of the store turned to stare at Zita. She waved at them, then at the security cameras. "Plus, lunch."

Wyn flounced out of the stall and glanced at her phone. "Time to feed you, I suppose? Have we really been here two hours? Don't forget it's my treat since I chose the place."

Has it really only been that long in this shop? It seemed like forever, or at least Purgatory since they'd throw us out eventually when they close up for the night. Or if I touch anything, based on how that manager was watching me. She sniffed. *As if I'd want anything from a place that doesn't even sell usable exercise gear. If Wyn hadn't insisted on shopping while she's here on her conference, we could've picked out some boots and gotten in the warmup to a good workout by now.* Zita mourned the lost time. She muttered something noncommittal though. A high percentage of the supportive friend schtick seemed to require her to agreeably say nothing when they were doing one of Wyn's preferred activities. Wyn had told her so, and it seemed to keep her friend happy.

Leaving a disappointed saleswoman behind with both overpriced dresses, they exited the shop and headed down the street. Since it was Saturday, the office buildings that normally produced hordes of workers were quiet and still above their more commercial brethren. The wide sidewalks held mostly shoppers, both local and tourist, hitting the trendy shops and eateries that lined the pavement. Somehow, it smelled different from DC, though both shared the core scents of eateries, exhaust, and busy sidewalks. Wyn paused to point and gaze into several of the windows as they passed, but Zita herded her friend along, guided by her stomach and a new, bone-deep fear of dress boutiques.

Wyn yawned, covering her mouth with a dainty hand. "Sorry, I haven't had much sleep up until the conference, and I'm still tired."

Because you've been wasting time shopping? Zita squashed the thought guiltily and asked, "Why not?"

"One of the librarians has a kid who spotted a cat living on the roof, so she's been feeding it to lure him down where we can catch him. They were going to have an exterminator come to get the animal off the library roof, but I couldn't let them do that. He's a sweet, healthy boy, so either he was keeping the local squirrel population in check—"

Zita had to laugh. "I've been to your campus, Wyn. Those squirrels are not in check, not even remotely. That Squirrel King guy who attacked it at the start of the semester probably picked it because of the millions of fat tree rats. So, you got three cats now?"

Wyn sighed and shook her head. "No, my cats refuse to accept him and have been acting out, though he doesn't seem to mind them. Poor baby. I have to keep him shut in my bathroom. I tried to get someone in my coven to take him, but nobody was interested." She watched Zita through her long lashes. "You know, you'd be a great pet owner with your superior understanding of animals."

Zita made a face. "Bad idea. Not only do I tend to be gone for months at a time, but that psycho Sobek likes to leave me animals and people he's tortured to death. Last time, it was a neighbor's dogs. If I actually had a pet, he'd probably enjoy his sick game even more."

Wyn's face fell. "No, that would be a horrible fate for the poor creature. It's a pity. He's really very sweet and lovable right up until you try to confine him in a cat carrier. I had to try."

She nodded. "Sí, but no worries. You'll find him a home."

Wyn studied Zita, her face thoughtful. "Are you going to keep living on Andy's couch or are you moving in with me until Sobek's caught?" As she let her hair down and then bound it back up into another casual bun, anchored by a little, painted stick, she gave Zita a sidelong glance.

"Is that your subtext face, where you say one thing and mean another? If it is, I'm not getting the secret message," Zita said. "He's not real thrilled to have me there, but his family's out of town, and you're safer if I'm not at your place."

Biting her lip, Wyn said, "I'm worried about Andy. When I've touched his mind—and no, I haven't been digging into it—his emotions have been very dark."

Zita nodded, wrinkling her nose. "Part of that could be the stench. I don't know how anyone could be in a good mood when they got that much stank. But yeah, he's down." She had a sneaking suspicion she was still missing something.

A small furrow appeared in Wyn's brow. "I'm really worried he's depressed or he might hurt himself," she said.

"How? I mean, that's probably part of his problem. He's put off accepting who he is now and his power, so he hasn't been bathing, cleaning his place, working out, hanging with awesome people like us, or bathing..." Zita waved her arms for emphasis.

A passer-by flipped her off when one of her bags nearly slapped them in the chest.

Wyn pursed her lips. "You said bathing twice."

"Words cannot describe the level of stink he was at when I showed up the other day. I got things cleaned up a bit, though." Zita made a face, sticking out her tongue.

Two more people raised their middle fingers in unison as they passed.

Wyn ignored the New Yorkers, perhaps accustomed to what Zita suspected was a rude competitive sidewalk sport. "I don't know, but his emotions are all so negative. I've tried talking to him, and he shuts down or leaves."

Suspicious of Wyn's line of comments, Zita jiggled the bags. "Pues, I tried talking to him, and it didn't work out."

Wyn considered her. "Did you talk to him like you or did you actually talk to him as if you were a real person?"

"Ow, burn. Aren't you supposed to be the nice one? I talked to him, told him to pull himself together. You know, dude talk." She shrugged.

Wyn winced. "Perhaps you should make another attempt and endeavor to use some form of tact? We have been working on improving your diplomacy skills, and his emotional state worries me. Perhaps he needs someone to care for or something."

Zita paced a few steps before realizing that Wyn had slowed, then held still to let her friend catch up. "Fine. I'll stay with him for now, so you don't need to worry that he's going to figure out how to—I don't even know what would hurt him—walk into an open nuclear reactor or something. His parents come back at the end of the month, and I have to go then to keep them safe from Sobek."

Relief shone on Wyn's face, though she wore a thoughtful expression. "Thanks, Zita."

"It's Andy. He's my mano. Not going to let him waste his life sulking," Zita reminded her.

They had barely gone another block before Wyn paused and dug out the buzzing phone from her coat pocket. Glancing at the screen, she said, "I need to get this. It's my boss, and I can't afford to alienate her. Hopefully, she won't want me to spend the rest of my free afternoon working—the conference picks up tomorrow with a very busy schedule. Why don't you go on without me and save us a table? Order some dreadful calorie-laden appetizer, my treat. I think the place is on the right past that park there."

Zita tipped a couple fingers to her in salute. "Órale, see you there." She hastened toward the restaurant, enjoying the ability to walk at her usual speed. Despite legs like a giraffe, Wyn always seemed to move in tiny steps like a mouse with arthritis.

Right before the large, open-air park that took up most of a city block, Zita stopped and leaned against a cement pillar, one of a pair that bookended the entrance to an office building. She scanned the area, idly cataloging it as she searched for the restaurant Wyn had wanted to try. In the park, ornate benches were scattered along pathways that converged on a fountain, still running despite the late season. Thin stripes and triangles of grass squeezed in between the walking paths wherever possible.

Right now, most of the people present ignored the benches in favor of striding by, except for a lanky teenager. His face shadowed by a cap, the skinny kid seemed absorbed in slumping on a bench and staring at a remote-control car he piloted in mindless circles near his feet. The only serious athlete she could see was a broad-shouldered blond man smoking by the other entrance to the park, whose attention seemed to be on his cigarette and watching the quiet park or a nearby office building. A ball cap, matching the one on the teen, shadowed his face so she couldn't make out his features. *Maybe he's the kid's dad? Something about him is off.*

The building the man studied was representative of the area, with offices on the upper stories and shops and restaurants lining the sidewalk level. Farther down, a garage entrance undoubtedly led to underground parking, though the lot had a keycard reader and wooden arms barring entry. Glancing inside the entrance to the offices, she saw a couple of sofas, a young man in uniform behind a security desk, and a strange pile of objects.

The weird collection of items stole her attention, as Zita tried to determine if the tangle of tennis balls, plastic water bottles, and crumpled shopping bags over a metal snowman was meant to be modern art or simply a pile of recycling waiting for pick up. As a result, she almost missed the blond man's subtle nod at someone. Turning her head, she glimpsed a slim woman with spiky hair wearing all black, save for a red poncho, slipping out of an alley and into one of the side doors to the office building with the sculpture. Oddly, she held the door open for a whole minute before entering, a bored expression on her face.

Her balance is really good, perhaps she does acrobatics or ballet? It's not the right walk for those, but it's not quite martial arts, either, Zita mused as the stranger stalked toward the reception counter.

The man at the desk rose to his feet, smiling and gesturing toward the street.

Her mind still puzzling out the stranger's workout regimen, Zita gasped when the woman suddenly Tased the guard at the reception desk.

When the man dropped, black, triangular cat ears rose on the odd woman's head, and she hurried behind the desk, her glance darting around.

Zita turned her back before the cat-woman could see her. From the corner of her eye, she noticed the blond man turn her direction and froze at the familiar face. She could feel the blood draining from her face. *Pretorius! Here?* As casually as she could, Zita scanned the area for the spot with the least camera coverage. An alley with a dumpster was likely her best bet, and she strode there quickly, ducking behind the rank trash receptacle and a stunted pine. She peeked out.

Pretorius continued to lean against a wall, but he appeared to be watching the front of the office building, not her.

Dios, I hope she's not killing that poor guard while I do this. After grabbing a balaclava from her coat pocket, she turned that inside out and shoved it over her face. Stripping off her coat and sweatshirt, Zita stuffed her things into Wyn's bags, then hid them behind the dumpster, wrinkling her nose at the reek. *Sports bra and jeans... less distinctive than my awesome bejeweled T-Rex sweatshirt by far.* After a quick shift to Arca, she sprinted back across to the building and burst through the pedestrian door. "Hey! You leave him alone!"

Inside, the cat-woman stood holding an interior door to the offices open and staring into space, a keycard in her hand. Above the door, a tiny light glowed green. At Zita's entrance, the woman kicked the doorstop into place to prop the door open and dropped the keycard on the floor.

The cat-woman whirled, and a long, fuzzy tail snaked from beneath her poncho. She sniffed the air and curled her lip. Sharp tips edged each finger as she flexed her claws. "You again? Didn't I teach you enough of a lesson when you stole that notebook? You won't stop me this time, and I will never forgive you!"

At first confused, Zita dodged another wild blow, sliding over the surface of the reception desk to land on her feet. The guard had been stuffed under the furniture. *Wait, all that acrobatic coordination, but no actual fighting skill or stamina? I recognize her now. This is the same cat-woman from way back when we first got our powers and wanted to steal the notebook with our medical details so the government couldn't figure out who we were. I guess when she's not robbing houses, she breaks into offices.* "Oh, hey, Kitty. How you doing? Did you leave your friend at home this time? You know, crime doesn't pay and all," Zita said, ducking another stab.

Wanting to get the fight away from the (hopefully) unconscious man underfoot, she ran her hand along the underside of the desk until she found a button. She pressed it and was gratified by the sounds of alarms and slamming doors from the depths of the building.

"Stupid woman! Do you know what you taking that notebook cost me? I'm done trying to make amends for that." Kitty growled as she kicked at Zita. Her breath was ragged, and her blows were starting to slow.

"We didn't get the book. We thought you did," Zita said, though she had no time to ponder the mystery. Ducking under the high kick, she vaulted over the top of the desk and flipped to her feet in the center of the reception area. Wiggling her fingers at the cat-woman, she backed toward the massive windows and the weird sculpture.

Kitty sneered and stalked out from behind the desk. "I should have known you and your friends were too incompetent."

Zita shrugged. "We were good enough to beat your asses." In the light, it was easy enough to evade the other woman's advance, a whirling flip that seemed to involve a lot of flailing with all her limbs.

The cat-woman landed on her feet despite the impractical move. "I chose to leave last time. I'll show you!" With that, she leapt up into the air and began calling out words in another language.

Zita rubbed her hands over her face as each word seemed to thud into her brain like physical punches. Vaguely, she felt pain as her knees contacted the hard stone floor. A corner of her mind shrieked a warning, and she rolled blindly.

A clawed strike ripped her sleeve, though it failed to penetrate skin.

Blinking away the shredding remains of the sudden headache, Zita kept moving.

"Star Freedom Cat Ginkgo Final Strike!" A corona of light appeared around Kitty, and she lifted off the ground, floating five feet up and revolving in midair. Spotlights from nowhere covered and uncovered her, changing her ordinary clothes into ribbon-like strips of fabric that slowly wound around her, almost revealing her entire body.

Even if she didn't know what the peep show and special effects were supposed to accomplish, Zita was not going to stand there and stare. She glanced around and ran up to the weird statue, ripping a pair of tennis balls from it. Zita aimed and threw the first one at the flying, revolving woman, aiming for her center mass, followed by with the second ball.

Zita's first attempt flew true and socked the cat-woman in the stomach. When she gasped and bent over her stomach, the second ball smashed into her face. The woman fell to the ground, once again dressed in her ordinary clothing. Rolling over, she got to her knees, hands over her nose and eyes streaming with tears. If she said something, it was lost behind her hands.

The back of Zita's neck prickled, and she whirled, half-expecting to see someone else there, but the two women were alone, except for the security guard, who had pushed himself into a sitting position and now gaped at them. This close, he seemed only a couple years younger than herself, and she could see a short ponytail peeking out behind his head.

He stared. "Oh, ouch! Did you interrupt her transformation sequence? That seems rude. I mean, she deserved it and all..."

"What?" Zita scurried to him and freed his hands from the handcuffs, an easy enough task to do with the odds and ends on his desk.

Rubbing his wrists, the guard shook his head. "Never mind." He lurched to his feet and staggered toward Kitty. As he passed the interior door, it flew open, knocking the man into the wall. No one emerged, and the door slammed shut.

With a glance to confirm Kitty was still occupied the injuries to her face, Zita scanned the room. She thought she heard the soft whisper of rubber soles on the tile floor but didn't see anyone. A strong scent lingered: clean male, leather, and expensive cologne. *Oye, how did I miss that stench earlier? Did someone come in to work on the weekend after dowsing themselves in an entire bottle?* Moving quickly, she ran to Kitty and yanked the other woman's arms behind her back. "Is someone else here? Don't fight me."

Blood streaming from her nose, Kitty spat a curse at her. "I will have my vengeance someday."

Zita handcuffed the other woman's hands behind her back and guided her to one of the sofas. "Whatever, drama cat."

His eyes still groggy, the security man went to stand by the captive woman. He scowled down at Kitty. "Thanks, Miss. The cops should be here any second now."

"If you're good then..." Zita said. After a wave, she ran to the door and took a moment to survey the room again. Shaking her head at herself, she slipped back outside, scanning the area for cops. The street seemed largely undisturbed as if the spat in the building had gone almost unnoticed, though Pretorius' gaze was on her. She marched that direction.

A car horn sounded off in the street behind her, a long, musical melody made discordant by approaching police sirens.

When she turned to glance at it, the office opened by itself.

Kitty tore outside, hitting the closing door open with a shoulder and an angry yowl. Her hands were still cuffed behind her. She flicked a glance over her shoulder, her gaze skipping past Zita and sticking on someone. Her nose dripped blood.

It was a quick call. Why are you not here stuffing your face? Wyn's mental voice intruded.

Zita ran back to check that the guard had survived, throwing open the door. *I'll meet you there soon. A cat woman attacked someone, and she's getting away.* Calling inside, she said, "You okay?"

Resignation filtered through the telepathic link. *Let me know if I should come heal someone or if you need me.*

Inside the building, the guard got to his feet again. "Yeah, yeah, she surprised me."

Relieved the man wasn't badly injured, Zita turned her attention back to the escaping cat-woman and Pretorius. *Will do, but stay inside and hidden for now. Pretorius is here, and the last thing we want is him getting his mitts on you.*

Pretorius strode toward the bench with the teenager, making a small hand gesture.

With a wild laugh, Kitty raced toward the street and leapt into an older-model car headfirst.

Wyn's mental voice was alarmed. *What? Why would he want me in particular?*

A cacophony of honking and obscenity erupted as the car cut off a taxi and merged into traffic, Kitty's feet still hanging out the window.

Dismissing her as the lesser threat, Zita focused on Pretorius, who stood beside the bench. *Why does that pendejo or those thugs he works with do anything? A couple weeks ago it was all about kicking puppies. Maybe kidnapping supers is the evil hot thing to do today, and Halja was in rough shape. You're a healer.*

The teen pocketed something from the top of the remote-control car, then picked it up and got to his feet. As he lifted his head, she recognized him.

Zita shot toward them, leaping over cars and dodging traffic. *That's Janus. I need to stop them before they—*

Pretorius dragged the kid behind a large pillar.

Although he didn't fight the older man, Janus seemed to turn his gaze to the alley where Zita had hidden her clothing.

She didn't need to see the incandescent edges of the portal appear and disappear to know that she'd missed them. Zita slowed next to the pillar and swore, then trudged the last step to verify. *Stop them before they do that. They got away too.*

Wyn murmured sympathetically in her head.

Screeching tires, flashing lights, and earsplitting sirens announced the police had arrived even before they began shouting at her.

Zita sped away on foot and ran a block before she spotted a likely building. After ensuring the men chasing her had lost their line-of-sight on her, she scampered up a pile of crates, jumped a few feet to a fire escape, and climbed up the building. *New York's made for rooftop parkour,* she thought happily.

Are you still coming to lunch? Wyn asked.

Lying down on the roof, Zita assessed the activity below. The alley where she'd left her bags still appeared empty, though the police standing guard by the office building would make it necessary for her to enter and exit cautiously.

A flicker of color caught her eye, brilliant and unseasonal green in all the grays and strident, unnatural shades of the city. Zita turned and watched a familiar, gangly form dart from a closing portal into her alley. His shoulders held tight as if expecting an attack, Janus scanned the area. He didn't check the rooftops though; she had found few did. To her surprise, he actually wrung his hands before bringing one hand to his mouth to gnaw at a nail.

I didn't think people actually did that hand-wringing thing. Remembering the unhappiness on his face the few times she had seen him, she made a decision. *Be there soon. Janus came back, and I want to see what he's up to. Maybe I can get him to stop helping those murderers.*

The police are swarming on that block, so I'll wait for you at the restaurant. Wyn sent back.

Janus cowered between the dumpster and a lopsided pine, with the craned neck out to search nearby. By some miracle, he hadn't noticed the bags crammed behind the trash. He shivered in the shadows of the tree, rubbing his arms and shifting from foot to foot. Although his beige T-shirt and khaki pants fit this time, it resembled the bland, inoffensive uniform of warm-weather resort staff, assuming said clothing had been crumpled up and left in a locker too long. Reddish-brown smears on the pant legs showed where he had brushed against damp underbrush in the park. No coat shielded his gangling form from the chill of October. He was the only other being in the alley, discounting the bugs and pigeons perched high above.

After a quick teleport to the ground when Janus' attention was elsewhere, Zita sniffed the air. Though the dumpster muddied scents, no guns or other people seemed to lurk nearby. *Probably not a trap, then,* she thought, *unless he's got an ability outside of the portals.* The thick and choking scent of his fear made that unlikely, and she wrestled down her sympathy. Caution being what it was, she made certain to have a wall at her back when she spoke. "Waiting for someone?" she asked, her voice quiet, though her fake Mexican accent ran thick in her voice.

He jumped, smothering a shriek, skinny arms coming up to shield his face before he lowered them. "Yes, I needed your friend. Is the white witch here?"

"She's busy. You lucked out and got me. What do you want?" she asked.

His face fell, but his shoulders relaxed as if he were both disappointed and relieved at Wyn's absence. The tips of his ears burned red with color.

As Zita bit her tongue to let him speak without interruption, she pondered the mixed messages of his body language. Finally, she decided on the simplest explanation. *Poor kid is a teenage boy, and Wyn's sweet, sympathetic, and gorgeous in either form. His hormones must drive him nuts around her.*

He shivered, continuing to check the area. "I'm called Janus. They... Zeus' people... you have to stop them."

Somehow, his continued jumpiness was soothing. *He won't even meet my eyes.* Zita glanced toward the street and eased more into the shadows. Those on the sidewalk and across the street appeared not to have noticed—this being New York—not to care about the pair skulking in the alley. She relaxed. "They already got away. As I recall, you were a part of that."

"Not by choice. They know about my mom and little sister, so I have to do what they say or else. I can't risk being here long, or they'll notice I'm gone. I'm supposed to rest in my quarters until they call for me, but I didn't have to do a lot of portals today and wanted to warn you."

Her stomach clenched. *That's exactly what I've been afraid of happening to me and mine.* "Pues, so you want us to rescue your family?"

Janus rubbed his arms, covered in goose pimples. "Yes! I mean, that'd be great, but I came about the others. My family'll be fine so long as I keep being a good lapdog."

Too malnourished for a lapdog, she thought, *more like an abused lab. This kid should be out flirting with girls and being told his pants are too low by his parents.* "Are you sure your family is alive? What others?" Her stomach knotted, acid filling her mouth as a horrid suspicion flared.

Janus nodded. With a wary glance toward the road, he whispered to her, his tone bitter. "Once a month, I get to talk to them. Zeus has been recruiting supers, especially the obvious ones or monstrous ones he knows have a grudge. A few are paid, but most are willing, at least until they figure out reality."

With a tilt of her head, Zita said, "The one where he's a pendejo in love with himself?"

Again, his smile started, then died. "He divided us into tiers by power and usefulness, with him at the top. Well, him and Gaia, but she's not all there since Zeus threw out her meds. Atlas plays keeper for her, so she's not usually dangerous. Halja's a rung down from Zeus, but she's got a lot of ideas he likes to steal."

"He's an idiot, then. The only ideas Tiffany has are bad ones." Zita wrinkled her nose.

Janus peered at her. "You know Halja hates it when you call her Tiffany, right?"

Zita grinned. "I had hoped as much."

He returned to his original topic. "If you're not as powerful or you don't have a combat-ready skill, you end up a slave. I'm... I'm in the upper ranks of those. The problem is the people at the very bottom. Even with the recruiting, Zeus couldn't fill all their needs with powered folk, so he took over a pair of villages in the middle of nowhere. Says they won't be missed. Mercenaries are a last resort or for short-term stuff, except for Pretorius."

"That's terrible. Can you tell me where they are so the cops or someone can raid them?" *Got to be some organization that does that.*

It sounds too big for just me and two of my friends. Zita's lips pressed together.

Janus shook his head. "No. I'm not allowed outside the main building, but the compound's in a jungle somewhere. It's hot and rains every night. Lizards are everywhere, and monkeys are always screeching. Listen, I only have a few seconds more before I have to get back.... In her old life, Halja did something with archeology grants. Zeus rescued her because he wants to unlock a temple that's supposed to grant godlike power. That Hades knife was going to get them into it. At first, it was Halja's pet project, so she paid for it out of her own money until she brought the first piece of the knife back and proved it worked by... by... never mind." Green tinged his face, and he swallowed.

Not a kind and gentle demonstration, then. Poor kid. "Deep breath," she suggested, changing position slightly so if he vomited, she would not get splattered.

He nodded and inhaled and exhaled a few times before continuing. "So, Zeus is now obsessed with finding and gaining whatever the power is. Originally, they had me teleporting to a crumbled pile of rocks they think is the real Necro-Necromantis... Hades temple in Greece, not sure which, but it's on the side of an active volcano. The inner section of the temple is sealed. Since the Hades knife didn't work out, they're now focusing on an old jungle ruin linked to a cursed gem. It's like a jagged pyramid with an altar and a small building at the very top. Steps run all the way up, but they usually just have me take them right there."

Zita blinked, remembering a summer spent translating on a cruise ship. *Could be Mexico, though other places might have that kind of ruin too.* "Could it be in South America?"

"Maybe? The villagers don't speak English, but they're not African. It feels close by, and it has the same disco monkeys that are everywhere in the compound. Zeus has slaves building a weird framework to try to force it open, but magic stuff is keeping them out. If they get inside, Zeus and Halja will sacrifice as many as necessary until they get the power, sparing only myself and one or two vital others. The closest village might get sacrificed too—those people have no powers, shoes, or even phones, so Zeus thinks they're disposable. The gem will let them shortcut past all the trials inside or something. I don't know much more than that."

For once, Zita regretted not having Wyn's encyclopedic knowledge of such things, but she suspected that even her friend would need more information. "That's not a ton to go on. Can you give me anything else?" She ran her hand over her hair, forward and back once, and tried not to swear.

"Nothing other than the gem's green and they're going to kidnap some professor soon to help them find it. I can't be missed. I have to go."

The need to move overwhelmed Zita, and she paced a few steps. "What if I captured you? Surely your family would be safe then?"

He snorted, but winced, a sleeve riding up enough to show a burn on one scrawny bicep, shaped like a few fingers of a hand. "I'd have an hour or two to get loose before they attacked my family. They have these special plaques I memorize so I can come right back if I'm captured. Or else. I tried delaying them once when they were stealing explosives, and Zeus had someone total my mom's car. He said if I ever run away, he'll let this pyro guy burn my family to ashes. Please, don't stop me."

Zita kicked at the dirt. "I need more than that. Can you tell me anything else that might lead me to the compound?"

He shook his head, too-long hair swinging. "I'm a slave, not a confidant. If you can save those people or my family or both... please, you need to do it. If you can't, you still need to stop Halja. If she succeeds, she and Zeus will just going to keep going after bigger targets until they have the world, or at least the parts with the nicest stuff."

"What's the power?" She dug a hand in her jeans pocket.

Janus shrugged. "I don't know. The power of the gods is all they ever call it. Goodbye, and I never spoke to you." He clawed at the air, and one of his portals opened. The other end revealed a plain room, with the long, tall, shuttered windows common in a tropical climate and a slate tile floor. A simple cot and a handful of books were the only decoration in the spare room. Janus stepped through the hole.

Zita flipped a protein bar to him, and he caught it, tore off the paper and dropped it on her side of the portal. When he withdrew his arm, the portal shut, though she could have sworn she heard him whisper an apology.

Alone in the alley, Zita snatched up the trash, folded it, and put it back into her pocket. "Well, guess I got a tip and some fingerprints to follow." *The only question is if I know anyone who could run fingerprints or who could get others to do it. I won't ask Wyn to flirt or magic someone into getting results as that seems wrong. Jerome and that Hound guy are both detectives. If TV is to be believed, they should have tons of cop contacts willing to run prints. I'll try Jerome first since he's answered questions for free before, and that's the top of my budget as is. Hound probably gets paid by those mercenaries he works with or by whoever pays them.*

Once she'd retrieved the bags, she pulled out her sweatshirt and put it on, shifting back to Zita. She crept quietly out the other side of the alley and stopped, sniffed, and groaned. *Hopefully, Wyn won't ask why her bags stink.*

Wyn's voice roused in her mind. *What do my bags smell like?*

Zita winced. *Like bags? Listen, I had an idea about that cat...*

Chapter Nine

Eight hours later, with a sense of déjà vu, Zita did a pop vault to get over the stone wall surrounding Jerome's tiny, landscaped garden. On the other side, she rolled to a crouch behind an evergreen. Rustling and whispers announced Wyn and Andy on the other side, waiting for her to give the signal, and the only other sounds were the occasional purr of expensive cars on the street and the soft buzz of a pump in the rectangular koi pond. Moonlight flashed on a patch of white scales when a fish darted under a rock, and a black net broke up ripples in the water in even patches. The minuscule waterfall that had burbled so merrily in the summer was dry and silent. A breeze nipped at Zita with cold and brought a whiff of wood smoke, old barbecue, and exhaust. The overpowering scent was that of the leaves and autumn mold.

Since she had already scouted the exterior of the house as an owl fifteen minutes ago, Zita waited a few more seconds. When nothing happened, she whistled two notes.

Probably boosted by Andy, Wyn appeared, clinging to the top of the wall. The stone was wide enough to hold her body, but the wild flailing of her arms and legs overbalanced her as she scrabbled for a stable position. The tall woman tumbled off and to the ground with a soft exclamation. Motion detector lights sparked on, reflecting from the moon-pale hair and glittery dress of the illusion she favored as a disguise.

Andy sailed down and landed with a loud thump nearby, knees bent. He straightened and turned to face them.

Zita winced. *Not exactly subtle.* "Are you okay?" She scurried over to Wyn, avoiding the lit areas.

Wyn hissed through her teeth, and tears glittered in her eyes. "No, I injured my wrist. I need to heal it if I can, but I've never cast one-handed..."

Taking most of the taller woman's weight on herself, Zita hauled her out of the spotlight and into the deeper shadows of a large potted plant nearby. A tiny glint winked at her from the foliage. *I swear he's added cameras in the topiary animals over there since the last time I was here in August.* "You'll broaden your magicky experience then. Here. Hide behind this pig bush with the tuning fork on its head and try."

"I think that's supposed to be Lockjaw. He's a mutant-ish dog," Andy whispered.

Zita glanced at the shrub in question and shrugged. *If you want to name a pig bush and claim it's a dog, whatever.*

Andy darted across the lawn and behind another plant, as the topiaries anchored in substantial stone pots provided the only real cover available. The three huddled in the meager shadows, waiting for the lights to go off and Wyn to finish healing. While Zita's small size and dark clothing allowed her to hide fairly well, Andy was a miserable hunched mass.

Wyn curled up on the ground, trying to shield the gentle green glow of her healing spell as she repaired the damage to her arm. Her silvery hair reflected the light, and her dress sparkled. When she finished, she rose and stared at the house. The lights stayed on.

"I still can't believe you didn't want to change up your illusion," Zita whispered. "It's fortunate your part of the plan doesn't call for hiding. Shouldn't you be wafting up his steps and turning on the charm instead of giving away our location?"

Wyn's pensive expression was replaced with amusement. Her friend chuckled, the sound like bells ringing rather than her natural warm tones. Silver-blond hair shifted as her head tilted, and her impractical dress fluttered, seeming as if it was one breath away from floating off in the breeze. Her body was the same as usual, but her face was a perfect, symmetrical work of art, highlighted by deep purple eyes and a matching stone in the coronet. She glanced at the house and back again. The chiming voice that accompanied the rest of the illusion said, "The spell is anchored in my necklace and can't be altered without substantial effort. I can't believe you two dressed like that."

Andy exchanged puzzled glances with Zita. He wore black sweatpants and a dark, inside-out T-shirt. A domino mask hid half his face, stark white against his warm skin even in the poor light.

In addition to a matching mask, Zita sported a cranberry, orange, and lime-green plaid flannel shirt and her favorite dark purple sweatpants over the special exercise gear. "Like what?"

"I look fine. All creepy trespassers are wearing this style, and you know there's no help for her wardrobe," Andy murmured, tilting his head toward Zita.

Wyn waved a hand. "I don't expect her to understand, but I thought better of you."

"Why are we standing around?" Zita hissed. *We're in his yard, and we'll be late if you insist on continuing to talk clothes.*

Wyn put a hand on Zita's arm. "Relax."

Zita tried to moderate her tone, but impatience and concern made her words tumble out like clowns from a circus car. "All you have to do is talk to him and get the info. Jerome's cool, so you have nothing to be afraid of. We have places to go and things to do. Let's get it over with, and you can alert us via party line if anything comes up."

Wyn nodded. "I suppose." Her eyes dipped down, and she turned toward the house.

The outline of a burly man stood behind the sliding glass doors, gazing into the darkness. As he unlocked and opened it, silver glinted in his hand. "Oh, look who it is! And you want a favor?" Jerome said, his voice jovial. "Why, it's the people who couldn't be bothered to bring me in on the action in New York."

Zita twitched. "We didn't know you wanted in," she called back.

"Well, you need to rethink things. Come on inside." Jerome tapped a saber on paving stones. "Most use the front door, especially when they've been invited to visit. I'm curious to hear what you think you're going to accomplish skulking around in my flowerbeds and making my gardener cry by stomping his favorites. Mind you don't step in the pond or unplug the cord."

Zita stepped out from behind the topiary and shrugged, lowering her voice. "You're the one who told us to be discreet when I called."

He stopped, put his hands on his hips, and stared at her. "Breaking in is not discreet."

"We didn't break in. We used the back way," she countered.

"My place doesn't have a back way."

As she strolled toward the patio, she shot him an impish grin. "Sure, it does. We just used it."

Wyn drifted behind her.

Andy stood still, indecision in the lines of his form.

"All three of you," Jerome ordered. He flicked a switch, and the entire backyard lit up so brilliantly that tears came to Zita's eyes.

A corner of her mind made a note of the shadowy spots for future use. They trooped inside.

Jerome shepherded them through a spotless kitchen that smelled of bleach and artificial citrus and pizza, then into an office stuffed with furniture, takeout bags, and gigantic computer monitors. He seated himself in front of a keyboard, the oversized leather chair creaking with his movements. His saber gleamed on the desk, within grabbing distance. One screen showed camera feeds around his property split into zones. The others held text, except for the one where a pixilated green woman with the face of a pig, muscles of a serious weightlifter, and the costume of a stripper revolved above a circle. Various toys promenaded in places of honor on modern glass shelves while discarded computer parts and accessories mingled on the ground with food bags. He propped his feet up on his desk. "Right, then. Why did you have to sneak into my yard instead of using the door like normal people? Under other circumstances, I'd be concerned about you three lurking in my garden, but Arca's visited me before. I'm guessing she likes using back doors." White teeth gleamed in a dark face as he grinned.

After a second, Andy gave a choked laugh over the party line.

I told you there were cameras, perv. Zita sent. She nodded at the split screen.

Wyn giggled.

"I am smarter than the average human, let alone bear, plus I paid for a security system, cameras, and sound, and enhanced it. Did you hear that song about busting up an ex-boyfriend's car? An extra-crazy ex got inspired by it, and here we are, one fancy security system and a restraining order later..." Jerome clicked a button, shutting down most of the outside lights.

Do I need to know that song? Zita sent.

No, Wyn answered. *It's about a woman who revenges herself on a former lover by committing illegal vandalism against his belongings.*

Is there legal vandalism? Andy wondered.

Wyn glared at Andy.

Just asking. Andy seemed fascinated by the ceiling and stuffed both hands in his pockets.

Zita smothered a laugh.

Ever the people person, Wyn smiled as if they had come for a casual visit. "May I say you have a lovely home and garden, Jerome? It's a pleasure to be here." *Be polite.*

Spotting a tiny figure in a yellow gi with a large head, Zita tapped the Jim Kelly bobblehead.

"Yeah, right." Despite his words, Jerome's face showed his pleasure at Wyn's praise.

Andy stared into space.

Zita made a stab at the gracious guest thing. "I still like the koi pond. It's all thinky and peaceful, even if it's shut down for the winter." *Is it Andy's turn to compliment his place now?*

Jerome smirked. "So you've said before. Remember the bobblehead's delicate, Arca. It's custom."

She withdrew her finger and watched the plastic head bob. "Jim Kelly got robbed enough. I won't break him."

Jerome smiled. "Damn straight, you won't. Thanks for the compliments. Now, what do you want other than to admire my home, toys, and handsome face? You probably can't afford my usual rates, but I'll admit I'm bored." He propped his chin on a meaty fist.

Might as well be direct and just tell him so we can leave faster, Zita thought.

Andy nodded. *Guess so. By the way, Zita, you've missed almost every reference we've ever made, but you recognize a bobblehead?*

It's from a classic Bruce Lee flick. Jerome and I talked about it last time I was here. I've got the movie in a couple different languages if you want to borrow it.

Wyn made what might have been a suppressed shudder. "That doesn't negate the need for basic courtesy, and your domicile is worthy of admiration. We assumed that as a private detective, you might be able to find an application for an archeological dig submitted to a particular foundation in a specific time frame. While we don't have the names of the archeologists, we do have some information about it," Wyn said. She lowered her eyelashes, then glanced up through them.

Her friend's expression was winsome, yet beseeching, and Zita had no idea how the other woman had managed it. *Maybe Wyn has girly magic, perhaps imparted by imbibing pastel alcoholic drinks or not sleeping during chick-flicks. You want that movie or not, Andy? I've got a version with English subtitles for the weak.*

Oh, all that and the joy of subtitles? Pass. His mental voice was dry.

Wyn interrupted before Zita could reply. *Focus, children.*

Jerome nodded and stroked a hand over his goatee. "Simple enough. Why would an archeological expedition be of interest? Thinking of branching out from vigilantism to theft?"

Zita snorted. "No."

Her eyes narrow, Wyn shot Zita a warning look. *Who was it that wanted me to be the speaker again?* She returned her gaze to Jerome. "You mentioned the incident in New York earlier, the one where a group of superpowered criminals held a museum full of people hostage."

He nodded. "What about it? I watched the videos and checked them for alteration. Little had been changed, other than when they bleeped out part of what Arca said."

Wyn continued. "The woman responsible for that attack was in jail, until her organization attacked the corrections transport vehicles and took her back."

"You might recall the tall, beautiful black man there? The one the cameras loved? When she arranged this meeting, Arca slipped up on the phone and asked me which name I wanted to use, so I know you know I was there." Jerome signaled for her to continue, the gestures sharp and impatient.

Wyn explained their plan. "We suspect she's going after another artifact, and we're trying to locate it first to avoid anything like their attempted mass murder in New York."

"Hiding it elsewhere in the same building didn't work with them before. If we find it, we'll take it and hide it for a year or two, then put it back when they're gone. They should lose interest by then. We're not thieves," Zita added.

Other than a raised eyebrow at Zita's interruption, Wyn continued. "If the gem isn't there, we'll leave. If they want to waste their efforts searching for it someplace we've already determined it's not, that's more time they're not out there terrorizing anyone."

Jerome drummed his fingers on his desk. "Could be interesting. What's she after this time?"

With a dainty cough, Wyn said, "That's what we need you for. We know her real name and the foundation where she worked, but not which grant or coordinates. The application process is confidential." She fluttered her lashes at him and fingered the strap of her purse.

Tapping his desk, Jerome said, "Fine, but why do we care?"

Wyn's face sobered, losing some of the flirty charm. "We got a tip that whatever they're planning requires a massive human sacrifice at some point. Preventing them from getting the object averts that massacre."

Jerome stroked his keyboard. "Good cause. Why don't you just tip off the police?"

Zita butted in again, "They're fine against most people, but metahumans make up Tiffany's group. Calling cops in to handle the lightning guy—or Pretorius—"

"Who?" Jerome asked.

"Pretorius was the one who tossed you against the truck and shot you in the chest with the laser beam," Wyn said.

"Plasma bolt," Andy corrected. He had lowered his voice and roughened it again.

Zita winced. *I must've missed that. Sounds painful. That fake head cold voice Andy's using sounds uncomfortable too.*

Making a face, Jerome nodded and rubbed his chest. "Right. Him. I don't like him."

"I don't think anyone does," Zita said.

Wyn nodded. "Also, without more details, we don't know which agency has jurisdiction."

"Fine," Jerome said, "I'm in. All the way in. Since that's the case, it's only fair that we exchange code names and get an idea of each other's powers." His eyes glinted with amusement. "We can do more exact plans later once that's all settled."

Zita felt stupid but had to ask. "Code names?"

"Unless you want to use your real names like Caroline Gyllen?"

Zita involuntarily made a face. *That woman is a government tool.* "We're not fans of using our real names, no."

"I do have some ideas as to what those would be," Jerome said, eying the three of them.

Before he could say any more, Wyn spoke hastily. "It's probably better if you don't guess at our identities so you have plausible deniability."

Jerome harrumphed. "You have a point. Since I have to call you something, should I use the names the press calls you? Arca, Muse, and Wingspan? Really, if you've ever watched anime or a superhero show, you should understand how the name game's played for masked people."

Andy started to protest, then closed his mouth. "You have a point, but good luck getting the girls into the scanty outfits the women wear in those." *Or to stay clothed at all*, he sent.

Jerome eyed Wyn and Zita. "Muse is almost undressed enough to be in a comic book. Arca, though, did you mug a bum? If you don't like those names, we could use Witchy McWitchface for Muse, Fluffy McFluffernutter for Arca, and..." He trailed off, thinking. "We'll come up with something for you. The Internet will love the girls' names."

Zita wrinkled her nose at Andy's thought, even though the others couldn't see it beneath her mask. She considered her shirt and pants. They were clean, lacked holes, and covered everything. *Why do you people keep ragging on my clothes? Wait, Fluffy Mcwhat?* "Uh, no."

You look like you borrowed your psychopathic lumberjack daddy's clothes, and you have a big lump in one pocket. Wyn flicked a lock of hair over her shoulder. "Perhaps we should skip the offensive epithets. Muse suffices."

It's just the one lump. While it could be a miniature giant space hamster, it's probably food. Andy flashed a sour smirk.

Zita squinted at Andy. *A what? It's a bag of trail mix and a multi-tool.*

Unaware of the mental conversation, Jerome chuckled. "Hope not. How about McGruff for Arca? The silent wonder here can be Matches Malone."

Andy shook his head vehemently. "Nobody would get the reference but DC Comics' lawyers, and I'd end up sounding like a kid trying to be cool if they did."

"He speaks, and lo, his words are filled with Bat-wisdom." Jerome grinned.

Wyn murmured, "We're skipping obnoxious sobriquets, remember?"

Zita flexed her biceps. Under the loose plaid flannel of her shirt and in comparison to the abundant muscle the man had, the gesture lacked something, but she thought the group could stand to lighten up. "Don't make me come over there and beat you up until you cry like a little girl. Arca's good for me."

He snickered, not taking her seriously for a second, as usual. "Sure, if you say so."

"Right then, you know Arca," Wyn interceded. Her voice faded as she swung toward Andy, and all eyes turned to examine him.

He squirmed. *Uh, Doctor, um, no, taken. Uh.*

Jerome hooted. "So just go with the names they're using on television? I guess that makes him Wingspan or Mano then. Glad we got that settled. Me, I'll be Chevalier." He grinned and tapped his saber.

Andy gave Zita an accusing look.

She threw her hands up in the air. "What? I didn't know they'd take it for your name."

"Whatever." Andy stuffed his hands into his pockets.

Although he watched them all, Jerome didn't comment on the byplay, instead leaning back and folding his arms behind his head. "Now, what about powers? If we're working together, it'd be good to be able to plan."

Wyn gazed at Andy and Zita. *I shall not press you, but he has a point. He doesn't need all the information, but he deserves something.*

Zita sighed. "You're already aware I'm a shapeshifter."

As the government would be far more alarmed by a telepath than a witch, I'd rather not admit to that or to our party line. Wyn folded her hands in her lap. "I'm a witch. This is an illusion spell, rather than a true transformation, therianthropic or otherwise. I generally heal others as you witnessed on the freeway."

Zita cocked her head at Wyn. *I don't think you're misanthropic.*

The answer held amusement. *Therianthropic. My magic makes me appear this way, but I have not shapeshifted. You're the therianthrope. I'm an illusionist.*

Unaware of the telepathic conversation, Jerome's attention was on Andy. "So, you could just be tagging along, but I doubt it since I'm pretty certain I saw you absorb lightning."

Andy's voice was quiet and bitter, even beneath the fake rasp. "I'm strong and tough, and electricity doesn't bother me, apparently."

Jerome snorted and cracked his knuckles. "So'm I, plus I heal fast. What do you bench press?" He flexed one of his impressive biceps.

Even if Zita knew she and Jerome would never work as a couple given their personalities, she took a moment to appreciate the results of his dedication to lifting. *If we need anyone to enter a heavyweight boxing competition, he's in shape for it.*

Please don't picture him naked. Andy fidgeted, breaking his stance. He rubbed his hands on the sides of his legs. "I maybe picked up someone's fridge with a couple fingers. Her weights don't go high enough to make me sweat."

Wyn doesn't own real weights, just the tiny three-pound ankle belts. The only other place he would've felt safe trying that would be... Hurt, Zita rounded on him. "You picked up my fridge and didn't mention it? I'm your friend and coach. You're supposed to tell your coach these things... plus, I need to sweep under there."

He flushed. "Coins fell from my pocket and rolled under there."

She sniffed. "You still could have told me. I'd have made sure you didn't miss any."

Andy rolled his eyes. "They were quarters. No way was I going to leave them there until you finished working out." *I need to stop talking. Messing with my voice like this will give me a sore throat if I do it too long.*

The tension left Jerome, and a laugh boomed out. "OK, you got me beat." He scratched his head and sat down again in his chair, turning sideways to see them. His feet reappeared on top of his desk, and he typed on the keyboard, not even paying attention to the screen where data zoomed by, too fast for her to read. "Somebody upstairs likes you, man. We're cool. I'm in. Bonus round, I've decided how you can pay me. I'm waiving my usual fees in exchange for a favor." White teeth flashed, and a hint of the clever teenager they had known peeked out in the mischief of that smile.

Wyn stiffened, and her voice dripped with ice. "That depends on what the favor is." Tension drew her form tight, and she crossed her arms over her chest.

Zita set her hand on her friend's shoulder, careful to keep her touch gentle. *You okay or did some bad history just slap you upside the memory? Whatever happened before, we got your back this time. Jerome's never hurt you, right?*

Right, but when someone asks for a favor, it's never anything you want to do, Wyn replied.

Although he remained silent, Andy stepped between Wyn and the other man. *We're here for you.*

Jerome's teeth flashed again. "Oh, you can afford it. I'm going with you. Why just be the man with the computer when I can be a better dressed and more dashing Indiana Jones?"

Silvery hair shone as Wyn shook her head. "That's unwise." Her mental voice was curt, but the stiffness melted from her shoulders. *I'm fine. Don't pry.*

Jerome tapped his sword. "It's a great idea. As I recall from the prison break, there's a lot more of the bad guys than of you. I owe a couple of those assholes a punch. I can find what you need and take care of myself." He polished his fingernails on his chest and examined them. "Also, I'm really bored."

Zita answered Wyn mentally. *Even if rummaging through heads were in my skill set, I wouldn't pry into minds. I assume people think stupid stuff most of the time like I do, and I can come up with my own garbage. If you want to talk later, I'll eat ice cream, nod, and sound outraged like you told me to do last time. Skydiving would take your mind off things better though.*

Yes, that would distract me, but mental paralyzation due to fear is not an acceptable replacement for ice cream. The hard edges gone, Wyn's voice murmured assent. "Simplicity is best."

Jerome had a familiar mulish gleam in his eyes. He spoke. "Yes, well, you have a deadline, and I have what you need."

With a mental flashback to hours-long arguments between her brothers, Zita sighed. *Let's cut this short before daylight comes so I can teleport Wyn back to her conference before the crappy hotel computer link cuts out and ends the video call or something. We don't need to tell him about party line, and an extra body wouldn't hurt.* "We may as well agree. If nothing else, he can't turn us in without incriminating himself that way. If he's got practice slinking around taking dirty pictures for divorces, he might be better at sneaking around than the rest of us." *Or at least you two.* "Though if we have to have him tagging along, he needs to find out a couple other things, too."

Wyn nibbled her bottom lip. "True, but..."

Jerome snorted. "Tagging along? You all are blessed to have me given that I can take and give punches better than most. Also, I haven't photographed other people doing the nasty since my days as the best-dressed PI apprentice ever. I'm choosy about what jobs I accept."

If he's that discriminating, he wouldn't attempt to accompany us. Why are you arguing on his behalf? Wyn pressed her lips together.

"That explains the boredom. Too picky," Zita said. "He'll just nag until we give in anyway, guys."

The man healed after getting hit by lightning and being shot in the chest with plasma. It couldn't hurt to have him between you and danger, Andy pointed out.

Narrowing his eyes at Zita, Jerome continued, "I don't nag. It's more of a bargaining thing. What else did you want?"

Zita made one more attempt at soothing Wyn. *We don't have to say more than we already have. It'll make logistics more complicated, especially for Andy, but we need the information.* Nodding with a firmness she hoped to feel later, she forced cheer into her voice. "I'm betting you nag like a diva. The second job is to identify the kid whose fingerprints are on this wrapper and locate his family. He's an American teenage boy, the one creating portals for Zeus." She pulled out the trash, now sealed in a plastic baggie. "The last item is to find is an escaped prisoner, Sobek. His actual name is Tracy Jones. He was kidnapping and shipping people with powers before. His men made a play to grab you when I was here last time. It'd be good to know where he is before he gets up to that again."

Jerome's eyes gleamed. "Done and done. It's settled then."

After a moment, Wyn and Andy nodded.

"Now we've got that squared away, give me what you have," Jerome said.

Wyn set the paper on the desk with all the details they'd managed to glean from the Internet. "We're interested in two applications that went to this foundation in the past few years and probably got turned down. Halja's real name, Tiffany, will link to the committee somehow. One application will be for a Grecian temple, perhaps the Necromanteion, and likely references the Key of Hades. The second application is the more important one, and the primary artifact sought is a green gem. It's in a jungle temple, possibly a ziggurat, probably in Central or South America."

Jerome glanced at the paper. "You have anything else?"

"If a professor associated with an application is missing, that's probably the right one. Our tip mentioned they were going to kidnap one to assist," Zita offered.

The detective tapped his desk. "You never have much to go on, but at least you've got a full name and correct business name this time. Give me an hour for the grant application searches, then, the scope is pretty broad, even if it's limited to one organization. The fingerprints I'll get to you later since I have to dig up my old kit. For Sobek, I'll have to check further, depending on how stupid he's been while hiding. Help yourself to something in the fridge and make yourselves comfortable."

Zita nodded. "I could do with a snack."

"That's a surprise," Wyn murmured. She headed toward the door.

Andy frowned. "How can you do that in an hour?"

With a sniff, Jerome settled the keyboard on his lap. "I'm that good. Are you forgetting who created the top three Internet search algorithms out there? I'll have the computer sitting up and begging for Snausages if that's what I want it to do. Now, you go wait in the living room. I need private time with my main baby here to get the work going." He stroked the monitor. Screens whirled.

With a shudder, Zita escaped to the kitchen. *The way he touches that machine is so not right.*

***

It took less than an hour for Jerome to come back. He offered them a sheet of paper. "Got your gem. Still narrowing down the other one and running searches on Sobek."

"Brazil?" Wyn said, dismay in her tone.

Andy grunted.

A huge grin broke on Zita's face. "Brazil! Whereabouts?" *I hope it's somewhere I've never been,* she thought, *some place with steep bluffs or cave diving or something awesome. Wouldn't it be sweet if we had to climb a sheer cliff, dive off the top of the other side, then find the temple underwater in a cave?*

Coiling a strand of hair around her finger, Wyn scanned the information. "This doesn't have any specific location listed other than Brazil. Well, I suppose Rio de Janeiro wouldn't be too bad. Perhaps we'll find this Heart of Canaiwari there." *Concentrate, Zita. While your idea sounds terrible, I wouldn't mind a trip to the beach with a nice book.*

Jerome coughed. "I may have redacted that to ensure you keep up your end of the bargain."

Setting down the fancy organic beef jerky she'd been snacking on, Zita said, "Oye, Brazil is the fifth largest country in the world and has a ton of microclimates. How can we prepare for the trip without more information?"

Jerome grumbled and gestured for her to follow him.

The trio trailed after him. Once in his office, he turned back to his computer. His hands brushed over the keyboard. The screen in front of him, mostly hidden by his broad shoulders, flashed and changed to a map.

Zita stepped to the side to see better.

Jerome zoomed out until Zita could make out a few of the words, and then he turned to face her friends again. Behind him, the monitor went dark. "Fine, it's northern Brazil."

"That doesn't narrow down the climate too much, but it's definitely not Rio. Sorry, Muse," Zita said, her eyes flicking to Andy and back again. "I guess it's somewhere in the states of Amazonas, Roraima, or Pará from what I saw, so it could be a tropical, highland, or mountainous."

Andy stared at the floor as if willing it to disintegrate.

"Well, if you were counting on me to get us there, I can't arrange a flight for tonight. How will we get through security without removing masks? Speaking of which, I've got to find a Halloween mask somewhere before we leave, so tomorrow is the earliest I can go. Cops don't like a big, beautiful brother like me wearing a ski mask, even if my fashion sense is impeccable," Jerome said.

Wyn coughed and coiled another lock of hair around her finger. "Can we have a moment to discuss timelines for the trip?"

The big man shrugged and put his feet up on the desk. "Sure," Jerome said. "I'll go check on the other searches."

"Thanks," Wyn called out to him. Releasing her hair, she touched Andy and Zita's shoulders, urging them into the living room.

Andy and Zita exchanged glances and followed her.

As soon as they were alone, Wyn whirled and whispered. "What do you two think? I can't leave for long. I need to stay near my aunt so I can keep her as healthy as possible and prevent her Alzheimer's from advancing. Additionally, I've got the conference and a meeting with my lawyer over that lawsuit. The office will need more than a moment's notice, and it wouldn't hurt to get background information on this Heart of Canaiwari gem. I don't think I can do it in less than three or four weeks." She collapsed onto one of the leather sofas and massaged her forehead.

"Let's just get it over with and go tonight," Andy said, his arms wrapped around himself. "There and done."

Zita thought it through, pacing from one side of the room to the other. Her words came slowly. "As much as I usually would be all over a spontaneous Brazil trip, we need to arrange some details first, so our regular lives don't suffer. On the plus side, they can't go after the temple too fast."

Andy barked out a short, harsh laugh. "What lives?"

Zita shrugged and continued to circle the room. "True enough for me. With Sobek loose, everyone wants me to hide until he's caught, especially since he stopped by my work to check for me the other day."

Lifting his head, Andy blinked, concern replacing his sullen expression. "Compulsive much?"

Zita kept walking. "I know, right? My boss called about it yesterday. She was already freaked about me being in quarantine before, but now I'm forbidden to come back until Sobek's in jail again. On the bright side, I got permission to do training classes remotely, so I've been cramming those in to get as many paid hours as possible before she finds a legal excuse to fire me. Quentin will stay with Mamá to keep her safe and because the prosecutors want him out of easy reach. With Jen Stone loca and missing, he's their star witness. It's been suggested I do the same—Miguel ordered me to do so, in fact."

"It's as if he doesn't know you," Andy said.

Wyn nodded. "Is he attempting to get you to camp out on Sobek's front doorstep?"

Zita grinned and vaulted over the back of a sofa, landing on the seat next to Wyn. She bumped her friend with her shoulder. "I know, right? So, I can go anytime."

Andy shoved his hands into his pockets. Something ripped, and his face darkened. "The university's decided to cut costs by having a graduate student handle the labs instead of a postdoc, so I've been jobless awhile, other than working for Dad."

Wyn gasped, fingers rising to her lips. "Oh, no. Are you serious?"

"Those pendejos," Zita said, more to support him than anything. *Praise Dios that he's finally telling her.*

He nodded. "Guess I've got the time, other than Dad wanting me to turn to HVAC full time. I told him I'm looking for a physics position, but... the odds are horrible."

"Major suckage, mano. You'll find something, though." Unable to sit still any longer, Zita hopped up and punched his arm. "If you need me, I got your back."

Eyes welling with sympathy, Wyn rose and hugged Andy, then stretched out an arm to include Zita. "I'll help with your resume if you want," she offered. "With both your resumes."

He shrugged, pulling free. "Whatever. Not a lot of physics posts out there, so I guess I'm stuck with HVAC and my website money."

Wyn took the hint and let her arms drop. "You have a site?"

Color rose in Andy's cheeks. "I maintain a special-interest site and receive a small stipend from fans. It's not enough to live on, but it helps."

This is the man who can't handle any innocent nudity? You think you know a person, then something like this comes out. Zita brightened and bounced. "So, you run a porn site too? If you want, I can recommend it to Quentin. He knows tons of sex shops you could advertise at."

Andy choked, and red rose in his face. "What? No, I don't have a porn site."

At least he's showing more animation than he has in a while. "Qué lástima. I hear those are profitable."

Fingers covered her mouth as Wyn tried to suppress her giggles and failed. "So, what is the site?"

"It's a physics site, where I post the latest Farnswaggle research and news. Geez."

Zita shrugged. "Just keeping it real. I forgot the fansite you mentioned before was that profitable, so I said what we were both thinking. That makes more sense than you getting naughty for a webcam, though."

Wyn looked away, roses blooming in her cheeks, but made no correction.

Andy scrubbed a hand over his forehead. "Wow. So not happening. The only thing naked on my site is the physics. It's been more popular lately since some of his theories explain people having powers and how they work." He paused. "Even if I personally know some of those theories seem to be true, I can't ever present any proof of it."

Zita sifted through his statements and pulled out the part she understood. "Well, I'm glad your web stuff does well. Now, back to the gem. If they're going after it soon, we should stop them. Nobody needs Tiffany pulling another stunt like she tried in New York. Andy, are you in? Wyn, I understand if you can't go. Do you want to check in on us mentally and do research while we're gone?"

After clearing her throat, Wyn announced, "I'm going. I don't know how we'll arrange things, but you aren't be leaving me behind."

"We don't even know where or for how long yet," Zita said.

Wyn narrowed her eyes at Zita. "I'm going. Neither one of you can see magic, and I'm also the best educated if the gem is in a temple. In the books, it's almost always part of a giant booby-trapped statue. I have the most chance of being able to recognize it and disarm any curse."

"It's going to be risky. Since you won't use your magic to fight, wouldn't it be better if you stayed safe and helped us from there?" Zita gave it a try. Beside her, Andy nodded.

"While my faith won't permit me to abuse magic to harm another, you will still require my assistance with any magical challenges. I accept this will be dangerous, but I have faith that between the Goddess and you two, I will come through it unscathed." Wyn folded her hands in her lap and gave them a serene smile daring them to continue that line of questioning.

Even recognizing that expression meant her cause was hopeless, Zita played her best card. "What about your aunt?"

Her friend exhaled. "I'll have to cast the healing spell on her right before we go, and limit the trip in length, or at least my part in it. I'll see what vacation time I have stored up."

Andy sighed. "Fine. Let's go tonight then. Get it over with and get back."

Wyn seemed distressed. "We can't. I have to see my aunt, find a catsitter, handle the lawyer meeting, and arrange things at work..."

"Even if I'm half-packed already, we can wait a few days. If Tiffany's driving this, she just got magic napalm burns and will need time to heal. They might not get around to leaving for months, so if we need to wait for Wyn to get things in order, I think we can."

Andy growled in protest.

Zita grabbed his arm and pulled him aside, holding up a finger to Wyn to give them a moment.

The other woman nodded and dug through her purse.

Turning back to Andy, Zita whispered, "Dude, it's me. Trust me, I'd rather go right away too, but our schedules are more flexible than Wyn's, and she has a point." She went for his weak spot. "If there's magicky witch stuff, do you want to deal with it without Wyn there?"

Color drained from his face. "Let me know when we're leaving, then."

Zita nodded, took his arm, and propelled him to Wyn. "Let's go tell Jerome that we'll go in three or four weeks."

Wyn beamed.

Chapter Ten

A half-hour later, the trio had returned to Andy's much cleaner basement apartment.

At the computer, Wyn linked up to the webcam she'd left running in her hotel room. A picture of her cats lay on a hotel bed, with a paperback book next to it.

Beside her, Zita was trying hard not to comment on the shirtless bodybuilder on the book's cover, or to ask why he was purple and angled to hide his face.

On the opposite side of the room, Andy puttered with a stack of papers, picking them up and putting them down again. "If we're not going to Brazil tonight, we should all say goodnight. Zita's up past her bedtime."

Speaking of bedtimes. Zita cleared her throat. "So, I should mention that dream auntie's back again, stomping through and ruining perfectly good dreams with all her warnings. You know, the lady in church clothes who was invading our sleep when we were dealing with the evil knife of evilness? I meant to say something before and forgot. What kind of world is it, though, when a woman can't even walk around nude in her dreams without someone getting all prissy about it?"

"Please don't be naked in my living room or any room of my place," Andy said.

"That'll make it hard to shower," Zita teased.

He didn't smile.

"The Key of Hades... the knife may have been used for evil, but it is a magical artifact with a no-doubt fascinating history." Wyn shook her head and assumed a more businesslike manner. "The dreamcatcher I gave you isn't keeping her out? I'll revise the spell and see if I can do more about that. The challenge is that she's not using magic to do it, instead invoking what must be her power. I'm hesitant to eliminate every dream pathway since I don't want to risk prolonged sleep deprivation for either of you."

Andy stared off into space. "Get her to leave me alone too," he said. His whole body folded in on itself.

Zita drummed her fingers on her thigh and squirmed. "I've been sleeping on Andy's couch, not in my bed with the dreamcatcher, though sleeping in animal form seems to keep her from stopping by as often. That'd be hard for Andy to try, though. I think his bird form's getting a little round from lack of flying. He might be the size of two jets these days instead of just one."

"I am not!"

"Relax, mano," Zita said. "I'm sure you're only the size of one and a half jets. Last time you sparred with me, you had me teleport us there. How about we switch it up, and you fly us somewhere next time? As far as I know, you haven't flown since our diversion to Vegas." She grinned at him.

Andy's answer was soft. "It'd be a bad idea. I won't risk it."

Zita frowned at him but went back to the original topic. "So, if this Heart rock is what Janus warned us about, what bad stuff will it do?"

"I'll investigate it," Wyn said, her voice quiet. The research librarian's lips tilted into a smile. "I can do a bit while I'm in New York using the libraries there, and when I get back home Friday, I'll claim the research is at a student's request. When work is slow, assisting students is an approved way to spend our time. Tiffany assaulted the department head in my subject with the Key of Hades, so I'm short of tasks these days."

"How is he?" Zita asked.

Drifting past Andy and Zita, Wyn sighed. "He's recovering well for his age, but he's decided to retire and move closer to his grandchildren. The university won't say who they want as a replacement, so my conjecture is they're dangling tenure as bait in front of someone they want to lure away from another school. I do hope the new person is less of a Luddite. It's so much easier to deliver reports via email, and I worked with him a lot. The new head hopefully will also have a knack for finding funding. My job stability relies on that department staying funded, and you know how my cats eat."

"Like real cats?" Zita said.

Andy snorted. "Not like you, at any rate, Zita. You've got sabertooth tiger tastes in a domestic house cat body."

Zita considered that. "Probably true, at least compared to Wyn's beasts. She feeds them that fancy organic salmon and everything."

Wyn looked up. "Zita, before you take me to New York, can we stop by my place? I need to pick up something."

She shrugged. "Sure. I've got your basement memorized at this point."

***

When Wyn and Zita returned to the basement apartment, Andy had changed into his favorite baggy sleeping pants and a T-shirt with a cartoon on it. Wyn's chin was high, and her eyes were bright as she clutched a giant cat carrier to her chest. One hand on Wyn and the other clasping a large bag, Zita struggled to keep her face noncommittal.

Wyn smiled and set down the trembling carrier. Plucking the bag from Zita's hands, she glided forward, hugging Andy, then pressing it into his hands. "Please thank your parents for me! I appreciate them agreeing to take the poor little thing in! My cats won't accept him, and it's cruel to leave him shut in my bathroom. Plus, I'm starting to worry about the sink pipes if he stays in there much more. I put enough food for a week or two in this, plus bowls and a toy he has claimed."

"What? I didn't agree... Zita? Is this your doing?" Andy said, shifting the bag aside.

She waved a hand. *This is not how I would have done it, but, hey. Can't stop the Wyn train now.* "Chill, mano. You just need to give the poor homeless kitten a safe place until she finds something better. When I talked to your dad yesterday—"

"Wait, why were you talking to my dad?"

"You were in the bathroom, and he called, remember?" she said. "He said you used to beg for a kitten when you were a teenager, so they were willing to try it. They didn't think you'd mind taking care of him until they got back."

Andy muttered, "I am never going to the bathroom again."

Zita bit her tongue to keep from commenting on that and eyed the size of the crate at her feet, misgivings growing. "Wyn, did you get a new crate? How much food is in there with him?"

Sheepishly, Wyn shrugged. "I borrowed this one special just for him."

The carrier, a clunky thing two sizes larger than Wyn's usual ones, vibrated with the motion of the furious cat inside, the plastic parting at the seams with each impact, and a low, steady growl emanated from it.

Setting the cage on the ground, Zita backed away from it. "Did you forget to mention something?"

Andy stared at it. "I thought you said a homeless kitten?"

"Don't worry, he's litter trained, and between two and four years old, so he's past the worst kitten craziness. I had him fixed and got him his shots before I left for the conference." Wyn darted forward and unlatched the front of the carrier.

A gray and white streak burst from inside, knocked over the bag on the sofa as it catapulted past, and disappeared into the morass of wires behind Andy's computer.

Wyn gave a weak smile and fluttered her lashes at Zita and Andy. She shoved a bag of treats into Andy's hand and a piece of paper into Zita's. "He's really very sweet and loving, but he loathes crates. Directions are on the note. Zita, I really need to get back to New York before someone misses me." She grabbed Zita's arm with a surprising amount of pressure, given her scrawny arms.

"Fine, I'll take you." Zita glanced at the webcam and teleported with Wyn.

After the hotel room formed around them, Wyn exhaled and shut the laptop humming on the desk. She collapsed on the bed, one hand across her forehead. "I hope this works. I just couldn't stay another minute longer for fear he'd talk me out of it."

"Coward," Zita said. "You know I'm going to get the heat for this."

Wyn waved a dismissive hand but didn't deny the accusation. "It was your idea."

"I thought we'd ease him into the idea of a pet," Zita protested.

After kicking off her shoes, Wyn massaged her arches. "It'll turn out for the best in the long run. Thank you for the assistance getting back, but I should shut off the computer and head to bed."

"I really hope you know what we're doing," Zita said. With a sigh, she braced herself to face her cranky temporary roommate and his new cat, then teleported to Andy's basement.

Andy hadn't moved, other than to fold his arms over his chest and scowl. "I blame you." He stared in the direction where the cat had disappeared behind his giant monitor. The tip of a solid gray tail poked out like a question mark.

"Mano, I never actually met him before, and you can't want the poor thing to suffer. I'd consider taking him in temporarily, but I can't. Sobek would disembowel him like he did my neighbor's dogs." She forced down nausea at the memory, grimacing. Her eyes drifted to the computer.

A white and gray paw lashed out, and Andy's mouse fell to the floor.

Andy glared. "Oh, I can blame you and I will. Are there any other strays I'll be taking in that I should know about?"

As they watched, the cat emerged. Even with his ears laid almost flat against his head, it was almost impossible to miss that one ear had several notches in it, and the other was half missing. The cat lifted a wide, round head to eye them through suspicious green eyes.

"It's like a drunk cat on steroids mated with a pony... or a battering ram. I'm not certain there'll be any room left on the couch for me if he's there. Pues, at least he's all muscle, like a cat bodybuilder. Nobody can accuse your cat of being a pansy," Zita commented, as a body, almost as broad and brawny as it was long, slipped into sight.

With a deep exhale, Andy said, "Maybe he'd solve the serial killer who's after your family problem for you if you kept him at your place. I can't just keep calling him Wyn's cat, so I suppose we should name him."

Zita scooped up the list of directions and turned a laugh into a cough. "Mano, he's got a name."

"If Wyn named him, let's see... Thor?" As they watched, the cat reached out and knocked Andy's keyboard off the desk with a casual swipe of a claw. His eyes narrowed. "Grendel?"

She cleared her throat. "Apparently, the kid at the library named him based on the shape of one of the spots in his coat. He answers to Cupcake."

The feline strolled over to Zita's feet, and meowed, his ragged ears rising. While most of his coat was white, solid gray patches were slapped here and there as if he had been splattered with paint.

Andy's jaw dropped open, and the bag of treats fell to the floor, scattering tiny triangles on the ancient avocado shag carpet. "Cupcake?" He shot an incredulous glance at the cat. "What was she thinking? Who's going to want this beast?"

Zita wrinkled her nose at the fishy, chemical scent rising from the spilled treats. "Those stink almost as bad as you did when I first showed up here."

Apparently not sharing her distaste, Cupcake sidled over to Andy's feet and gulped down the treats. A low purr like a Harley engine revving rose as he dined.

"I feel like I shouldn't watch, but he eats even faster than you," Andy said, staring at Cupcake.

Zita picked up the treats and sealed them shut.

Cupcake eyed them both, crouching on the carpet. His eyes darted to the canvas bag Wyn had brought over, and he inched that direction.

"Oye, you need to find somewhere to put up his food. No more jerky storage on the couch for you." Zita scooted over to remove it from Cupcake's reach and tucked the treat container inside. Considering the brawny animal, she added, "Better make it someplace secure."

"Fort Knox?" Andy said.

A rusty, rumbling sound emanated near her feet, and a hard shove against her ankles had her looking down, where the big cat now rubbed.

Cupcake chirped like a kitten.

Zita exchanged glances with Andy. "You're in luck. He's food motivated. Cesar Millan says that's the easiest kind to train."

Andy slapped his forehead. "He's a dog expert! This is a cat. You don't train cats, you just hope they're not hungry enough to eat you yet!"

She grinned. "Well, you've got a way to bribe him to stop him from eating you."

"Nice, Z. Just set up the bowls and some food for him." Andy stomped into his bedroom and slammed the door shut.

At her feet, Cupcake purred and wore an expression that seemed suspiciously like a smirk.

Chapter Eleven

In retrospect, she should have bought the rock candy and lost the man.

That Friday night, the wind tugged at Zita's brown bomber jacket with frosty fingers as she considered giving into temptation and abandoning her blind date. It would have been easier to do earlier, but she had been on her best behavior. Around and above her, the dead corn rustled and whispered, rising higher than her head. Occasional mad laughter and clumsy movements of others in the maze broke into the constant susurration of the stalks, but for all intents and purposes, they were alone in the dark.

Given that her date—*Ivan? Isaiah? Isaac? Something with an I—* had gone running around another bend in the path, she was by herself in the unlit place. Honestly, being without her date for a few minutes didn't bother her. Zita snickered at the thought, though she would have brought her compact flashlight had she known they would be roaming outside this late.

Checking to ensure she still had her wallet and keys, she touched her fingers to the tiny penlight attached to her keyring, her hands stroking the body-warmed metal. The weight of her phone was in the opposite pocket, balancing her jacket. *The starlight and full moon are more than enough to navigate by, and this is easier than the awkward conversation expected on a first date, especially a blind one set up by one's brother. I suppose I could've delayed this, but I won't let that psychopath Sobek ruin my whole life.*

The walk barely counted as motion to someone who exercised multiple hours daily, but she didn't make a habit of pursuing men who ran from her. Unless, of course, she wanted to hand them over to the police or stop them from mass murder. She made a face at that thought and continued walking. *This is a date,* she told herself, *and I'll be a normal woman on it. Nothing's going to happen that will give away my powers.*

She entertained the idea of allowing her date to escape and going home. *Is he trying to ditch me or is he just really bad at walking with another person? I didn't think the date was that terrible. It wasn't going well, but nobody's been beaten up, swarmed by mind-controlled squirrels, or fallen asleep, which puts it ahead of my last two. At least the walk is fast enough to keep me awake. I was afraid he would insist on a leisurely stroll, and while it's pretty and all, it's just dead corn and the occasional hay bale with a pumpkin on it. Perhaps he's bored, too?* As she mused, her muscular legs carried her forward with little effort.

Mentally running through the date, Zita tried to figure out what she'd done this time. Or what he'd done. Her date, Igor—*No, that doesn't sound right. He seems like an Isaac, so I'll call him that until he says his name again*—had sprung the surprise of attending a Maryland harvest festival on her after they'd met at a DC coffeehouse. Although she was certain she could take him in a fight, as he lacked the coordination or the situational awareness she expected in a field agent or someone who had trained in martial arts, she had ridden her motorcycle separately.

Once there, the silences had been more of the uncomfortable variety. While he had insisted on paying for dinner, he had frowned the entire time she had eaten. At least the food had been good, with the meatloaf and chicken being exceptional and the apple cider donut making the whole evening worthwhile. Zita had wanted to check out the rock candy, having never tried it before, but he had dragged her away when she'd headed for the table, even when she offered to pay for it herself.

Running down the list of events, they could agree on very few. They had compromised by stopping by the "petting zoo" of overfed farm animals and walking through the corn labyrinth.

Speaking of puzzles, Wyn should be back from her librarian conference and might have found out something about the Heart gem. I'll just check in and make sure everyone treated her right. Since her date was still absent, Zita flipped open her phone. She continued to stroll forward as she laboriously typed in a message to her friend. When she rounded the corner, as had happened before, her date waited there for her. *Pues, he really looks like an Isaac, one who's gotten into his grandpa's moonshine.*

She pressed Send and shut the phone.

"There you are," probably-Isaac said, his voice too loud and jovial. In the limited light of his big flashlight, his eyes glinted. He laughed, the sound a little feral, a little nervous. Sweat stood out on his forehead.

Perhaps he got a bad piece of chicken and needed a bathroom? It might explain why he had gotten more and more wound up as the evening progressed. My brother said he was a prankster, but Miguel is so straight-laced that most people are jokers in comparison. Zita plastered on a smile. "Sure, here I am."

He checked his watch again, the numbers glowing green in the dark.

Her eyes narrowed. *Bizarre. If he weren't a federal lab tech with a high clearance, I'd think he was on something. Maybe it was the chicken.* "Did you want to turn around? You seem to be in a hurry," she said, strolling up to him and tilting her head up to meet his gaze.

"No, I'm in no hurry," he said. "If you're scared we can go back." In the quiet field, his voice was nearly a shout.

She laughed. "No, I'm fine." In the dried stalks nearby, someone stumbled. *They should've brought a flashlight too if they're that blind. I'd lend them mine if my keys weren't attached.*

Isaac drew close, looming over her, easy to do given the disparity in their heights. His pace slowed to match hers, and an arm touched her side, sliding around her shoulders.

She sidled away from him automatically. *Oye, I don't know you that well, and I don't like annoying strangers touching me. Carajo. I'm supposed to be trying to give him a chance.* With a sigh, she decided to try talking to him again. "So, do you work out? What's your favorite? Mine is aerial acrobatics and—"

The thrashing in the corn drew closer, and her date finally noticed.

"Did you hear that?" Isaac said, interrupting her attempt at conversation. One corner of his mouth twitched as if it wanted to smile and the other half disagreed.

She cocked her head to the side and listened. "Whoever's busy falling through the corn? Sure. They've been roaming around for a while, and this is the closest they've gotten. Did you want to see if they're lost? If they are, we could at least point them to the barn or take them back ourselves if you're tired of the maze."

Isaac seemed disappointed, though he hid it after a second. "No, I'm good. It's a beautiful night, and the stars are coming out. Look there..." He pointed upward.

Zita obediently tilted her head up. *Still the same stars as earlier.* Her phone pinged, and she glanced down at it, flipping it open to read it. "Could be work," she lied as she took a few steps away, "so I'll just check it real quick."

Wyn's text was simple: Jerome says emergency, we need to meet him at Rock Creek Park ASAP.

As she prepared to text back, a blur of motion nearby drew her attention.

A man wearing a stupid white mask with black holes for the eyes and mouth lumbered out between the corn stalks. Metal gleamed in his right hand, and he slashed upward.

Zita was already in motion, shoving Isaac to one side and hurling herself in the other direction. She cartwheeled to her feet and came up into a defensive position.

The knife must have clipped Isaac because her date made a choking sound and dropped his flashlight. His hands grasping at his stomach, he fell to his knees and collapsed.

"¡Ni madre!" she shouted, hurling her phone at the attacker's head.

He jolted forward when it hit.

With a weird laugh, the attacker turned to lunge at Zita in an absurdly telegraphed overhand strike.

No skill, he's holding it badly, and he doesn't move as if he has any fighting ability. Not big enough to be Sobek, but still tall and moves like a laborer. Something was wrong, but her body reacted before her mind caught up. Her low back kick hit his ankle and swept him off his feet.

Arms flailing, the knife still dangerously clutched in one hand, the attacker fell with an incoherent shout.

Before he could do anything else, she spun again and jumped on his wrist with both feet.

He screamed and released the weapon, curling into a ball around his injured hand.

Zita kicked the knife away and fell into a defensive stance, prepared to knock him down if he tried to rise. "Stay down," she said, her heart pounding.

"Stop! What are you doing?" Isaac cried, standing.

She kept her eyes on the attacker. "Don't move too much, Isaac, you don't want to make the injury worse. We can call for..."

Isaac grabbed her shoulder and shoved her away from the downed man. "Jacob, are you okay?" He knelt over the attacker, tearing off the mask and touching the other man's shoulder. "Are you okay?"

"Dude..." Her brain caught up with everything. "You know this loser?"

Her date snarled at her. "You're no prize yourself. Jacob's my twin brother. This was just a prank."

After a moment to process that, Zita took a deep breath, struggling to keep her temper under control. "Seriously? Did Miguel not mention the whole serial killer on the loose issue? The real one who favors a knife and wants to use it on my family?"

Isaac lifted his head and scowled at her. "He said something, but I figured he was joking. He hasn't been in the Department of Metahuman Services long enough for me to really know him."

Anger hit. *I could've killed him if I had followed through on that move the way my tía taught me...* "And you thought this would be funny?" She let them know what she thought of their joke, first in Spanish, and then in English.

Turning away from her, he assisted his brother to his feet. "I should've listened when Dr. Smith mentioned you were a head case."

"Justin Smith? Save a man once, and he bears a grudge forever," Zita grumbled as she picked up his flashlight and used it to search the ground. She stepped over the knife, obviously a prop with painted-on blood in the better light and knelt to pick up her phone. It was in two pieces, and she turned it over in her hands, biting her lip. *Ni madre. Just what I needed, another expense.* His words sunk in. "Wait, DMS? Miguel's FBI."

Isaac panted with effort, his brother's arm around his shoulders as they moved toward the barn. "Not anymore. He's been with DMS for the past couple of weeks and moved to the New York branch. Good riddance, if he's as nuts as you. By the way, my family owns this farm."

His brother spoke, "Consider yourself banned for life."

Why didn't Miguel mention he'd been transferred to DMS? Zita shrugged and handed him the flashlight. "No big loss. Your animals are all overweight, and I don't know why anyone would pay to pick fruits and vegetables, anyway. I certainly wouldn't. Sorry about the hand." She turned away and marched through the stalks ahead of them. *At least now I don't have to make an excuse for a quick exit.*

Chapter Twelve

An hour later, Zita, Andy, and Wyn, in their respective disguises, strolled up a park pathway in DC. Stretched out on a bench under a light, Jerome wore beige clothing so new that the creases still showed the original folds. Sunglasses hid the top half of his face, despite it being nighttime. A wide-brimmed hat sat next to a massive, overstuffed backpack, which sported the logo of a high-end travel store.

Skipping a greeting, Zita said, "So, what's the emergency?" She scanned the area—the flyover she had insisted on earlier hadn't revealed any lurking police, but her mother had ingrained caution in her. *Does he have a cooler hanging off the end? That backpack needs to be repacked and balanced right. Must be nice to be extra strong, but then again, you don't get the kick of working out to build strength.*

Jerome waved. "Hi to you too. Why don't you check your phone more often, Arca? I texted you yesterday. Your friends hadn't given me their numbers, at least not until Muse contacted me today."

"I only turn it on a few times a week when I'm somewhere outside of my daily routine. A friend told me that phones have trackers inside that only work when you have the battery connected, so I just leave it disconnected most of the time. So, what's the problem?" Zita said.

The big man sighed and nodded. "Makes sense."

"If you're paranoid," Wyn murmured.

"Or running around playing vigilante in masks," Zita shot back in an undertone. "So, the problem?"

Jerome continued. "I've been monitoring keywords relevant to your questions all week. The professor who applied for the grant to find the Heart has been kidnapped. They grabbed her in front of the university security cameras two days ago, so I can verify the blond dick who shoots lasers was there. He smirked at the camera right before he shoved her through a portal."

"Plasma. Pretorius shoots plasma," Andy corrected in his fake raspy voice. "Lasers are different... never mind. That poor woman."

Wyn inhaled and rubbed her arms. "We've got to help her."

Trying to loosen the tense muscles in her shoulders, Zita squashed down her pity for the professor and focused on the oddity. "Any chance she could've staged it? It's a little too convenient that so much of the abduction was on cameras. Pretorius didn't seem that stupid. Evil, yes, but not stupid."

Jerome grimaced. "When I spoke to her, the department head's secretary said the professor would never have left in the middle of tenure negotiations. Does that make any sense?"

"It does, actually. No way it's staged, Arca," Andy muttered, seeming interested despite himself.

Closing her eyes for a moment, Wyn blanched. Her voice was somber. "If the negotiations were going well, no professor would walk out on a guaranteed job."

That, Zita understood. "Bad omen, then. So, she was definitely kidnapped or murdered."

Nodding at her, Jerome said, "Her travel bags are missing from her home, so they must've stopped there at some point."

"They must be going without Tiffany because she still had second and third-degree burns since Muse didn't get a chance to finish the healing spell. No way she's recovered yet," Zita said.

Andy shrugged. "Or they have their own healer who treated her."

Zita and Wyn both blinked at him.

He spread his hands apart. "What? Being practical, here. I saw how messed up she was when Pretorius carried her through the portal. If Tiffany's still alive, she'd have to be magically healed or be a patient in a burn ward for the next few years."

"Makes sense," Jerome said. "I've been periodically checking the best US burn centers and one in England for someone with her name or general age range and haven't found a match. From what I dug up on her country club lifestyle before she got her powers, she wouldn't accept anything less than the best."

Zita swore. "I thought we had more time."

Her mouth in a thin, tight line, Wyn massaged her forehead. "We leave tomorrow. If we are to save the professor, we lack the time to wait for me to be fully vaccinated or to have everything settled."

Jerome hefted his bag. "My stuff is ready now."

Over their mental connection, Wyn fretted. *My aunt. I can't get in to treat her Alzheimer's before visiting hours tomorrow, so we need to wait at least until then. I don't know how long this will take us, but she was due for another round of spells next weekend. And I need to set things up at work, with the lawyer, and for the cats.* Aloud, all she said was, "Great, but I need to arrange a couple things before I go and none of us are ready yet."

I wanted to leave and get this over with days ago. Andy stared at his feet and tried to covertly brush white cat fur off his pants. *We probably won't be able to shake Jerome now, and now I'll have to get someone to take care of your cat.*

"I'm packed," Zita said. *Cupcake's been sleeping in your lap since he got to your place, mano. Pretty certain he's not Wyn's cat. If necessary, I can sneak you in to see your aunt, Wyn.*

"We weren't supposed to leave for—" Wyn cut herself off. "I forgot who I was talking to. Very well. It's already near midnight. Shall we meet tomorrow afternoon then and go? I did research the gem this past week."

Jerome nodded. "Tomorrow afternoon's fine, so let's get the quick version of the Heart's history and go home for the night. And don't try to leave me out of this or I'll use my considerable skills and free time to find and harass you."

Wyn sighed. "Can we accomplish this without acrimony? The Heart of Canaiwari is an emerald, a huge, uncut trapiche emerald. It was found on a sacred mountain, Paremiyan, in Brazil or Venezuela. Conquistadors heard about the giant gem and promptly confiscated it, taking it back to Spain due to its size—hundreds of carats—and pattern. Apparently, they slaughtered a large portion of the tribe they stole it from while doing so."

Did gems come in patterns? Why did no one tell me? I just assumed any gem with a pattern was fake. Maybe I should pay more attention to jewelry, Zita thought. "Pattern? Like leopard print? That's a cool ass gem."

"A trapiche emerald has a carbon impurity running through it forming a six-spoke pattern on it like..." Wyn paused. "Like a shadowy daisy imprisoned in the stone. The Heart has the additional distinction of being shaped like a heart."

"Dramatic," Andy murmured, still brushing at his lap.

With a shrug, Wyn said, "I could talk about the radial spokes and the origin of the word trapiche, but I figured Arca would fall asleep somewhere around the second sentence."

Her friend knew her far too well, but Zita made a token protest anyway. "Oye, am I supposed to just stand here while you insult me? So, it's a big green shiny with a black flower pattern. Why would they care beyond the monetary value?"

Wyn sighed. "I'm uncertain. It's not an obvious weapon like the Key of Hades dagger. I see two possibilities. The first is the more dangerous as it supposedly grants dominion over the great monsters. It could summon something other than the walking piles of putrefaction that Tiffany already uses or grant her power over anything deemed monstrous enough. If that includes control over, say, other witches or shapeshifters or anything even remotely close, that could be a real problem for us."

Andy finally lifted his gaze from the study of his shoes, his face grim. "That includes all three of us."

"I'm good," Jerome said, folding his arms over his chest. "All man, all the time." He grinned, flashing his dentist-perfect teeth.

Zita made a rude noise at him and shook her head. "We're not monsters, but Tiffany don't need that rock."

"Without evidentiary information otherwise, the gem might treat us as such. The other alternative is that it radiates some form of death magic."

"Death magic? Is that magic magic or radiation?" Andy asked.

"No way to know until I see it," Wyn replied. "According to the legends, the Heart is cursed. Every owner met with a gruesome death until the last one returned it to the remnants of the original tribe and built a new temple to contain it. Supposedly, a powerful local shaman put safeguards on it afterward, and that's why nobody knows exactly where it's at. Periodically, people search for it, but it has never surfaced again. Most of the expeditions don't come back. The last recorded attempt was in 1978, but nothing official since then until the grant proposal that Tiffany's foundation denied."

"I don't know whether to hope for radiation or not," Andy mumbled. "I suppose I should go pack a duffel bag."

Zita exhaled. "If you want to carry stuff, use a good backpack like Jerome's—"

"Chevalier's," Jerome corrected.

"But weight it so it balances evenly and leaves your arms free. I'd loan you one of mine, but it would drive you nuts since it wouldn't sit right." Zita surveyed Andy. "Your torso is way longer than mine and shaped different, but I might have a friend I could borrow one from... but we'd need to make sure he got it back in one piece."

He sighed and rubbed the back of his neck. "Thanks for offering. But given that we're chasing after Tiffany or whatever thugs she's farmed the job out to this time, we couldn't promise to return the pack undamaged."

She nodded. "Good point. It's a shame you and Muse are both so freakishly tall that I can't lend you more gear." A thought struck her. "It's spring in Brazil right now, so make sure you pack long-sleeved, light-colored, gauzy breathable shirts and long pants for heat. Both of you will want a coat or layers too, in case we have to climb a mountain. If we go high enough, the temperature will drop, hopefully no more than twenty degrees, but still. Hard to say with what little Chevalier has given us."

As he folded his arms behind his head, Jerome didn't seem repentant. "I like to hedge my bets."

"Long sleeves in the heat?" Wyn asked. "Also, my height lends me elegance and class, unlike you, whose squat form can be squashed under my dainty feet."

"Mosquitoes. Those chingado things love them some sweet tourist blood, and we don't have time to get you guys—well, Muse, since a needle won't make it through Wingspan's skin—shots. Some plants can be sharp or irritating, too, and don't forget about all the ants. I'm up-to-date since I've been there before. You still certain you want to come?"

Jerome made a rude noise. "Your lack of concern has been noted. They can still bite me."

"With your ability? Walk it off, hombre." Zita grinned at him, though her eyes turned toward Wyn, the one she was really concerned about.

Nibbling her lower lip, Wyn played with her hair before responding. "With that tempting description of a journey of a million mosquito bites, how could I resist accompanying you? I forgot about the insects. You'll need me to point out the gem and deal with Tiffany if necessary."

Jerome cleared his throat. "Speaking of dealing with people, no updates on Sobek. He's fallen off the radar. I found the kid though. He didn't have a record, but I ran facial recognition and got hits off social media. I've got an address for his family. What do you want to do with the information? I'm not thrilled about handing it over to just anyone."

Zita froze. *Miguel's DMS now.*

Dismay filled Wyn's mental voice. *Oh, no. Now you really can't ever tell him about your abilities.*

I know, right? He's the only government person I'd trust to do the best for the kid, but I don't want to tie him to us nor do I want to have to talk to him more than necessary as Arca. Zita rubbed her hand over her hair and moistened her lips.

Let's go with Miguel. At least that way we might be able to find Janus later. Andy spoke up. "We've clashed with a DMS agent... he's a pain but honest. Arca, do you have his number in your phone? If you want to skip giving us the information, Chevalier, tip off the DMS guy on the kid's family. The government should be pretty interested in getting them to safety in order to cut off the portals."

Jerome grunted. "I'll check into whoever you recommend."

"Yeah, it's Garza or something. Give me paper and let me check my phone for his number," Zita lied, trying to keep the unhappiness off her face.

Once Wyn handed over her things, Zita walked a short distance from the others and snapped the battery back into the disposable phone. The blue smiley face sticker tickled the palm of her hand as she turned it on. To her surprise, she saw a message from a vaguely familiar area code, in addition to five missed calls and a text from Jerome.

Curiosity got the better of her, and she pressed Play instead of Delete.

***

When she returned to the others, she handed the paper to Jerome with her brother's work number on it. "That's the DMS guy. I got an interesting call from someone else, though. Muse, do you remember when I got into that fight in New York?"

Wyn nodded. "Yes, you said a feline woman attacked a security guard without apparent provocation."

"Something happened in New York last week, and you never said anything? How do you keep running into these things?" Andy said, scowling. "More importantly, does the story have a point?"

Zita wrinkled her nose at him and flipped him off with no real animosity. "Chill, I'm getting there. The call was from that New York detective, Hound. The cat woman was just the lookout for the real thief, who stole secret computer files from General Aetherics. His partner thinks the theft was committed by a super who can turn invisible, and they called me to see if I had noticed anything in particular about the invisible person because everyone got away."

Jerome blinked. "Hound? That man gets around."

"An invisible super? That's not good. If they start joining in fights, it's going to be really hard to protect you guys." Andy scowled at his feet again, glanced at Wyn, then at Zita.

Wyn shot a worried glance at Andy, before turning to Zita. "Did you notice anything useful?"

Zita nudged him with her shoulder. "I don't need that much protecting, but yes, it'll cause problems," she said, carefully not looking at Wyn. "All I could tell him was that the invisible person is probably a dude in rubber-soled shoes, who wears an expensive men's cologne. Hound didn't know Pretorius was there, but I mentioned it in case that helps him. The real question is why steal computer files to find a gem in the wilds of Brazil? What are they going to do, wire the old temple for cable?"

Jerome shrugged. "Beats me. Do you want me to find out more about what was stolen? General Aetherics is known for making SNARC balls, but it would've been all over the news if a billion-dollar clean energy source was stolen. They make a pretty wide swath of cutting-edge technology, so it could be anything."

Andy's head shot up, and he didn't speak, but panic covered his face. *General Aetherics is going to produce and sell Brandi's fabric. Do you think the thief stole the formula? It could ruin her reputation if someone else patents it first!*

Setting a hand on his shoulder, Wyn gave it a squeeze. *General Aetherics is notorious for their speed and efficacy when it comes to patent applications. She'll be okay.* "If you have a chance, that would be appreciated, Jerome. It might help us understand their end goals and make countering them easier."

"Consider it done, though it may have to wait until after Brazil. General Aetherics is known for their tight security." He smiled. "If we're not leaving now, I'm going to go home, check out this DMS agent, and pwn a few noobs."

"Do I want to know what that means?" said Zita.

***

When they arrived at the tiny, closed air park the next afternoon, Andy took one look at the runways pitted and broken by the persistent and inevitable stab of weeds reclaiming the asphalt surface and turned to squint at Zita and Wyn. "We're not taking a plane that Jerome paid for with all his sweet Internet money, are we?" His backpack sagged to the ground, slipping over smooth fabric of the plum-colored sportswear he wore.

Wyn batted her lashes at him and gave him a winsome smile. Her illusion was already in place, and she had assured Zita that it would remain up, even when she slept until she chose to remove it. "No, we're counting on you to fly."

He turned away. "I've given that up."

"But you love flying," Zita said, tugging down the hem of the top of her own sportswear, identical to Andy's. "It's wicked awesome, so much work to do, and the freedom." She smiled at the memory of her last flight and flexed her shoulders.

Andy shoved his hands in his pockets and scowled. "For you, but you're in control of yourself. I don't know what bird-me is going to do, and he is too big to risk him getting loose. Me getting loose. Whatever."

"He's still you, so it'd only be you running wild, which means there's nothing to fear. You're a good person, kind of boring sometimes, but a good guy. You wouldn't hurt anyone innocent. We either need to name your other form or use Wingspan for it, if only so you don't have to call yourself Bird-you. It sounds funny. Hey, I bet Birdseed Pervert is still open!"

"Shut up Zita," he said, but his tone held no real rancor. "All the good names are taken anyway, and it won't matter since I'm not using that form."

Zita tried to imagine giving up her powers. Even though she'd only had them a few months, they were as much a part of her as any of her limbs at this point. "No mames, mano. If God gives you a gift, you don't throw His work away."

"What she said, with fewer overtones of patriarchal and theological oppression," Wyn murmured.

"Pagan," Zita teased, smiling.

"Quite." Wyn grinned.

Zita elbowed the other woman gently. "Don't mind her. She's jonesing to meet my priest, deep down."

Her tone dry, Wyn said, "I'd make the facetious suggestion that Zita is jealous of my ability to sing and dance naked in the moonlight, but you've met her. She's probably already done so."

Zita donned an innocent expression that quickly morphed into mischief. "A few times, actually. I usually refrain from singing unless I want to scare away predators. Pues, predators and friends."

Andy winced and paced to the edge of the closest runway. "Can we please not be nude in spirit or otherwise?" His head lifted toward the clouds.

Wyn touched Zita's shoulder. When Zita turned to her, she put a finger on her lips. *Hush. Let him process,* she sent.

Exhaling a huff of air and unsaid words, Zita took the hint and stayed silent.

With a sidelong glance around, Andy squared his shoulders, set his feet, and narrowed his eyes at her as he faced the women. "So, why did you decide to let Jerome in on your teleportation?"

Zita blinked. "I didn't. It's too big of a risk to me and my family, especially given Janus' example. Why would you think that?"

He folded his arms over his chest. "That's the only other option to reach Brazil unless you've got cash to burn that I don't know about."

Holding up a hand to stop him before he could continue, Zita said. "No."

"What?" His chin jutting out stubbornly, Andy glared at her.

With a deep breath, Zita reminded herself to be gentle and tried to curb the torrent of words that escaped her in answer. "Just no. You think I don't know you're trying to pick a fight? You have to fly us to Brazil and you know that's what I meant. It's not what you want to do. I get that, but it's our best option to get there fast and keep Tiffany from getting the Heart of Whatsis."

"Canaiwari," Wyn murmured.

Zita shot the other woman an exasperated look, then set her hand on Andy's shoulder. "If it makes you feel better, the two of us will stop you from eating anyone. Wyn can use her mind tricks or a spell or some juju, and I'll do my best to keep people out of your grasp if you start drooling. Neta, mano, I couldn't teleport there if I wanted, which I don't. You know I can only go to places I know really well or someplace I can see. A set of coordinates means nothing, and if there's a webcam, we couldn't find one closer than a twelve-hour drive away."

Andy paced a few more steps, his head movements short and sharp like the bird he could be. He folded his arms over his chest and scanned the area. "You've got your aunt in Brazil. Don't you have a teleport spot there?"

"Two. One is in her house, which won't work for obvious reasons, and the other is a beach near there that I really like."

"Let me guess... free food there?" Andy gave a sour smile.

Zita smiled at the memories and shook her head. "No, it's just a beach. Paolo and I had sex everywhere there as teens. Frequently."

Andy grimaced. "Way TMI."

"Keeping it real." Zita scrubbed a hand over the long hair of her Arca guise. "In any case, neither is near where we need to go in Brazil, and I thought we were in a rush to save this professor lady.

Jerome seems solid and all, but we don't really know him an more. I mean, Aideen used to be much more bearable, and now she's burning people to death when she gets pissy."

After a moment, Andy gave a curt nod.

Zita cleared her throat. When she continued, her voice was gruff. "Besides, I went to Brazil earlier today while you guys were packing. I checked flights out of the local airport. Nobody goes up that way without a lot of cash we don't have, and we don't want to sponge money off Jerome more than we have to."

Wyn tilted her head, a chestnut curl sliding off her shoulder. Her mental voice slid like a whisper into Zita's head even as she laid a hand on her shoulder. *Is that all you did?*

Zita felt her ears flush warm and blessed the mestizo complexion that kept her blushes less obvious. She tried to deflect, knowing what her friend was suggesting. *I peeked in on my aunt, my buddy Paolo, and his wife. She's pregnant again! I think it's kid five or six, but she seems happy.*

New leaf. Wyn reminded her. *Did you go to your friend's grave and say goodbye? The one who died and the reason you're so overprotective of me?*

Zita scowled. *No, I didn't go to my friend's grave. Her family blames me, and my presence would be unwelcome.*

Her mental voice gentle, Wyn sent, *You have the power now to visit without them knowing, and it might help you resolve a few things if you went. Aren't you Catholics big on cemetery visits?*

Wrinkling her nose, Zita shook her head at Wyn. *It's not about visiting the dead, it's about praying for their souls. Pretty certain the whole sacrificing herself to save others let her right into Heaven.*

Snapping his fingers, Andy said, "If you're going to have telepathic conversations without me, can I leave?"

"We're done," Zita said, fighting the urge to hug him for the interruption. She gave the other woman a stern glance. *I'm finished on that subject for now. You're going to respect my privacy, sí?*

As you wish, Wyn sent, a little smile on her lips.

"So, we okay, mano? Will you fly us, or do I have to spar you for it?" Zita perked up at the thought. *A good sparring session might cheer both of us up. I'd definitely enjoy it, and it might help him.*

He closed his eyes and nodded. "No sparring, Zita. I'll do it this once. Twice. There and back. When we get there, it's all on foot or car. You guys will stop me from eating anyone, right?"

"Promise, mano," Zita said.

"You have my word as well," Wyn said. She cleared her throat and began digging in the cavernous magical depths of her purse.

"Whatever. Let's just get this done," Andy said. "I'd like to be home when my dad and stepmom get back from the big anniversary cruise."

Zita shrugged. "I'm supposed to be in hiding, so I just told my family I was leaving the state for a few days. When we get back, I'm to call Miguel so he can let me know if they caught Sobek yet. Since Quentin's gone to hang with Mamá, I don't have to worry about leaving him undefended."

Andy squinted at her. "You do realize your brother is a former Marine who made it out of an overseas tour of duty alive? Despite being a bomb guy?"

"Sí, but I don't see your point," Zita said. "It's Quentin. While Sobek's not in your weight class, he still has powers, and Quentin doesn't."

Clearing his throat, Andy said, "He survived a tour in the Middle East. I'm pretty sure his ability to shoot things evens the playing field. Given that Sobek kidnapped Quentin and his date, and then held them captive and tortured them for days, your brother probably wouldn't even mind shooting Sobek a few hundred times."

"He can't take a gun everywhere, not legally," Zita said, "And the rules against actually using a firearm to defend yourself are pretty harsh in Maryland. Not to mention, he hasn't been himself since the kidnapping. Killing people probably isn't the best way to solve mental health problems."

Wyn murmured, "The probably in that statement is worrisome, but you're right, violence isn't the answer. How about we focus on more practical matters? Do we have everything? Zita, did you need to put another unlabeled butter container into my purse for the trip? I think you only stuffed eight or so in there. Andy, did you want to unload some of that while I'm here?"

Opening his eyes, he shook his head and scuffed a foot on the ground. "No thanks. We'll seem really weird if we don't have any backpacks, and I'm the one best suited to carrying the luggage, assuming I can keep from breaking anything."

"Should be good on food now, thanks," Zita said, "though if we have the time, I could grab—"

"Forget I asked," Wyn said, smoothing her illusory dress.

His voice echoing as he strode up, Jerome said, "Man, this place is dead. I see now why you said nobody would notice us here." His massive backpack, still unbalanced, swayed on his back as he passed the locked door of the only hangar, a small one ribbed with rust. "This must've been a private airstrip. How did you know it was here?"

He really needs to redistribute the weight, so it lies even and redo the knots on that cord, so his cooler doesn't fall off, Zita thought. Tearing her attention away from how she'd fix his backpack, she shrugged. "The owner of the land has a house in that forest over there. I scouted out his property a few months ago when we needed to talk to him without the cops getting involved."

Jerome harrumphed. "So, breaking into backyards again?"

"He got it in one," Andy said with his fake head cold voice.

Before anyone else could bring up another sore subject, Zita stepped onto the runway. "Time for Air Wingspan! Let's go find us a big ass gem!"

Chapter Thirteen

One day later, Wyn and Jerome grabbed the rollbar as the ancient Jeep jolted to a stop on the muddy lot surrounded by the rainforest's spill of a million shades of green. Jogging next to the car, Zita took a second to admire the area before studying the tiny Brazilian medical clinic they'd found nestled in a clearing. Tall trees shot upward, supported by thick buttresses of roots, the bark covered by layers of smaller plants. Mosses, lichens, and other epiphytes hid the original colors of the trunks beneath their fuzzy jade blanket. Brown leafy detritus on the ground only peeked through gaps in ferns; flowers and fungi interrupted the endless green with splashes of brilliant red, purple, and yellow. Her mouth watered as the breeze brought a whiff of the chocolate, lime, and pineapple scent of a nearby flowering cupuaçu tree. Birds laughed with monkeys in the distance.

White and rectangular, the medical building squatted in the jungle like an exotic and aging toad. Two screened windows with planters formed wide eyes above a fiberglass double door. A capuchin monkey, brown with a ring of golden fur circling its head and neck, reclined in one of the elevated flower boxes. At their arrival, it pounded on the window frame and gave a series of barking screeches.

"Are we there yet?" Andy called from behind the vehicle, his voice low and raspy. Presumably to dislodge dirt and possibly to straighten his bedraggled mask, he swiped a hand over his forehead. The plum color of his sportswear was covered in mud from a moment of inattention when he (and the Jeep) had landed in a ditch after too hard of a shove.

Despite the heat, Zita was happy to be on foot. A few miles at a sustainable jog had been far better than the hours preceding it. Her own purple sportswear and mask might have been dirtier than she liked from the exercise, but she couldn't have stayed still any longer, especially on the padding-free and cramped back bench she had shared with all the luggage and Andy.

"Just a bit more so we don't block the entrance," Jerome said. His khakis and sunglasses bore a thin layer of sticky dust, the tidy folds long ago having wilted. Wyn had offered him one of the sportswear sets, but he had preferred his own clothes. He hopped out of the front seat where he had been steering the Jeep, a decrepit rental that had crawled along a boring highway for a few hours before sputtering and abandoning any pretext of running when they steered it up the mountain via the dirt road.

Zita was certain when the others had insisted on renting a car, they had pictured a Hummer or something that hadn't been scraped out of a junkyard for the occasion.

With a heavy sigh, Andy followed Jerome's directions, pushing the Jeep until it sat next to an even more ancient Chevy pickup with bald tires rusting in one corner of the lot. Mud painted the truck, allowing only slivers of white to peek out beneath. When their vehicle slipped into place, a wave of vivid sapphire and emerald burst around the vehicles as a flock of macaws took flight in a soft thunder of wings.

After the birds were gone, Wyn tapped at the equipment in her lap, tilting it this way and that. "GPS is working for the moment.

We're near the coordinates, but not quite there yet," she said in the gentle, chiming voice of her blond disguise. Thanks to her illusion, the only visible sign of her discomfort on the trip was the perspiration that glimmered on her brow. Although Zita had enough survival instincts to avoid mentioning it, Wyn smelled just as sweaty as everyone else beneath the suffocating eucalyptus of her overpowering homemade mosquito spray.

Before anyone could reply, a man emerged from inside. Scrubs encased a stout form with a habitual hurried stride and fine, strained features. In Portuguese, he said, "You're early. Good thing. There's been troubling..." At the sight of them, he stopped and stared, raking a hand over his natural, close-coiled hair. "How may I be of aid to you, travelers?"

Jerome stretched. "Arca, can you translate?"

Before she could answer, Wyn looked up from the GPS and unfolded her long legs from the front seat, slipping to the ground. "After mistaking us for someone else, he asked if he could be of assistance."

"Forgive me, I thought my supplies had arrived early," the man said in slow, hesitant English tinged with the music of Africa. "I had not expected Americans. My English is excellent, if rusty. Which of you requires help?" As his gaze slid over their faces—Andy and Zita's hidden behind masks, and Jerome's behind a pair of wraparound sunglasses—his welcoming expression switched to a polite, cautious one, and he retreated a step toward the door. "I am Doctor Mwangi, and will do what I can, but I have little here." He folded both hands together at his waist, his shoulders tense and drawn up.

Zita took a second to consider her group through a stranger's eyes. She swore mentally and grimaced. *He's too young to have been here long, so he might not know anything useful. Wonder what he did to piss off people enough to end up in a clinic way out here?* "We're not here to rob you," she said.

Jerome rolled his eyes and leaned against the Jeep, hands relaxed and at his sides.

The monkey in the window planter hooted and leapt down onto Mwangi. It clung to his shoulders, waving a piece of fruit over his head and picking at his hair.

The doctor disentangled the animal with practiced ease and set it down, murmuring to it. When his attention returned to Zita and her companions, his eyes were flinty, like dark mahogany against the lighter brown of his skin.

As it devoured its food, the monkey scurried away from her group and perched on the old truck, watching them with bright curiosity.

Dr. Mwangi continued to survey them, his attention lingering on Jerome. "Of course not," the doctor said, his shoulders still pulled tight. "What did you need?"

Let me do the talking before you scare the poor man to death, Wyn urged.

Andy sent his silent agreement, *Yes, let's not draw this out any longer than necessary or give him a heart attack.*

What? He doesn't know us, and you'd be alarmed if strangers like us showed up at your remote workplace. You and I are in masks and dirty pseudo-Spandex, Jerome has serious money clothes and a boxer's build, and Wyn is ready to party at a nightclub. Zita held her hands up in the air and retreated toward the truck. Absently, she cataloged the monkey as a juvenile male with interesting gold markings, like jewelry on his chest and wedge-capped head, from some offshoot subspecies she didn't know. The monkey watched her approach, but he did not seem to object to her proximity.

Andy grunted. *I don't have a job, and he might not be able to see the mask under all this mud. At this point, I may never be clean again.*

The illusion in my pendant is static. It doesn't update my clothing or appearance; it just mimics whatever actions or expressions I take. Beneath it, my apparel is depressingly drab, sensible, and in dire need of a wash, Wyn sent. She inclined her head to the doctor and proffered him a sparkling smile. "This may sound odd, but we're trying to find a mountain known as Paremiyan. It's supposed to have an old temple on it?"

The doctor pursed his lips, steepling his fingers together, though his eyes darted to the side. "Haven't heard of that one, and there aren't any temples around here. Monte Roraima National Park is right over the border, and I can direct you there. Maybe they can identify your mountain or sell you a map of interesting places for tourists. Is there anything else you need?"

He's lying, Wyn sent. *He thinks it's safer for us if we continue on, so he's pretending ignorance.*

Andy snorted and brushed ineffectually at his clothing. *At least he didn't say it out loud. That'd be like waving a red flag in front of a bull with Zita here.*

Wyn bit her lip. *Do you think he'd let us borrow the facilities?*

The thought slipped out before Zita could stop herself. *Didn't you go in Boa Vista?*

Some of us cannot turn into camels when our bladders become too pressing of a need. Wyn tucked the GPS into her purse and put the strap over her shoulder.

Unaware of the mental conversation, Jerome stretched and said what the others had begun to argue about. "Hey, doc, we've been cooped up in the car a while, and I'm starving. Do you mind if we stop here for a bit? Maybe let us use your bathroom?"

"What are you complaining about? You're male," Zita said.

He shrugged. "I'm not too hot on the idea of peeing on a palm tree swarming with those vicious bullet ants you warned us about or with the spikes on the trunk. Manhood also doesn't mean I want to whip it out with all the snakes, bugs, jaguars, and who knows what else here. For all I know, they've all just been waiting to take a bite out of me. I have it on excellent authority that I'm delicious as well as talented, brilliant, and attractive."

"Modest, city boy. I did tell everyone to use the toilet before we left," Zita teased, though she preferred flush toilets herself. She grinned. "Point taken. You good with that, doc?"

Mwangi nodded. He frowned at Andy, who continued trying to brush himself off. "You are all welcome to use my restroom and eat before you turn around. I have drinkable water should you need it. This road does not lead to the park, and you will have a long drive to get there. I can offer your friend a bucket of water and some rags to aid in cleaning himself."

"Thank you, doctor." Wyn darted through the doors of the clinic with amazing fleetness.

"Is anyone else going to mention the car's dead?" Zita asked.

Mwangi's face fell.

Jerome shook his head. "Don't worry, doc, we'll manage. You won't be stuck with us forever." After digging out his backpack, he opened the attached cooler and pulled out a bunch of wrapped squares. "Since I'm waiting until Muse is done, I might as well eat. The ice packs won't last much longer, so we'll need to have these before they spoil. Anyone want a mystery meat sandwich?"

"Do you need to ask? Bauru is roast beef, which is what I told you when you ordered them." Zita licked her lips, mouth flooding with saliva as the aroma of cheese and meat rose in the air. She held out a hand. "Happy to solve that problem."

Andy shrugged. "Sure."

Jerome nodded. "How about you, doc?"

Staring at the doors to his clinic, Mwangi opened his mouth to speak but stopped when a small form shot from the forest and ran up to him.

Naked feet flying over the uneven ground with the grace of one born to it, a boy in shorts with red paint on his face shouted the doctor's name. Slim and lightly muscled in the way of someone who always has more work than food, he burst out of the foliage and almost flew to them. When Mwangi smiled at him, a river of liquid syllables tied together with a lilting intonation and a familiar cadence poured from his mouth.

With each lyrical syllable, pounding agony streaked through Zita's head, throbbing in time with the words. Her ears rang, and her hands rose to her forehead. She gasped, bending double.

The world narrowed to pain, and Zita forced herself to breathe. As suddenly as it had come, the headache disappeared. Blinking her eyes a few times to refocus, she realized someone held her upright and noticed an unfamiliar hand on the pulse point on her arm. She tensed but stopped herself from lashing out until she realized what was going on.

During her inattention, most of the others had crowded closer, with varying expressions of concern. Andy had his arm around her, and Mwangi held her wrist. Jerome had bauru in each hand, a concerned expression on his face. Although the young boy had retreated to stand behind the old Chevy, he peeked out at her from there, curiosity shining. The little monkey had returned to his window, but he crooned at her from his lofty seat. Thankfully, Wyn had missed everything.

Zita's cheeks burned with the attention, and she stepped away from Andy's support and freed her arm from the doctor. "I'm okay," she said, her voice gruff. "Just hungrier than I thought. Can someone toss food my way?"

The other adults relaxed though Andy seemed less convinced than the others. Shooting Zita a glare that promised an uncomfortable conversation later, he passed her a sandwich.

"Thanks," she muttered as she unwrapped it and ate.

"You're welcome," Jerome replied.

After Zita started shoveling in the food, Mwangi turned his focus back to the boy. In an odd intonation, he said, "She will be fine. Am I needed in the village? You said witches kidnapped your grandfather?"

The kid still surveyed Zita's group with a suspicious expression, but he crept out from his hiding place, darting to the doorway. He answered the doctor, his words carrying the same strange lilt. "Unless you can return the dead to us, you aren't needed. The men tried to run them off, but their magic was too strong. One woman turned the ground into monsters, and a man shot fire from his hands! They also had a great beast who roared and batted away our arrows like nothing. They would have killed all of us, but the man-faced woman spoke angrily, and they stopped. After they took my grandfather and left, I followed. The Death Spirit that travels with them noticed me and warned me away, but I heard they meant to go to the Temple of the Forbidden Goddess." He shivered. "The spirit spoke directly to me, and I can't go home until I am cleansed. Do you think your medicines can save me?"

After patting the kid's head, Mwangi said, "None of us can evade death forever, but what did the spirit do? You seem uninjured."

The boy rocked from foot to foot, his eyes downcast and his face contorted with worry. His eyes blinked rapidly, and thin shoulders shook for a moment before setting into a determined stance. "When they went to ascend the forbidden mountain, he rose out of the bushes with one of the guns the miners sometimes have, but his was longer and thinner. He said he hunted today, and if I did not wish to be prey, I would go."

Mwangi squeezed the boy's shoulder, then released it. To his credit, he did not laugh at the tale. "You obeyed him, so I believe you should be safe since he sought another. I'll check you to ensure you have no symptoms and to, ah, clear any bad magic. Did the man who shot fire wear metal all over his body?"

"No," the boy said. He started to enter the clinic.

Zita held out a hand to him, sending a tomato flying from her sandwich. "Wait! Can you describe these witches? We were trying to reach the temple before some others and had hoped to stop them before they could hurt anyone."

The kid and Mwangi fell silent, turning toward Zita.

She took a bite and chewed, shifting under their scrutiny. "What?"

"You speak my people's tongue, but I don't know you," the boy said, his brows lowering.

Jerome frowned. "That sounds different. What are you saying?"

"It's just Portuguese," Zita said. "I mentioned we wanted to head off Tiffany and her group. We should have brought a picture of them..."

Zita, that's not Portuguese, Andy sent. *I speak enough high school Spanish that Portuguese at least sounds similar.*

You're wrong, mano. I've never been in this exact area before, so I don't know even a few words of his language.

What are you two talking about? Wyn sent.

"I've got a few images. I might have one of the professor too," Jerome said. He dug an electronic tablet from his bag and switched it on. After a second, he set a finger on the screen, then turned it around to face the boy and Mwangi. "Do you recognize any of these people?"

Andy's mental tone was bleak. *A bunch of outsiders with powers attacked a local village. Zita's pretending to speak Portuguese to a kid who survived.*

Wyn's reply bore her horror and sympathy. *Oh, Goddess. Those poor people. I'm coming.*

Mwangi translated and gave the boy's shoulder a squeeze.

After examining the images, the kid pointed to the missing professor, Pretorius, and Halja. "The witch hides half her face in a skull now though."

Zita tried not to think about Halja's mask too much and instead indicated Garm. "What about the wolf?"

He shook his head. "Their tame beast was bigger and had fur like a queixada, claws like a sloth, and teeth like a jaguar. It walked on two legs, close to the man-faced woman with yellow hair and a black mustache."

Zita took a moment to process, fitting animal pieces together and eliminating anything native as the kid would've recognized it. Suspicion raced down her spine. "Chevalier, do you have an image of a bear on your computer? Grizzly or Kodiak would be best."

With a frown, Jerome stroked the screen. "Let me see... Yes, here's one." He showed the image to the boy.

His eyes widening, the kid could not nod fast enough. "That is the creature!"

Jiggling her leg as she thought, Zita frowned. *The blond woman might be Trixie, but I won't say her name in case I'm wrong. It could be someone else. I have no idea what he means by her having a mustache. Jerome doesn't need any more clues to our identities and recognizing her would be a real tip-off, since he met her in quarantine with us.*

Wyn inclined her head as she rejoined them.

Andy narrowed his eyes at Zita. *You think the bear shifter and Trixie are here? Are you going to assume your imaginary friend—*

Her words came tumbling out before he could finish. "The bear's probably a shifter we've met before. He travels with a blond woman and a very dangerous sniper. The gunman waltzes around all masked and goggled and ripped, so he might be the one the kid thinks is Death."

Andy groaned. "Mind you, nobody's seen the shooter or evidence of his existence except Arca."

Jerome's eyebrows rose behind his sunglasses.

"Don't mess with me right now, mano, you know I'm not making it up." Zita tilted her head at Andy.

The boy watched them, wide-eyed, and turned to Mwangi.

"They might be siblings. You need not worry about it. Go on inside and wait for me," the doctor told him.

With the solemnity of his many years, the boy nodded. "Ah, I see." He scampered into the building.

Turning back to Zita's group, Mwangi said, "I can lead you where you need to go on Paremiyan. It is half a day's steady hike from here. The boy's village is about a day's walk from the tepui, so for him to have followed them and then reached my clinic, the people you seek are at least two days ahead of you. When I've finished examining the child, we will go. If we leave soon, we should get there before nightfall."

I told you he was lying, Wyn sent. "So, you have heard of it? Why didn't you say so before?"

The doctor pressed his lips together and studied her, his eyes hooded and measuring. "Most maps don't include it because the locals believe it sacred to a bad-tempered goddess and don't speak of it to outsiders. They say her storm clouds hide the forbidden peaks so mortals will not spy on the land where Canaiwari lives with her monster children. Out of respect for their beliefs and the dangers of the trip, I don't encourage visitors."

"That's the name of the rock the others want, right?" Jerome said.

Wyn nodded.

His arms wrapped around himself, Andy lifted his head. He rasped, "What changed your mind about helping us?"

Mwangi gestured toward Wyn. "Your masks, her ridiculous outfit, your nonchalance about the others exhibiting powers the boy mentioned... you're all magic bearers, aren't you?"

"We're not all magical, but we have powers, yes," Zita said.

Only Zita's proximity allowed her to catch the soft words Mwangi muttered, "Even those who remain still and quiet in their mouse holes must expect cats."

"What?" she said.

Mwangi stepped away from her, toward his clinic, then swung around to the group again. His dark eyes sparked with unidentifiable emotion, and his voice increased in volume. "It is better if you face these people and be gone, before more like yourselves come. Those of power attract others of ability, like a gathering of lions and just as dangerous. The closer together they are, the more often they clash. I bear you no ill will, but this is a poor area that cannot support so many predators."

I've never read that, but it would explain why our lives have been so odd lately, Wyn mused.

Andy chimed in. *It's not covered in anything I've read either.*

Listen to you two, doing all that reading. Your school teachers would be so proud, Zita sent.

"We're not here to cause trouble, just to stop the others," Jerome promised Mwangi. "Believe me, we'll be on our way as soon as we do that."

The doctor gave him a brief nod. "Good."

"How do you know?" Zita asked. "Who said that?"

Mwangi pursed his lips and stared at the distant mountain. "In the late Seventies, my mother was part of an expedition that passed through here. It included the Paladin. He said even though the odds of their paths crossing were low, every single one of those with power had met most or all of the others with gifts."

Jerome's eyebrows rose. "The Paladin? Did you mean Joe Paladin was part of the expedition? Are we talking about the same guy who wore armor and flew on Pegasus? This would have to have been right before he disappeared."

The doctor acknowledged with a curt nod.

Andy frowned. "The probabilities of the ten to fifteen people with power all meeting each other when scattered across the world are..." His lips moved as his eyes became unfocused. When he caught everyone watching him, he flushed. "They're astronomically low, especially if you consider that the Cambodian plant lady has never left her country and hasn't been seen since she killed Pol Pot."

Fascinating if it's true. "That we know of," Wyn said. "What happened to the Seventies expedition? Records are sparse." She imbued the last sentence with all the disapproval of a born librarian.

Mwangi's face was stone. "Out of thirty, only four survived, including my parent and the boy's grandfather, who was a youth at the time. They only made it because Paladin helped them. Every year, we'd come here to remember the fallen, which is why I know where it is and a deciding factor in my clinic's location."

Jerome gave a low whistle. "Good for you that your mom survived, but that's a real body count."

"What a lovely omen," Wyn said.

Preferring to focus on the practicalities, Zita asked, "What can you tell us about the trip?"

With a glance toward his clinic, the doctor said, "The rainforest ends nearby, and we ascend through highlands for a couple hours until the grasses disappear. At that point, if the ledges remain, we take an animal trail up the tepui to a cave. A rockfall sealed the entrance forty years ago, but if it is open, you must pass through a series of tunnels to the other side. I will not go in the caves as I would enjoy continuing to live."

"Pues, if we're lucky, it'll still be closed off, and the professor and the kid's grandpa will be milling around after the bad guys have gone home to play evil board games or something." Zita took a fortifying bite of her sandwich.

"That'd be convenient," Jerome said. "Dibs on the bathroom next."

Andy stared at his feet. "I expect to go caving with our luck." *I hate caving.*

Zita smiled and rocked on her feet in anticipation. "Yeah."

***

After the small group passed through the rainforest and highlands, Zita led the way on the narrow ledges that made up a makeshift trail to the cave. By the time they were only about four thousand feet up the tepui, nowhere near altitude sickness territory, the height bothered her less than the slow rate of travel caused by the others' need to flatten themselves to the rocks at the narrowest parts... or most of it, as it turned out. She felt they were being overly squeamish because the trail was uniformly one to two feet wide most of the way.

"Geez, Arca, are you part mountain goat? Wait up," Jerome complained. With his broad shoulders and overall size, he'd had the hardest time fitting on the trail.

"No, she's always like that. When she's part goat, she eats the scenery," Andy said from where he trudged at the rear of the group. After Zita, he seemed most comfortable, neither winded nor spooked.

Biting her lip and sweating, Wyn limped along ahead of him. "Literally." Other than a few comments about not being a hiker and missing her library, she had been stoically silent, although her color and energy had faded as the hike progressed. Her face remained resolutely turned toward the rock wall, away from the long drop beside them.

Jerome snickered.

Dr. Mwangi frowned. "You are joking, yes?" Once they had settled into a pace everyone could keep, he had handled the exertion well enough, especially once they'd started taking brief stops to allow Wyn to catch her breath.

"Sure, make fun of the shapeshifter. Yes, they're joking. They think they're hilarious." Despite her words, Zita paused and spent the time appreciating the mountain. Sheer, steep sandstone walls loomed, speckled with verdant green sections where plants spilled off the natural terraces that otherwise interrupted the forbidding surface. Drifting mists of thick white and cranky gray clouds hid everything above a certain point, teasing her, and never delivering on a solid view of the top it crowned. Her fingers itched to touch it, to dig in, and to climb, to feel the sweet release of exertion and effort winning over the unforgiving terrain. When the others drew close enough, she continued walking, excitement surging through her.

Just ahead, the ledge they traveled widened enough for all of them to stand if they remained within a few feet of each other. She suspected their destination was the six-foot-tall hole that yawned between two great walls of sandstone. Jagged stone rubble covered nearly half of the surrounding ground. Lines of green lichen streaked from the opening as if running away, and a nasty stink, like burned garbage, clung to the area.

Clambering onto one of the less pointy rocks so the others could pass her, Zita balanced there and waited for Wyn, so she could help the other woman get past without injuring herself.

Jerome and Mwangi trudged ahead.

Zita hopped down. Once she had helped Wyn over the worst of the debris, she released her friend next to the wall. "Take a minute. You earned it," she said.

With a whimper, Wyn slid down and ripped off her hiking boots. As she mumbled the now-familiar refrain of her healing spell, her hands lit with verdant green around her fingers, then danced over her feet. She closed her eyes and sighed in relief. Discordantly, her illusion still showed she wore silvery shoes with a needle-like heel, despite the hiking boots sitting next to her. Other than a small crust of mud and crushed greenery around the soles and wet marks from the grass, the boots were pristine.

I told her to break those in before we left, Zita thought with disapproval.

It's unbecoming to say I told you so, Wyn replied primly. Even her mental voice held overtones of weariness.

Zita rolled her eyes. *I didn't mean to send that to you, but it doesn't make me any less right. If it weren't for your spell, your feet would be in big trouble. Now get what rest you can before we continue on. We can't camp on this ledge, so we'll have to keep going soon.*

Wyn did not deign to reply.

Jerome stood by the entrance, examining it with the doctor beside him. He frowned, bringing his hand away from the wall and rubbing his fingers together. "The rock has scorch marks and soot on it. What were they doing? Mind the edges, some of them are sharp."

Andy inched past the others to the far end of the ledge and gazed out. Both hands hid in his pockets, and his back was tight and stiff, though the top half of his body swayed toward the edge.

"I see," said Mwangi, bringing a finger to his mouth. He pulled it out and dug out a package of wipes from his pocket, flushing beneath his dark skin when he saw Zita watching. "Perhaps just an artifact of the explosives those doomed fools used to blast it open? I had not expected it to be so sooty."

"What if they weakened it with a bolt of lightning or plasma, then packed the hole with explosives?" Zita asked. She joined Andy and admired the long drop, the grassy highlands interrupted by slashes of rock and straggly shrubs, and the distant lush rainforest.

Jerome rubbed his chest. "Both of those do nasty damage."

As if realizing they were talking, Andy turned and blinked at them, then studied his feet. "That would work."

"Right, so they went this way. Doc, you got any tips on how to get through to the other side?" Zita stretched, enthusiasm building at the thought of exploring the caves.

He sighed, brow furrowing. "Don't stray from the main tunnel into the side rooms. If you keep going up, eventually you'll find the murals. Follow those, and you can't miss it." Rubbing his chin, Mwangi added, "Or so I've been told."

"Be nice if we knew what we're up against," Andy muttered.

"That I can help with," Zita said. Taking off her shirt, socks, and dollar-store purple shoes, she shifted to a bloodhound and picked her way to the opening, sniffing it. As she sorted through the barrage of olfactory information, she began to differentiate individual scents. Beneath the heavy sting and lingering burned smell from the damage to the rocks, she sorted out impressions, ignoring the quieter odors of sun-warmed stone, lichen, and wind. She changed back to Arca and dressed again. "They reopened the cave at least partially using some kind of bomb. Tiffany and Pretorius are here. I've got bad news, too."

"Worse than Tiffany and Pretorius playing with TNT?" Andy asked.

Sotto voice, Jerome asked Wyn, "Do I want to know why she knows what explosives smell like?"

"They hired Freelance and the bear from the museum—their scents I recognize." *The bear's scent always makes me hungry for burgers. More than usual, anyway.* Zita tried not to think about the sniper's masculine odor. "Two other women are with them, one of which is probably the blond who hangs with the mercenaries. The other is likely the missing professor. I also picked up what I'm guessing is the kid's grandpa."

"Everyone's alive then," Jerome said. "Why is that bad news?"

Zita exhaled. "The mercenaries are competent, versus the thugs they usually run around with."

Andy grimaced. "So much for beating them here," he said. "Are you certain you're not just smelling what you want to find here?"

With a roll of her eyes, Wyn confided in Jerome. "Arca has this thing where she thinks an imaginary mercenary, Freelance, is stalking us."

Stung, Zita said, "Not true. I never said that. He follows us around sometimes, though, and he's shown up at the biggest fights we've been in, other than the highway prison break. If he was there, I didn't sense him."

"I stand corrected," Wyn said, giving Jerome a look.

Raising both eyebrows, Jerome paused. "Okay. I'm staying out of that debate. What are we up against since I don't know these people?"

After a deep breath, Andy said, "Let me bring Chevalier up to speed. Tiffany's a summoner and throws potions. Pretorius is the DPS blaster who hit you in the chest at the highway. He also has slow flight and extra strength and toughness."

Jerome pursed his lips. "Yeah, I'd like another chance at him."

As if he had not been interrupted, Andy continued. "The bear is a shapeshifter, basic brick, don't know about regeneration. Freelance and the blond woman both shoot guns, but she also throws weird things really well, according to Arca. We've seen the bear and the woman before."

Zita rolled her eyes. "You guys are just yanking my chain about the sniper, and he disarmed at least one bomb I know of, so he could be who was playing with explosives over there." She waved her hand at the opening.

Jerome cracked his knuckles. "Right. So, Pretorius and Tiffany are the big threats, followed by the bear, then the other two."

His mouth hanging open, Doctor Mwangi stared at the group. "That's who you're up against? I didn't think the latest round of people who gained powers had anyone amazing, other than that pretty American, Carol. No, Caroline."

Zita almost growled at Caroline's name. *Has everyone heard of that attention-seeking glory hound?* "Pretorius has the strongest powers in that bunch. Our Muse here has the best witch championship title sewed up, but I'd say Freelance is the biggest threat. Most of us are vulnerable to head shots at a distance or being blown up."

"What a lovely thought. So much for avoiding any conflict." A line furrowed Wyn's brow, and her shoulders slumped. "I'm sorry my concerns prevented us from taking this journey sooner. We could've avoided all this."

Cocking her head to the side, Zita blinked at the other woman. "Are you kidding? What you had to do was necessary, and we had no way of knowing they would act so fast. Don't beat yourself up over it. And if I'm saying that, it must be true. I'm Catholic. Feeling guilty over all sorts of stuff is one of our things."

Andy never moved his gaze from the horizon. "She's right. It's a religious obligation to be guilty. My priest tells us so most Sundays."

Zita concentrated on sending a thought over the party line without speaking. *Your aunt needed you. That's important, so lose the guilt.* Out loud, she said, "Besides, even if we had gotten here first, they still would've kidnapped the grandfather and the professor, and we wouldn't be in a position to rescue them."

Andy nodded.

Wyn smiled a little. *Thank you. I could hug you both.*

Twitching her shoulders, Zita rubbed her hands together. "Right, then. Let's go check out the caves!"

His tone hesitant, Dr. Mwangi swayed from foot to foot. "I'll go no farther. There's nothing I need to see in there. Are you certain I can't dissuade you? At least promise you'll turn back if it's too dangerous?"

Wyn smiled at him and patted his shoulder. "Don't worry, doctor. We all have obligations that will keep us from making stupid, life-threatening decisions, right, Arca?" Her attention switched to Zita.

Distracted from calculating how she would climb up to the next cliff ledge, Zita agreed amiably. "Sure, whatever she said." After a second, she eyed Wyn suspiciously. "Momentito, why am I the only one you asked that?"

"Maybe she's just keeping it real," Andy offered.

Zita harrumphed at him. "Hater. Is this the only way in, doc?"

He gave a slow nod. "To the best of my knowledge, it is, but there are many branches and caverns off the main tunnel, and I don't know where those go. If you stay to the passage with the cave paintings, I'm told you will find yourself at the heart of the tepui, where the goddess dwelled with her monsters. I'll camp in the highlands over the next few days, but I have to ensure my young patient is well and spend part of every day in my clinic in case someone needs me."

"Cave paintings detailing the tale of this mother goddess and her monsters?" Wyn perked up, a familiar gleam in her eye and almost rubbing her hands together. "I can't wait."

You're such a nerd, Wyn. With a tight smile at the doctor, Zita said, "Pues, good thing we're stupid enough to go in anyway. You take care of that kid, doc. Let's get going, guys." She clambered over the rocks and headed inside.

Chapter Fourteen

Zita led the disappointingly easy way through the mountain, calling out whenever the floor got too uneven, or she ran across evidence of Tiffany's group. While the path held few surprises, the red dirt and stone cave floors seeming almost as groomed and tidy as caves open for walking tours. Besides footprints, she found a tiny chalk arrow at every intersection, verifying the others had preceded them. Periodically, the sandpaper-rough walls teased bits and pieces of ancient, embedded bone—the curve of a wing here, an arched spine the length of a room, and the jaw with serrated teeth still clinging to it there. Behind her, a sober-faced Andy walked beside Wyn, helping her over the occasional hole. Jerome brought up the rear. Swirling diamonds in sparkly pastel colors drifted above their heads and illuminated the tunnel. They all carried flashlights anyway, in case Wyn had to cast a spell.

Jerome and Andy had both laughed when balls of light appeared over each person like bobbing lanterns, claiming it made them feel as if they were playing a video game. At first, Wyn had seemed offended, but then she reshaped the lights to diamonds and mumbled something nonsensical, and all three had gone off in peals of laughter while Zita blinked at them. When they were done with their hilarity, they returned to the trek.

"I've always wanted to be a player character, but I've always felt like such an NPC." Andy sighed.

"What?" Zita said.

Jerome clapped her on the shoulder. "He lives a sad life. Let's keep going."

After an hour, she spotted a flash of color ahead. Switching on the cool, heavy flashlight she held in her hand, she aimed it at the wall. "Órale, we got old graffiti here," she called out, panning her flashlight along a mural. Squiggly lines interspersed with pictures in a gruesome image.

A pain started at the base of her skull as if someone had hit her, and she spun to defend herself, holding her flashlight like a sap.

Wyn and Andy stared at her, having come up behind her while she was studying the art.

"You okay?" Andy asked.

Zita squeezed her eyes shut and nodded. "Fine." Her head throbbed, and she wiped a bead of sweat off her forehead.

"If you say so," Wyn said, her tone dubious. She opened her mouth, perhaps to say more, but then stepped to the side, staring at the mural behind Zita. She squealed and hustled forward, stopping in front of the wall.

Rubbing her head through the thick knot of her hair, Zita turned to watch her friend. Andy stopped by her side.

Wyn gestured to the others, excitement sharpening the movements. "Come see this! Pictographs, so well preserved, and they get more numerous as they go on! If the professor's traveling with them, I'd be surprised if they got her past this willingly. Does anyone have a camera?"

Jerome grunted. "My tablet takes photos. Light's bad though." He stepped up to stand beside Wyn and grimaced. Setting his pack down, he plunged his arm inside and came out with the electronic device.

His tone uneasy, Andy murmured, "Whatever it says, it must be pretty brutal. Those monster shapes are eating humans and dropping people bits everywhere. Ugh. That one even looks like a giant bird." He swallowed and turned away.

The bright flash from Jerome's toy intensified the pain in her head, spreading to encompass the area around her ears. Stubbornly, Zita pushed the discomfort aside and continued on, shining her light on the path ahead and refusing to look back. "The next section opens out into a cave and has a lot more pictures," she said with no great enthusiasm as she entered. Stalactites and stalagmites, some broken, littered an otherwise empty cavern the size of the exercise room in her apartment. The floor was reddish dirt, and the wall between the only two openings had more pictographs on it.

Wyn squeaked happily.

Jerome laughed. "You sound like me at a technology conference. Don't worry, you go on to the next and have your nerdgasm, and I'll finish this one and then get the next."

"Thanks." Wyn rushed forward with more enthusiasm than she'd shown so far during the trip. The light above her brightened the mural closest to Zita.

Agony exploded in Zita's head, wrapping completely around as if she wore a circlet of fire. Gasping, she dropped to her knees, shielding her eyes with both hands.

"Z—Arca!" Andy called out, and she felt warm arms surrounding her. "Another headache?"

Squeezing her eyes shut, she waited out the latest paroxysm. "Stupid headache. Thanks for the assist, mano." When the pain receded, she pushed away from him. "I'm good. Must need to eat."

"Another?" Concern warred with irritation in Wyn's tone. *Are you keeping secrets, Zita?*

Don't say anything, Zita sent. *I'm fine now.*

Andy smoothed his hands on his pants and refused to meet either woman's eyes. "She had an episode like this at the medical clinic when you were in the bathroom. Once she recovered, she talked to that kid."

"In Portuguese," Zita said, unable to restrain herself.

"You keep telling yourself that," he said.

Even as she dug in her bag for food, Wyn frowned at Zita. "I don't like those headaches." With a glance toward Jerome's tablet flashing in the corridor, she sent a question as she handed over a container. *Could you be developing telepathy?*

Zita shuddered at the idea and opened the repurposed butter tub. Plucking out the fork she'd stored inside, she shoveled the food into her mouth. Spicy rice and beans, cold as if eaten from the fridge, exploded on her tongue while she contemplated the horrific thought of gaining telepathy. *Dios, I hope not. I mean, you do okay with it, but I'll stick to misinterpreting what people say instead of what they're thinking, thanks.* "Not much I can do about it. The pain goes away after a few seconds. It's already gone."

"If you're certain you're all right, then." Wyn sounded dubious but brightened again when her attention turned back to the mural. She touched below the painting reverently. "Perhaps we should stay here for the evening? We're all hungry and tired from the long hike here, and I don't want to encounter whatever the monsters are at night. It'll also provide an opportunity to examine these wonderful glyphs more."

Jerome entered the cave and let his backpack slide onto a rock. "Sounds like a plan. There's enough space for us to spread out and sleep in here. I'll check what's left in the cooler when I'm done with this batch." Light flashed as he started another round of photos.

Andy hovered near Zita until she threatened him with a forkful of beans. He moved a few steps away and busied himself with his pack.

Zita opened her mouth to vote to push on, but when the usually graceful Wyn stumbled, she frowned. *The guys and I could continue, but Wyn's wiped. The other group has to accommodate Tiffany, who is a lot less athletic than any of us, so they can't be that far ahead.* "Rest sounds great."

Despite turning to check Zita every few seconds, most of Wyn's attention was on the mural, a more elaborate one than in the previous corridor. "I wonder what these could tell us if we only understood them."

Zita sighed. "They're pictures. You don't have to wonder. The first one was a warning. Keep going, and you'll be monster food. This one's not about religion. It's about how a teacher married a magic farmer-king."

"What?" Wyn said. "But it shows signs of classic female fertility goddess..."

"Teacher," Zita said. She jabbed a finger at a chunky figure surrounded by smaller ones. "See? Here she's teaching kids about monster bones while she watches the guy on the mountain over there." She squinted and gestured at the symbols as she spoke. "See the squiggly lines shoot out of his hands? He's a magic farmer because all the trees are dripping with fruit and the grain's as tall as a person. In this spot, dudes are bowing to him, so he's a king or noble or really rich, which would make sense with all that food."

Andy pursed his lips and rubbed his neck. "As much as I hate to disagree, Muse, the first image does resemble the storyteller figure that's popular in the Southwest."

Her eyes narrowing, Wyn seemed thoughtful as she gestured to the next panel. "How about here? Where she's on an altar and turns into a monster. They clearly show her accepting offerings and being given gifts."

Zita glanced at the scene and took another fortifying bite. "She took a nap for a few days, and when she woke up, they were being invaded. After she chased off the army as a monster, the farmer-king married her, and it was total party land."

Jerome wore an odd expression. "She napped for a few days and awakened as a shapeshifter? Sounds familiar. At least, I'm assuming you all caught the coma sickness."

With a slow nod of his head, Andy nodded.

Wyn's illusory purple eyes sparkled. "This may be almost as good as a goddess myth. Don't you see? It's proof metahumans existed before the Seventies, which were the earliest known incident. To find evidence that it happened however long ago this was drawn... This is amazing even if it's not as much in my field as I thought."

The others took the opportunity to eat, even Wyn, though she insisted on nibbling a packaged protein bar while studying the wall. When they had tucked away the debris from their dinner, they set up blankets and settled in for an uncomfortable night. At least the constant temperature of the cave kept them from getting too cold or too hot. By whispered consensus, Wyn was the only one who did not take a watch shift overnight.

***

The next morning, they continued down the corridor until they reached another cavern. After calling out to alert the others to the ancient graffiti on the walls, Zita paused to check out some flattened areas and a few bits of trash. "Tiffany and company camped here."

Andy sighed. "Was it too much to hope they got lost in the caves? I mean, I don't wish any harm to the professor or the local guy, but life would be simpler without Pretorius and Tiffany."

Jerome shrugged. "At least they had to stop. It'd suck if they'd already come and gone and all this was for nothing."

Gesturing toward the walls, Wyn turned to Zita. "While we're here, what do these say? They have more people... and the king and queen seem to be exploding?"

Zita scanned the mural. "The invaders returned, bringing outsiders, probably gringos, who tried to take over with bad magic."

"Gotta hate those gringos getting into messes everywhere." Jerome snickered.

Andy huffed. "Sounds like a familiar pattern for this continent, though."

Frowning, Wyn said, "How do you get gringo out of this?"

Zita pointed to the mural again. "See here? This person is black all over, and this one has yellow hair, and all of them are wearing white dresses. Nobody else has colored hair or wears that outfit. Yellow hair guy threw lightning, too."

Wyn waved at another panel. "While evidence of conflict between competing supers is fascinating, I'm almost afraid to ask what's happening here, given the number of discarded limbs."

"They had a war." Zita skimmed the picture, glossing over the weirder stuff, like plants eating people. She tapped an image she thought her friend might like.

To her surprise, Wyn batted at her arm. "Don't touch it! Ancient art like that is notoriously fragile, and the oil from your skin could damage it!" After a moment, her face filled with curiosity. "Who won?"

"Not this guy," Jerome said, pointing at an invader who appeared to explode in fire.

"Or that one." Andy jerked his chin at a native being hit by lightning.

Removing her hand from the wall, Zita gestured at various parts of the mural as she read aloud. "Lots of death all around. The farmer-king cast a spell as he was dying, and their land became forever green and fertile. After he died, the teacher flipped out and accidentally turned most of their surviving tribe into monsters. The invaders fled... at least the ones the monsters didn't eat, anyway."

A hand fluttered up to cover Wyn's mouth. "How sad! And then? Did she perish from heartbreak or did her tears bring him back to life?"

"What, you think this is a telenovela? No." Zita left out the bit about how the teacher traded hearts with her dead husband because that made no sense at all. "Since the teacher couldn't change her people back, she shut them away and instructed the few humans remaining in the area to never to come here or face a horrible death and whatever. She sealed herself and the farmer-king's' body in with them."

Wyn sniffled. "Your delivery is sub par, but it has all the hallmarks of a tragic love story and a standard mythos."

"What do you think really happened?" Andy's voice was soft.

Zita shrugged. "Who knows? Could've been any number of things. If we find people, we need to avoid them. We don't want to accidentally infect them with viruses they've never been exposed to."

"Prime Directive, then?" Jerome said.

"What?" Zita blinked at him. No one answered.

Andy nodded gravely. "Yeah. I don't want to introduce smallpox or something if uncontacted people live there."

"Dr. Mwangi didn't mention any people, just tried to convince us it was too dangerous," Wyn said. "Though I concur, if there is an untouched civilization living near the temple, we skirt around it to avoid passing any contagions to them. I doubt Tiffany and her group will be that considerate."

"The doc might not know. His mom went, not him," Jerome pointed out.

After another moment of examining the wall, they continued further up the passageway. Green-tinted light and a warm breeze teased flowers at the end.

Excitement sparked. Zita rocked on her feet. "We're almost there! We might have to put on some extra clothes for warmth, but let's see before we go rummaging through the bags." She rushed forward until her toe hit something rectangular and metal and sent it skittering across the floor. When she bent to pick it up, she noted the way the ground was churned up, as if multiple people had dragged large objects around. Darker blotches marred the dirt.

The others crowded near her to see what she'd found.

"Well, that's a lot more recent than the wall art," Andy said.

Zita wrinkled her nose. The faintest scent of decay clung to the thin sheet of worked metal. While it had the shape, white frame, and green background of a street sign, it displayed a series of emojis instead of words.

"Why would they haul this all the way here and then abandon it?" Jerome asked. "Not to mention, why have a sign with a tiger, a fish, and a skull and crossbones on it?"

"Not a clue." Zita set it face down on the ground. "If it's still here when we go to leave, let's grab it. It smells like something dead was on it, though, so I don't want to carry it longer than we have to."

"Eww, agreed. I don't want that in my purse," Wyn said.

"Fine, I'll carry it out when we go. Sissies," Jerome said.

Neither man objected, so Zita left it behind and headed to the exit. She pushed aside massive ferns and stepped out.

Heat and humidity wrapped around her as she stared at the vista unfolding before her, and the thunder of an enormous waterfall nearby pounded her ears. "This is all wrong."

Chapter Fifteen

Andy exited the cave, holding an oversized fern leaf aside for Wyn and Jerome. A moment later, all three came to stand beside Zita, and they stared over the tepui.

The mouth of the cavern spat them out onto a ridge overlooking the main plateau. From that vantage point, Zita saw a plain of unfamiliar ferns reaching upward, some taller than any of the humans based on the size of similar plants nearby. Butterflies skipped along above the swaying fronds. The occasional tree, conifers of some sort, struggled out above the mass of greenery. Broad, empty swaths of dirt as wide as suburban streets crossed and meandered through it all. Farther out, the ferns ended before another cliff, atop which rose a mix of cycads with their palm-like leaves and more pines, with flowers splashing color on green and brown of the trees. Several hundred feet away, an enormous waterfall thundered down from the highest edge of the rim, spreading into a river that wound its way down the wall and through the ferns. One bank came within a hundred feet of the base of the ridge where they stood. Reeds and marshy grasses blurred the lines of the waterway, and brief splashes of silver and bronze swam past and disappeared under the clear liquid. The warm, moist breeze carried the scent of the river, the spiciness of the nearby plants, and the earthier undertones of rotting vegetation and animal life.

"Toto, I know we aren't in Kansas anymore," Andy murmured.

Jerome stared. "You said it. Wasn't it supposed to be cooler up here? It's just as hot as it was in the rainforest." He wiped sweat off his forehead.

In the distance, the rim of the tepui was only a misty grayness on the horizon, with a sea of verdant life between them and it. Thick clouds crowned the tips of the walls and carpeted the sky overhead, allowing only the occasional glimpse of blue.

"It's huge," Andy offered.

Turning in place, Zita assessed the area and frowned. "It's too big. It shouldn't fit."

"That's what she said," Jerome stage whispered and snickered.

Andy snorted and broke into a smile.

Zita waited until they were done to continue. "The size and microclimate are all wrong, as is all the vegetation. It should be cool and rainy with lots of carnivorous plants, bromeliads, and orchids. While every tepui does its own thing, I've been to Monte Roraima and Auyantepui, and they're not like this." From the corner of her eye, she caught Wyn retreating toward the cavern. "Muse? You okay?"

Raising her arm, Wyn wiggled her fingers in the air next to the entrance. Her gaze skimmed the wall, the sky above it, then returned to the same spot to begin again.

She looks like she's reading bottom to top, left to right and using her hand to keep her place. Is it time for her to do a spell? "Well, I'm guessing we're here. How long do you need to do your ritual thingy to find the temple?" Zita cocked her head. "Or did you already start?" She had to repeat her questions before her friend responded.

"What? Oh, you mean you don't see it?" Wyn fondled the rock, her attention focused on it.

Zita and the men exchanged a glance before scanning the area. Andy shrugged, Jerome shook his head, and she spoke for the three of them. "No?"

Wyn gestured at the wall and sky. "Around the cave and going up into the air, as far up as is visible, everything has this really intricate spell on it. It all leads that direction, toward the massive glowing pillar of light surrounded by a multicolored mushroom cloud."

Jerome swore. "What is this, every modern superhero movie ever?"

Obediently, Zita checked again. The stone remained the same, save for where a few lizards and insects had scurried a few feet, and the sky was clear all the way up to the thick blanket of white clouds that hid the sun. A brilliant bird in shades of blue and red flew from one tree to another at the edge of the distant forest. "Pretty macaw, but no, I don't see any magic," she murmured.

Andy had an odd expression and started to speak but stopped when Wyn gasped and pointed upward.

"Guys? Is that?" Wyn's eyes were huge, and she had lost the geeky absorption she'd had since spotting the spell.

Zita and the two men turned their attention skyward. A pterosaur swooped down and captured the colorful bird in its mouth. With a few shakes of its head, it flapped its wings to rise high again. Once it soared above the ferny land, it tilted its neck back to swallow its unfortunate meal.

"Holy Land that Time Forgot, Batman." Andy gaped. "Is it just me or does that pterodactyl needs a shave? Is it wearing a jaunty blue beret?"

Taking a second, Zita began to shift to eagle but stopped when her vision sharpened. As the creature soared off, she admired it.

"That's not a pterodactyl, but it's some kind of pterosaur. The blue hat's a big crest, and the beard is hair-like filament things—pycnofibers, that's it. With those legs and the giraffe neck, it's probably an azhdarchid of some kind. Sucks to be the macaw, but isn't it cool?"

Andy grunted in agreement.

His hands on his hips and his feet spread wide as if to take on the entire landscape, Jerome stared at it until it disappeared into the cloud cover overhead. "If we see a Tyrannosaurus Rex, dibs on taking it home as a pet."

"Have you gone insane, or have I?" Wyn asked. "At least those hairy things over there are cute from a distance, an extensive distance." She waved at a trio of thirteen-foot-long sloths, one of which reared up on hind legs to stare their direction, before dropping down and continuing to move away.

Zita snorted and returned to her usual Arca form. "No way, hombre. T-Rex never partied this far south. Not to mention, who wants to poop-scoop after one of those? Or even after the furballs Muse prefers. Though now that I think about it, giant sloths and the dinosaurs never coexisted, so this place might be messed up enough to grant your wish."

Jerome laughed. "So, you're secretly a paleontologist?"

"I wouldn't want a giant sloth as a pet, but it'd be preferable to a T-Rex." Wyn turned her head, and the warm sensation of party line sprang up. *I'm curious too, how did you know the respective dinosaur eras?*

"No, I just like animals, including the extinct ones. Why would you want a giant, ravenous predator anyway? I mean, it'd be fun to see one, provided it's not attacking, but they're a bad idea anywhere near people," Zita said, her eyes scanning the area. *My college scholarship required me to have a sciencey major or minor. I liked dinosaurs and took a class on them, but paleontology wasn't for me. I don't have the patience for all the grids or a taste for all the academic backbiting.*

Andy's tone was dry. *No, you lacked patience for something? What a surprise.*

Unaware of the mental conversation around him, Jerome grinned. "I wouldn't actually take one home, but if I did, there'd never be a question about who the man is because it'd always be me. No matter what anyone else said, I'd be all 'yo, I don't have time for this. My T-Rex, Bowser, needs dinner, so I got to jet and feed him before he eats the maid.'"

Really? I knew you had to have a degree to be an accountant, but... Wyn sent. Her face flushed a rosy pink, and she seemed to forget her preoccupation with the walls.

Zita turned toward her friend. *But what?*

"You've already named your imaginary T-Rex?" Andy said. "And you named him after a bad guy?"

Jerome made a face. "Sure, haven't you? And what else would you name it after? Big Bird?"

Andy colored, and his gaze darted away. He coughed. "Maybe." *What she's saying is we're surprised you were able to last through classes at all, let alone long enough to take a minor.*

Setting her hands on her hips, Zita made a face at her friends. *Pues, I'm not a total idiot just because I like to move. The college didn't have zoology, so I got a minor in biology because it had the most hands-on classes. I don't know how you people stood getting more than a bachelor's degree. College was hard and not in a fun "ay, papi" way either.*

Andy grimaced and chose to speak aloud. "So, what about those dinosaurs, huh?"

Zita jiggled her leg as she thought. While she moved, her mind raced, categorizing the area. "Everything's stuck in a mishmash of prehistory. Flowers and butterflies mean Cretaceous period or later if I remember right. Giant sloths weren't around until after the dinosaurs died out, so for them to coexist with the pterosaurs... it's more than one era." Zita said, her eyes returning to the flying animal. "I couldn't tell you if the pterosaur is a known species or not. It's gigantic though. That wingspan's got to be thirty feet. Again, not an expert."

Wyn shuddered. "We are not taking a massive meat-eater home with us."

Zita winced and nodded. "Military equipment would take them out eventually, but they'd terrorize the area for a while first." In the distance, she could make out four-legged dinosaurs with elongated necks, bulky bodies, and plants hanging from their mouths. They had to be between fifty and sixty feet long, but she refrained from pointing the herbivores out since they wouldn't cross paths on their way to the temple.

Andy watched the pterosaur. "We have to ensure none of these things leave this place."

"Man, why do you all have to get your reality all over my fantasy?" Jerome asked.

Wyn withdrew a can of eucalyptus bug spray from her bag and covered herself again. "To return to our previous conversation from before the pterosaur interrupted us, I won't need the ritual."

Jerome stomped forward a few feet, then stopped. "Great, so where are we going?"

Zita pursed her lips but kept the majority of her attention picking out a route down to the ferns. Waving her hand at a small trail, she said, "This way. It's the only safe path without climbing gear or the boys doing their crazy jumps. Then we take that big animal path at the bottom. Given that it's wide enough to drive on, I'm not in a rush to meet the creatures that created it."

Andy and Jerome started down the small trail, their heads turning as they scanned the area.

Wyn tugged at a lock of her hair as she fell in beside Zita. "Our destination, the temple, is probably somewhere among the trees since it's not visible amongst the ferns. The spell funnel and cloud are also over the jungle area." She pointed to the mix of conifers and cycads above the distant cliff.

With a shrug, Zita descended from the ridge a few feet and tapped the ground. "Tiffany and company left footprints heading to the bottom, so they must've decided to follow the wide path too. It's an easier walk than slashing through the ferns and goes in the right direction. Do we want to follow them or try to parallel it, maybe go more direct if it loops? We could cut off a lot of time if we go up the cliff instead of around it."

Biting her lip, Wyn eyed the path. "I hadn't realized... Are you certain they came this way, and we won't be following some animal around?"

Before Zita could reply, Andy barked out a laugh as he unearthed a plastic water bottle from beneath a stubby cycad frond. "Not a lot of these from the Seventies, and it wouldn't be so clean. They headed that direction down the big path. And really, do we want to be doing any of this? It's just one more thing in the way of rescuing the kid's grandpa and the professor... and stopping Tiffany from getting the Heart." He pointed his chin toward the distant jungle.

Jerome frowned at the other man and leaned his upper body away. "If you're dead enough inside to not enjoy the fact that we're in a land of dinosaurs, you've forfeited your man card. Come on, when you were a little boy, didn't you want to see dinosaurs?"

Andy didn't answer.

"Animals don't wear shoes, so Tiffany's group has definitely been here," Zita said. "If the magic thing's that huge, can you smell the gem or something?"

Wyn shook her head. "I keep telling you, it's more visual than scent. I can't see it right now, and the odds are good that I won't be able to unless Wingspan takes us up and hovers. Once we get closer, I can pinpoint it better, but the edges of the spell go funnel-shaped somewhere among the trees."

"I don't really hover. We should walk and take the shortcut," Andy said. He twitched, pushed aside a fern, and continued down the first, smaller trail Zita had indicated. "This mountain is creepy. I don't feel the Southwest or the Pacific Northwest. Normally, anywhere I go, I can tell where I am in relation to those places. But here? No. They're just not there."

Wyn tapped a finger on her chin and delicately stepped around a plant. "Interesting. And Arca mentioned the area is much larger than the map allowed as well as disobeying whatever the norms are for this valley."

"This type of mountain," Zita said absently. "A tepui is a tabletop mountain or mesa, and while the ecosystems vary wildly, this one doesn't even hit all the basics."

Wyn made a humming noise in the back of her throat and glanced at Jerome, who was busy scanning the horizon. Digging out her GPS, she held it up for a minute. *Not that I want you to try it, but I'm going to guess you couldn't teleport home from here if you tried, Zita.*

Zita blinked. *Why not?*

"GPS doesn't work either. I think this place is similar to my purse." Wyn switched to speaking aloud. "My theory is that this is an instance of dimensional transcendence, possibly a pocket dimension, that contains a massive chunk of one or more prehistoric eras. If it's all a giant spell construct, that might explain the odd magical signature surrounding the area. To keep it going, however, it has to have some renewable source of energy..." She tucked away the device.

After a moment to wade through all that, Zita interrupted. "So, the Heart supports all this? Guess we know why Tiffany wants it, now."

Andy and Wyn stopped to stare at her.

"What?" Zita said defensively. "It's a spell that needs a lot of mojo. The bad guys were trying to collect magic last time by hurting people with the evil knife. Janus said they needed to bust past some barrier, which takes power. If they can get a nuclear-level gem pre-loaded with juice, why wouldn't they go for it? I don't know why they aren't after a SNARC ball or something more modern instead—no offense, Muse, but everything breaks eventually, and this rock is super old."

Wyn had to watch her steps as the trail grew steeper where it met up with the bigger one. "Magic and electrical power aren't interchangeable, but well-reasoned. We do have a larger problem, though..."

"The fact that Tiffany's group is ahead of us?" Zita suggested.

"The dinosaurs?" Andy and Jerome said.

Wyn stared at them as if she could will knowledge into their heads. "The Heart likely powers the spell sustaining this place. Tiffany taking it might break the link between this plane and our own. That could release the dinosaurs on our world or seal us in here permanently if Tiffany's group leaves with the gem. Or this entire construct could end with us in it."

Zita winced. "Well, all of those options suck. How long would it take you to know?"

Jerome exhaled. "I'm too pretty to go all caveman."

"If I'm really going to decipher it, I'd have to hold still and concentrate on it. Attune to it and perhaps perform some rituals. Right now, knowing the old legend gives me a way to guess what's woven into the spell, but not enough." Wyn fretted with the strap of her purse, currently slung across her body, and scurried to keep Andy in sight.

Zita touched Wyn's shoulder and slowed her own pace to fall back next to the other woman. "You're doing fine," she said. "If you can tell where the gem is or see anything magicky we should know about, like, oh, the spell breaking, drop a word to the rest of us?"

Wyn gave her a small, tight smile. "Be assured of it."

Jerome hurried to catch up. "Magic isn't my thing, but I understood enough to know that we don't have time if these losers are after the Heart, so let's take the cliff shortcut. Walking works for me for now, but I'm still disappointed there won't be a T-Rex. Even if I can't ever say anything once we leave here, it'd be cool to see one from a distance."

Zita didn't even have to think about that. "Sorry, I told you they weren't native. South America had similar predators, though, and if we're lucky, we might see one of those."

Andy interrupted in his raspy voice. "The word you want is unlucky, emphasis on the un."

Waving a hand in dismissal at his back, Zita continued, "Normally I would have said the tepui was too small to support a viable population of huge predators, but clearly this place is giving the usual rules the middle finger."

With a shudder, Wyn asked plaintively, "Can we stop talking about things that might eat us? The amount of magic you'd need to do something like this... I have no idea how someone could have managed it, let alone why."

Zita snorted and followed others onto the wide trail. She paused for a second. The dirt had a mishmash of scuff marks, as if the other group had held a dance-off or squabbled with the local wildlife. "Why is easy. Somebody like Chevalier wanted to be the man. The others are definitely following this trail. There are more footprints here."

Jerome snorted from his position bringing up the rear. "Or the story on the cave walls is true."

They walked for a couple minutes in silence.

Andy glanced over his shoulder, yelped, and ran back. "Dinosaurs behind you!"

Falling into a defensive stance, Zita whipped around.

Five dinosaurs, all the size of jaguars, burst out of hiding with an earsplitting series of screeches. They had slim, narrow bodies, shaped somewhat like plucked chickens with claws instead of wings and a sharp-toothed lizard snout replacing a beak. Their scales were green with white spots, the sleek lines softened by protofeathers at some of the joints. Rather than assaulting a single person in a coordinated attack like a pack of wolves, they separated to swarm all the humans.

One pair, more ambitious than the others, went after Jerome, despite him being the biggest in the party. He punched the first, turning it into a gory display of broken flesh and bone. While he was distracted, however, another snuck in and bit his leg.

Zita put herself between the closest animals and Wyn and urged her friend back as she kicked off her sneakers.

Andy ran past her.

Jerome ripped the dinosaur off himself, sending blood spraying out. As his leg gave way and he tumbled to the ground, he swore, his tone vicious. Almost as an afterthought, he punched the one that had bitten him, pulping its chest.

Another dinosaur assaulted Andy, and its teeth scraped along his skin and off. He stomped on its head with a sickeningly squishy crunch.

The fourth beast ran at Zita, probably because she was the smallest.

She shifted to an Orinoco crocodile and let out a warning growl, showing her own sharp teeth. Her tail lashed behind her.

When it was five feet away, the creature made an abrupt leap sideways toward Wyn instead.

Wyn screamed and fell down when she tried to escape.

Throwing herself forward with a burst of speed, Zita seized its tail between her teeth and jerked it away so fast that it made a sound like the crack of a whip. The dinosaur went limp in her jaws, and she spat it out after putting her bulk between it and her friend.

The last one tried to veer around Andy and go toward the women.

"I got it," Andy called, grabbing it.

Seeing no more of the creatures, Zita changed to Arca and wiped her mouth on her arm, offering Wyn her hand to help her up. The hair on the back of her neck prickled in warning, and she shoved her friend aside. A large form clubbed her, sending her to the ground with a shock of pain and a sick snap followed by absolute agony. She choked as her throat filled with liquid.

Wyn shrieked.

Andy turned white and ran to her side, pushing a lizard off her. "Oh, God. Z—Arca, are you okay? I am so sorry! That last one was so fast, and I just threw it, and with my strength..."

Zita struggled to breathe and sit up. Coughing tore through her, and something inside ripped loose, sending her crashing back to the dirt. She fought the urge to shift... into what, she didn't know.

Wyn hurried over. After a few words, her hands lit with the soft sparkling green of her healing spell.

Since she had to concentrate on continuing to breathe, Zita sent, *What happened?*

Jerome tapped Andy's shoulder. "The one at your feet is still twitching."

Andy glanced down. "Right." He picked it up and hurled it over the ferns toward the river. *I can't apologize enough, Zita. I accidentally threw it at you.*

Something splashed, and a flurry of thrashing came from the waters before relative silence returned.

"Right then. No swimming today," Jerome said. Despite his joke, his face was grim.

As magic spread through Zita, the pain receded grudgingly, and she took a deep, shuddering breath and spat out a coppery mouthful that suspiciously resembled blood. She rubbed away liquid that had gathered at the corners of her eyes. *Dusty here. No hay bronca, Andy, it was an accident.* She managed to choke out a few words. "I'll survive. Thanks, Muse."

After a few minutes, she experimentally tried to sit up, and a warning twinge in her side reminded her that Wyn's spell wasn't finished yet. Zita held still. Very, very still.

Wyn continued healing.

"Take all the time you need to get back on your feet. I am so sorry," Andy said, hovering over her. His arms were wrapped around himself.

"It's okay, mano, it was an accident. We need to get going and fast," Zita said, squeezing his ankle, the only part she could reach. The action did not incite any discomfort, and hope grew.

He didn't reply, but Jerome said, "Why the rush?"

Wyn released her. "I'm through. She's fine now."

Zita took another breath and did a cautious stretch, then flipped to her feet. Since her body felt normal again, she replied, "We're surrounded by snack-sized meat on a mesa filled with dinosaurs, some of which are known carnivores, and we just made a lot of noise."

Jerome stood and jogged in place for a moment, the smooth, unmarred flash of his muscled thighs visible through the shredded remains of his pants. "Shit, I'm going to have to wear the purple Spandex, aren't I? My regular clothes won't hold up against dinosaur teeth, and you said the special outfits heal when torn?"

"Yes, they do," Zita said. "You might need to press the edges together if it's a big tear. Wingspan and I have tested that a ton, right, mano?" She flashed him a smile to show him she held no grudge, but he didn't respond.

"We've got two in navy," Wyn offered, color seeping back as she pulled a set out of her purse. She managed to give Zita's shoulder a squeeze in passing.

"How about anything in stylish?" Jerome made a face but accepted a pair and waded into the brush. From his position behind the rock, he called out, "We're not going to want to pick any flowers here."

"Not that I was planning to, but why? Some are quite pretty." Wyn gestured toward a large burgundy pitcher flower whose deep throat had a delicate tracery of yellow over it.

Jerome emerged, pulling the tight shirt over his impressive chest as he walked. The matching pants already adorned his lower half. "The one back there is eating a cat-sized lizard."

Wyn winced and made a moue of distaste. "Ugh, disgusting."

"I am so sorry," Andy said again from beside Zita. He rubbed the sides of his thighs and shuddered.

"No worries, mano, it was an accident." As she walked around the rock to see, she raised her voice so the others could hear. "Carnivorous plants are normal on a tepui. At least something is right here."

Moving slowly, Andy stepped to her side and shuddered at the plant. "You don't recognize it at a glance?"

She stared at the striking maroon pitcher flower, speckled with green and white, save where the dark form of a lizard pressed against the side. It stunk like rotten meat and stale peppermints. "You can't eat them, so, no, I don't."

Wyn muttered something about priorities under her breath.

Now dressed, Jerome waited next to Wyn. "At least it's not talking. Or singing. You sure you're good to go?"

"I'm fine. Don't fuss. Accidents happen all the time," Zita said, returning to the trail with Andy as her shadow.

Wyn gave the plant only the most cursory of glances. "Shall we go?"

As she approached Wyn, Zita tried again to soothe her friend's ruffled sensibilities. "I think it was dead soon after it fell in."

"Can we stop talking about the plants?" Wyn asked.

Jerome passed Zita. "Since I wasn't the one bleeding out a minute ago, I'll take point."

Irritated, Zita said, "Muse healed me. I'm fine. It's over. Pretty certain this is a deer path... or at least an herbivorous dinosaur path. A really huge herbivore, most likely, that might not even notice us underfoot."

"Please stop being so helpful," Jerome called over his shoulder as he jogged ahead. A moment later, he returned at high speed.

"What's wrong?" Andy said, walking forward.

"T-Rex!" he shouted, running back toward them as fast as his powerful legs would allow.

Ferns crashed to the ground, releasing a spicy, leafy scent as an enormous creature raced onto the trail. Built similarly to Jerome's coveted T-Rex, it had tiny arms tipped with three nasty claws, taloned feet, and a gigantic mouth filled with unabashedly carnivorous teeth. Mottled shades of sun-faded green striped with blurred stripes of a rosy brown let it blend into the surrounding plants, save for the gaping black maw. Unlike the previous dinosaurs, this beast was easily forty feet from head to the tip of the long, narrow tail.

Even as Zita put herself between Wyn and the dinosaur, her mind spun, eying the lean muscles visible despite the thick skin. *How do I fight that? Andy, you got Wyn?*

The creature leapt forward with impressive speed toward Zita, who was already moving out of its way, but veered to the side when it was within five feet. It nearly trampled Andy but snapped at him instead. While its bite would have ripped anyone else in half, its teeth skittered along his skin, rending the fabric of his clothing.

With a horrified squawk, Andy jumped to the side.

It tilted its head, then bit again with a burst of crocodilian speed, but this time did not release him.

Andy's lower half dangled from the dinosaur's mouth, his feet kicking so hard that Zita had to duck as one sneaker flew off. Another scream emerged, angry and slightly less shrill than before, and then he fell silent.

The dinosaur stepped backward, its jaw working.

Zita froze for a second before she remembered Andy's abilities and moved again, backing away with Wyn as she tried to figure out a way to help him. "Don't hit it! We don't want to get him swallowed."

Jerome retreated to the other side of Wyn, lowering his arm.

The jaw and mouth of the creature made a horrible grinding sound as it attempted to bite down on her friend and failed. As she watched, another shred of cloth and a yellowed, curved stone dropped from it—a serrated tooth, she realized.

"Mano, force its jaws open and get out!" she shouted, before realizing he likely couldn't hear her. She repeated herself on the party line.

A dinosaur is trying to eat me. Andy's words carried both disbelief and equanimity.

It isn't having much luck with that, so get yourself out of its mouth, Zita sent back.

I can't! Not without possibly ripping off the top of its head and sending pieces flying.

Zita moved back a few more steps, keeping Wyn behind her. *Mano, you can do it, just moderate your strength. It'll be a lot more gruesome if you have to bust out of its stomach.*

"What do we do?" Jerome asked.

If I do anything, it'll be like that other dinosaur earlier. I won't risk the rest of you. Andy's mental tone flowed with a grim self-loathing.

Dude. Mano. That was a freak accident. I'm not mad at you. Sensing she wasn't going to change his mind in time, Zita seized Wyn's arm. "Can you make the dinosaur drop him? Make it think we're nasty-tasting frogs or something?"

Her friend shook her head. "How? It doesn't speak English, and I don't know what a poisonous frog tastes like! Do you?"

"No."

"Well, at least we've found something you don't want to eat." Wyn stared, fingers twisting together. *I'm not certain how well that works without words. If I just send it bad feelings, it might decide to destroy us all or run off with Andy.*

Zita scowled. "I don't like chocolate covered raisins either. Hey, it should be pretty happy with Wingspan playing pacifier. Can you put it to sleep?"

"What if it falls on him?" Wyn asked.

Zita winced. "It won't hurt him, and he can get out from under it."

The creature rendered their conversation moot by shaking its head and spitting out Andy.

Andy's upper half gleamed wetly as he staggered to his feet with a whimper.

After flexing its jaws, the dinosaur took a step forward, its dark eyes on Zita and her friends.

I can't normally become anything but real animals, but if it's real enough to slobber on Andy, it's possible. To avoid a repeat, especially one that included someone less invulnerable in its mouth, Zita shifted to mirror the beast, praying she could copy something that big. After a second of uncertainty, she figured out how to use the tail to balance and shambled forward, cutting off its sight of her friends. *Don't ask me to run like this.*

The big carnivore lumbered to a stop, then approached her, its head bobbing from side to side in an odd cadence. Now that it was no longer attempting to eat her friend, Zita could appreciate the sheer scale of the creature; her skull (the dinosaur smelled female in this new shape) alone was a few inches bigger than Zita's natural human height.

Zita blinked, shaking off her distraction, and the dinosaur stopped in front of her.

The creature breathed on her... hot, spoiled-meat scented air.

Other than curling her three-fingered claws into fists, Zita didn't move. *Oye, at least Nibbles here has breath better than Garm's. Not like minty fresh or nothing, but better.*

Don't name it. We're not keeping it, Wyn sent.

Too late, Zita sent back, sidling left to keep Nibbles from eyeing her friends.

Whispers came from behind her. "I can't tell them apart, and they're just standing there breathing on each other." She thought that was Andy.

Deeper tones answered him. Jerome. "Maybe she's going to kiss it into submission?"

Zita gave a congested snort at the ridiculous comment. *So not happening.*

As if she had made a suggestion, Nibbles stretched out her neck and focused greedy eyes on Jerome.

He retreated, but he and Andy kept their bodies in front of Wyn.

The reptile took a step toward him.

Zita head-butted Nibbles to retain her attention. Concentrating, she engineered a small change to her form, choosing the colors she wanted. *Back away, haters. I'm trying to buy you time to get to safety or attack it or put it to sleep. I'd rather keep it alive to avoid screwing the local ecosystem or putting a huge carcass in our path home. The smaller dinosaur corpses will attract enough scavengers as is.*

Andy sounded half-strangled. "Arca's the one who grew neon orange stripes in the last few seconds."

Wyn made no comment, just whispered under her breath, her words rapid and wispy.

To Zita's relief, a pink fog twined up around Nibbles' legs, climbing past the stunted-seeming arms and embracing the head. Snorting and snuffling, the dinosaur twitched, then turned and staggered a few feet, lowering herself to the ground. She finally closed her eyes, oversized lower jaw resting against her chest in an odd partial sit.

Zita backed up, her steps mincing to avoid stepping on the others.

Giving Nibbles a wide berth, her friends crept around the sleeping beast.

Did it snore? Andy sent.

Zita changed to Arca, falling behind the rest of the group. *No, I think that was me trying not to laugh.*

How about we let sleepysaurus sleep and get as far away as possible? Wyn sent.

As she passed, Zita snatched up the broken tooth and tucked it into a pocket, after touching the edge. "You're still pretty cool, Nibbles," she whispered to the slumbering dinosaur as she turned and bounded after her friends.

The four humans jogged for about ten minutes before slowing to a fast walk.

"I can't believe we fought a T-Rex," Jerome said as he reclaimed the lead position.

She considered it, even as she slowed her pace to allow Andy and Wyn to keep up. Wyn still seemed breathless from the jog, and Andy was sticking close. "No, they didn't live this far south. I can't tell for certain, but I think the nose was too long, and the tail was too skinny, but Nibbles was definitely a theropod. Could've been a Mapusaurus or Giganotosaurus, though."

Jerome twisted to look at her, "Are you telling me that wasn't a T-Rex because T-Rex got more back and a nose job? Maybe this one's been on a diet."

"Probably?" she said. "It's not as if I had time to check a reference book or do measurements."

"Spoilsport." He made a flippant noise and sped up to take the point position.

They had been walking for twenty minutes when Andy cleared his throat. His voice low and worried, his face held concern. "Z— Arca, you said the shapeshifting teacher turned her tribe into monsters. Were the dinosaurs her people? Did we just slaughter five people and leave the sixth one sleeping?"

Wyn paled even as she got the distant expression that meant she was checking her prodigious memory. "I didn't think to examine Nibbles' mind like that, but yes, that's what she said."

Zita's stomach turned over, and she fought to keep from losing her breakfast. "Dios. They just attacked, so I assumed they were animals, but... Is there a way to verify one way or the other?"

As she bit her lip, Wyn said, "I'll scan the next dinosaur we see and let you know if they've got animal thought patterns or not. Returning to the sleeping creature would be foolish. My spell was meant for humans, so I don't know how long it will last on the dinosaur."

"Do we tell Jerome?" Andy's body was tight and his voice unhappy.

Zita nodded. "It'd be wrong not to."

"Agreed. I'll talk to him." Wyn raised her voice. "Chevalier? Can I have a minute?"

Chapter Sixteen

Later that day, Zita shoved away a dangling vine. The coniferous forest opened into a sunny clearing, a perfect circle of light breaking the perpetual shadow they'd been straggling through. "We made it to the temple! I told you going up the cliff instead of following the trail all the way around would make it faster," she called over her shoulder as she studied the ancient building. She felt more than saw Wyn, Andy, and Jerome as they caught up with her.

"Thank the Goddess, a rest from the hiking!" Wyn panted and leaned against a nearby tree trunk. Even though Andy had carried her up the cliff in a prodigious leap, the walk had winded her.

Similar to the old mission buildings that littered the Brazilian countryside, the temple was no more than thirty-five feet wide and one hundred feet long. The spare, sturdy structure had smooth, flat white walls softened by the embrace of a profusion of vines and flowers along the sides. In addition to the greenery, other colors peeked out from it: a vibrant spill of turquoise and yellow tiles around the remains of the arched doorway, the bright blue windowsills and shutters, and a red-tiled roof. Two-thirds of the building resembled a townhouse with a curving roof and pretty little shuttered windows. As if the architect had remembered that this was supposed to be a holy place at the last moment, it had a solitary tower slapped on it, rectangular save for the Arabic flare of the onion dome at the top. A bell, sans rope, dangled from the belfry. The door was missing, with only a few remnants of striped hardwood dangling from the frame, but the scorch marks and obvious violence of the entry were new enough to have a lingering burnt wood odor. An uneven gray lump filled most of the opening. Spicy with the aroma of the unknown white flowers that dotted it, grass covered the grounds around the temple as if a flowering golf course had been transplanted into the middle of the Cretaceous jungle.

"Anywhere else, this would be cute. Here, it's creepy. Either someone just built this—which would be totally weird given the man-eating dinosaurs and the whole sealed for forty years thing— or this is one of those magicky things? That grass is not native even if the rest of the plants match some we passed on the way in," Zita mused aloud.

Wyn stared at the temple, then directed her gaze farther upward. Her brow furrowed. "This building is the center of the magical construct. Or was. The lines of the spell have gotten tangled and are curling in on themselves. The others must've gotten here first and stolen the Heart."

Andy groaned. "So, we would've run into them if we didn't take the shortcut?"

Zita grimaced and hurried toward the temple, the others trailing behind her. "Is there any chance you're wrong? Maybe we should check inside, just in case."

"Did you notice the freaky statue? I'm afraid to blink around it." Jerome pointed to the shape filling the doorway. A disturbing stone man blocked the entry, surrounded by the wooden shards of the door. Horror screamed from his face and posture, and a gun drooped from his hand as if he were in the process of dropping it. Detail on the carving was amazing, not only showing a knife strapped to his side, but also revealing tiny granite chest hairs curling at the unbuttoned top of his shirt.

Andy gave a half-smile. "Where's the Doctor when you need him? Or even a Companion?"

"Doctor Mwangi stayed back in the highlands," Zita said.

Jerome rolled his eyes and exchanged glances with Andy. "Man, she is bad," he commented. "Does she miss every reference?"

Andy nodded. "Most of them. We tolerate her anyway even if we're not sure why. It's not for her charm." Tilting his head like a bird, he cleared his throat. "Guys? Look over there." He pursed his lips and nodded at one side of the temple.

When they checked, the ground held headstones—twenty-three of them—and the small white flowers blanketed most of the graves as if planted there. Two other statues, also of men with guns, stood guard over the dead. Zita crossed herself, muttering a quick prayer.

Beside her, Jerome made an unhappy sound and took off his hat, worrying the brim with his thick fingers.

"Are the statues going to come after us?" Andy asked. He kept several feet away from the graveyard.

Wyn gave the stone men a glance. "No, they're no more magical than the dirt or grass. Let me take a break and study the spell holding this place together, and we can resume the mad chase after the others in a few minutes." She limped over and sat on a lumpy granite rock near one grave. After she murmured the words of her spell, light streamed from her hand as she healed her feet again.

Still twisting his hat, the last bit of his original costume other than his sunglasses, Jerome kept guard over her.

Zita touched Andy's bicep. "Sorry, mano, but if we're going to keep Brazil safe and avoid getting trapped or killed here, you have to give us a ride back. It's the only way we'll beat them to the cave entrance."

His face unhappy, Andy glanced up, then at the ground. "This clearing isn't big enough for the bird without stepping on the dead."

Zita glanced at the graves. "Pues, then we'll go to the base of the cliff where you'll take your big form on the plains and fly us back from there. Easy enough for you to carry Wyn down with you."

He nodded. "We make it as fast as possible."

"Let me scout the temple while Muse is figuring out the spell." Zita did a quick lap around the building. "I see trash, but no signs of them now and no more graves," she shouted.

"Hello? Is someone out there? Please, you have to help me!" A female voice called out from inside. "In the temple! I was kidnapped and trapped here!"

Jerome strode closer to the building and stopped. "Why do I want to quote Admiral Ackbar right now?"

"Because you're smart and understand how our luck works?" Andy said.

Hurrying nearer, Zita could see muddy red slide marks where the one stone man had been shoved into place. Flashes of varying shades of brown moved on the other side, a woman's face appearing at one point.

Zita stepped aside. "Wingspan, would you move the statue for the lady?" In a lower voice, she said, "Just in case, nobody else stand in the direct line of fire."

"Paranoid, much?" Wyn said, though she rose and retreated to stand near Zita. *The professor is the only person in there.*

Andy shuffled forward, and after staring at the statue for a moment, lifted it and set it next to the doorway. Nothing happened, and he returned to stand beside Zita.

You did your mind thing? Zita queried.

Wyn sighed mentally. *Yes, I did.*

Before anyone could speak, the missing professor scurried out of the building like a quail rushing away from danger. Once out, she slowed, taking off her hat to mop her brow and letting a backpack droop toward the ground. Sensible khaki clothing held numerous smears and a few grass stains, but still covered most of her skin.

She's carrying extra weight, but her legs are pretty toned, and that pack can't be light. No obvious movement styles, so probably goes to a health club regularly instead of focusing on a martial art or sport, Zita absently assessed.

While strain etched lines in the fine teak planes of the professor's long face, short, tapered hair curled tight in abandon above. Glasses reflected sunlight every time she tilted her head to examine another person. Jerome seemed to require the most scrutiny. "Thank you. I'm Professor Santos. Who are you and what are you doing here? Wait... have I seen you on television?" Her gaze settled on Zita. "Didn't you rescue a puppy?"

Órale, I've rescued a bunch of people, but she remembers the dog? Zita managed to resist rolling her eyes.

Smothering a grin, Wyn stepped forward. "I'm called Muse, and these are Arca, Wingspan, and Chevalier. We've been searching for you, Professor. Did the ones who took you get the Heart of Canaiwari?

Santos nodded. "Yes, they did."

Even though she'd expected that answer, Zita swore.

The professor blinked. "I don't understand... they had someone who claimed to have seen my grant application, but how did you hear about an obscure rock?"

Wyn cleared her throat. "We've been chasing your kidnappers and got a tip that led us to your application. When we sent someone to ask you about it, we found out you were missing and decided that following the information in your grant might be the best way to find you and stop them. The murals on the cave walls were also instructive."

The professor's eyebrows rose. "One of you could read those?"

Andy rasped, "Arca."

"For the last time, they're just pictures. You don't have to be able to read to understand pictures. Toddlers do it all the time," Zita mumbled.

"Denial... river in Egypt," one of the men muttered, and the other snickered, but when she glared at them, both had similar noncommittal expressions.

Her face lighting with Zita recognized (and feared) as academic fervor, Santos leaned toward her. "No, they're a complex series of pictographs in an ancient dialect—"

Wyn touched her arm. "Don't bother. No power on this planet or in any alternate dimension could help her. We need to find out where your kidnappers took the Heart."

Shooting Zita a look that promised unsolicited educational lectures later, the professor shrugged. "I believe they were returning to their homes. The mercenary woman who told me to stay in the temple told me they'd come back and take me home once they got rid of the homicidal maniacs, but then they shoved that awful statue in the doorway and left me in there to die! As if a few canned meals and canteens would make up for sealing me in there!"

Wyn's face was a mix of sympathy and outrage. "That's terrible."

"I might've done the same thing. Professor, are you armed with a big gun or superpower?" Zita said.

"Of course not!" Santos blazed.

I don't think she likes me, Zita thought.

Probably not, Wyn sent. *Not at all. You just said you'd leave her in a room to starve.*

"Since you can't defend yourself, it makes sense to put you in a place where the local wildlife can't eat you until someone can come back for you. If the only other option was letting Pretorius or Tiffany kill you, it'd be the sane choice to make," Zita explained, frowning. *She shouldn't jump to conclusions about people so fast.*

Pot, meet kettle. Andy's mental voice was dry.

Zita frowned at him. *What?*

Amusement sang over the party line from both her friends. *Never mind,* Andy sent.

"Tiffany? Vaudeville and Halja were the only other women." Confusion and concern warred on the professor's face.

We know who Halja is. Vaudeville must be Trixie. I wonder why she chose that name? Wyn mused.

"Tiffany is Halja's real name," Jerome said, taking pity on Santos.

The professor stretched and flashed a smile at him. "Ah, thank you. It's good to be out of there. Let me take a quick gander at these things... if only I had more of my equipment!" She hurried over and began reviewing the tombstones.

A line appeared between Wyn's brows. "We have a minute, but we need to catch up to the people who left you here. We can't let them take the gem out of the area." Despite her words, her face tilted upward, and her lips moved as she stared at something only she could see.

She's either studying the spell on this place again or watching the clouds. Oye, that one resembles a stack of pancakes. Food would be nice, Zita thought.

Santos glanced up from the tombstone she was examining, light reflecting off her glasses. "While I abhor artifact theft as much as the next, I'm not in a hurry to meet up with any of them again."

"You don't understand," Wyn said, her gaze still skyward, a hand tugging at the pale strands of her illusory hair. "The spell that sustains this land is collapsing because the Heart—the power source—isn't where it should be. In the best case scenario, the boundaries will dissolve when they cross back into the normal world and all the creatures inside will be ejected into our world. In the worst-case scenario, we all die immediately after they cross or are imprisoned here forever."

The professor jolted into motion. "Prior to this trip, I would've scoffed at the idea of magic, but after this place... I don't think I'll be writing anything I've seen for fear of becoming a laughingstock in a straightjacket." She tapped a tombstone. "This is strange."

"More bad news?" Jerome asked, twitching uncomfortably.

Somber, Santos traced the letters on the last monument with her fingers. "These graves would be a major find even without the cave murals, dinosaurs, or mummies. They're for everyone on the last missing expedition, except two. Three of the known fifteen people with powers from that decade went on this expedition. Alchemist died here. Clockwork flew off into space sometime later, so we know he survived. While Joe Paladin was never confirmed killed, his name is missing."

Crossing his beefy arms, Jerome said, "That count's off. We know someone who said four people escaped, including his mom and Paladin."

"Locals tend to get hired as guides, porters, and guards, and they wouldn't be on an official list. At least one of the survivors was from a nearby village, so the expedition probably had others from around here. That might account for it," Zita said.

Wyn raised her eyebrows. "Wouldn't they just hire a guide to help them find a place like this and skip the others given that they'd want to keep an undisturbed site secret from looters?"

With a snort and an internal wince at the memories it evoked, Zita vetoed that. "You think fancy archeologists carry their own crap?"

The professor shot Zita a glare, pursing her lips. "Unfortunately, true. Proper scientific equipment and excavation gear can be quite bulky."

"You sure you're not a paleontologist or something?" Jerome said in an aside to Zita.

Zita shook her head, bile burning her throat at the memory of just how willing one scientist had been to abandon his local guides to thugs, and how her friend had died as a result.

Santos tapped her fingers, chipped fingernail paint and all, against a stone. "That's all beside the point. Your friend must be mistaken. The only female member of the expedition, Patricia Wanjiku Mwangi, is listed right here." She patted the monument she stood beside. Unlike most of the graves, only a few flowers decorated the grass by the stone.

"Mwangi?" Jerome said. "Maybe his aunt? The doc couldn't be more than his early thirties, tops, so his mom had to have survived."

"Who did your friend say escaped?" asked the professor.

"Joe Paladin, his mother, a local boy, and a fourth person he didn't specify," Wyn said.

Her eyelids lowering, Santos scanned all the gravestones again. "Except for the metahuman Clockwork, all the scientists recorded on the expedition have headstones."

While they debated, Zita's eyes rested on the creepy statues, and she finally figured out what bothered her most about them and the surrounding graves. "Guys? If these are the remains of the people from that expedition, where did they get marble headstones from? And more than that... The statues have guns and sunglasses. I'm not all up on that history stuff, but the conquistadores did not wear shades. How and why would they bring that stuff up here?" She gestured toward it, remembering Andy's aversion to pointing at the last minute and ending with a weird wave instead, as if she were a beauty contestant.

The professor straightened her glasses. "While he never did it that anyone knows about, it was hypothesized that the Alchemist could turn people to stone. We can't ask him since he died on the expedition. The headstone next to your friend's aunt appears to be his or at least that of the man suspected of being him."

Zita rubbed the top of her head. "We are so chingado. If the temple is right for the supposed era of the legend of the dude who returned the rock here—"

Pushing her glasses up on her nose, Santos nodded. "I've had more than a day to examine the interior, and it seems authentic other than the remarkable preservation." She wrapped her arms around herself and shuddered. "As much as possible with no real gear or food. At least I had the one mummy to examine, but I couldn't get back to the other one."

"This climate is too humid for mummification," Wyn said, perking up. Interest gleamed in her eyes, and her tones held an excitement Zita couldn't understand. "You'd need extreme aridity and temperature extremes for a mummy—even the human-created ones—to preserve them."

Her face warming with enthusiasm, the professor nodded. "That's exactly what I said when we saw the first one on the altar in the temple. That one is female, I think, but she had no offerings around her, so perhaps a servant. In the caverns underneath, we found a wonderful mummy, a male noble given the finely worked clothing and grave goods surrounding him. While he was curled up in the style of Incan or Aztec mummies, he was on his side rather than sitting. This represents a whole new mummification ritual process. When the big blond man, Pretorius, took the Heart from him, he broke a few of the mummy's fingers."

Jerome crossed his arms over his chest. "That's never good."

Andy nodded in agreement and sidled another step away from the temple.

Wyn frowned, coiling a strand of hair around her fingers. "How could they defile the mummy like that?"

"Exactly!" Santos flashed an approving smile at Wyn.

"It could be the teacher and the farmer from the wall pictures and yes, very uncool," Zita said. She ran a hand over her hair, wondering how she had gotten drawn into the conversation. "Unless we want to join those in the graves, we need to get our culos in gear right now to stop that gem from leaving."

Wyn shook herself. "Of course. Sorry, Professor, we will have to postpone the academic discussions for another time, but if you all don't mind, I'll just take a quick peek at the mummy." She struggled back to her feet, her eyes beseeching Zita not to argue. *Besides satisfying my curiosity, it might help me understand the spell on this place if the interior has anything different from the exterior.*

Santos shivered. "I've spent enough time inside contemplating her. I'll wait here."

Zita sighed. "Fine, let's make it fast though, and everyone grab food to eat on the go. We probably won't have another chance before getting back to the entrance."

The others agreed and passed lunch around.

"I'll wait at the perimeter," Andy said hastily, retreating to the tree line. Nibbling their food, Jerome and the professor joined him.

The first to finish eating, Zita tapped fingers against her thigh while she waited. She eyed the temple. "Hey, Muse, can I get that candy I gave you? If another headache starts, I can gnaw on that and see if it keeps it away."

With a nod, Wyn withdrew the fist-sized chunk of rock candy and handed it over. "I doubt it'll help, but good luck."

"Thanks," Zita said, stuffing it into a pocket in her pants and closing it. She trailed Wyn as her friend entered the building.

Dim and cool, the interior seemed bare without the usual Christian symbols and pews for worshippers. White walls swept upward, with simplified versions of the pictograms from the cave painted in red at eye level on all sides. While the nave was empty, the chancel bore a long sandstone altar engraved with local animals. Her eyes stung from the unpleasant odor in a corner, confirming the professor's story about being locked here for more than a day. On the altar, a still form, dried skin stretched over bone, formed a huddled shape. One withered arm was flung out toward the back wall as if the person had lain on their side to sleep and had forgotten to wake.

Zita crossed herself.

Wyn spent a couple minutes studying the place and the body. "I suppose it's only to be expected of a commission by a European with a conquistador's stolen gem, but I'm disappointed that this building is pedestrian and Christian, rather than an example of ancient religious architecture. While the mummy is part of the spell, the focal point is somewhere beneath the temple." Even though her words focused on the magic, she withdrew a scarlet cloth from her purse and draped it over the huddled form on the altar like a blanket, her eyes sympathetic.

Zita glanced down at the hard-packed dirt floor and shook her head, retreating to the doorway. "We don't have time to find and explore the undercroft."

After one more moment, Wyn joined her. She trudged toward the trees, a sigh escaping.

Zita patted her friend's arm. "No worries, Muse. Plenty of chances to geek out later." Raising her voice, she called out, "We're ready, vámonos."

With a groan, Jerome shouldered his backpack. "Right, no rest for the wickedly handsome or you guys. Let's go."

Andy muttered under his breath.

The professor cast a lingering glance at the temple and nodded.

Once Wyn was back at Andy's side, Zita took the lead on the deer trail—small dinosaur trail?—they'd followed to the clearing. She grinned. "On the bright side, we get to go down the cliff this time, not up. Should be fun, even for you bumbly sorts! The boys can jump and carry people, or we can rappel down with my ropes."

"Cliff?" Santos asked. "We took a dinosaur track of one of the larger species to get here, though we saw none of a size to create such a track. It took almost two days."

Zita beamed and held aside a fern. "If they moved that slow getting here, we can beat them back to the exit. I find the best shortcuts."

"Be still my beating heart. I can't wait to be thrown off the cliff," Wyn murmured.

Chapter Seventeen

On the ledge outside of the cavern entrance, the small group camped all night, with Andy, Jerome, and Zita taking alternating watches. Wyn and the professor had both been too exhausted to do more than eat, chat, and sleep once they had arrived.

Perhaps her sensitivity had been heightened by the expectation of an imminent fight, but Zita found herself unable to sit still even more than usual and slept only lightly. To her, the waterfall's thunder seemed to have changed cadence to a sound less regular, and all the scents around them were too sharp. All else was as they had left it.

As she nibbled, her expression unenthused, on a late breakfast, Wyn lifted her head. "They're coming."

Zita cleaned up the food and trash as fast as possible. "Does everyone remember the plan?"

"Is it bad I want to make a joke about having the high ground?" Jerome said.

Andy shushed him, but he gave a small, slight smile.

Practically vibrating with eagerness to end the waiting, Zita stepped out of her shoes and handed those and the refuse of their meal to Wyn.

Wrinkling her nose, Wyn tucked it all into her purse.

Zita took a deep breath and ran through the strategy they'd sketched out during dinner the previous night. "Muse, you take cover and put the bear and Vaudeville and whoever else you can catch to sleep when you're not undoing Tiffany's spells. Chevalier goes for the shooter and Wingspan takes Pretorius and blocks the trail up. I'll hide at the bottom until they get close, then steal the gem while they're distracted. Professor Santos said Tiffany has it in her bag." Each of her friends nodded as she detailed their part. *At least this spot is reasonably defensible, with only the trail up as an option without climbing gear or flight, and the tepui walls covering two sides. Even if the ledge is only the size of a one-bedroom apartment, it's got enough of the squat ferns and rocks to provide cover.*

The professor rubbed her arms, her face uneasy. Her pack had been stored inside the cave as soon as they'd arrived. "I'm to conceal myself in the caverns. If you lose or don't come after me, I follow the murals out and ask the doctor camping on the highlands for help to go home," she said.

Zita nodded. "Right. I'll get going." With hope that the green feathers would make her hard to spot, she shifted to a mealy amazon parrot and flew down from the ridge.

As she picked a place where she expected to be overlooked, Wyn called out from above. "The spell is becoming more unstable. The Heart needs to go back to the temple as soon as possible. Did I mention immediately would be good?"

Before she could do more than nestle in the crown of a fern, Zita heard a familiar giggle. *They're here! Be ready.*

I only sense five minds incoming, Wyn sent. *That is an ill omen for the poor local guide.*

Apparently forgetting their plan, Jerome charged down the path, rushing toward the approaching large Kodiak bear.

As she watched, Jerome slipped and fell on his butt, skidding to a stop in a mass of greenery.

The bear roared and slashed at him.

With a cackle, Tiffany emerged from behind a clump of ferns. Long black robes, the bottom tattered and splattered with mud and broken greenery, hung off her skeletal frame. An embroidered mask hid half of her face. White gloves covered hands that wove in jagged patterns. The visible part of her face was haggard and worn, the first time she had ever appeared lacking makeup.

It would've been wiser to be silent, but Zita's mouth had even less patience than the rest of her. "How can you dress like a Halloween witch without the hat? If you lost your hat, we can help you find it." In her parrot form, her voice was high and screechy.

Soft chanting came from above. *Tiffany requires a reminder of her schooling. She's trying to summon her nasty creatures again, so I'll put a stop to that foolishness.*

Andy slid down the trail and into a bush bristling with spines. He gave a girly yelp, then shouted, "Bananas!"

With a shove to get the bear out of his way, Jerome stood. Distracted by the shapeshifter, he stepped on two peels and fell again. "No shit. Did someone bring bananas just for that?"

Zita scanned the area. *Where are Freelance and Pretorius?*

"Mine is the strength of ten men, for my heart is ridiculous," Trixie said, giggling. A flash of yellow gave away her hiding place behind a tree. She wore boots and khaki jodhpurs with a man's evening coat in green camo colors, topped by a pith helmet. A small spike on top of the hat speared what was probably a plastic banana. Ignoring the gun strapped to her back, she instead dug through her backpack and threw a cigar at Zita. A lavender one that smelled like artificial grapes and sugar.

Zita dove from her spot and flew through the ferns, inching closer to Tiffany. She'd seen Trixie throw things before and had no desire to be a target.

The candy sliced off fronds along its path and stuck, quivering, in the plant where Zita had been hiding.

"Watch out for the gum! It's dangerous!" she squawked.

"You bet your bubbles it is! Cavities are no joke," Trixie sang as she launched another. Her face came into focus; beneath her ridiculous helmet, she wore thick glasses with thicker eyebrows atop them, a fake nose, and an enormous false mustache.

"Surrender—" Tiffany called out. She stepped into Zita's line of sight, her hands moving in a familiar series of gestures.

"If she says Dorothy, I will laugh," Andy gasped as he ran by and pushed Jerome out of the way of a bolt of plasma. A few spines stuck out jauntily from his now-disheveled braid.

Tiffany continued, unaware of his interruption, "Surrender the white witch, and we might let some of you live!"

Close enough. Andy snickered and charged Pretorius, who had moved from behind a fern to stand in front of Tiffany. Clad in sensible, long-sleeved green camouflage gear and boots, Pretorius drifted a foot from the ground... one hand glowing

"Did you raid a Day of the Dead closeout sale for that mask?" Zita called out. "Come on, put the gem back! If you don't, the spell holding this place together will fail!" To be safe, this time she changed her hiding place before another cigar flew her way, moving closer to Tiffany.

At the sound of Zita's voice, Tiffany snarled. "Forget mercy. Nobody cares. Get the white witch alive! Kill the others."

"I got Muse covered," Jerome called out, hustling back up to the ridge.

Tiffany finished waving her hands, but nothing happened, and she stomped her foot. "You can't keep that up forever!" She dug through her bag.

A rifle sang out.

As he reached the crest, Jerome fell, blood and brains exploding from his head. His body disappeared from her view as it collapsed.

Time slowed and almost stopped as Zita stared at Jerome's body. *I'm too slow, just like before when...* She yanked her mind away from the remembered horror. Controlling her breathing, she forced it into the cadences of a capoeira ginga and flew to another bush. Her eyes scanned the area, searching for the source of the shot. Her stomach churned and threatened to revolt.

Jerome's down... And... Dios, I hope he can heal from that. I've seen him get better from worse, but those weren't head wounds. Zita fought to force her thoughts to coherence. *Deal later, fight now. There's the shooter.*

Leaping down from the leafy crown of one of the taller bushes, Freelance carried a rifle, a second long gun on a sling over his back. He dragged a barefoot man from behind a rock.

Freelance's prisoner, a lean fellow with the stringy muscles of a serious runner, glared at the mercenary. His hand dropped to the waist of his sensible shorts, his only clothing as if reaching for a weapon no longer there. Every line of his weathered face shouted his relationship to the boy at the clinic. After a moment, Zita realized he was middle-aged, not elderly as she had first thought.

Gracias a Dios, the guide's alive. Wyn, you miscounted. There's six of them. Zita readied to teleport onto Freelance if necessary to stop him from hurting the kid's grandfather.

Pushing his prisoner toward the path up instead of harming him, Freelance took cover behind a different rock.

Wyn's mental voice held concern. *Are you certain? I still only detect us and five others.*

Red tattoos formed new shapes on his face as the local man gave a fierce smile and darted nimbly up the narrow trail with fleet, practiced movements that mirrored his grandson's earlier run.

Don't hit him, the kidnapped grandpa is making for the exit, Zita sent. As she readied herself to snatch the bag, her instincts screamed a warning. Letting her small body drop below the crown of the plant, she flew to the ground.

A blast of light whooshed by and destroyed the fern where she'd been seconds before.

"I hate headshots," Jerome growled.

Alive? Gracias a Dios! The painful knot in Zita's stomach loosened at the big man's complaint. Launching herself from where she'd landed, Zita wove an indirect route through the ferns, her feathers blending with plants.

Jerome stood up, then went down again under another bullet.

A thud and a high-pitched squeak announced Andy falling somewhere nearby.

Trixie's laughter cut off.

Zita glanced that direction.

Her pith helmet visible on the ground next to her, Trixie sat slumped at the base of a tree. A dainty snore escaped her open mouth.

With a roar, the bear abandoned the fight against Andy—where he'd been aiding Pretorius—and limped to Trixie. He lifted her inert form and carried it farther from the combat.

Another shot rang out, and Wyn screamed, mentally and physically.

Wyn? Fear raced through Zita, and she flew toward her friend.

Throwing Pretorius aside, Andy thundered through the brush behind her.

On the ridge, Wyn curled up in a ball, cradling one of her hands.

Zita changed to Arca and knelt beside her. "You okay?" She glanced all around. "Get the shooter or Pretorius," she told Andy.

He nodded but remained next to Wyn. "Will you be okay?" he asked.

"My hand. I can't cast." Dread and pain clouded Wyn's eyes, and she pushed at them with her good arm. "Don't let Tiffany get away with the gem. The spell keeping this place together is in a precarious state already. If she leaves the zone of effect, it will dissolve. I can do a quick illusion to appear to be brush, so don't worry about me."

Andy relocated to the ledge at the trailhead, crouching as if to spring on someone coming up the path. On the ground, Jerome's body tensed, but he remained prone.

A massive boom rang out, and something hit Andy on his forehead just as he was about to jump. He flinched and stepped onto a banana peel while off balance. As if choreographed in a kung fu comedy scene, his arms windmilled, and he fell backward off the edge of the ridge. A painful sounding splash echoed from below.

Andy? Are you in the river? Watch out for protocrocodilians and get back as soon as possible. After giving Wyn a squeeze on the shoulder, Zita flexed her shoulders and ran to see what she could do.

Pretorius and Tiffany appeared at the top of the path, near Zita. They stepped over Jerome's inert form.

Light flared, and the ground shook. Distant dinosaurs and other creatures roared or screeched or screamed. Everyone staggered, and Tiffany tumbled to her bony hands and knees.

Andy's reply included a few profanities Zita hadn't known he knew. *Screw that, I'm in quicksand! Let's just say strength is not the way out.*

A big gun boomed again somewhere though Zita didn't see the weapon or the target.

Jerome grabbed Pretorius' ankle. He pulled, and the big blond man fell, but not over the edge. Rolling over on top of the mercenary, Jerome began punching.

Tiffany scurried forward, scrambling to stand.

In Zita's head, Andy lamented, *Ah, yes, and here comes a monster crocodile. That guy keeps shooting me every time I'm about to get out. I hate my life. On my way.*

Zita dove at Tiffany, knocking her down again. Rolling to her feet, she grabbed the satchel, yanking it from the evil woman. "The gem has to go back before anybody dies." She stepped away with the bag.

As she lurched back up again, Tiffany screeched a profanity and batted ineffectually with her wimpy arms at Zita.

Zita brought an arm around to strike Tiffany with an elbow— not using her full strength, as she still had no intention of killing the other woman—while her other hand dug through the contents.

Tiffany fell back, gasping. When she recovered her breath, she switched to clawing at Zita's face and pulling hair.

Careful not to jar the many glass bottles while she searched the satchel by touch, Zita dodged. Her fingertips touched a rough, uneven fist-sized surface among all the glassware. An idea sparked, and her free hand scrabbled at her own pants and tore the Velcro fastener on a pocket open. *Dios, don't let anyone shoot the crap in this bag. I really don't want magic napalm on me,* she prayed silently, moving fast. Aloud, she covered her actions by taunting Tiffany. "At least slug me or kick me. Come on, you're making all us women look bad."

Her words seemed to redouble the witch's attempts to snatch back the bag.

Wyn shrieked and bolted out of her hiding place, pointing at the sky. "The spell is breaking! We're all going to die, or the dinosaurs will get loose and decimate the villages! Put the Heart back in place to reset it! I won't be able to hold it long, especially resorting to brute force!" She ran to the walls and placed both hands on them, lowering her head. Chanting, soft and almost inaudible, rose from her lips, and silvery white light emanated from her fingertips.

Another gunshot sounded.

Runes appeared, ones that spread over the mountain and spilled into and across the sky, hiding the constant screen of clouds overhead. They faded, melting into the rock and disappearing.

"Pterodactyl, incoming!" Jerome shouted, pointing up before continuing to pummel Pretorius. A blast of plasma caught him in the stomach, and he slid down the trail, out of sight.

Wyn gasped and threw her head back. Light flared and went out, except in her eyes, which were luminous but unseeing.

Following the direction Jerome's finger had indicated, Zita spotted a pterosaur dipping toward the fight and the edge of the tepui, perhaps having glimpsed the unsuspecting world outside.

Another gunshot rang out, and the massive winged beast fell.

At the whisper of movement nearby, Zita dropped the bag as she hurled herself to the side in time to avoid a charge by Pretorius. She flipped to her feet, one hand over her pocket.

Tiffany snatched up her satchel. She rifled around inside, panic on her face. Tension leaked from her, and she visibly relaxed. "I still have it. Pretorius, come!" She ran for the cavern entrance that led back to normal Brazil.

Pretorius turned, one hand glowing.

With a nod to the witch, Pretorius unleashed his bolt on Zita.

She leapt aside and rolled into the field of oversized ferns. "Oye, Pretorius, we never talk no more. Are you trying to hurt my feelings?"

In the tunnel, Tiffany held a large clay disk, covered in symbols and a nasty brown smear. The sorceress smashed it on the ground as Pretorius threw another blast, though his aim was off enough so Zita couldn't be certain who he had aimed at.

A wavering portal sprang up in the passageway, glowing bright in the darkness. On the other side of it, a familiar barren room waited. A howler monkey screeched.

With a jerk of his head, Pretorius ran to join Tiffany. Frowning, he grabbed her arm. Proximity allowed Zita to hear his growled words. "It's not time."

With a smirk, Tiffany nodded and said, "They'll all be dead or busy when the spell breaks. We don't have to worry about keeping the nosy idiots tied up until Thursday or paying the other mercenaries. Don't complain. It's more money for you." They stepped through the opening together, and it closed up behind them.

All sounds of combat ceased.

Jerome hauled himself up the trail again. He swore and scrubbed a hand over his shaved head. "How the hell are we going to catch up with them now and get the gem back before anyone dies?"

"Hey, Freelance, how about a truce?" Zita called out. She risked a glimpse. He either wasn't where he had been, or he had hidden even better.

"Why?" came the groggy-sounding answer from Vaudeville.

Sand dripping from him, a damp Andy jumped onto the ridge. He ran to Wyn. "Are you okay? Muse? Muse?" He touched her shoulder and gave it a light shove, but she remained motionless.

As she scanned for Freelance's new position, Zita said, "Well, are you getting paid to kill us or guard them? Tiffany and Pretorius just portaled out, and we'll stop fighting if you quit attacking us." When Zita hurried to her friends, she blanched.

Wyn's eyes had gone completely silver, matching the light that still shined where she touched the rock and the occasional rune that glowed to life on the wall. The scent of sweat drowned out the fading eucalyptus sting of her mosquito repellent. Plants twined around her ankles, and her arms had sunken into the rock up to her elbows.

Andy glanced up at a rune that sparkled with Wyn's magic and down again, his shoulders twitching. He eased his body between Wyn and the ferny forest.

"So, can we assume we got a truce for now? Your employers left, and I don't think we have any reasons to murder each other." Zita crossed her fingers.

Jerome muttered though the words carried to Zita, "Oh, I don't know. I'm not a fan of the bastard who shot me in the head."

Trixie, followed by the bear, ambled up the path with her arms in the air, though she had a bubblegum cigar ready in each hand. "Speak for yourself, but we'll go with that because that's what the boss says."

A soft whirr came from behind Zita. She twisted in time to see Freelance land on the ridge and retract his grappling hook and rope. "So, you got a name? Or should I keep calling you Freelance?"

The masked man inclined his head.

"Seriously?" Zita asked.

"Oh, can anyone make up nicknames? Can I call you Freelance, boss?" Trixie giggled. She pointed a thumb at the bear beside her. "He can be Beary Sexy, no, Bearlicious."

The bear hid his face in his paws.

Before Zita could speak again, Freelance's goggles turned to the mustached woman.

Trixie composed her face, making a motion as if she'd zipped her lips shut, but a snort escaped and her shoulders shook.

The bear sighed. "Every time. Adrenaline drunk."

With herself, Jerome, and Andy all surrounding Wyn's immobile form, Zita pasted on a smile and gestured toward the exit. Noting Freelance's attention seemed to focus her direction, she angled her hips away, hoping he wouldn't notice the lump in her pocket. "Well, then, I guess you can go on home. We'll wait here, so you feel safe and all."

"What's wrong with this picture?" Trixie asked.

Zita eyed the doctor and her costume. "Your mustache?"

"No, no, that's perfect," Trixie said. "What are you hiding? You're not even mentioning glowing coma girlfriend over there." Her head tilted, and she touched her ear.

She must have an earpiece, Zita thought.

Trixie's eyes widened. "You've got the gem! You know, if you give it to us, we can part ways peacefully."

"At the cost of how many lives when these creatures break free and ravage the countryside? Or if we all die because we don't get out fast enough and this place collapses once Muse stops whatever she's doing?" Zita glanced over at Wyn and shivered involuntarily.

The bear rumbled. "The earth moved when Halja set foot up here. They might have a point."

Trixie visibly bit her tongue twice, then spun one of her candy cigars. Holstering it, she unwrapped the other and chewed. Artificial grape perfumed the air.

Zita tapped her fingers on her leg and shot a worried look at Wyn. "So, you just go on your way, and Wingspan can take me to the temple. I'll return the gem. It's easy enough for me to get down and put it where it belongs if someone tells me where you found it."

"I don't hover," Andy said.

"You don't have to stay in place long," she said. "I've jumped out of planes before, so this'll be pan comido, a piece of cake."

Andy winced. "Please stop using that expression. Nothing good ever comes of it."

Trixie laughed. "Fat chance. What's to keep you from stealing the gem?"

"My innate honesty and awesomeness?" Since they seemed unconvinced, Zita continued, "Even if the dinosaurs didn't pose a threat to the local villages, I wouldn't take it and leave my friend here. She'll die if I don't get her to stop whatever magicky thing she's doing. If you can extricate her from the spell without hurting her, let us know. I'm assuming putting the rock back will do it. I'm no thief, and I don't do my friends like that. Carajo, I don't do my enemies like that, and I earn what I have."

With a snort, Trixie said, "We don't know you or anything about you other than what's on television. Your friend dying might increase your split of the loot so you might be fine with her death. You should give it to us to return."

"Because mercenaries are more trustworthy with a jewel than vigilantes working for free?" It was Zita's turn to snort.

To her annoyance, Freelance nodded.

Kodiak, still in bear form, studied everyone. He lumbered past them to the tunnel entrance and bounced off an invisible wall. "We're stuck here."

Zita sighed, giving in to the inevitable. *Wyn can't advise me, and I've got no telepathy, so I can't use party line to talk privately with Andy.* "Right, let's pretend to have our act together and try cooperating. Chevalier, Bear-dude, and crazy chick, guard Muse from the dinosaurs. Once she's not busy being a wall, she can figure out how to get us out. If we don't put the Heart back, Muse said the options were instant death, a life trapped inside here forever, or all the dinosaurs being loosed on Brazil. None of those are acceptable."

Trixie sniffed. "I prefer Vaudeville, and tall, dark, and hairy goes by Kodiak."

Ignoring that, Zita continued on. "Freelance, you're with me, so your team knows I didn't run off with the rock. You're probably the least likely to trust me anyway without proof. If Wingspan gives us a lift, we can be there in minutes. We'll replace the Heart where it belongs, and hopefully, the spell will reset before the tepui eats my friend." To her dismay, no one seemed to recognize the wisdom of her plan.

Andy stared at his toes. "I can't land in the tree zone, not without risking toppling the temple and the trees and hurting you. If I take off below the ridge, I'll just be crushing ferns, so that's not too bad, but... I can't hover, and I can't predict what effect the downdrafts from my wings would have."

Zita touched his shoulder. "Wasn't expecting you to, mano. We'll make our own way back. You keep watch, and if you see us in the plains, come pick us up in your claws or wait for us to walk."

Andy opened his mouth, then closed it, frowning.

"Right, let's focus on business," Zita said. "Is everyone happy now? Can we go? I don't know how long Muse can hold the spell, and I guess you all want to go home too."

Sobering, the others nodded.

"Can I talk to you, Arca?" The part of Andy's face visible beneath his mask grimaced, set into unhappy lines.

Zita punched his shoulder. "Always. You don't have to ask. What's up?"

He eyed the rest of the expanded group, his gaze lingering on Freelance. "Ah, privately?"

"Chevalier, you got Muse covered, right?" Zita said.

His normally sunny face solemn, Jerome nodded and walked to stand next to Wyn.

"Gracias." Moving as far away from the rest as the small ridge allowed, Zita leaned against a tepui wall and watched Andy shuffle up to her.

Andy said, "Are you out of your adrenaline-loving mind? We can't trust them." He jerked his chin toward the mercenaries.

Zita shoved a long strand of hair over her shoulder in an irritated gesture. "What else do you expect me to do? I'm open to suggestions, but we need to get the Heart in place before Tiffany realizes the switch and comes back with reinforcements."

"We get them to leave and take it back. If Tiffany returns, then we handle it." He glared at the three newcomers and brushed sand off his arm.

She closed her eyes for a second and exhaled, opening them again. "Take a close look at W-Muse. Do you think we can detach her from her creepy rock hug? Even if we did, she's in no shape for a fight. If Tiffany comes back with helpers or another group of dinosaurs attack, all it takes is one shot or bite to kill her and bring the spell down on all of us. Not to mention, the bear tried to leave and couldn't, so whatever's going wrong has already started. Muse has my shoes and most of our food in her purse. If I didn't climb and do acrobatics barefoot all the time, my feet would be shredded right now."

In unison, they both glanced down at Zita's dirty bare toes, then swiveled to check their friend. Sweat glistened on Wyn's pallid face, and her lips moved constantly. Her only other motion was the occasional tilt of her head as if studying something on the walls. Plants twined around her legs, and she was now ankle-deep in the soil, though her arms still only disappeared into the rock up to the elbows.

Zita marched over, took a breath, and plunged her hand into Wyn's bag. Her fingers scrabbled around and found nothing. Withdrawing it, she shrugged at Andy and stepped away from Wyn.

Jerome and Trixie hovered nearby, watching Andy and Zita curiously. The bear—Kodiak—was inspecting something on the ground, and Freelance stood alone, though his goggles appeared to follow Zita and Andy.

Shoving aside an errant lock of hair, Zita paced a few steps and back. "So. Limited food and water to split between all of us, and no shoes for me. I have no idea what Muse is doing, but she can't keep it up forever. She said if the Heart goes where it belongs, everything should stabilize. If nothing else, taking one of their team means they can tell me where the gem came from. Muse said the source of the spell was in an undercroft we didn't have time to explore."

Andy rubbed his eyes. "Fine, but I can't fly you there."

Feeling herself burn under the mercenary's goggles, Zita turned most of her back and face away. *Oye, I bet he can read lips or something.* "Dude, that's our only option. They won't let me go alone, and you're the best choice to protect Muse for a longer period of time."

"Won't they?" he said.

"We totally won't," Trixie said, striding up and putting her arms around Zita and Andy's shoulders. "How did you fool Halja into thinking she still had the Heart, anyway?"

Zita wrinkled her nose at the gum scent and shrugged out from under Trixie's arm. "Rock candy in her bag." She turned away. "Chevalier, I need to borrow a canteen."

Andy pulled away, retreating until he almost stepped off the ridge again.

Her eyes wide, Trixie stared at her, then howled with laughter.

Going over to where he had stashed his pack, Jerome dug a bottle out of the cooler. "Will this do?"

Trixie brushed tears from her cheeks as she finished laughing. "Rock candy. Not a bad move for an amateur."

Accepting the water, Zita rolled her eyes. "You guys keep calling us amateurs, but it's not like there are training classes on being vigilantes who don't kill. I mean, what would that even be called?"

Another rumble from the bear. "The military, but the not killing part might be an issue?"

Her pitch horribly off-key, Trixie sang something about the Navy and clapped her hands. When she started to dance, her larger companion seized her shoulder before she could high-kick herself off the ridge. "What?" she said, "If you're going to do it, you need to go all in." She mimicked twirling her mustache.

With an exaggerated shake of his head, Kodiak released her.

"Teen Titans or Xavier's School for Gifted Youngsters?" Jerome suggested.

Soberly, Andy said, "Hogwarts. Of course, Arca's a terrible Muggle or maybe a Squib."

As he stroked his goatee, Jerome snickered. "Pretty much any heroic sidekick position would count as training." His dark eyes twinkled as he paused, then said, "Would you like to be my sidekick? I have studied many ancient video games and cartoons and am a master of the subject."

"Shut it, Chevalier. You can all be my chingado sidekicks someday." Zita shook her head at the silliness. "Freelance, you're with me. Why don't we just go? These guys can giggle it out while we're gone."

The masked man inclined his head.

As she, Andy, and Freelance walked away to allow her friend the space to transform into his bird form, Jerome had to have the last word. "Luchador training!"

Zita flicked her middle finger at him and kept walking. "At least luchadores are awesome and real," she muttered.

Chapter Eighteen

Andy's bird form circled above the temple, just under the perpetual layer of fluffy white clouds. After motioning Freelance to stay where he was with his backpack, Zita scurried along a massive wing until she felt the warm, misty wind and the slight yield of the feathered limb beneath her bare feet. Jerome's water bottle was lukewarm as she rolled it back and forth in her hands and scanned the area.

Below them, the canopy of conifers crowded so close together that from above they seemed a single lumpy expanse of emerald with a few holes. The largest gap held a splash of red, the Spanish-style temple roof, as well as a lighter green patch dotted with specks of white and gray beside it. In the distance, the pterosaurs hunted, though they kept far from the gigantic golden eagle with the glowing eyes and lightning chasing over it.

I would stay away too if I were them, Zita thought, distracted by the flying creatures for a moment. *If Freelance were more trusting, I could've done this and been back within a half hour. How hard can it be to slap a gem into a statue or a hole or something?*

As she padded to her silent companion, she said, "Good news! He's gotten right above the temple, though he can't hover more than a few seconds, so he's circling. On his next loop, we need to be ready to descend. How do you want to handle it?" Even if she knew he'd make her friends uncomfortable at the cave entrance, she attempted to ditch him one last time. "I can fly down, but what will you do? Wingspan can take you with him, and I'll meet up with you all later once the Heart's in place again."

Black goggles considered her for a moment, then the man walked along the wing where she had been a few minutes ago and peered below. Setting down his large backpacking frame, he removed half of it and strapped it to his back. The remaining part, complete with stiff metal poles, he attached to his front. His head tilted toward Zita in what she assumed was a disdainful glance though his mask hid his expression.

"What?" she said.

When Andy was at the point of his loop farthest from the clearing, Freelance leapt.

She swore and raced to the edge, preparing herself to teleport if necessary to save his life.

A parasail unfolded from his pack and Freelance glided to a controlled landing in front of the temple door, using only two steps to bleed off speed.

Zita blinked and shut her mouth, licking her lips. "No, don't answer my question. Just go on with your sweet toys and bad self. Why are the unavailable ones always so hot?"

The massive bird chirped, a sound that's volume belied its resemblance to the cry of a newly hatched chick.

"Are you laughing at me?" Clearing her throat, she said, "Once I'm off, go watch over Wyn, okay? She can contact me later to figure out if you'll pick us up or what."

Andy did not reply.

Taking that as his agreement, she shifted to a gavião-real, grabbed the water bottle in her talons, and dove over the side. She winged to a stop next to Freelance and returned to her Arca shape.

Zita patted her pocket to ensure the gem remained inside, grateful to feel the rough, uneven edges through the fabric.

The clearing brightened as Andy sailed away and his avian body no longer blocked the sunlight.

In the time it had taken her to land and reclaim a human form, Freelance had folded and stowed his parasail in its backpack again.

She squinted at him. "Right. You could have mentioned you had that. I don't suppose you'd let me—"

"No." His voice still held the mechanical overtones she remembered from their last meeting. He connected the halves of his pack to the frame and shouldered the entire thing.

After pushing errant hair from her face, Zita rolled her eyes, not hiding it from him. "Oye, no fun. Okay, Mister Professional, let's go get this done."

He was already disappearing through the door.

She sidled past the creepy statue that might've been a man a long time ago and into the temple again. Other than improved smell, as if someone had cleaned up the one soiled corner, it seemed unchanged.

At the big stone altar, Freelance pressed a section of the ornate stonework, and the back of the platform slid away to the side. The still form of the mummy, draped with Wyn's red cloth, remained above.

Zita hurried over to see. Rough-hewn sandstone stairs led down into darkness, and she broke out in a sweat as a wave of humid air poured heat and a strong, earthy sulfuric scent over her. She wrinkled her nose and began mentally running through her catalog of shapes for one that would not mind the stench or the darkness. Water trickled and bubbled somewhere below.

He held up a hand and shone a tiny flashlight down the hole. The beam illuminated another dirt floor, one with the uneven dips of a natural tunnel. Above that, a concave rock, like a natural birdbath, bore faint brown stains.

With a deep breath, Zita shifted partially to an owl, hoping the changes would be useful. Her vision sharpened, as did her hearing, and she caught the sound of a soft rustle. The weight of her long hair disappeared. Touching her ears, she found feathery tufts. Reaching back farther, feathers cascaded where her hair should have been. She smoothed her hands over her clothes, running one over the pocket with the Heart, reassured by the slippery feel of the fabric and the comforting irregular lump.

As she descended the ancient steps, marks on the wall attracted her attention, and she rolled her eyes after deciphering the pictures. Etched above a cave opening, the giant symbol of the farmer king glared down at her. "Whee, more warnings of gruesome death to those approaching the trials. What trials?"

"Traps," Freelance said, striding a few feet ahead of her and stopping. His goggles whirred when he tapped the side of them.

As Zita walked through, she got only a few steps before halting. A forty-foot wide gorge separated the halves of the cavern. Two long, rounded logs, secured with vines, formed a narrow bridge over the chasm. At irregular intervals, a sap-like substance oozed from short black spines the length of her smallest finger and only a tone or two darker than the rest of the wood. A handful of stone spires held up the contraption.

Peeking over the edge, she discovered the source of the odor and heat. Water seethed below, bubbles roiling and popping on the surface of the red-brown waters. Sweat dripped down her face, and a burst of steam left her skin painfully tender. She withdrew. "Pues, no hot tub today."

Her companion crossed over the bridge and waited on the other side. Another dark hole yawned behind him, and he kept his body turned sideways, as if to minimize his outline to anything farther ahead.

She hurried across, watching her feet to avoid the suspect spikes, absently noting the vines grew wrapped around the logs, rather than being tied there. "Are we there yet or is something waiting to pounce on us?"

Freelance pulled two handguns from holsters and checked to see if they were loaded. He flexed his wrists and shoulders and strode toward another opening, this one emblazoned with the symbol of the teacher-shapeshifter.

"Oh, joy. This place gets better and better." Zita sniffed the air again. The sulfur overwhelmed most other scents, including her companion's subtle masculine one, but an unpleasant undercurrent of decay, death, and burnt meat penetrated. "Did someone die? Can you give me an idea of what's inside?" As they exited the cave with the hot springs, the temperature dropped in the tunnel that followed, and she shivered. The cool, gritty dirt between her toes was almost a welcome relief.

His robotic voice finally answered. "Small dinosaurs."

Zita repositioned herself at his back as they entered, the lumpy feel of his backpack poking her with each step. She readied herself to switch to another form, but their caution was wasted.

The corpses of spotted dinosaurs lay scattered in bloody heaps around the cavern. They seemed to come in two varieties: a winged creature, turkey-sized but with vicious teeth, and variants of the group that had attacked her friends earlier. All of them had feathers and their bodies demonstrated the many ways to die. Claw marks spilled entrails from some, others sported neat bullet holes, and a few had half their bodies burnt away. A winged one appeared to be pinned to the ceiling by a purple bubblegum cigar.

Zita tried not to stare at it as she passed, though the artificial grape rose chemical and sweet among the more charnel odors.

"Why are all these things in one cave, anyway? Wouldn't they just eat each other and eventually starve? Why would anyone have a random room of prehistoric attack chickens? This makes no sense at all. Besides, I thought magic had rules or at least guidelines." She felt offended on Wyn's behalf.

As they left the grisly scene and entered another sloping tunnel, she exhaled in relief and filled her lungs with fresher air. "So, are we there yet?"

Freelance shook his head and returned the guns to their holsters.

Swearing internally, she followed.

When they passed through the next opening to the last cavern, she was rewarded with the sight of another altar... no, a wooden bier upon a stone cairn. A wizened, mummified body lay on its side as if sleeping curled, one arm thrown out and the fingers tipped open. Two ancient digits barely remained attached, but the position was otherwise a mirror image of the mummy above. A hole gaped in the middle of his chest. Zita assumed he had been the king, since he'd died first, and a lump in her throat had her swallowing hard. *I don't want to touch him.* The walls displayed more painted pictograms, but she ignored them.

Other than the tense, defensive posture he always exhibited, Freelance seemed unmoved by the scene. He stopped inside the doorway. "The gem was in his hand."

She frowned, Wyn and the professor's half-remembered conversation rising in her mind. "Not one but two mummies? This place is just wrong. Muse and the professor were gabbing about that earlier."

Like all of his other thoughts, he kept any on unlikely mummifications to himself.

Zita's fingers slid over the uneven surface of the Heart. Either she was sweating more than she thought or had cut herself without noticing. She carefully advanced and set the rock into the mummy's hand, leaping back in one fluid motion.

The rock teetered, then fell off onto the floor with a thud.

"Does that look like a reactivated spell to you? Because it seems like a dud to me."

Freelance's silence practically shouted an accusation.

"Don't even start with me about switching gems again. It's been in my pocket since the camp, and this outfit makes it pretty obvious I'm not hiding another rock or any candy on me." She gestured to the Spandex-like material covering her.

Despite his goggles, his gaze was intense enough to feel like a thorough pat-down.

Zita whipped the multitool out of her pocket and set that and water bottle on the ground. "Fine, you examine my stuff. I'll try to put the stone back again, but if it falls out, you can be the one to touch the dead guy next time." She scooped up the gem and tried to place it into the mummy's hand, even gingerly trying to wrap the desiccated fingers around it as much as possible without damaging them.

It fell again with a clunk and a phalange.

She turned to her companion, who replaced her belongings on the floor. Pretending she didn't care if he trusted her, she pocketed the multitool and said, "No luck. We have to figure this out."

Another tremor shook the room, and her eyes flicked upward. *I can't teleport home from here, even if I were willing to abandon everyone else. Wyn? If you can hear me, I need a hint.* Zita swore inwardly when she got no response, not that she had expected one.

His steps nearly soundless, Freelance's warmth and scent brushed her as he stepped around her. Stiff cloth gave a faint creak as he moved.

A thud, identical to the two times she had tried to put the stone back, sounded.

She turned and frowned. "Maybe we're doing this wrong. It's called the Heart of Canaiwari right? We've been putting it in his hand."

He nodded.

"I don't suppose you want to?" Zita gestured toward the fallen gem. When he made no move to pick it up, she sighed. "Fine." After retrieving it, she approached the mummy and hesitated. Finally, she thrust it into the cavernous hole in the mummy's chest, squinching her eyes shut.

It clicked against something else as if it had hit another rock.

She stepped away, brushing off her hands. "Does hand sanitizer work on mummy cooties?"

Nothing happened, though the gem did not fall out this time.

Her companion also did not offer any cleanser.

Zita had half-hoped he would, if only to find out if his smelled like guns or money. Battling down the urge to giggle, she smothered the irrelevant thoughts and focused. She took a deep breath and peered inside the mummy's chest cavity.

The Heart sat beside a smaller trapiche emerald. "Did you know there were two of them? Do you think that worked? My friends haven't contacted me yet..."

"What if his heart isn't the gem?" Freelance said.

"What?" She gawked at him like an idiot. "But that's the name of it... in English." Zita whirled, her eyes scanning the pictographs on the walls. "It says the spell will last eternally when the king's heart returns. Riddles. I hate riddles. They should just say what to do and not expect people to figure out cutesy word problems."

The mercenary took out a gun and checked the ammo inside, then returned it to the holster. "The words predated Pretorius' theft of the stone."

Her eyes wide, Zita stared at him, her mind churning. "Two rocks. His physical heart is probably one of the withered organ things in his chest I had to push aside. Do you think they could mean his wife? He died first, how would he even know where she was?"

His head tilted.

"His queen. The rock we've been carrying around isn't his heart, it's hers! Canaiwari is her name, and the rock's called the Heart of Canaiwari!" Trying not to think about what she was touching, Zita removed the gem from the mummy's chest and bolted, sprinting through the room of dead creatures. Rather than risking her bare feet on the bridge, she leapt up onto the narrow handrail and scurried along that. When she reached the other side, she jumped down, rolled to the stairs, and bolted up them.

Freelance was only a few steps behind her, his stride longer but his passage across the bridge slower.

The thin red cloth Wyn had covered the female mummy in earlier remained, and Zita pulled that away. Up close, this mummy's chest also had a hole in it, almost hidden by the drape of an arm. With a shudder, Zita thrust the gem inside.

When nothing happened, she wound the fabric around the corpse to keep any bits of it from flaking off. *When his heart returns...*

Her grasp as gentle as possible, Zita picked up the red-shrouded body and took a second to get used to the weight and balance. *I'm bathing in sanitizer when I get home. At least she's lighter than a full-grown person should be and thankfully not too tall,* she judged. "You might've been drawn chubby, but you're not that heavy anymore," she said.

The ground chose that moment to shake again.

Zita sped back down the stairs, pushing by Freelance.

A faint, mechanical sigh followed her. She sensed, rather than saw, him following. Despite her burden, Zita danced quickly around the spines on the bridge. She jogged to the burial chamber, ignoring the gruesome sights along the way.

Zita skid to a halt and lowered the wrapped form to the thick stone slab, setting it on the outstretched arm of the other mummy. For good measure, she scooped up the finger that had fallen and set that in the male mummy's hand. The dry bones were redolent with an odd stink, and she was happy to move away and pick up her water. "I hope this works because I'm out of ideas after this."

Her companion grunted. Even through the voice changer, it sounded like agreement.

She shot him a smile and heard scraping behind her. As she twisted around to view the mummies, Zita inhaled and stepped back. The two bodies were now intertwined, their arms around each other and the Hearts hidden from view.

Her voice came out a bit squeaky, and she retreated to the entrance to the cave. "Okay. That's... something. How about we go now?"

His goggles focused on the corpses, Freelance joined her, and they escaped into the passageway.

The welcome warmth of party line touched her mind, and Zita stopped moving.

You did it, Wyn sent, her mental voice slow and exhausted. *The spell is stronger than before. Hurry back so we can leave. On the bright side, while I was part of it, I altered it a little. In the future, no one should be able to get in here without a skilled magic-user, not even if they sacrifice every descendant of the original tribe, as the conquistador attempted. Tiffany would need the blood of at least three different supers and a great deal of good fortune to manage it, based on the sloppy work I've seen from her so far.*

Touching her ear, Zita beamed and turned away from Freelance. *I can't tell you how happy I am to hear you yapping in my* head again, even if it's about awful stuff like mass murder. We're on our way.

We have to rest before we leave, Andy sent. Wyn is sick.

I'm tired, not unwell. I don't require medical assistance, though a chance to nap would be welcome, Wyn admitted.

You were half-buried in the dirt. We couldn't—even I couldn't—dig you out, and while you're free now, you are barely able to stand, Andy sent. Trixie said you were having seizures and if it continued, you would die.

Zita ran a hand over her hair, forward and back. Carajo. Get some sleep.

We'll wait at the battle site. After my close acquaintance with the spell, I can open the entrance to let us out, but it would be easier to do only once. Wyn's words were careful and precise, like a drunkard trying not to slur.

After you rest, Andy sent.

Zita added her mental voice to support his argument. Freelance and I can make our own way back. If Andy sees us once we get clear of the trees, he can pick us up as the Birdseed Pervert. If not, we can find the camp again.

Please use Wingspan instead of that awful name, and I'm not taking that form again in this place unless I have to. Strangely, Andy's words carried a strong wave of self-disgust and upset.

You sure you guys are okay? Zita glanced at her companion and mouthed words as if she had an earpiece.

Amusement and weariness accompanied Wyn's acquiescence over the party line. Yes, fine. We'll see you soon, Zita, or we'll come searching for you. The warmth of the connection died.

Something whispered behind her, and Zita turned.

Freelance stood there, his head tilted to the side. Through the doorway, she saw the stone slab with the corpses.

"It worked, but we're on our own getting back. Muse is wiped and... did you cover both mummies with the cloth?" Her eyebrows rose. It seemed oddly sentimental for the mercenary, but she had left the one corpse rolled up in the fabric.

He turned to study them, then turned back to her.

Cold chased down Zita's spine. "Right. Magic is creepy. You know, they can keep it. Let's get going." She scooped up her bag and headed toward the cave with the dead dinosaurs, pausing when her instincts insisted something was wrong.

One step ahead of her, Freelance pulled a shotgun and a handgun, both with suppressors attached. "They're healing."

Zita didn't know where he'd gotten the long gun, but she abandoned that line of thought as she realized the reek of death was receding, replaced by a dry, scaly odor somewhere between that of a reptile and a bird. As she set foot in the doorway, she saw wings shivering as the creature pinned to the ceiling fought against the bubble gum. The candy fell out, and the feathered animal dropped to the floor where it rolled to its feet.

"They animated only after we entered before."

Zita flexed her shoulders. "Feel like a run?" A quick glance at the doors showed her the openings were too narrow to exit or enter as anything much larger than a sheep. Praying they'd get through it without being eaten or killing anyone—if the creatures were people—she handed him her water bottle. "I'll try to clear a path once we're inside."

He tucked it into his bag and ran.

Just inside, Zita became a rhinoceros and charged toward the door, knocking aside everything in her way except her companion.

By the time they had reached the center, the cavern seethed with newly reanimated dinosaurs showing no indications of their previous deaths. Only the ones that Freelance methodically shot or that she tossed lay still on the ground. She sent up a brief prayer again that they weren't really people.

Thanks to the almost constant roar of Freelance's guns, Zita was three-quarters deaf as she head-butted away a creature that had been diving their way. With a bellow, she dashed around Freelance, smacked another dinosaur with her horn and barreled through the swarm. Right before leaving the cave, she whirled to defend the exit, backing up one step too far. Her wide hindquarters got stuck in the narrow opening as she slashed at an attacking animal. She wiggled, trying to get free.

Only seconds slower, Freelance seized her horn and used it to vault onto her back and over her.

Zita's ears rang with the close discharge of his weapon as he fired it behind her. The air was redolent with the coppery scent of blood, and warm wetness dripped down her side. With another swipe to clear space, she switched to Arca and backed out of the cavern.

The creatures, several them injured, paced inside, but none moved to follow them, as if the entrance to the passageway were an invisible line they would or could not cross.

Gracias a Dios, they're limited to that cave. Saying nothing, she and Freelance hurried farther down the tunnel.

After they had gotten out of sight of the animals, Zita checked herself for injury. Her arms and sides were unmarked, but she frowned at the blood on one bare foot. She pulled up her pant leg to find the source. Long, narrow scratches greeted her, and those were already scabbing—her thick hide had protected her from serious injury. Her pants had either avoided being torn or had already mended themselves, so she pushed them back down to cover it. "No major hurts here, but I should clean it when I can. You?" The sharp bite of rubbing alcohol stung her nose, and she turned her attention to Freelance. Her breath caught.

Her companion leaned against a wall and appeared to be pouring a flask on his leg. An empty canteen sat in a bloody puddle on the ground next to him. Freelance had propped his bag in the way so she could not see the severity of the wound, but the large square of bandaging he had prepared told her it was more than a scratch.

"You want me to wrap that?" Her voice might've been louder than she intended, but her ears still rung from the firearms.

His shoulders stiffened even more than before.

Zita exhaled. "Look, I know you don't know me, but given all the predators running loose, we can't afford to leave a blood trail all the way back."

He stilled and set down the rubbing alcohol.

Taking his inaction as permission, she picked up the bandages and eased in closer. "I don't suppose you have a knife I can cut off your pant leg with?"

"Roll it over the top."

Narrowing her eyes at him, Zita stopped and sighed at the apparent prudery. "It'll attract carnivores, but if that's what you want... Once we reach the others, I'll get Muse to heal you, which should remove any infection and fix it up. Keeping the bloody pant leg is still a bad idea though."

His shoulders lifted once, then dropped.

After that, she knelt and dealt with his injury. Although blood and the tattered remains of his pant leg obscured part of it, the rubbing alcohol and water had rinsed away enough to see a nasty gash in a firm, muscled light-skinned calf, one that already had a thin tracery of white scars. *Sweet definition. I still want to know his exercise regimen, but whatever messed up his leg before this was extreme. Some of those scars might be surgical, but the others are too irregular. Maybe he shattered the bone at some point? Wonder if metal detectors beep if he walks through them unarmed.*

As she applied butterfly bandages to keep the edges of the wound together, then taped a pad over those, she found she couldn't picture him without weapons. Nude, yes, but even then, her imagination supplied him with a gun. *My pervy libido needs a cold shower. This is so not the time.* "If you're a total idiot and refuse to let Muse heal you, you'll need stitches and actual medical treatment later," she warned.

After he packed up his supplies, Freelance inclined his head once. He offered the water bottle to her.

"At least we're through the worst of it," she said, rising and taking a long drink.

He didn't reply.

Por supuesto. Zita strode the last few feet to the cave with the bridge and stopped. The interior was pitch dark, though she still heard the hot spring bubbling. It felt warmer than before, and a strong wind gust tugged at her, its hot, greedy fingers redolent with sulfur. The square of light from the open trapdoor in the temple was not visible. Shifting partially to an owl did not help with her vision this time.

"What now?" she groaned.

After changing into a large bat, Zita rose in the air, opening her mouth to use sonar. The resulting information had her head spinning, and she landed again with a thud.

Once she returned to Arca's form, she rubbed a hand over her hair. "Something's messed up. I can't echolocate in there, and the wind makes flying almost impossible. Why is there wind when we're underground anyway? How did your team get through this before?" *If it weren't pitch dark, I could teleport to the other side. I don't know anywhere in this land well enough to go without seeing it. Stupid magic.*

He was silent. "Halja cut our guide's hand and dripped his blood on the bowl before the chasm. The bridge appeared."

Zita inhaled. "Muse said the spell liked blood sacrifices. I'm not from this area, and I'm guessing you're not either?" She paused for him to confirm.

After a long moment, he shook his head.

As if not being a native to one of the local tribes narrows down anything about him... Based on my glimpse of his leg, he's white or mixed with it, so no real surprise, she thought. "Well, if I go slowly, I can find the bridge and walk along the railing of that, since I'd rather not risk the spikes."

His voice was like a gunshot. "No."

"What?"

He gestured toward the impenetrable darkness.

Zita followed his movement, her forehead wrinkling. "What? I can't see a thing in there."

A half-twitch at her words suggested he might've been surprised by her statement. "The bridge is gone. Five stone spires have small wooden disks atop them made of the same thorny wood at irregular distances apart."

She twisted to eye him. "You can see through that? Is the railing gone too?"

He nodded and tapped his goggles.

"Right. Do you think you can get across?"

Freelance flexed his injured leg as if testing it. "The disks are not secured to the spires. Someone would have to jump on them in rapid succession before the disk falls into the water."

"Someone. You mean me. So, you can't?"

His shoulders stiffened, and he said nothing. Instead, he took a few steps forward, disappearing into the inky cave. A familiar hiss, whirr, and thud revealed the use of his grapple gun, followed by a scraping sound and a wet splash.

"You okay?" she called out.

Freelance emerged, winding up a rope. His grapple gun had returned to his belt. "Stalagmites are too wide and the winds too strong."

Dark where it had been immersed in water, the rope steamed and radiated heat when she reached for it. She let it drop. "Here, lend me your goggles."

His fingers curled.

For a minute, they stood there, her hand outstretched.

Turning away, he dug through his pack.

"You brought an extra set? Awesome. If I can see, it's a done deal, pan comido," she said.

His back to her, he pulled off his goggles and slid something else on his face. When Freelance checked the dark cavern again, the ones he wore were twice the size of his originals. He stared into the cave, then turned away and switched eyewear again.

Zita waited.

After he faced her, once again in his original pair, he handed her the oversized ones.

Excitement mounting, Zita took them and slid them over her head, adjusting the strap for her smaller size. She turned to the cave and couldn't help the expletive that escaped her. "These don't work."

"They did." Even with the distortion by whatever voice changer he used, he made it sound like her fault. Freelance tucked away the old eyewear.

"It's not me, it's you." Zita pushed hair out of her face as she paced. *This is like one of those awful trust exercises at a company meeting, only instead of accountants who drop me so they can see me fall on my culo, I've got a mercenary who might kill me.* She stopped in front of him and placed both hands on her hips. "So, you can see... and I can jump. If you direct me across, I'll attach a rope to the stalagmite nearest the door, and you can slide over on that."

He set down his pack, glanced into the cave, then inclined his head at her.

Zita rubbed her hands and offered him a lopsided smile. "Let's do a practice run in this tunnel, then go for it before my adrenaline fades. I'll warm up with some jumps, and you start in with your advice when you're ready." She sprinted almost to the doorway where the dinosaurs seethed, and ran back, leaping randomly and trying to make her feet land together in as small a footprint as possible.

"Close your eyes," he called out.

She obeyed and tried to relax her body. *He's a sniper. Being a good judge of distance is a requirement for that.*

He barked a measurement.

She jumped and crashed into a wall.

"Dead." Freelance tried another.

This time, she smacked the wall hard enough to bounce off and stagger a step. "Carajo," Zita said, holding her shoulder where it had hit.

"Dead." He gave her another measurement, one very close to what the previous ones had been.

She leapt, and though an elbow bumped the wall, it did not slam into anything.

"Dead. Poison spike. Again."

They continued until the routine got her down the length of the hall without hitting anything.

Her muscles warm, loose, and slightly sore from collisions, Zita took a deep breath and a long drink of her water, almost emptying it. She tucked the bottle into a pant pocket. "If I fall, I'll try to switch to a bird, but those gusts are brutal for small birds, and there's not enough room for a large one."

He nodded and disappeared into the cave for a moment with his rope. When he reappeared, he handed her the end of the line.

She retreated until she was as far back as the corridor allowed and could still be lined up with the darkness of the cave opening. The tight weave of the rope she gripped bit into her palm, and she squared her shoulders. "Nice rope. Ready."

"Four paces, jump eight feet to eleven fifteen o'clock, feet tight left."

Zita inhaled, ran, and jumped.

He called out the next set of directions as she flew.

She landed hard on a wooden object that sloped under her weight and launched herself again.

Freelance gave another order.

They managed to make all of the leaps up to the last one.

Her feet hit the edge of a support, and she wobbled. *Not going fast enough to make the next one.* Taking the extra second, even as the wood tilted downward under her, she crouched to bring as much force to the last jump as possible and sprang out. After curling into a ball, she flipped and stretched out her arms.

When her hands touched the very edge, she pushed off it. Bringing her legs over her head, Zita landed on her feet, though she staggered and banged one knee into a stalagmite. *If this were the Olympics,* she thought, *I'd lose points for not sticking the landing.* Exhilaration streaked through her. She pumped her fists in the air. "We did it! Where to now?"

Freelance gave her directions and soon joined her once she'd set up the line for him. Lapsing back into silence, his hand was surprisingly gentle on her arm as he guided her to the steps and released her.

Visibility returned when she got high enough up the stairs for her head to be in the temple. She hopped the rest of the way out and stepped aside so he could follow.

In economical movements, Freelance exited, winding up his rope.

They stared into the pitch black below.

His goggles glinted as he studied her, and he pressed the carving on the altar, closing the trapdoor.

Zita was more interested in another fact. "Wasn't there a hole where your team blew away the door before?" She pointed to the smooth, clean, windowed wall where the destroyed wood had been. The air held no sign of the professor's unwilling stay, and she licked a finger, holding it up. "Wind's still fresh and coming from the tower though."

Freelance's head turned to the missing entry. Pulling his grapple gun from his belt, he fired it at the belfry. It connected to something, and he tugged it. When it didn't come down, he pressed a button, and the rope hauled him to the bell. As the silent mercenary perched on the edge, he glanced down, then left the building.

"Is my team the only one that talks too much?" Zita changed to a gavião-real and followed.

Unsurprisingly, Freelance had already reached the tree line by the time she exited the building. His backpack was on the ground, and he had turned away to drink from a canteen.

Zita swooped over and shifted, landing on her feet in her Arca form. "It's me, don't shoot." Retrieving her water, she took a swig from own dwindling supply. As she replaced it in her pocket, she handed him his pack.

He shouldered it and walked without a word. His step had a hitch to it, but he showed no other sign of injury other than the swollen, torn pant leg over his bandage.

As she brought up the rear, Zita tilted her head to let the warm sun caress her face before she entered the perpetual shade of the trees. After a second, she realized the direction and called out. "Wait! Following that trail will take forever. My group got here and back faster than yours, and I don't think either one of us wants to be separated from our friends any longer than necessary. It's not a bad trip unless you're afraid of heights... are you?"

He did not deign to answer.

Choosing to interpret that as a no, Zita continued. "Didn't think so. This way then. There's a big cliff where the track veers around, and we'll just go down that. I can even retrieve your rope afterward if you want," she said, heading down that path instead.

He did not reply, but she felt him following her, even if he made no more noise than her.

Zita cleared her throat. "So why were you working for Pretorius and Tiffany? They usually only hire brainless thugs, and that doesn't describe you or your team."

His head tilted.

She snorted. "Please. They abandoned you in a hot second. Was it for the money or because your powers are subtler than his?"

"Not a metahuman."

Zita made a rude noise. "I get that you're professionally mysterious and all, but I've seen proof otherwise."

His goggles glanced at her, then away.

"What, you don't believe me? I know a little about guns, like which way to point the muzzle. You're a sniper, so that tells me you're an expert."

Slowly, he inclined his head.

"When we were in combat, you hit my friend with a rubber bullet at the exact spot necessary to numb her hand for a while but not destroy it. Any number of shots would've disabled her, but you went for the trick shot nobody actually does in real life. The only reason you'd do that is if you're stupid or you know you'll make it." She raised her eyebrows at him, forgetting she wore a mask until it rubbed against her forehead.

His mechanical voice droned, "I never miss."

Not caring if it was rude, Zita pointed at him. "You missed me. Twice."

Freelance walked.

"Everyone misses sometime, thanks to wind and sudden movements if nothing else. I'm guessing if your average is that good, you've only not missed since May or June of this year when superpowers manifested again. You could be an unknown power from the Seventies, but you don't move like an old guy." She resisted the urge to eye his magnificent body... again. *Be businesslike, Zita,* she told herself. *Don't ogle the nice—don't ogle the competent sniper.*

He remained silent, so she gleefully interpreted it as an invitation to keep talking.

Zita proceeded to her next point as they continued deeper into the forest, where the odor of decay rose from detritus mingled with the rich scents of the conifers, a spicy blend of pine and cedar. "Since our last run-ins, I may have researched grapple guns. Yours is too sweet to be real. So, either you or whoever you get them from has powers."

"It's modified."

With a snort, she waved that excuse away. "Sometime after May? I bet it turned out better than expected. Also, I don't care how prepared you are, there's no way you knew to bring so many different calibers and types of bullets, especially given the weight of your pack. My arms are sweet, but I'm not supernaturally strong. Even if you bought nothing but the lightest, most expensive brands, your backpack should be heavier with all that ammo, guns, and other supplies in it."

He didn't acknowledge her in any way.

"What? You don't like your power? Not big enough?" Her mind, steered by her libido, took an abrupt detour, speculating on the possible size of things she would never see. Licking her lips,

Zita forced herself to focus. "Maybe you don't need a bigger power. Maybe you have more that I haven't figured out." *If having a really nice culo is a superpower, you've got that too, in spades. Oye.* Even though she was fairly certain he couldn't read her thoughts (he hadn't shot her yet, after all), she cleared her throat.

He increased his speed.

When Freelance began to outpace her despite his injury, she glanced behind them and noticed trees shaking. Zita sped up, until they traveled at a fast walk, almost a jog, through the shady forest. Their feet were silent on the damp mosses that filled the spaces in between the gnarled roots that crisscrossed the ground.

They ran for all of a minute before he spoke. "It's closing." He pulled his long gun around on the sling and rummaged in his pack as they bolted over the terrain. Black and silent, his goggles turned to her as he loaded cartridges into his weapon. Somehow, he managed not to drop anything.

"Don't kill it if we can avoid it! It could be a person stuck in dinosaur form. Even if that's wrong, this has got to be a closed ecosystem by definition, and we don't want to mess it up when we went to all that trouble to set it back to the way it should be. There's no time to discuss it, but it might catch us at the rate we're going."

He sped up again.

Chapter Nineteen

As Freelance and Zita reached the top of the cliff, she stopped
and turned to face the thundering footsteps growing ever closer.

A forty-foot long theropod crashed into view, either the same
one that had failed to eat Andy earlier or an identical creature.
With a crocodilian rush of speed, the massive toothy beast snapped
at the dark-clad man, catching his pack in its serrated teeth.

Quick and agile as a mongoose, Freelance slid his arms out of
the straps and let his body drop to the ground, rolling to absorb the
impact and coming up with a gun in his hands.

Zita prepared to shift. *Pues, the secretive sniper's a parkour or
free running fan. That move was textbook.*

The creature bit down on the backpack, dropped it, and paused.
Its muscles tensed for another attack.

"You get to safety. I got this," Zita shouted. *With luck, he can
find a good spot to hide until it's gone or at least descend far enough
down the cliff to be out of the dinosaur's reach.* Jumping between
them, she changed shape to match the dinosaur and clonked heads
as it—she, her reptilian senses told her—lunged for Freelance again
and Zita got in her way.

Having spent part of the morning in this form to discourage
flying predators, Zita had no problems keeping her balance, but she
shook her head to clear it.

Startled, the beast reared back, teetering before she stabilized. Her mouth opened, showing a newly broken tooth in the front of the capacious maw.

It's Nibbles, Andy's friend! Let's see if we're still buddies. Zita bobbed her head. From the corner of her eye, she saw Freelance pick up his pack one-handed, the other arm still aiming his long gun, braced against his shoulder, in their direction.

Nibbles retreated a few feet and copied the motions, though her eyes followed something behind Zita. Her breath was no better than before, and something greenish brown glinted at her gum line.

"Oy, you got spinach or lizard or something stuck in that tooth there, girlfriend," Zita said, though it came out as a querulous series of clucks and chirps. She waved her tiny clawed hands toward her own mouth.

Another glance revealed Freelance backing toward the edge of the cliff.

Let's make sure he knows which one is me. Zita concentrated, altering her pattern to use the neon orange stripes she had used earlier.

Nictating membranes closed and opened again as Nibbles stared at Zita, her posture more uncertain than predatory.

Doesn't anyone around here like a little color? Even the reptiles are critics. Zita sidestepped, making it impossible for Nibbles to charge, then glanced at her companion.

With his pack over a shoulder and the long gun on a sling, Freelance grasped his rope, leaned out in a perfect L-shape, then rappelled down the side of the cliff in smooth, unhurried motions. While she couldn't see it, she heard the quick, measured staccato as his feet tapped the rock on the way down. When the sounds stopped, she checked the rope. It had lost the taut tension, so she assumed he had reached the bottom. *Of course, he's an experienced*

climber and can go down a sheer cliff with a bulky, heavy load. Silly me
for worrying he'd be trapped or hurt himself.

The dinosaur lumbered next to her, head wagging as Nibbles
also checked for Freelance. She made a disappointed hiss and
groan.

Zita snorted and tried to use the scaly claws of her foot to
unhook the climbing line and drop it over the edge, but she lacked
the dexterity in her current shape.

Nibbles turned away and ambled toward the coniferous trees.

Switching to Arca, Zita grabbed the rope, freeing it from the
rock.

Whirling at the sound, Nibbles spotted Zita and lunged back at
her.

Zita grinned and jumped off the cliff. As she fell, she dropped
the rope and became a magenta and neon yellow pterosaur,
swooping up past the startled Nibbles. Gliding high, she checked
the path back for other giant lizards, then spiraled to the ground.

At the base of the cliff, Zita whooped as she shifted to Arca. She
grinned at her companion, not caring if she seemed foolish. "Oh, sí,
pretend that wasn't awesome. I know the truth. Anyway, I did a
quick check of the way ahead. No more big dinosaurs, so we only
have to watch out for Nibbles up there chasing us down, the packs
of roving small predators, and any lurking protocrocodilians by the
river. Pues, and those flowers that would eat us given the chance.
Pan comido, hombre."

With admirable swiftness, Freelance finished coiling the line
and put it away.

For a second, Zita was distracted by the smooth flow of rope.
The man's got serious climbing skills.

A roar came from above. At the edge of the cliff, Nibbles
surveyed them, drool dripping from her mouth

Zita grimaced. "Right, as soon as you've got that done, let's go before she finds her way down. It couldn't hurt to put some distance between our hungry buddy up there and us."

He jogged toward the ridge, his movement marred by a small limp.

She took off after him, running to catch up with his longer legs, but settling into a jog once she matched his speed.

Given his apparent dislike of conversation, it was a surprise when he broke the silence a few minutes later. "Why didn't you kill Pretorius?"

Zita nearly tripped over a root. "What?"

"When we fought, you didn't become a dinosaur."

"Of course not. However tempting, it would be wrong." She made a face at the thought.

Disapproval radiated in the lines of his body.

She raised her eyebrows. "If you kill someone in defense of yourself or others, that's one thing, but killing them just because I could would be murder. I got the Heart without anyone dying."

His head tilted.

Zita eyed him, then grinned. "I could blab about allowing people a chance to choose redemption, but I'm no priest. Gracias a Dios on that, as I plan to get laid again someday. I know you're not interested in the morality of it, so consider the practical aspects. Faced with you and me, who are people going to think the bigger threat? Who will they kill first?" In case he missed her point, she pointed at him.

He scanned the area, tapping the side of his goggles. She caught the faintest whir of electronics.

I'll take that as a win. Go me. She smiled as she vaulted a log and continued to move, the jog a comforting exertion, despite the collection of scratches and bruises she'd picked up. "We got the gem, so we stopped them. Additionally, us not killing your team encouraged you guys not to murder us. If our teams keep running into each other, it's good to know we're all reasonable and don't have to kill each other." As her adrenaline receded, tiredness crept in, and she forced it away.

His head might have inclined.

She tallied another win in her favor. "Can you ride a horse?" she asked, her mind whirling. "I want you to ride me. It'll be hard since you'd be bareback, but if you hang on, I think you can do it."

His steps faltered.

Her brain caught up with her mouth, and Zita felt her ears burning. She prayed her dark skin would prevent him from noticing. "As a horse. I wasn't offering... Ignore the fact that I sound like an idiot and listen to what I'm actually saying. We can increase speed for longer if I'm in another shape and you're on board. Since we've got a head start and are on a nice cleared path in these plains, I should be able to outrun most predators along the way. It'll give us a chance of getting back before dark, too." *Plus, it'll put less stress on your injured leg.*

Reflecting the sunlight, his goggles turned to her, and Freelance stopped moving. "Dinosaur. Little will attack."

She blinked. A grin spread across her face, and she bounced on her heels. "Or we could do that."

***

By the time Zita and Freelance reached the tiny trail up to the ledge, it was midafternoon. She stopped at the base as it was too narrow for her to navigate as a large theropod. To ensure the others recognized her, she'd again used neon orange stripes on her side.

A gigantic, hairy man stood guard at the trailhead, and Jerome held a position on the opposite end of the ridge. *The hairball must be Kodiak's human form.*

When they got closer, Jerome whooped and called out, "The prodigal returns! And whoever the masked guy is too."

Kodiak raised a massive hand in greeting, seeming unfazed at his employer returning on dinosaur back. "Boss man. Arca."

Andy appeared behind Kodiak and waved, his mouth dropping open a little.

In a smooth, economical motion, Freelance leapt off and headed up the trail.

Had Zita not been observing him closely, she would have missed the slight hesitation in his step after landing on his injured leg. She huffed, switched to Arca, and followed.

The camp seemed much as she had left it, although someone had hauled a second log by the blackened and cold ashes of the fire. Backpacks, two of them unfamiliar to Zita, lined the tepui wall in a tidy line. Nestled in blankets, Wyn slumped between the logs. She giggled at a comment by Trixie, who sat nearby. Andy had retreated to the precipice overlooking the river.

Wyn lifted her head and relief shone on her face. A smile tugged at her lips, and though her illusion was as perfect as before, the set of her shoulder revealed a deep weariness. "There you are! We were growing concerned."

"Let me clarify," Trixie said. Her fake nose and mustache were even worse for wear. "She was worried you were hurt. I have happy feelings in all my places, especially the naughty ones, because you're not hauling a dinosaur to gut, clean, and cook. Hunting dinosaurs is not my favorite thing. I'm way too fascinating to be bait. Again."

Deciding to ignore Trixie's commentary, Zita hugged Wyn. "Done with your nap, Muse?" She grinned.

"If you insist on putting food on your head, you should expect someone to want to make it useful," Kodiak called out, in all the tones of a long-running debate.

"Hey, we're nothing without a good theme," Trixie argued. "I think the Marx Brothers could work for us, though I can't decide if the boss makes a better Harpo or Zeppo. I'm leaning toward Zeppo, even if that's a speaking role."

The big man considered Trixie. "If you're picking a permanent theme, lose the gum. It stinks. I'll save the boss the effort of ignoring you by saying no, we won't be dressing up to play along."

Trixie pouted. "Aww, but he has it down to an art form! You don't want to deny him the chance to express his artistic side, do you?"

Choosing a log that put his back to the wall, Freelance set his backpack down and picked through it.

"See? He's working on a masterpiece now," Trixie said.

Zita glanced over at Andy, then at Wyn. The other woman gave her a helpless shrug.

With a sigh, Zita strolled over next to Andy and studied the drop. "Good to see you, mano." She bumped him with her shoulder.

He elbowed her back. "You too." His tone was even quieter.

She took a deep breath and tried for a neutral topic. "It's a pity we can't trust the stuff here enough to eat it. I'm certain I saw a giant pirarucu a second ago."

If anything, her comment made Andy withdraw further.

From his post, Kodiak lifted his head and gazed at her. "A what?"

"It's a type of fish... Paiche, it's called in some places," Zita explained.

The big man licked his lips and eyed the water. "I've had that once," he rumbled. "It's good eating."

She nodded in agreement and returned her gaze to the river for a moment. Warm saliva flooded her mouth. "It's a nice big fish too, so it's more than a few bites if you catch it. Good dried or fresh. Mix it up with some fried bananas and potatoes..." she trailed off.

Pleasure trip to Brazil soon, she thought, *I think I need pirarucu à casaca, pão de queijo, and maybe brigadeiros.*

Andy shot a glance at her. "Are you drooling?"

"No judging. It's been a very long day, even for me," Zita said.

"Fried bananas? Sounds good. Some good garlic and a light breading might work on it too," Kodiak added, his voice dreamy and a bit lustful.

Zita's eyes met those of the big man, and they both smiled in understanding.

Charging over, Trixie inserted her body between Zita and Kodiak. "What's going on here?" she asked, her gaze narrow and accusing. Her posture was aggressive, and her muscles were braced as if for a blow.

"They're talking food and slobbering," Andy said.

Trixie's mouth opened and closed. Tension left her shoulders. "I should've known. Well, they probably didn't stop and eat a dinosaur on the way back like you did. Birdbrain took that thing down and didn't even bring us a piece."

Andy turned away, but not before Zita saw the shame on his face.

Pues, that's what he was afraid of. Zita gestured toward the cave. "The professor might be waiting for us on the other side, so let's pack up and get going. I'll just go see if Muse can get us through the magic wall. If everything works out, we'll have everyone home by tonight." As she left, she saw Trixie relax and take Kodiak's arm.

As far away as she could be from Freelance without leaving the fire pit, Wyn had moved to perch on the edge of a log. Her face was wary as she watched him clean a partially disassembled handgun.

"Muse, do you have the energy to let us back through to Brazil today? Professor Santos may still be there," Zita asked.

Wyn grimaced. "It's been long enough that she might've already left to see if she could meet up with the doctor. I'd be willing to attempt it, but I'll need rest afterward."

Frowning, Zita noticed Freelance's leg still bore a bandage. "Do you also have enough mojo for healing? Freelance has a serious injury, and I've a couple scratches too. It'd be good if we could heal those before infection sets in. Lizards got nasty mouths, and I'm guessing dinosaurs have the same."

As she squared her shoulders, Wyn nodded. "I'll cast the spell for you, both of you, once we're in Brazil, but I might be too tired to heal it all. We can go anytime you're ready." *His companions are okay if a bit weird. I gave Kodiak a set of the special sportswear since he shares your problem retaining clothing after shifting. Andy might be scarred for life from that view. I don't think my spell will work on an android or cyborg or whatever Freelance is though.*

Zita glanced at Freelance, then at Wyn. *He bleeds human blood, and his scent is all man, with nothing I'd associate with a robot in it other than the persistent gun oil part, which has an obvious reason.*

After he finished assembling his weapon with that graceful economy of movement he brought to everything, Freelance stood. "Healing only," he warned. He hefted his backpack.

Wyn blanched.

Andy's mournful mental voice wound its way into her brain. *And here I'd hoped my nightmares about the T-1000 Terminator were a thing of the past. How is it that he didn't look ridiculous riding a giant orange and green dinosaur? Did he have food on a stick in front of her nose to steer? Did I just send that to Wyn and Zita?*

Yes, yes, you did. I steered myself. Zita lowered her voice before she spoke again, Andy's prehistoric snack on her mind. "And here I thought we bonded, Freelance. Did you have time to use that spell to find out if the dinosaurs are people or not, Muse?"

For a moment, Wyn seemed confused by the new topic, but then she shot a glance at Andy. "Oh! So, you heard about Wingspan's brontosaurus aperitif. Yes, I did. They're just animals."

"Sweet. That takes a load off." Relief poured through her. Zita gave a shout, "Let's pack it up, people. We're heading home."

Wyn rose and sloppily folded her blanket, avoiding anyone's gaze. *Freelance still creeps me out, and not just because he's invisible when I check the area with telepathy.*

Andy wandered over to pick up his things, followed by the others.

Unable to help herself, Zita strolled over and refolded the blanket, then worked on getting everything else ready to put away. "So, why're professionals like you slumming with a bunch of sleazebags like Garm, Tiffany, and crew? You don't seem the types to work for slavers," Zita said. *Not that I've ever met slavers before. Or professional mercenaries wearing a fake nose and mustache, but there's always a first time for everything.*

While Freelance did not bother to respond to her question other than to tilt his chin in her direction, Trixie lifted her head. "Slavery? Nobody mentioned anything about that. As to why? They paid us."

Zita snorted. "Didn't you know? They recruit metahumans—though I have no idea how they can make joining sound anything but stupid. Those in power only give you rank if you've got sufficient power to beat down others. Anyone who doesn't make it high enough becomes a slave and doesn't get to leave or pick their role. It's one big, vicious, predatory pyramid scheme. At least a few of their recruits are blackmailed to force them to stay."

Kodiak, Trixie, and Freelance exchanged glances.

"News to me," said Kodiak. "Ours was a straight professional contract that passed all the usual vetting. That said, it wasn't the most fun we've ever had on a job."

Trixie giggled. "I'd love to divulge what was the most fun, but then I'd have to kill you, and you're all such cute little idealists. How would a bunch of squeaky-clean innocents like yourselves know their recruiting practices, anyway?"

Careful not to divulge her vulnerable source, Zita shrugged. "What can I say? I have one of those faces, I guess. People tell me all kinds of things I don't want to know."

Kodiak huffed, absently scratching his back against a wall before shouldering a large pack. "Glad I didn't take them up on their job offer, then. Is it just metahumans they're after? You're in the clear then, boss."

Jerome said, "Why is that?" The big man snuck a glance at the silent gunman.

"No powers." Freelance must've been unconvinced by her near-monologue earlier in the day.

Zita couldn't help it. She laughed and shot a grin at Freelance. "You keep telling yourself that, but it won't change anything."

Trixie pouted and fiddled with her fake glasses, making it even more crooked than it had been before. Her false mustache tilted crazily, limp and the worse for wear and humidity. "They tried to hire you away and not me? I'm insulted. Don't they realize I'm the brains of this group?"

Kodiak rumbled, deep, low, and brimming with amusement. "Only if they want brains that are cracked and fried. Besides, you spent most of the trip antagonizing Halja."

"Someone that humor deficient is a cry for help I can't ignore. Why do you think I work with you guys? He's an ongoing project," Trixie said, pointing her thumb at Freelance. She withdrew another of her bubblegum cigars.

Zita pressed the subject and did the bear shapeshifter (and herself) a favor. "How did you get a job with them, anyway? Did you threaten to trap them in close quarters with that chemical grape smell? That's just torture for anyone with a sensitive nose."

Trixie's eyes slid to Kodiak, and she tucked away the cigar she had been about to put in her mouth.

Kodiak shrugged, but his face held sleepy amusement. "People contact our secretary and make an appointment to discuss details. The boss decides what we take." He shuffled to stand near the cave entrance.

Andy fidgeted. *Do we really want to leave the mercenaries running loose behind us? What if they figure out how to get back in?*

Wyn's face wore a suspicious expression as she considered the silent Freelance. *I concur, though your bird form is the only person here with magic other than me.*

Their paychecks have left, so I doubt they'd do that, but, sure, I'll see what we can do. "As we're all leaving, do you guys want a lift somewhere once we're out of the caves? Where do you need to go? It's a long hike from the tepui to anywhere else," Zita said.

"Manaus," Freelance said.

Kodiak added, "Set us down a mile outside, so the Brazilian Air Force doesn't come after us. We don't need to be associated with you, especially since we haven't received the second half of our pay yet."

"Sounds good, though I can't believe you beat us to the temple from there," Zita said.

The bear shrugged. "Our employers had that teenager open a portal from there to the village. Speaking of which, where'd the old man go?"

"Escaped during the fight," Freelance said.

Trixie snickered and skipped over to the bear shapeshifter. "Funny how often that happens when our employers are on the bloodthirsty side."

Kodiak tried to smother a smile.

See? They're not so bad. Zita smiled. "That explains it. You three be careful once we set you down."

Trixie stretched, reaching her long arms up to the sky. "Where's the fun in that?"

Kodiak rumbled but didn't bother with words.

Freelance didn't even do that.

Chapter Twenty

By the time they had dropped off the mercenaries, the Jeep, and the professor, they didn't return to the Maryland airpark until late. Twenty minutes after Jerome left, the trio was back at Wyn's house. Despite the full food bowls and sparkling water in their dishes, Siamese cats met Wyn, Zita, and Andy at the top of the basement steps, complaints about their abandonment clear in their disapproving expressions and whiny meowing.

As they reached the living room, Wyn pursed her lips and continued the discussion that had begun at the airpark. "I'm telling you, I don't have your disposable phone, Andy. You never handed it to me. My bag is enchanted to give me what I'm searching for when I reach in, and it's not giving me your cell." Tapping her amulet, her illusion disappeared. She emptied the purse of Zita's belongings, piling up the butter containers on the living room table.

Zita changed to her natural form and separated the food from the other supplies.

"Great. It must've fallen out in the quicksand or something. At least it's not my regular one, just the vigilante phone. Z, seriously, stop tapping your foot. You're driving me crazy," Andy said.

Blinking, Zita glanced down, not having realized she had been jiggling her leg. "Can't drive you to a place you're already at," she shot back in reflex, but she quit moving. Her pocket beeped.

"Carajo, I forgot to turn off Arca's phone, and someone's texted." She flipped it open and checked it. "Jerome? You'd think he'd have had enough of us by now."

"Congrats! You've gone viral! I love the video, especially the close-ups on Wingspan. It never hurts to have fan service for the ladies. LOL," the text read before a line of characters she recognized as a web address. Since she hadn't sprung for a data plan for the little, unregistered flip phone, she handed it to Wyn so the other woman could memorize the URL.

Zita sorted the containers into piles based on which still had food in them and which were empty.

"It's a video of some sort," Andy said, glancing at it. "That's a popular video-sharing site. I've got a bad feeling about this."

Wyn sighed. "I'm sure it can't be that horrendous... can it?"

Nothing like the faith of your friends to reassure you. Rolling her eyes, Zita shrugged. "Not a clue. Shouldn't be. I haven't done anything in front of the camera that I'm ashamed of, so it's probably just another news anchor with more all kinds of crazy guesses about our identities. Maybe now I'm a teenage gangbanger stripper with six kids who lives in Rock Creek Park. Wyn's my baby daddy, and Andy's my gang leader, no doubt."

Folding her hands in her lap, Wyn raised her eyebrows. "I believe I lack the equipment for that task."

Andy widened his eyes and slapped on an innocent expression. "I thought you lived at the zoo, only coming out at night to raid the trash cans and dance nude. If you have a paying job, we need to up your gang dues."

"Why you got to be a hater?" Zita said, ensuring the containers were in tidy columns. "Mano—"

Wyn interrupted, "Let's get my tablet so we can see what amused Jerome so much."

Zita snapped the flip phone closed and pulled out the battery, handing both to Wyn, who tucked the pieces into her purse.

A few minutes later, the three friends squashed together on the velvety scarlet sofa. Sitting between Zita and Andy, Wyn held her small tablet, a sleek white and silver thing in her lap. She typed in the address.

Her stomach rumbled at the sight of the apple on the back of the computer. *I could eat before I crash,* Zita thought, then forgot in her surprise at seeing Arca's masked face on the still screen.

"Well," said Andy, "it was posted by a DJ and labeled 'Vigilante Party,' so it's not a news report."

Then Wyn pressed play.

"I'm here to fuck," Arca's voice declared, and music started. It boomed out of the tiny speakers, a strong bass beat trying to shake its way out of the depths of the machine. The video exploded into action shots of her running and jumping, interspersed with random images: Arca rolling her eyes, cuddling the dachshund puppy, and putting her hands on her hips. Clips of her speaking (mostly the same phrase that had begun the song), a woman moaning, and weirdly, the bellows of a wildebeest comprised the lyrics.

Zita's jaw dropped. "Caramba. Was that a cross-eyed platypus?"

Andy and Wyn howled with laughter.

"Excellent. You finally showed up, mano," Arca's voice said. The video switched to a shirtless Andy, turning his back on the camera. Editing made it seem as if he boogied across the screen, slapping his own rear, the camera zooming in and out on it. Zita could make out fragments of the New York museum in the background.

Andy's laughter stopped.

"We're here to fuck," Arca said onscreen.

Distorted by electronic manipulation, Andy's voice sang, "How cool is that? Did I just do a superhero?"

He hid his reddening face in his hands. "I was brushing dust off, not spanking myself. Shoot me now."

The screen split, and Andy bopped at the bottom of the screen. A wildebeest galloped across the top making lame yelping sounds. In the center of it all, Wyn's illusory shape, Muse, floated with her arms spread and a beatific smile as the new chorus repeated.

The video ended with Arca declaring, "I got places to be."

Zita blinked. "Well. That's special. Catchy. Might make a good workout tune but not how I'd prefer to be remembered."

"That was awful!" Andy said.

Zita shrugged. "It's just some Internet video. I bet nobody saw it."

Scrolling down, Wyn cleared her throat and giggled again. "It has twenty million views and quite the comments section. Our physical assets have received significant admiration, though some are debating if Zita's chest has been artificially augmented and if Andy is wearing some derriere enhancement. A few are calling for a version cut with a porn. Several people offered to party with us, and the DJ has promised an eventual follow-up. We may wish to consider our language on camera in the future."

"By we, she means you, Zita," Andy said. "I knew I should've kept my jeans on."

Zita harrumphed. "Then all of your clothing would have been gone, Andy, after your walk through the electricity. Would you have preferred to be naked?"

He grumbled.

"Now, children," Wyn said, tapping on her screen.

Andy rose and picked up his pack. "Well, now we've headed off another weird magical threat and been publicly humiliated on the Internet, I need to go home. Some of us have HVAC in the morning."

Zita bounced to his side, touching his arm with her hand. "Oye, mano, your dad's still out of town, so no, you don't. We'll get a pizza and just hang to unwind. Maybe a kitchen sink one where they throw a bunch of different stuff on it and don't tell you what! Last time, the toppings were anchovies, broccoli, extra cheese, Canadian bacon, chicken, and pepperoni."

Pulling away from her, Andy grimaced. "No thanks."

"Fine then," Zita said, "we'll do a pepperoni for you and me, and a broccoli for Wyn and me. After that, we can all go home and crash. It's late."

Even with that enticement, he shook his head. "I'd like to just go."

From the couch, Wyn made an unhappy sound. "Guys? I don't think we did win. We need to postpone that celebration, as tempting as a 'kitchen sink' pizza undoubtedly sounds to someone."

"What?" Zita frowned at her friend. "We stopped them."

Wyn gnawed on her lower lip. "To keep an eye on what people are saying about us, I had a program collecting news on metahumans. I just checked it, and you'll want to see this. I believe Zeus wanted us chasing Tiffany..." Her voice trembled, and she waved the tablet at them.

His shoulders slumped as Andy sighed and walked back toward the sofa.

Zita trailed after him and plopped down on Wyn's other side. They scanned the article in silence.

Andy rose and went to stare out the window.

When Zita finished reading, she swore. "You're right. We got played. Hard."

Wyn tapped a video of a report on the heists and closed her eyes. She gnawed her lip, and a tiny line appeared between her brows. "While we were in Brazil, Zeus and his accomplices were quite busy, but it seems like a pointless collection of objects. Six motorboats? A lab's worth of scientific equipment? The entire contents of an electrical supply warehouse? Somehow, they also found time to break out a hundred convicts from that maximum-security prison as well."

Zita scrubbed a hand over her short hair. "The prison is close to the taqueria where I ran into them in Jessup. We encountered them at two of these other spots."

Andy rubbed his forehead. "The office building I saw them at housed the lab they robbed." He stared into space for a moment. "It's possible they haven't finished whatever they're doing. While you were gone, Vaudeville said their contract ended Thursday or whenever Tiffany and Pretorius declared it."

Wyn nodded. "Tiffany mentioned something about Thursday as well. I'll text Jerome and let him know so he can work on it, too. It's Monday, so we have until Thursday to discover their goals."

Exhaling, Zita rubbed her forehead, her joy over a successful mission fading and leaving only weariness behind. "I'm wiped, and it's past my bedtime. Let's pick up our stuff and head out. We'll figure it out after some rest."

***

Back in Andy's apartment, Zita set down her bag and stack of containers and flopped on the overstuffed sofa. Her mind spun in circles deciding what to do: sleep, bathe, or clean her travel gear. Andy pulled away from her as soon as they had arrived, and he tossed his backpack on the floor. While he hadn't hit any of the furniture, the pack had split open and spilled things all over. Cupcake appeared out of nowhere and was exploring the items now, purring.

Normally, cleaning up the mess would have been Zita's first instinct, but pondering Zeus' crime spree warred with weariness. *I don't think I'm going to come up with anything that we haven't already considered, at least not without some sleep.*

Muttering from her roommate broke into her contemplation.

I need to do something about him. Well, being blunt didn't work, so I'll try Wyn's way. If this keeps up, I'll be working just to afford fancy treats for my friends. After collecting all the containers that still had food in them, Zita trooped upstairs to the kitchen. A few minutes later, she returned to the basement with two bowls heaped high with the ice cream she had stashed there earlier. She set one in front of Andy and dug through her duffel bag. "You're upset. So, in case I haven't been clear, I'm being supportive right now. I'm all willing to listen and nod my head and say noncommittal stuff. We can watch this romantic comedy, and you can laugh it out." After finding the DVD, she put it next to him. *Maybe he won't notice if I doze off during it.*

Andy glanced at the food, the bag he'd started to unpack while she was upstairs, then the movie. "You do know that not everyone... *Wing Chun?* This is a kung fu movie. It's not even in English, Zita."

"It has subtitles. If you'd prefer a tragic love story to cry it out instead, I also brought *King Boxer.* You might remember it as *The Five Fingers of Death.*" She found the box and waved it at him.

His tone dry, Andy said, "I'm certain I don't recognize it, and I'm a little frightened by a love story using either name. Pass."

"I can translate that one for you, but it's old-school kung fu, so you don't need the dialogue. Pick one and start talking. I'm ready to be agreeable and not offer advice. See? Not offering any practical tips right now," she said, cramming a massive bite of triple chocolate something cheap ice cream into her mouth.

Andy made a choking sound. "You do realize I'm a guy, and we don't do the ice cream and nodding and movie thing. Why are you? Did Wyn put you up to this?"

Zita stared at him, the treat chilling her. "I wanted to help you. She suggested the techniques she's had me using on her might work better than telling you to man up."

He kicked his water bottle, sending it flying across the room, where it knocked over the desk lamp. "She needs to let me be, and so do you. I love you, Z, but you have to stop talking to yourself and listen to others. Treat them like individuals based on that instead of whatever's backflipping around in your head."

Her cold fingers tightened, squeezing so much the smooth, slippery bowl almost slid from her hands. When she replied, her voice sounded far away. "I wanted to help."

"I know. You always do. Even if I needed it, you couldn't do anything. You're lucky enough to not have to worry about breaking the world, so why don't you go back to wasting your powers and leave me alone?"

She blinked. "What are you talking about?"

His voice was tight. "Most of your life is exactly as it was before, if you substitute shapeshifting and teleporting for obsessive exercise and extreme sports."

"I'm not hurting nobody. What do you expect me to do? Go loco like Tiffany and Garm and try to rule the world, crushing all the unempowered under my sneakers? Not cool. Cutting out family and friends is even more uncool." Zita exhaled, trying to catch her breath and remembering his description of her activities. "And I am not obsessive. I'm dedicated."

His chin jutting toward her, he lifted his head. "We should go do superhero things! Or at least I should."

Her arms flew wide with exasperation. "What did we just do in Brazil? Before that, what about Sobek and New York? Your life isn't wrecked, mano, unless you want it to be."

Andy stared at the avocado green carpet. "We've been reacting to things that fell in our paths. Since I've got nothing else left, I should do more to help others."

She picked up the dirty clothes that had spilled from his bag and tossed them into his laundry basket, hoping he'd catch the hint. "Is this about farting around on rooftops being cranky again? I'm not a cop or military person trained to handle soldiers and criminals. I'm an athlete and a tax preparer. You're a physicist. Mano, if your response to getting a new baseball bat is to wander the streets searching for someone to beat down, you got serious issues and better go see a shrink. I mean, sure, if a killer breaks into your house, hit them with it, but it's not meant for fighting."

Either scowling at her—or at the amount of wash he had to do—Andy's voice held a sharp tone. "We didn't get new equipment. We got superpowers. I'm invulnerable, or almost so, and super strong. Plus, I turn into a psycho bird willing to eat a person!"

"That was a dinosaur, and Wyn said they're just animals," she reminded him.

"I didn't know that at the time!" His face was tragic.

Zita ran a hand over her head. "Maybe Wingspan-you knew. Wyn mentioned you're magic in that form."

Andy refused to be comforted. "Doubtful. How is any of that comparable to baseball gear, anyway? I mean, your powers are better suited to playing, but there has to be more to our abilities than just selfish amusement."

Hurt laced her, and she flexed her shoulders. "I don't just play. Sure, I don't go hunting for trouble like you seem to think I should, but I've been trying to help people when I can."

"The best way you can do that is by leaving them alone," Andy shot back. His face fell, and he winced. "I'm sorry, I didn't mean that. I'm just tired. It's been a long day, and I want to sleep and forget about that video, eating that dinosaur, and everything else for a while. Goodnight, Zita." He disappeared into his bedroom, closing the door behind him. The lock clicked.

Zita slumped before she forced herself to stand up straight. "You know that lock won't keep Cupcake or me away, right? Fine, goodnight, I'm tired of the drama anyway," she told his door, her voice louder than necessary as she swore at herself mentally. *Esta de la chingada. I screwed that up, big time. Why do I even try? I'm making things worse. No wonder Quentin was avoiding me. He's probably afraid I'll try to help him too, and we'll get into another fight. It's a sad day when tight-ass Miguel is the brother I'm getting along with best.*

Hinges creaked, and she turned, but Andy merely gathered the cat up and stalked back into his room. The door snicked shut behind them.

Appetite gone, she set the lamp upright and got rid of the ice cream. When she returned to the basement, she moved the backpack and became a large, fluffy black cat. *At least in animal form, I don't mind not bathing first as much.* Leaping lithely onto his overstuffed sofa, a decrepit brown monstrosity with a faded orange, purple, and cream plaid pattern, she curled up on the pillow. When she caught herself kneading, she admonished herself for being careless. *Animal instincts can be sneaky, though they're not as calculating or cannibalistic as Andy seems to think.* She wrapped her tail around herself and let possibilities swirl in her brain, hoping for the right one. Her eyes may have sunk lower and perhaps even closed in the dark room.

***

The tinny sound of music broke the silence a few hours later, jolting Zita, still a cat, awake. For a moment, she was grateful. It was frustrating enough to not know how to stop Zeus and his team without some dream-walking metahuman nagging her about it in her sleep. *Though hadn't dream auntie said something about checking on my family? That was new.* She glanced at the clock. *Hours to go before dawn. They'll all be tucked up safe in their beds. Or in Quentin's case, in someone else's bed.*

She surveyed the area through slitted eyes, seeking the source of the noise. Andy's room. Her tail whipped against the sofa. *Did I oversleep? Was that an alarm? He's like a brother, so he could be who dream auntie meant.*

A groan echoed from behind his door, and the song cut off during a verse asking who had let the dogs out. Andy shuffled in a minute later, wrapped in his worn black bathrobe, and plunked himself into the chair in front of his computer.

Zita arched her back and enjoyed the sensual pleasure of a full-body feline stretch before she dealt with whatever had awakened her friend. She changed to her usual human form.

His eyes bleary, Andy stared at the glowing monitor, his shoulders slumped. Despite his indolent stance, his hands flew over the keys once he had logged on, and another window opened.

Even if his poor posture dismayed her, Zita was in awe of his speed. *Look at him using all his fingers like a crazy typing genius.* She flexed her wrists as if that would grant her the ability to do the same on her laptop. "Why are you up?" *Please don't say you need to play a game. These middle-of-the-night marathons are killing me.*

"I have a raid," he said, grinding her hopes underfoot ruthlessly. "Since I don't have a job, I've got time. My ex-girlfriend kept our original guild in our breakup, so now I have to earn brownie points with the new team. They have a mission due to start in fifteen minutes, but they're not organized, so it'll be at least twenty before they get their acts together enough to go out." His hands danced, and another screen came up.

Email, then more video games. Lucky me. I hope I can sleep through this one. She fluffed her pillow with little enthusiasm, returned to her cat shape, and circled several times until she found the right spot. Her eyes closed, and she sought rest, only to open them again a few minutes later when Andy growled to himself.

His voice was higher pitched than usual. "Noticed you're falling behind on the site. Hope you aren't ill. Anticipating reading the latest soon." He dropped to his usual register and continued to grouse. "Listen, you passive-aggressive jerk, if I want to take time off, I will. Perhaps I don't want to jump on the first paper available..." His words trailed off into indistinct cranky muttering and additional key presses.

After resuming her natural form, Zita said, "Are you talking to me? Because nobody's ever accused me of being passive-aggressive in my life. Aggressive, yes, though people usually follow that up with something irritating that makes it clear I'm cute instead of intimidating." She rubbed the sleep from her eyes and yawned.

Andy squeaked like a twelve-year-old girl, jerking back from his screen and almost falling off his chair. Next to an open email window, a costume shop site and another website displayed, with a stick figure man scribbling equations upside down at the end of a banner reading "Farnswaggle Fysics!"

She squinted. *Why is he so jumpy? It's not like I caught him drooling over porn.* "Did you spell Fysics wrong?"

"No, it's a joke about the physicist this site is dedicated to keeping up with. Even someone like you knows who Farnswaggle is, right?" He wheeled his chair closer to the computer.

Zita cocked her head to the side, her eyebrows raising. "Someone like me? You mean an awesomely fun person? Farmwiggles is the guy you like with the guesses about the source of our powers."

Andy sighed. "Why don't you go back to sleep?"

Because the past week has taught me that you talk to yourself and sometimes shout whenever you get annoyed with your games, and I can't snooze through that. Zita shook her head in frustration and rose to her feet. "Pues, I'll run home, shower, do a load of wash, then come back and crash later." She hefted her gear and clothes. "Plus, I want to put my camping stuff away where it belongs."

Andy raised his eyebrows, though he did not seem upset at the idea. "Thought you had to avoid your apartment."

She brushed the short hair on the top of her head with a palm. "Nobody's going to be sitting around my empty apartment on the off-chance I'll come home. It's been closed up for weeks." Opening her eyes, she checked the clock on his computer. "At this obscene hour, no less. We've just spent the better part of the week marinating in each other's company, plus Wyn, Jerome, and the mercenaries. I think we can both do with some quality alone time. Órale, my workout clothes have to be washed before they throw themselves off a bridge without me. Besides, I need a few hours of uninterrupted sleep."

He grunted and turned to his keyboard. "Fine. My raid is starting. I'll be here if you need me."

Zita scooped up her duffel and gear. "Por supuesto, you'll be here. You don't leave the basement anymore of your own free will unless someone's life is at stake." She teleported home.

Chapter Twenty-One

Zita reappeared in her bedroom. The sight of the soothing green walls, rainforest mural, and her mink-soft purple bedspread should have soothed her, but her disquiet only grew after the first second. She tensed, shouldering the bag she had been about to drop. The door hung partially open, and the air lacked the stagnancy of an apartment that had shut up for weeks. Everything else seemed untouched: the corners of her bed were still perfect, no scent but hers lingered on the pillows, and her knife remained in its hiding place behind the headboard.

Something clunked in the living room, and she heard a man's laugh, a little wild, a lot familiar. When the same voice murmured again, she couldn't make out the words but recognized who had invaded her space.

Quentin! He's supposed to be safe at Mamá's! Zita padded to the window and peeked out. Glimpsing the stairs, she teleported there and stomped up to her floor, anger growing with each step. *Why is he here? If Sobek had caught him here, I wouldn't have been around to protect him.* As she leaned her bag against the wall, she absently tried the doorknob. To her surprise, it turned under her hand, but a deadbolt stopped it from opening.

Zita stared at the blue door, rage mounting as she fumbled for her keys. *Quentin didn't even throw all the bolts. Did he bring home a one-night stand and get too busy dropping his pants to even lock it all the way? He's always after me to secure all four deadbolts, and he can't be bothered to close them himself?* After a moment, she realized she was growling and squashed it. She unlocked the door and pushed it open.

"¿Qué pedo, Quent—" she began, cutting herself off as she saw what awaited inside.

Sobek, a.k.a. Tracy Jones, the sadist who had held her brother captive in August, smiled at her so widely the pointed edges of his teeth were visible. "Well, this is convenient. Hello, sweet thing."

Zita stared. Quentin stood with his back to the balcony doors, his Kimber Warrior in his grasp. At this distance, she couldn't see if he'd already thumbed the safety off on the gun or not, but she hoped so given that three burly armed men surrounded him. Another man guarded Sobek, who lounged close to the door.

"Run, Zita!" her brother shouted, eyes wild and wide.

Before she could react, the thug by Sobek took a step closer and tried to backhand her. Light flared on the switchblade in his other hand as he moved.

Without thinking, she blocked the slap, pain radiating up her arm from the force of the blow. Zita hit his hand to knock it away from her face, reversed direction to strike underhand at the nerves in his knife arm, and spun back into the hall.

Recovering from her hits, he followed and stabbed at her.

A gun boomed twice from inside.

Dios, please protect my brother. She shoved the massive bag between herself and the switchblade, so it was buried in her supplies. *Caramba. I hope he didn't hit anything expensive.*

The guy fell back a step when she pushed the heavy duffel at him.

Another gunshot roared from inside.

Zita threw her bag (and his embedded weapon) aside. The duffel slammed into the metal railing by the stairs. She spun into a diagonal handstand, kicking his collarbone with both feet in a meia lua de compasso dupla. Something crunched and gave under her hit.

The thug fell backward, hitting his head on the wall. He slid to the ground.

Zita flipped to her feet and slipped into a cautious ginga, darting close enough to deliver a quick kick to his side. *Por favor, Dios, let my brother be okay in there.*

He moaned and curled up but made no motion to rise.

"Quentin, I'm coming to help!" she shouted, bounding over him and moving toward her apartment. She stopped dead when the doorway filled with a tall, stocky form.

Sobek waggled his Colt M1911 at her, his shooting stance relaxed, as if choked exclamations and meaty thuds weren't drifting out behind him. "Ah, now, we can't have that. Stand still, my pretty little pet."

Zita backpedaled, hopping over the groaning man, toward the stairs as her mind raced with the best way to disarm him and get to Quentin.

Sobek paused by the downed thug. His eyes were hooded, almost lost in his face, as he stared down his nose at his employee. After stepping on his hand with a disdainful sniff, Sobek shot him.

Ears ringing with the close discharge, Zita gaped at him. Her stomach revolted, and while she wrestled that into submission, her mouth ran free. She avoided using the fake Mexican accent, but it took effort as every nerve screamed at her to check on her brother. "You know you just killed your own dude, right? Most people give out pink slips when they want to fire somebody."

Sobek sniffed. "Not my man or my problem. Other people's help is terribly unreliable. If I told them once, I told them a million times... I'm the artist with a knife... They're hired thugs who should obey orders and leave their own shoddy equipment at home. My men would know better." He brought the firearm back up to center it on her again.

A gun roared again inside, once, twice. Ceramic shattered, and Quentin cried out, pain in his voice.

Her heart clenched, and she licked her lips, her throat dry and painful.

"Hmm. You might be down a brother, so I'll have to slice up your other one. How sad. Guess I'll just pin this one's death on you, then. Unless his employer wants to lose the only source of the pink ice, they'll have to believe me when I tell them you did it." Sobek faked a pout that dissolved into a cackle.

Zita gave him a dubious look and tried to lure him away from her place and, more importantly, Quentin, by sliding sideways onto the top step. "Pink ice? Like diamonds? You run a drug ring, kidnap and torture people, *and* sell jewelry. You're a busy psychopath these days."

Ignoring her gibe, Sobek raised this gun, clasping it in both hands in a Weaver stance as he stepped over the dead man and moved toward her. "I grow tired of the oh-so-righteous Garcias. Come along quietly now, or I'll shoot you where you stand. And, Quentin, inch any closer and your sister will enjoy a lovely gut wound. It could mean a beautifully excruciating death for her, though nowhere near as perfect as the one I could grant her, but that's a risk I'm willing to take."

His voice ragged and hoarse, Quentin growled. "Or I could shoot you first."

As she eased to the side, Zita glimpsed her brother as he peeked around the corner with the tip of his gun just visible. Relief poured through her. *At least the body is between them, so Quentin can't do something stupid like rushing an armed man.*

Sobek paused, then sidled away, moving back enough where he could see both siblings. "A crocodile never forgets. You can shoot me, but you might also hit your baby sister," he taunted.

Hoping her brother would catch the hint, Zita let her mouth run free as she inched out of the direct line of fire. "Elephant. Elephants never forget. You can distract a crocodile, and it'll forget about you, but an elephant? It'll take your distraction and go back to what it was doing before. And, just saying, you don't smell like a crocodile." She pursed her lips as if thinking and tapped the side of her chin, then pointed at him. "Maybe you could be a sick frog that's been rolling in its own shit, psycho shit in your case, but you don't got the reptile tang."

As she had hoped, her words focused Sobek's attention on her, and he turned his head away from Quentin for a moment. "You're begging to be cut open. I wonder how long before you scream?" He rushed her.

Quentin's firearm boomed, echoing in the hallway and interrupting whatever threat Sobek had been about to spew.

Sobek let out a wordless exclamation and staggered, losing his forward momentum. He lifted his gun at Zita. "If I can't vivisect you..."

She burst into action, twisting her torso as she stepped and kicked, hitting his wrist with the sole of her foot.

The weapon flew from his hand, clattering against the wall.

She whirled back into a ready position and fell into a slow ginga, careful of his greater size and the supernatural strength she had witnessed before. *Need to keep him away from the gun and Quentin.*

Sirens screamed in the distance.

Sobek crouched, wrapping one arm around his side, where dark red bloomed. A droplet ran and dripped on the floor. He grabbed the railing at the top of the steps with his free hand and coughed, an ugly wet sound that ended in a gasp. "You wouldn't shoot an unarmed man, would you?"

"¡Zita, muévete! You're in the way," Quentin hissed, altering position to keep Sobek in his sights.

Feinting left, Zita attacked low, trying to sweep Sobek's feet out from under him. Her kick rebounded off his ankle, and she flipped off a wall to avoid a vicious swipe of his good arm.

"I'll hear you both screaming sometime soon," Sobek hissed, grabbing the railing again and leaping over it, down the three flights of stairs. He landed with a loud thud and a groan.

She ran to the railing. Bloody footprints emerged from a larger splatter and trailed into the darkness.

Quentin swore and headed for the steps. His right arm bled freely and hung limp at his side. "He can't be far. If those pendejos hadn't shot my gun arm, I'd have gotten him, and this would be over. Are you okay?"

When he tried to push past her, Zita grabbed his uninjured arm. "Oye, I'm fine, but you're hurt! Don't even think about running off after that chingado psycho, gun or no."

He grimaced and winced, pulling away. "I'm fine."

In reply, she poked the shoulder above his wound.

Quentin gasped and paled, staggering.

"Yeah, I can see that. Your shoulder's probably dislocated, and you're chingado bleeding all over. You're not going nowhere, mano. You want me to clean that and get it bandaged so we can put your arm back into joint?" Zita steered him away from the steps.

With a last glance down the stairs, he acquiesced. "They winged me, but I'll let the EMTs handle it."

"You got a solid hit on him, you know. Sit down and keep the neighbors back," she said as she stepped inside and surveyed her apartment.

Two men bled on her carpet, one conscious, the other not, and a third sprawled bonelessly like a grim lap blanket over the wicker chair by the futon. Blood stained the white furniture red, and shiny pink plastic and blue curls peeked out from the other side of the chair. A clay parrot was smashed, near the soil leaking from a crack in the giant container that held her magically enhanced pepper plant.

She gulped, queasiness almost taking over, but curiosity propelled her toward the body and whatever the blue curls were near it. *Please don't let Quentin's date be dead,* she prayed. Her second thought was more practical. *Where am I going to find a new chair at a good price? I'm not keeping the death cooties one even if someone gets all the blood out.*

"Zita, you don't need to see all this. We should wait outside for the police," Quentin said, coming up behind her. "Why don't you take a minute and rest, and I'll handle everything?"

The remnants of her nausea burned off under his patronizing tone, and she turned to glare at him, hands on her hips.

Before she could say anything, he sighed. "Never mind, I sound like chingado Miguel. How about you sit on the steps and fend off your neighbors while I grab my phone and call the cops?" He offered her his second-best smile, the one he used when conning their older brother. His gaze darted past her. Pain etched deep lines around his mouth, adding years to his face.

She narrowed her eyes. "If anyone's handling them, it's you. I'm not injured and dripping all over. What are you hiding, mano?" After shoving past him, she drew closer to the death cootie chair, hating every step, and finally identified what hid behind the dead man. Whirling, she glared at Quentin.

Her brother held his hands out. "Oye, Zita, cálmate. I can explain."

Zita's temper rose, and she took a step toward him.

Quentin recoiled at her expression.

Zita slashed a hand through the air. Since the shots had to have awakened the neighbors, she hissed her words. "Oh, you don't need to explain nothing, you pinche pendejo. Instead of being safe at Mamá's where you said you'd go, you dressed up a chingado blow-up doll like me with a clown wig and some of my clothes to set a trap for Sobek and his boys. Were you just going to kill them all?" She threw her arms up and swore at his stupidity in every language she knew.

Perhaps sensing how upset she was, Quentin let her vent. When she paused, he said, "Are you okay?"

Her mind racing, Zita seized the wig. "I'll hide this stuff before the cops make it more complicated and send you to jail forever. We'll leave it out of our statements, but believe you me, mano, we are talking about this first chance we have. While we're at it, we'll also cover how you've been a regular man-whore since you were kidnapped in August and how that's screwing up your life."

Quentin's mouth compressed. "There's nothing to discuss, and even if there were, you hate talking."

Furious, she waved the blue hair at him. "That's how you know I'm serious. The world might end since I'm the one suggesting a talk about feelings, but this is important. You can't keep ignoring that you're messed up and need to handle the damage. I've kept my mouth shut for months, but this isn't working, and I'm not losing you to an STD or another stupid plot like this. You need help, so you are going to talk to a priest, or a shrink, or a talking circle of talking therapy people. Whatever. I'll help you find one, but you need to do this."

Sirens roared in the parking lot.

Zita swore, snatched up the doll, and hustled into her exercise room, throwing it and the wig into her equipment closet. She slammed the door shut. By the time she got back, Quentin was talking to a cop. Extreme weariness seeped in as her adrenaline ebbed.

***

Since she'd been sleeping on the sofa, or trying to, given Andy's weird late-night gaming habits, Zita knew she could teleport to Andy's basement apartment if she wanted. Leaving her violated home was the sensible thing to do.

Which was, perhaps, why she hadn't done it yet.

She was also supposed to stay out of it until the police gave her clearance to return, but she'd ignored that too. Despite her defiance, she hadn't been blasé about staying and had partially shifted to allow herself better senses. All four deadbolts were thrown, and she'd left up the police tape. The door would have to be replaced since a bullet had carved a lethal peephole in it. The forensics team had cut out a square around it to preserve the bullet's passage. To keep out insects (and her nosier neighbors), she'd filled the hole with putty and duct-taped over it on both sides. *The cops can deal. It's my place. Well, technically, it's Miguel and the mortgage company's, but I rent it, so I've got rights.*

Even though her apartment sang with her scent and her belongings, the acrid chemical odors of the fingerprint powder and the miasma of the men who had been in her living room still intruded. Especially the dead one. Her stomach threatened to rebel again, but she forced it to settle back down. *Hopefully, Mamá will have tips on cleaning that up since I don't have the funds to hire anyone.*

Anger coursed through her, and Zita stalked down the hall and entered the exercise room. She clenched her fists. Despite her exhaustion, more than anything she wanted to push herself on a hard run—or flight—then beat the crap out of someone, preferably someone named Sobek, so he never endangered her brother again.

Instead, she took a deep breath, focusing on the familiar scents in the room: her own sweat, the metal and leather of her equipment, and the strong vanilla tang of her favorite soap in the nearby bathroom. One by one, she relaxed each of her major muscle groups to avoid getting sore from tension, watching herself in the mismatched mirrors that covered a wall. She prowled the confines of the room, senses high, even though her nose told her that no one else had entered the space recently. The brilliant blue walls, mirrors, and gleaming silver equipment were untouched. Her breathing and pacing was the only movement that disturbed the long vines of the cheery fake plants, and her careful ordering of the bright rainbow wash of color from her DVD collection had not changed.

She scrubbed a hand over her hair, rubbed her gritty eyes, then turned back to the closet where she kept sports gear. When she opened the door, Quentin's blow-up doll stared at her with its perpetually surprised face. Yanking the valve harder than necessary, air escaped it in a hiss. "You need to go away. If the cops realize Quentin tried to lure Sobek in, it's not self-defense. I don't know whether it was suicide by serial killer or Marine bravado, but I'm not letting him go that easy." While she waited for the doll to deflate, her mind drifted from one brother in trouble to the other.

As she stared at the contents of her closet, her eyes fell on a newly washed canteen. Her mouth widened in a smile. "Pues, it won't solve Andy's problems, but it'd at least help his mood."

Chapter Twenty-Two

On Wednesday morning, Zita lasted all the way through three renditions of the song, then threw down her headphones and jumped off the treadmill before it could grind to a halt. The poor old thing had struggled to keep up with her, anyway. She stomped over to Andy and tapped off the power button on his computer. The deep bass and peppy electronic music cut out, and for a moment, the only sound was Cupcake's purring and the droning voice from her headphones.

"Hey!" His fists clenched, Andy rose to his feet, dumping Cupcake to the floor.

The cat glared at them, then began cleaning himself vigorously.

Zita gestured with both hands for Andy to stop. "You're done with that. You said you hate it, but you've been playing it constantly. It's drowning out the tax crap I should be studying, and for what? All you're doing is making yourself more miserable. I won't stand by and watch it happen."

He folded his arms across his chest. "Then don't. You can always leave."

Hurt sliced Zita's heart for an instant before anger pushed it aside. "Oh, hell, no, mano. I won't psychoanalyze whatever's up your ass or pull any more of Wyn's tricks, but you don't get to keep punishing yourself. We're going out."

"You can't make me. You're not my mother." Thunder boomed overhead.

Zita beetled her brows and frowned at him in the best imitation of her mother she'd ever done.

Andy slapped his hand to his forehead, closed his eyes, and winced. "Did that sound as childish to you as it did to me?"

As she chortled, Zita clicked off the tax instructions she'd been listening to. "Yeah, but I have that effect on people. Since you're like a brother, I forgive your lame ass this time. Now, we're getting out of here for a while and climbing. No real conversation required from you, just listen to my instructions and ask any questions you have. The other day, you mentioned that you damaged a building when you tried to climb it. After a few lessons, you'll do better, plus it'll give you a new way to practice controlling your strength."

"It's going to rain," he said.

Sensing his capitulation was imminent, Zita pressed, "It does that a lot here these days. No worries, we'll go somewhere without rain. Throw on jeans, a shirt, and sturdy shoes and let's go. I'll fill water bottles." After a quick rummage through her duffel bag, she pulled out the canteens she had brought from her apartment.

He glared at her, suspicion on his face. "Last time you surprised me, you ambushed me with the cat."

She put her hands on her hips. "Technically, that was Wyn, and if you'd talked to us, it wouldn't have been necessary. No hay bronca, this will be you and me and the mountains. It'll even be in the Southwest. You know you want out, and if you don't go, Wyn will come over later to explore your feelings. If you turn this offer down, I'll text her and encourage her to do so." Her foot tapped so fast it almost vibrated.

Andy acquiesced with a nod. "Just us guys, then."

Zita beamed. "That's right! Wait! I'm not a dude."

He muttered under his breath, but she didn't bother to listen.

"I'll pretend that was an apology," she called, racing up the stairs toward the kitchen.

When she came back down lugging a full cooler, Andy held up a hand. He still wore the same faded T-shirt and the fuzzy pajama pants he slept in. A smug Cupcake curled in his lap again, batting at Andy's fingers. "If we do this, if I go with you, I'm not interested in talking."

"Don't worry," she said. "I tried Wyn's methods, and they didn't work. Screw that, I suck at it anyway. So, this is just us hanging out. I picked out a nice, easy, obscure mountain we've been to before, so if you wuss out, you can take yourself home. Climbing is a great exercise choice. You can't hurt anything too much with your strength, and it's excellent practice for control. Unless you want to miss out on the thrill of doing it right, you can't just claw your way up the rock. Plus, cheating like that makes Baby Jesus cry."

He blinked at her, one hand absently stroking the cat. "We wouldn't want that."

"Nope. Come on, you've got to be dying to move. I know you haven't been working out any, and that would drive me nuts." She eyed him and wrinkled her nose.

He narrowed his eyes. "Not all of us get itchy when it's been more than six hours since our last workout, and we did go to Brazil a couple days ago."

Did he just suck in his gut? Zita made a derisive sound, air escaping her mouth in a disdainful hiss. "You were an Olympic-caliber judoka once, and you can't tell me that you don't miss exercising, even if it's sporadic. Go get dressed. I don't care what you wear so long as you're comfortable, it can be washed, and your boots have traction. When we get back, send Wyn a copy of your resume so she can pretty it up. Having that will keep her from pestering you about your feelings or girls or merging your troubled chakras or whatever."

Andy squinted at her as if trying to find a trap for a moment before he nudged the cat from his lap, rose, and ambled into his bedroom. The door clicked shut behind him.

I hope that means he's changing his clothes and not going back to sleep. She double-checked the cooler and stole a nibble from the carrot sticks she had packed for their lunch.

Fifteen minutes later, Andy emerged dressed in what she assumed were hiking clothes. "Okay, do your worst."

Zita smiled evilly.

He blanched. "You do know I didn't mean that literally, right?"

***

Even if the dry air sucked all the moisture away before she could feel it, Zita sweated on top of a large boulder, her own scent mingling with the local sage and dust. The Arizona sky stretched overhead, clear and blue and filled with the distant sounds of quail and other birds calling each other and taunting the coyotes. While her preference would have been to climb in a greener, more humid area, her companion had a definite fondness for the desert. The gritty sandstone dug into her forearms as she brought her legs out perpendicular to her body and considered Andy, who struggled to his next handhold on a similar rock nearby. She kept her motions slow and uniform, both to combat her own impatience and to increase the challenge of the moves.

Silently, she acknowledged he wasn't the only one who had needed an outing. Going to Brazil had been a fun change, but most of it had been at either a sluggish walk to accommodate the others or riding in the back of a cramped Jeep.

"I think I'm getting the hang of mountain climbing," he said. "Do you have to do upside-down yoga stuff while I'm doing this?"

"You're doing good for your first time, mano, and yes, I do. I wouldn't want to miss an opportunity to combine disciplines," Zita said. With effort, she refrained from correcting him; since he was only climbing a thirty-foot rock, not an actual mountain, the technical term was bouldering. Under normal circumstances, she would have restricted a total bumbly beginner like him to smaller rocks, but he couldn't hurt himself or anything other than a spindly patch of teddy bear cholla that sprouted out of a sparse mat of desert weeds. They were far enough up that even if he fell and rolled a few feet, he would not break one of the rarer, massive, and slow-growing organ pipe cacti.

"Agh!" Andy shrieked, pulling away from the boulder. His arms waved, frenzied, and a small brown form flew by, just inches from Zita's face. Twisting his body, he fell off, landing hard on his back next to the spiny cholla.

She grimaced but held her position without a quiver. "Cálmate," Zita said. "Remember to keep your focus, or you'll fall. It might not hurt you, but it could announce your position or injure something below you."

He dragged air noisily into his lungs and sat up, his hands on his thighs. "I was doing so well until a scorpion crawled onto my hand."

She nodded. "They do live here." Her tone was philosophical as she stretched her legs skyward over her head. "Did you realize you almost hit me with it?"

Andy's shoulders slumped. "What? Again? I'm so sorry. Did it sting you?"

"No hay bronca, it missed. Next time, watch where you're flinging irritable wildlife. Some of us are squishier than others, you know." She moved her legs into a scissor-like position.

He made no attempt to get up, continuing to sit and stare at the dust-covered toes of his boots. "I forgot it couldn't hurt me."

Karen Diem

"Try to remember, since out here you don't got to work hard to pretend to be normal. Most people would get all upset about a scorpion if they weren't climbers. If you're used to it, you learn to deal, preferably by watching where you put your hands. Have a drink of water, and we'll give it another go. You'll get it up this time, I bet." Realizing what she'd said, she smothered a snicker in case he thought she laughed at him.

Flushing red beneath his bronze skin, Andy wiped his forehead. "Maybe this was a bad idea." He leaned forward, putting his head in his hands and hiding his face from her.

In the distance, thunder grumbled.

Zita snorted. "Seriously? You relaxed long enough to forget about that bug up your ass."

"Smooth, Z. All that time with Wyn has really improved your diplomacy skills." Even though he mumbled, she could still make out the words.

At another growl from above, she pushed herself up into a full headstand and checked that direction. *Monsoon season ended in September. This is October in Arizona.* One cloud struggled to form in the sky overhead, managing a few strips of sullen gray against the greater blue. *That's odd, though no weirder than the month and a half-long rain in Anne Arundel County where Andy lives and has been pouting for... Wait, I may not know much mythology, but... I shouldn't say anything until I'm sure.* Despite her decision, her traitorous mouth ran ahead of her. "Dude, it's you! It tries to rain when you're cranky. It's just having more trouble here because there's not much water."

Frowning, he looked up at her. "What?"

Enthused by her idea, she lowered her legs and stood upright. She bounced and waved toward the clouds. "You turn into a giant, magic, lightning chicken and it rains whenever you're upset and not controlling your power. You should reconsider calling yourself Thunderbird."

His hand sliced through the air. "I will not call myself that. It's disrespectful. Would you call yourself Jesus Christ, our Lord and Redeemer?"

"If my parents named me Jesús, yes, but not that whole chunk. That'd be sacrilegious. Oye, I see what you're saying. Aren't you Catholic? You came to Mass with me last week and took Communion and all." Zita frowned.

He shrugged. "I'm mostly Catholic, but it's just wrong."

Zita contemplated that. "So, is Thunderbird like the native Jesus Christ then?"

Andy exhaled. "Depends on the tribe, but generally not. Usually, Thunderbird is a powerful spirit, a protector, and rain-bringer. My mom's people have legends of a tribe able to turn into thunderbirds, but they were people with gifts from the spirits."

"So, if you turn into something very similar to one of these big guardian birds, even if you're not calling yourself that, why are you afraid of your other form?" Zita stretched, lifting her arms above her head and bending backward.

"Shut up and climb down."

She eyed him and smirked. "I'm already on top of the world. Oye, you could combine Thunderbird with another name. You could be the Thunderbirdseed Pervert!"

"I refuse to call myself by any version of that and have no idea why you think it's so funny." Andy folded his arms across his chest.

"Suit yourself, Wingspan," she said.

He winced.

Zita brought her arms down and stood, tapping her hip. "Honestly, I think you're smarter in your bird form."

"What?" He was so surprised his head shot up, his voice cracked, and their eyes met.

Zita held up a finger for silence. "When you've been the bird in the past, have you ever hurt anyone?"

"Well..." He cleared his throat.

She didn't wait. "No, you haven't. When I've been with you, your bird hasn't even done any property damage, unless he was saving people in an area too small for it, like when you kept Wyn from dying at the hospital or your mom on the street in Vegas."

"It shredded that pod!" He mimed tearing something apart.

She clucked her tongue at him. "Evil robot pods don't count, especially when they're attacking people, and your bird shape figured it out before I did. Faster than Wyn did too, which is impressive because that woman is scary bright. Did you have to fight yourself to keep from hunting in any of the places we've been, like Manaus or Boa Vista? Or stop yourself from eating the mercenaries?"

"The bird might've just been full from the brontosaur." Andy folded his arms over his chest.

Zita rolled her eyes. "Hombre, I've been a bird. You burn through calories like nobody's business, so if bird-you wanted to eat more, he could've. Bird-you figured out dinosaurs were animals and ate rather than subtract from our supplies. Since Wyn had the bulk of our food in the purse we couldn't access, eating it ensured we'd have more for everyone else. So. Bird-you is smarter and not the mindless beast you keep treating him as." Swift and sure, she climbed down her own rock, being careful to avoid insects on the way.

His hands clenched into fists. "What if it's about how I have no control over my own body as a bird? You can't know what that's like! When it went to Vegas..."

"Are you forgetting you're not the only one who had cancer? I even got tied down when I was on the drug that gave me seizures."

Her voice might've been sharper than she intended, but even now her muscles tightened at the memory. She forced herself to relax.

His face went red, and he was quiet when he replied. "It's not the same."

"No, it's not the same as bird-you deciding to save your family and thousands of others instead of going where your human shape wanted one single time. You're lucky. Your other shape can sense when your family is in danger from a distance and protect them even better than your regular one. That's not bad, that's chingado awesome. If I had that kind of power, Sobek would never have gotten his claws into Quentin. So, suck it up and deal, mano." She offered him a hand up.

He took it, swinging to his feet, and brushed off some dust.

Enough seriousness. Zita laughed. "You got a big ball of cholla stuck to your butt. This last time, you got fifteen feet up, so next time you've got a good chance of succeeding. Then the real fun begins!" She flexed her fingers.

With a groan, he attempted to bat away the cactus spines, finally just plucking them out and tossing them back into the cholla patch. "Oh, no. What are you planning?"

"Lunch?" She grinned at him.

He relaxed.

"After you have some water and give it one more try. Then we'll eat, and I'll up the ante a little, so you can do it again," she said, crossing to the big, battered orange cooler that sat in the shade of the rock. She opened it, pulled out a sweating canteen, and tossed it at him.

Andy fumbled with it but caught it. "A warning would be nice next time," he said. His tone lacked any real censure. He took a long swig.

Following a drink from her own bottle, Zita dusted off her hands, preparing to climb again. "I used some of that pot roast your family left for you and made us juicy sandwiches, so maybe that'll motivate you. If your parents came home and found out you'd been subsisting on beef jerky and cheese curls, it would break their hearts. Your stepmom must've cooked forever to stock that fridge."

"Fortunately, you rescued them from that fate by coming over to help empty it." After chugging most of his bottle, Andy capped it, set it in the shade, and went back to his rock.

She grinned as he started up again. "I'm a giver, what can I say?"

As they climbed, Zita enjoyed the warmth pooling in her muscles and the challenge, choosing to go up a different side of her boulder. She reached the top first and had just contorted into a yoga pose when he spoke.

Andy clung to the stone, twenty feet up. "I don't know if I can get to the top of this thing. Why am I here? Why am I even trying?"

Somehow, she doubted he meant climbing. *I thought he didn't want to talk?* Zita settled on telling him, "Have faith in yourself, mano, because I do. You can do this. You could be way cooler than you are."

"Wow. Did you just try to bolster my self-confidence by simultaneously insulting and complimenting me?" Andy stared at her.

Her mouth opened and closed as she tried to defend herself, but she changed the topic. "I'm pretty certain you'll master shifting with regular clothes before me."

He blinked at her. "What?"

She shrugged and let her body flow back to a normal standing position. "The little rubber band that keeps your braid in sometimes stays in your hair after you change shape. Once or twice, your boxers were still on after a shapeshift when you weren't wearing the special sportswear. My underwear and braids don't do that."

He touched his braid, running his fingers down the length of it, and tossed it over his shoulder. "I never realized." His back arched too far, she noticed with disapproval, and he wasn't paying attention to his handholds. One foot inched sideways, losing traction, and the other had only a partial toehold.

"Yeah. That's because you don't shift enough. I'm a terrible person to give advice, but I'm a decent wingwoman and an excellent coach. I notice all the important stuff, like how you're mucking up your position right now. Stop leaning back. Fix your feet," Zita said.

"What?" He overbalanced and fell off his rock into the same patch of cholla.

Zita dropped from her boulder, landing in a crouch to bleed off energy from the landing.

He groaned. "I hate my life and my stupid abilities."

She snickered. "Dude. You're not really upset about having powers, especially the whole part where you didn't break your back and suffer from the cactus. Sure, the job and girl thing, they suck, but that'll get better."

From his cradle in the cholla patch, Andy's face darkened. "Aren't I? And what do you know?"

Zita tilted her head. "I've hardly enough job to feed my active metabolism, am stuck mooching off my friend for a place to stay, and don't have a boyfriend either. Plus, I've got powers of my own."

"So?" He sat up, picking off cactus bits with an annoyed expression.

She offered him a hand up. "According to you, I break the laws of physics all the time. Do a lot of trespassing too, but that's beside the point. Or not. Maybe it illustrates my point."

Andy waved her away and got to his feet. "Is this going somewhere?"

She nodded. "The problem isn't your power or what to do with it—for all your whining, you've still had my back and done your best to help people no matter what laws we break, physics or otherwise. Your issue is you enjoy your power, even though you don't have total control over it, and you feel guilty that you're not doing enough for others with it."

"What?"

"You're so busy beating yourself up over what could happen that you're not seeing what does happen. You're missing all the good." Zita strolled over to the cooler and extracted wipes. "And that you've got cactus on your butt again."

Andy swiped at himself enough to get off the prickly plant and crossed his arms over his chest. "Good? Like when I almost killed you with a dinosaur? Or a few minutes ago when I threw a scorpion at you?"

She cleaned her hands, fastidiously getting out the gunk beneath her fingernails. "Details, mano. Those were accidents and show you need to keep practicing, so it doesn't happen again. I'll remind you that you don't break things often anymore. In fact, you've bitched about Cupcake walking on your face and licking your eyelids in the morning when he wants to eat, but the cat doesn't have a scratch, bruise, or—" She shot him a sly look.— "unpampered spot on him."

"I wouldn't hurt... Fine. Point made."

Zita touched his arm. "You can do it. We practiced, and you've had my back before. You'll have it again."

"I almost killed you," he said, his eyes on the ground.

"Past is done. When you get your head out of your culo and believe in yourself, you'll chingado fly." Zita pulled out another handful of wipes and offered them to Andy. "So, you going to clean your hands before you eat or be gross?"

"Are those baby wipes? Somehow that seems appropriate." Andy snatched the material from her and scrubbed the brown dust off, dropping the filthy cloths into the trash bag. "Practice isn't the answer to everything, Z. You almost died, and I won't risk you or anyone else again."

Her hands flew to her hips. "You really think that's your decision to make? Or that you could stop me? You should ask Miguel how his attempts to run my life are working for him before you try the same thing." She snickered and strolled to the cooler, where she pulled out the sandwiches. "I'll probably be illegally climbing a building at night somewhere when you do. Maybe the Bassiter one since neither you nor Wyn wants to climb it with me. Here, catch."

Grabbing the food, Andy tilted his head down to meet her gaze for a moment before he looked away, but a corner of his mouth twisted. "Point made. I won't try to make your decisions for you, and you won't try to make mine for me. I won't use my powers anymore, and you can't stop me." He took a big bite and glared at her while he chewed.

"Nope," she agreed and continued chowing on her own sandwich.

Andy blinked at her and swallowed. "You're not fighting me on that?"

"No. An aerialist who doesn't want to be in the air shouldn't be, and this is like that. You should consider something though." Zita waggled her sandwich at him.

"What's that?" Suspicion clouded his face.

She made him wait until she had eaten another mouthful. "The way things are going, people will get into trouble, and I'll go help them. Since I promised to do so, I'll probably call you, because you won't turn them down. Or me. Then you'll have to use your powers without the habitual control you need, and someone might get hurt."

His head turned away, and he muttered a curse under his breath.

Placidly, she pressed her point. "You haven't injured anyone in your other form—which you just told me is a protective symbol in your mom's and stepdad's peoples, not a raging monster—and you're making great progress on controlling your strength. I won't make you practice, but I won't hesitate to call out where you can improve either."

"As if you could make me."

Refusing to accept the bait, Zita shrugged. "No, I can't, and I'm okay with that. You figure out yourself. If it helps, talk to Jerome or someone else with super strength and see if they got tips for you. I'm working on figuring out why Zeus wanted us busy until tomorrow. Why steal all that weird stuff and free a hundred killers, none of whom have been seen since then? Which reminds me, Wyn said they added a giant lab-grown diamond to the list of missing items."

He frowned. "That could help if they're building a massive drill or a really crappy cartoon laser. Most of the companies they stole from manufacture assorted electrical or mechanical parts. Did you ever find out what they swiped in New York robbery you failed to stop? It wasn't sharks, was it? If it was, I don't know if that'd be appalling or hilarious or both."

"Just rub in the failure part, why don't you?" Zita said. She wasn't certain why he was talking about sharks, but he at least seemed more animated.

Andy lifted his head and stared at the sky. "The New York theft is the standout, since they attempted to be discreet. Most of the others had a bunch of thugs with guns busting in, instead of a once-removed invisible person and a cat girl. We should contact Jerome and see if he'll research what was stolen."

She waved her hand. "No need. Hound said they grabbed a copy of some software that measures high energy outputs and regulates things."

"Things. Nice and specific there, Z." Andy scowled at his food.

"What crawled up your ass and died? He was vague, and I'm interpreting. General Aetherics didn't specify in any more detail than that," Zita said.

He stopped, hands poised in midair. "Wait. The software was from General Aetherics?"

"Yeah, so? I mentioned that before," she said around another mouthful.

He turned to face her. "I missed it. I mean, I heard it, but all I could think of was Brandi's patents for the sportswear. The equipment combined with the software they stole... I can't tell without a list, but they'd need to pour cement and rods, and none of the places I saw listed would have that."

"Wait, Zeus does have a cement mixer and a bunch of big steel rods." Memory tickled at her. "Remember when they busted out Halja? The trucks they used to block off part of the highway had those things, and they rolled them through the portal when they escaped."

Andy's moroseness disappeared, and he slapped his forehead. "I thought they took them because their guys were inside, but you're right! We don't have time to eat. Put away the food and teleport us to Wyn's house."

"Why?" The word was garbled around a massive bite of sandwich.

"I think I know what they're after."

She took another mouthful and packed away all but the half she'd almost finished. "What's that? Peace, love, and good will to men?"

"Balls."

"If nothing else, the number of heists they've done proves they have some of those." She snickered.

He snatched her food and tossed it into the cooler. "Let's go, funny girl."

"Hey!" Zita grabbed the container in one hand and Andy's arm with the other. "Fine. But I better get to finish my lunch soon."

Chapter Twenty-Three

Zita teleported both of them to Wyn's basement. As soon as the stacks of cardboard boxes and the altar appeared, Andy pulled free and ran up the wooden stairs, shouting for Wyn.

While only pausing long enough to pick up the paperback he'd knocked over—this time the shirtless man on the cover had wings and tattoos—and put it back on the wooden stool, she followed behind him, lifting the cooler so it wouldn't bang as she followed him, bemused.

"Andy?" Wyn's voice carried curiosity. "Is Zita here too? Of course, she is." Snuggled up on the rich crimson velvet of her dramatic sofa, Wyn had a stack of printouts around her, a blanket over her legs, and fragrant, steaming green tea in a minuscule floral cup. Her tablet glowed on the table nearby. She nudged one of her cats, distracting the animal from its previous occupation pulling strands of duct tape up from the back of the couch.

Andy paced the length of the living room in the small house, his color high and eyes bright.

"What are you two doing here? Didn't I get a text that you had somewhere to be today?" Her nose wrinkled as she noticed the old cooler Zita toted and the layer of red dust it had picked up in the desert. "Ah, and I see she brought a light snack."

Recognizing Wyn's cup as one she'd repaired after it had been broken in a home invasion in August, Zita smiled at her handiwork. *Not a crack visible and holding liquid. Score.* "Hey, Andy had a brain fart."

As she toyed with a chestnut curl, Wyn offered untidy stacks of papers to the others. "If you're free after all, you can assist me in determining Zeus' actual goal, since the Heart was either a diversion or a side project. I haven't figured out the pattern, but perhaps you will have more success. I'm baffled. The best I could do was determine that most of the companies they targeted manufacture electrical or mechanical parts."

Andy beamed at her. "No need, I think I know. In addition to the parts you noticed, they have cement, metal rods, and software they stole from General Aetherics. Wyn, what is General Aetherics known for?"

Excitement on her face, Wyn inhaled. "Self-Normalizing Aetheric Reactor Cores!" She pronounced the words as if swearing.

Her forehead wrinkled, and Zita tapped fingers on her thigh. "Zeus wants a SNARC ball? What, he ran out of batteries and decided to replace them with the priciest one possible? He doesn't have a city to power... I hope."

Andy ignored her questions. "General Aetherics keeps the technology close to their chests and even insists on using their own installers, or each one wouldn't command a billion-dollar price tag. Nobody else can build SNARC balls. It's still cheaper than nuclear overall since you don't have to install as many safety measures or requisition as much land. If we assume not all the robberies have been reported, the theft of that software, plus the diamond, the cement mixer, and the other heavy equipment, means they're building an aetheric power plant somewhere!"

Zita absently jogged in place while she thought. "Pues, it's great to know you could put all that together and get a solution, but... why would we want to stop them from building it?"

Wyn said, "If they have a plant but can't construct a SNARC ball, they have to steal one. Once a SNARC ball has been activated, you can't touch or move them, so they need a ball before it's used. Since General Aetherics doesn't release the location where they're built, they'd have to catch it in transit." Her milky skin turned paler still. "Rani... she took a job as an apprentice with General Aetherics as an installer. They offered her unbelievable money because of her electrical immunity. Since they're installed so infrequently, she's supposed to help with one—or watch, anyway—today in Brazil. Manaus, Brazil."

Zita blinked, then swore. "That's where we dropped the mercenaries. It's also the biggest city in the northern half of the country and a major tourist hub. Millions live there."

Andy leaned toward Wyn. "Do you know where and when they're installing it? And can I use your tablet?"

Wyn handed him the electronic device, but shook her head hard, sending curls bouncing over her shoulders. "No, she didn't say other than Manaus. General Aetherics is handing it off to the military somewhere."

As she used the cooler to do bicep curls, Zita thought aloud. "The Brazilian Air Force has a base in Manaus. They'd be set up to counter a strike by the local cartels so they wouldn't risk bringing it in by river, and they'd minimize land travel. They've got to be flying it in. Boats... Is the airport right by the Rio Negro?"

After he pulled up a map, Andy nodded, his lips pressed tight together as he bent over the tablet.

"I still don't get what they need a SNARC ball for, though," Zita said. "Based on the snooze-worthy speeches, Zeus is all about Zeus.

He won't be doing a charity project to light up poor neighborhoods."

Andy's fingers stilled, and he glanced at her. "That's a good question."

"Energy," Wyn said. "He and Zita must've had the same thought."

"Well, that's frightening," Andy said.

Wyn continued as if uninterrupted. "Halja tried to sacrifice multiple New York blocks to gather power using the Hades knife. SNARC balls are almost unlimited power. If they can figure out how to hook it up, they can blast through that temple Janus said Zeus was obsessed with and find whatever they're searching for. Perhaps the boy seeded truth with the fiction that sent us on the wild goose chase."

"Makes sense. Evil sense." Andy nodded. "Having failed with magic, they're now going for a scientific solution."

Zita lifted the cooler and held it up, her expression dubious. "I know I suggested it before, but that's a lot of effort to open a decrepit temple that might be empty. The SNARC ball is worth a small country, and the waiting list takes decades so they could get more money than anyone can spend in a lifetime if they steal it. They could sell it, retire, and use the other stuff to build a tricked-out mansion."

"What about the giant industrial diamond in this fantasy?" Andy asked.

She had to raise her hands in the air at that one. "Maybe Zeus wants to teach the escaped inmates a trade making flashy jewelry? Or he wants a disco ball for the mansion? It's more likely than a crazy plot to use a reactor to crack open an old temple for magic powers."

Andy laughed. "These are supervillains, though. It's not that farfetched for them, though I haven't ruled out sharks with lasers on their heads either. I double-checked the list. Everything is exactly what you need to set up a power generation system. Most of the equipment they stole measures output and temperatures. The cement is a common part of most nuclear reactors, and I can only assume SNARC ones are similar. The only outliers are six motorboats and a scientific prototype monitor."

Wyn managed a weak titter.

"Let's not forget the hundred criminals they pulled out of the Supermax prison," Zita offered.

"Shock troops." Andy shuddered.

Zita put down the cooler. "Stick the escapees in stolen boats as a diversion while the main force portals in and takes the SNARC ball."

His expression turning thoughtful, Andy said, "Do you think the ball can go through a portal?"

"Why not?" Zita tapped fingers on her leg.

He paused. "I guess it's the idea of putting something more powerful than a nuclear reactor through a portal powered by an unknown energy source... but it's inactive, so it should be fine, just a lump of electronics."

Wyn sipped her tea, her eyes contemplative. "That explains the boats, but what about the prototype equipment that measures dark energy? Does a SNARC ball produce that?"

Andy shook his head, but his face warmed with enthusiasm. "No, but Professor Farnswaggle posits that dark energy is related to our powers. While there's a lot of speculation on that subject, he has the only equations that mathematically support his theory. Nobody else has even come close to proving an alternative. It's not a popular theory, though, since many discount him as a crackpot, especially after the Stephen Hawking meatball fight. He can be a little out there, but most of his stuff is genius."

Wyn's eyebrows rose, and she tapped a finger on her rosebud lips. "So, he's like Tesla? The bulk of his work is solid, but he's known for the more outré ideas?"

Andy nodded. "Close, but Tesla was an experimentalist, and Farnswaggle is all about theoretical physics."

"Either way, where do we look for them? We can assume they're in Central or South America since Janus mentioned they were staying somewhere hot and jungle-y, and I heard howler monkeys twice when the portals were open. That doesn't narrow it down much." Zita paced the room, her steps rapid with her frustration.

His face intent, Andy said, "We'll have to catch them when they make the play for a SNARC ball. When's the one being installed today? That would explain the timeline—get us out of the way until they're done."

Wyn pursed her lips and shook her head. "Rani didn't say other than she was leaving yesterday and expected to install early this afternoon."

Zita glanced at the clock. "It's almost noon, we need to go now!"

Andy said, "Whether they steal it to sell or install, they'll need the special technicians too, not just the SNARC balls."

After a deep breath, Wyn went pale. "We should warn General Aetherics. They can cancel the install and keep Rani and her trainer safe. They're the only ones who'd know the real names of SNARC ball installers and where they all are." She set the papers on the table and leaned forward, catching both of the others in her gaze. "We also need reinforcements."

Realizing her chance to eat was slipping away, Zita retrieved the mangled sandwich before offering her opinions. "We can call Jerome and try Remus, though Remus was real uncomfortable with all the violence at the museum. No Aideen. That girl's loosely corked right now. If she loses control, Manaus is packed with people who could get hurt in a blaze and a jungle that'd be hard to put out. If we hit up Jerome for money, which I don't want to do, we could try to hire those mercenaries and see if they want a piece of their former employers. We'd also have to hope that detective I called last time to contact them actually has their number."

Her voice tight, Wyn said, "Not the mercenaries. They're creepy and could be working for Zeus. We don't want to warn them that we're onto their real plan. I agree on calling in the boys and leaving out Aideen."

"Agreed, especially on the creepy," Andy said.

"You might have a point. Freelance—besides being both incredibly competent and hot—did say they don't do freebies." Zita concentrated on eating, rationalizing that the last thing she needed was to sneak somewhere and have her rumbling stomach give her away.

"Did he say freebie?" Andy asked. "For some reason, I feel more masculine if he used that word."

Her forehead wrinkling, Zita gazed at him. "No, he didn't. I was paraphrasing."

He sighed. "Figures. We need to hurry, too, or we'll miss them."

"Pues. Well, I'll teleport to the National Mall and see if Jerome and Remus want in. While I'm there, I'll try to call and warn the Brazilians and General Aetherics, if one of you can find the phone numbers. You want to throw on your costumes and come with?" Since she had her special sportswear on already under her hiking clothes, Zita shucked all the extraneous clothing, put the phone in her pocket, and wolfed down the last bite.

Wyn rose, walked over to her purse, and rummaged in it. She pulled out a mask and tossed it to Zita. "If you don't mind, I'll wait here. I need to powder my nose and retrieve insect repellant from where I put it away for the spring."

Even knowing the probable answer, Zita had to ask in the vain hope her friend would be reasonable. "Sure you don't want to stay here? The Brazilians might not believe we're on their side. Almost everyone will have guns. You don't hide well, and bullets hurt you."

Setting aside her bag, Wyn narrowed her eyes. "That's exactly why you need me there. I can persuade them and heal the injured, which, let's not forget, might include you since bullets injure you too. Not to mention, if they bring Tiffany, I can undo her spells. That said, I'm content to cower in a corner somewhere for most of it."

"Don't even ask me to stay home, Z." Andy crossed his arms over his chest. "Though, I should eat and get something from home, so could we do a side trip?"

"Sure," Zita said amiably. "Wyn, find your bug spray. I'll teleport us all to Andy's so he can eat, you can pee—"

Wyn winced.

Undeterred, Zita continued, "And I'll go make my calls. When I get back, we'll meet up with Jerome. You're good flying, right, Thunderbirdseed Pervert?"

His tone gruff, Andy said, "Wingspan will do. I'll have lunch while you're making your calls. If I have to fly, I don't want to eat a tanker or city bus on the way."

"You'll love the lunch in the cooler," Zita said. "Nice and hearty."

Wyn smiled, and her mental voice spoke in the depths of Zita's mind. *He didn't argue being the bird this time.*

Plus, that was almost a joke, such a good sign, Zita sent in agreement.

After a short search for Wyn's spray, they teleported to the familiar confines of Andy's basement apartment.

***

When Zita returned to Andy's a few minutes later, a cloud of eucalyptus scent assaulted her as soon as the room formed around her. Coughing, she waved a hand in front of her face. "You two good to go?"

Wyn tossed a lock of hair over her shoulder and touched her amulet. Her illusory form sprang up. "Ready. And hopefully bug-proof."

"I can tell. The mosquitoes can probably smell you from Brazil," Zita said, wrinkling her nose.

On the opposite end of the room from Wyn, Andy nodded, a mask over his eyes and empty plastic wrap in his hands. "I have to agree. That's the first time I've felt like a koala when eating a pot roast sandwich." He tossed the trash into the can.

As Andy moved to her side, he shook out something blue and fastened it on himself. A long piece of fabric flapped behind him as he caught up to the two women.

Zita frowned. "Why do you have a sheet tied around your neck? And did I hear Velcro?"

"It's easier to concentrate in a cape. Besides, capes are cool, like superhero bling. Velcro means I can take it off, so I don't get sucked into a jet engine or something." Andy crossed his arms over his chest and stuck his chin out.

"That'd be tough on the plane," Zita murmured. "And since when have you ever cared about bling?"

Wyn giggled. "Is this because of the 'Vigilante Party' video?"

He glanced away. "I'd rather the cameras not get a good look at me."

"That's a yes, then. Mano, if they're ogling at your culo, they won't be staring at your face. Your usual jeans are so baggy that people wouldn't connect you and Wingspan anyway." Zita's mind raced. *If he's determined to wear one, perhaps we could make it useful.* She came up with a few attractive options. "We could use the cape as a rope or a protective blanket for when he has to jump somewhere with you, Muse. Does it have pockets?"

Andy rolled his eyes. "No, and even if they did, I wouldn't carry your snacks."

"It was just a thought," Zita protested.

Wyn's laughter rang out. "Very well, though I still think it's sad that you feel the need to wear one. Where would you even find one of those, anyway?"

"Ordered a bunch online, next day delivery. It's close to Halloween, so everyone's got them," he admitted. "Had them delivered to Chevalier, then picked them up when Zita was out buying a new cell phone."

Try as she might, Zita couldn't imagine Jerome in a cape. "What, he's going to wear one too? He didn't even bother with a mask last time, just big sunglasses."

Andy coughed. "His actual words were that he wouldn't be caught dead in one. He said if it wasn't illegal or smelly, he didn't care what I ordered, and I should rent a mailbox next time." He shoved a corner of his cape over his shoulder. It crept back as he moved. "Takes getting used to, though," he mumbled. When he twisted to push it into place again, he tripped.

Catching him before he could smack into the ground, Zita steadied him until he pulled away. "Other than that caveat, he's a good friend to have." She mused, "I'd totally not care what was in the boxes because I'm full of trust and shit."

Andy grinned, a hint of his old self peeking through. "Especially that second one."

She gave his arm a light punch. "Vámonos, funny man. Remus didn't answer his phone, and I'm certain both the company and the Brazilian military blew me off. On the bright side, Jerome is coming. He also said while we were in Brazil, Miguel got DMS to put Janus' family into the Witness Protection program. Apparently, his little sister refused to go without taking Janus' favorite stuffed toy with her own."

Both of her friends smiled.

"Thank goodness. That poor boy has suffered enough under the threat of Zeus' retribution against them."

Andy nodded. "That's great. Let's get to the airstrip. Wyn, you driving?"

Zita cleared her throat. "Since it'd take Jerome too long to reach the airstrip we used before, we're meeting up at Rock Creek Park by the zoo, not by his house."

The smile dropped from Andy's face. "I thought you wouldn't teleport—oh, no. DC is a no-fly zone."

Wyn gave a high-pitched cough into her fist. "Technically, we're not flying an aircraft, so we're not in violation. Also, the decrepit airstrip we've been taking off from? That's in the restricted zone too."

Andy moaned and buried his face in his hands. "I thought it was far enough out... Jerome better be ready."

"Be strong, mano. I have faith you can outrun a couple of stodgy military jets if need be. They haven't even gotten close the last few times, and we don't have time to wait. It's almost noon. If they're installing in the afternoon, they could land any minute now. Besides, it's not like we're buzzing the White House, though we could if you wanted." Zita patted his shoulder.

He grunted. "Sometimes I hate my life. Let's go."

Chapter Twenty-Four

From the broad, feathered back of Andy's bird form, Zita took a moment to admire the view on the all-too-short flight to Brazil. *How high up are we? We're way above the clouds, but the air and pressure are the same as at sea level.* The stars were brilliant overhead, a multitude of shining lights and pastel swirls against the pitch-black sky. At whatever the altitude was, it seemed as if nothing was between them and the dark expanse of space and galaxies.

Jerome and Wyn also tilted their faces upward, at least until Andy sloped into a gradual descent toward Manaus, cutting down through the thick cloud cover over the city. While Wyn had her standard blond club-goer illusion as a disguise, Jerome had bowed to the inevitable and upgraded his outfit to a real costume. While he still wore the navy version of the tight sportswear that would work with his powers, the letter "C" now began at the top of his impressive pectorals and stopped above his tapered waist, echoed in the ornate belt buckle. A saber hung in a hand-tooled leather scabbard from the matching belt, and a three-quarters mask replaced the sunglasses he had worn before.

Zita padded out to peer over the edge of Andy's wing. As if someone had thrown a bustling metropolis down in the middle of the jungle, the unnatural and geometric shapes of Manaus shoved hard against the organic borders of the surrounding rainforest and the river, with tendrils breaking through in spots. As they neared the ground, she saw the famous confluence where the dark mirror of the Rio Negro and the silty brown Solimões met to flow side-by-side as the Amazon. "We want near where the rivers join," she said aloud.

Andy banked and drew closer.

After a partial shift to eagle, Zita's long-distance vision sharpened. She ignored the soft rustle of feathers on her head and neck, pleased she had the sight enhancement she wanted. *At least the Manaus Air Force base is obvious. This is the right area, and it's far less busy than the other one with all the traffic and the swarms of baggage trucks.* "There, see those four hangars in a row with helicopters parked in the circles out front? They're south of the swimming pool. Unless they're renting the airport out for private parties, that jet has to be it, since it screams corporate, not military. Wingspan, squawk or something when we're low enough for me go scope more out. They might've noticed us, so remember not to eat anyone and try to let the others off close by."

The high-pitched chirrup that Andy made in response sounded like a giant-sized, newly hatched chick that had just been insulted.

"Dude, not trying to diss you, but you asked me to remind you eating people is bad. I'm keeping my word here." She continued studying the base. Individual cars were now visible. Small hordes of soldiers swarmed every chokepoint on the roads leading in. On the river, military boats blocked both directions. Other fortifications resolved themselves as her friend drew closer.

"Are those tanks? Did they actually listen to me? That'd be a first." Zita stared, and as she watched, the tank shuddered, and a massive flash of light emerged from the muzzle, followed by a cloud of dust and smoke. The corresponding explosion of a car approaching the base was echoed a moment later by a second near the other major road blockade as it belched forth its own attack. Down by the river, a third tank aimed at the tributary that came closest to the airstrip. On the Rio Negro, the naval barricade exchanged gunfire with a group of motorboats.

Behind her, Jerome stirred. "They have a tank? For real? Are we even necessary if they have those? I doubt it was your warning. It's probably standard military procedure when an item worth billions flies into your airport." His tone grew thoughtful as he joined her in peering over the wing, though he stayed closer to the main body of the bird. "Do you think I'd need a special license to drive a tank in DC? Parking would be so much easier."

Andy flew lower still, and she could make out each person. By a hangar, Brazilian soldiers fanned out into a large circle around the corporate jet. One clump of soldiers formed a smaller oval around a pair of officers (or the most decorated grunts she'd ever seen). Multiple squads patrolled the immediate area. All the uniforms had automatic firearms on their back with the ease of people who'd worn the weapon many times.

Zita summarized for the others. "Oye, the Brazilian military ain't playing. They got three tanks and started without us. Since fighting's already underway, the SNARC ball must be on the base, probably in that fancy jet, so let's hurry. I'm still trying to decide if attacking the checkpoints is meant to draw off some of the military forces or be a distraction or both. They have no reason to use the roads when they can just portal in."

Rotors spun up from rest on two helicopters parked outside the hangars, and more worrisome, an armored vehicle emerged from one of the other hangers, missiles bristling on an attachment at the rear.

She ran a hand over downy feathers covering her head. "And now they see us, so they're mobilizing helicopters and a souped-up armored car with eight million rockets on it. Be careful, mano."

He chirped.

Zita readied herself at the edge of Andy's wing and glanced over her shoulder at Jerome and Wyn. "We're good on the crappy plan? Chevalier, you get Muse to safety, so she can talk the Brazilians into not shooting us. You go fight once she's set somewhere and not a target. Muse, you be all diplomatic and healer-y and kick magic culo. Wingspan, get down and punch the bad guys back to sanity when you get the chance. We can't handle all the people attacking, so focus on the ones with powers. Trust the Brazilian military to stomp the regular thugs."

Wyn took a deep breath, visibly steeling herself. "I am as prepared as I can be," she said. Party line rose, bringing her warm presence and Andy's more distant one to Zita's mind. Even though it was invisible beneath her illusion, she wore a small earpiece that matched Jerome's so they could all communicate. As shapeshifters, neither Andy nor Zita had received one for fear of accidentally destroying it.

"Uh-huh." Jerome's reply was distracted as he focused on the helicopters, which had taken off and angled to meet them.

As Zita became a gavião-real and flew from Andy's back, she heard Jerome asking from behind her, "Are those missile launchers next to the giant machine guns on the copters?"

She soared down, searching for the telltale glimmer of a portal when she heard a whoosh and a high-pitched whine. Whirling, she noticed two streaks of light detach from the helicopters and hit Andy, once in the stomach and again on the wings. When she spun back around to a normal flying position, a piercing screech escaped her. *Andy! Wyn! Is everyone okay?*

Sounding confused, Wyn replied, *Did something happen? They missed.*

No, they didn't. They scored direct hits on Andy. When Zita risked another glance, she saw no evidence of the attacks, save for the dissipating smoke.

To Zita's surprise, Andy's bird form spoke over the connection, his voice echoing and resonating, eerily like multiple people speaking in perfect unison. *We are fine. I won't risk the village below getting hit.*

Studying his feathers, Zita could see no damage, though the helicopters hovered near him as if they were foxes outside a henhouse. *Anything over a million people is more city than not, but I'm glad you're good. The ground rockets will be their next gambit, I bet.*

Andy released a series of high-pitched sounds that resembled giggles, if said laughter included a roll of thunder. *Let them.*

After a moment of silence, Wyn's mental voice was prim. *Jerome says he's impressed that you didn't even flinch, Big Bird. Zita, can you ask them to not fire on us, so we can land? I'll mediate once I'm down and perhaps stop them from wasting their energies after that. We'd all enjoy returning home tonight.*

I'll do what I can, but you know me. Zita turned and flew toward the corporate jet.

Wyn's reply held both fond overtones and resignation. *We'll expect more trouble, then.*

Haters. Zita sniffed.

Between two of the hangars and a large outbuilding, the sleek plane would've been hidden from anyone on the ground, unless they approached from the runway. A truck nestled under one wing. As she watched, a vaguely familiar man placed traffic cones around it, then handed off a set of rolling stairs to the passenger area to someone else. Another man attached something to the plane. An honor guard maintained defensive positions in a loose circle. Pushback tugs pulled fighter planes to the edge of the runway, leaving them in a position guaranteed to allow a faster takeoff. Between those, the cordons on both land and river, and the armored anti-aircraft weapon, most of the approaches to the hanger were blocked if attackers used a vehicle. Irregular bursts of gunfire broke the air, punctuated by the deep, guttural booms of larger weapons, likely the tanks. Despite the noise of combat, Zita could still hear the unending frog and bird chorus that characterized the Amazon.

The military has it handled for large groups, but a few people on foot could sneak in if they hid in the local flora and the stacked piles of crap. Zita landed behind a tiny, red-roofed outbuilding, east of the hangars.

From her new position, she could see one of the more decorated officers and the squad led by the oldest sergeant (or at least the guy with the whitest hair), bunched up between the hangar that hid the plane from her sight and the helicopters to the southwest. A blue Jeep was parked north of her on the side closest to the city. Thick rainforest of mixed palms and other trees was to her east. With relief, she noted crates that could provide temporary hiding places for when her diplomacy failed. *If my diplomacy fails. I've been practicing so I might be able to talk them into not shooting us. Weirder things have happened.*

After shifting to Arca, she wrinkled her nose at the expected, but nasty, scents of coarse, hot asphalt and the tang of airplane exhaust up close. The stink drowned out the far more pleasant smells of the nearby jungle. Before she could do more than straighten her mask, her pocket rang. She jerked back and withdrew into the shadows thrown by a crate. A frown creased her brow at the name on the display. *Andy? How can you be calling me? I didn't think we'd get service here on these.* Glancing up, she still saw his shape circling.

As she opened the phone, Zita said, "Hello?"

"Nice ride if you can get it." Trixie's voice greeted her without preamble. "Boss man said to tell you the portal's at three twenty from the Jeep near you."

Zita glanced around, calculating the angle. Her eyes scanned the area, but she couldn't decide where the mercenaries were. *Freelance would have to be on a building or tree, and I didn't see him on a hangar. He could be on top of that military hospital or all the way in the city, but that's close to a mile away.* She whispered, "Gracias. Are you guys on our side this time?"

What? Andy's still flying. Wyn asked.

A dinosaur didn't eat Andy's phone like we thought. Trixie has it and is babbling on it now.

Trixie complained, "You know, this could have gone smoother if you'd shared info with us. No worries, even when Ms. Halja pays her bills, we won't be working for her again. We have firm rules against repeat contracts with customers who attempt to kill us and loot our stuff. Strangely, it's more common than you'd think. It's so hard to find good employers these days."

Zita paused, drawn in despite herself. "I'd assume it happens pretty often."

You're being facetious, right? You never check your phone. Why would you answer it in the middle of all this? Wyn sent.

"Well, you've got a nasty, suspicious, and surprisingly realistic take. Boss also has us abiding by boring rules about no freebies, no collateral damage, no participation in invasions, and no working for criminal causes. Our most important rule is no white chocolate. It's the real stuff only because life is too short for fake chocolate. We have standards. That was my contribution." Trixie sniffed.

While she had been distracted, the military had been busy. Four men, including the grizzled sergeant, burst out from around the corner and jogged toward Zita's hiding place, barking orders in Portuguese for her to drop to the ground and spread her limbs.

"This isn't a good time, but we didn't know whose side you would be on. If you can, get them not to kill us." Zita raised her arms in the air, keeping the hand with the phone closer to her ear, and tried to appear harmless. *No need to shoot the nice masked lady with the sweet muscle definition trespassing on your base while it is under attack.* She grimaced. *Now that I think about it, I hope that being fun-sized, obviously unarmed in this pseudo-Spandex stuff, and whatever makes people not take me seriously will help me for once.*

"Sorry, out of my bailiwick! This was amusing. Chat soon!" Trixie hung up.

"Down, now!" the men ordered.

All of them held their guns right, she was gratified to see. Zita got to her knees but posed her back foot to let her dodge or spring up if needed. *If this is how I will go out, I'm happier to get it from someone who knows what they're doing and not just some idiot who can't even handle his gun.*

What? Wyn squawked.

Not now. Busy talking so you can land without getting shot up. Using her thumb, Zita flipped her phone shut. "Hey, guys," she said in Portuguese. "I'm glad you're here. Listen, I called in a warning earlier about people attacking? My friends and I came to back you up against anyone with powers, even brought a healer for the injured. The bad guys are using a portal to bring in troops. It's in position three twenty o'clock from that Jeep over there. You need to get men there, especially if you've got other metahumans on your side. By our count, the bad guys are throwing hundred criminals at you plus whatever super-powered thugs they had before that. I don't know what you've taken down at the checkpoints, but they're on your base." Keeping her arms raised, she angled them toward the supposed portal location.

The sergeant hefted a radio from his belt and spoke low into it. A three-man squad emerged from the other side of the hangar and advanced past the Jeep, melting into the jungle.

Carajo, they would've hit me from behind if I didn't cooperate. They really aren't playing, but at least I'm still alive. Zita inhaled and offered a weak smile.

A screech broke out from behind the car and gunfire erupted.

Keeping close together, the three men who had walked by earlier raced back in a retreat. "Monsters!" someone shouted in Portuguese, his attention never lifting from whatever he was blowing rounds at. Of his companions, one supported another, who bled from a leg injury.

"That sounds like the people I was trying to warn you about. Are they man-shaped and made of mud and stank?" she asked, her words trailing off as a familiar jaguar-sized dinosaur leapt on top of the Jeep.

Two more came around the sides, hissing. Although they retained their speed, these were almost clumsy in contrast to the living ones. The creature on the top teetered on his perch. Their scales were a sickly gray-brown vomit color, and white covered their eyes, as if spider webs obscured them. A couple were missing an eye, and the third had a hole in the center of its forehead, in addition to neat clusters of bullet holes in the chests and a growing collection of wounds that made their muscles shiver as the creatures continued forward, snapping their deadly teeth. Oddly, they all wore small collars. From her position near the ground, she noticed a brown gem inset in each collar, invisible until the dinosaurs lifted their heads to charge at the soldiers.

Remembering the ugly brown magic amulet that had animated a statue in New York, she shouted, "Shoot the gem in the collar!"

Two of the uniforms by her turned and fired at the creatures.

"Stay down," warned the sergeant. "We don't have time for you." He withdrew a handgun and aimed, his men falling into a tight formation around him.

The bodies of the dinosaurs jerked as more bullets tore into their flesh, but the injuries seemed only to slow them.

Before she could do more, the head of the monster on top of the Jeep exploded in fire and flying brains, then she heard a rifle bullet. The headless creature jumped from its post but landed feet away from anyone, where it rolled on the ground before careening upright and clawing the air.

The remaining monsters on either side of the vehicle darted around the headless one to attack individuals. Another dinosaur dashed out from the trees and headed north.

After forming back-to-back pairs, the Brazilian soldiers kept them off everyone in the small group.

Zita started to get up and help, but the men focused on her waved their guns in her face in warning. As she fumed, she opened her phone and punched the call back button. She got up to a crouching position so she could spring out of the way. *They're not stopping the dinosaurs, but they're at least keeping them from killing anyone.*

His gun in a tight grip, the sergeant shot the gem on the collar, and the headless one dropped.

"Phone duty is so boring," Trixie announced as she answered. "For a job that sounds so much like lazy, liaising is a lot of work and leaves so little chance to borrow a tank for a joy ride. On the bright side, my hat has fruit on it, so at least I can have a snack—"

In English, Zita cut her off. "Whatever. Is Freelance on zombie dinosaur duty?"

"Yes, but we're not cleared to enter the base until the dinosaurs appear to be escaping, so we're sidelined. Should be nine of the scaly lovelies running around unless they held some in reserve. Did your team have any luck with them?"

Her brain whirled at the count and Zita recalled offhand comments back when they'd been with the mercenaries. "You guys killed the dinosaurs the first time, before we caught up with you. That's why the passageway smelled like dead things and how you know how many, isn't it? Tell Freelance to shoot the collars. They've got a brown gem under their chins like that statue that came to life in New York."

The continuing gunfire made her ears ring, and Zita could barely hear Trixie, even when she cupped her hand around the phone.

"Hunting dinosaurs is not illegal," Trixie said, her voice prissy. "Even if it were, how could we know they would return in a Night of the Living Dinodead?"

Another volley obscured anything else she said.

"What?" Zita yelled.

"I don't have the right costume for this conversation!" Trixie shouted back. The rest of her comments drowned beneath the gunfire.

"I don't care what you're wearing!" Zita raised her voice. She made a small movement to get up. This time the soldiers were too busy focusing on the animals to notice.

The closest soldier reloaded his weapon, and his gaze flickered to her, but his focus returned to the undead creatures.

"Boss says get their..." Another barrage ate the rest of Trixie's words.

After wrapping both arms around her head to muffle the noise, Zita tried again. "What? Get their collars off?" *I could do that, but it'd be a real challenge to avoid getting shot or ripped apart.*

Trixie shouted again. "Chins up! Get their chins up!" She hung up again.

Swearing, Zita flipped her phone shut and got to her feet. "I'm told there are nine dinosaur zombies. That's three. Where are the others? They're on your base already, you need to put more people on the SNARC ball!"

The guy holding a weapon on her growled, and she slowed her movements.

Zita studied the sergeant, who was barking orders into his radio and had taken up a shooting position. "I'll distract the dinosaurs before they get your men. You decide what that says about me." While she spoke, she ran through forms in her head, settling on a gavião-real again and launched herself into the air. *This should be both maneuverable and big enough to get attention from those things. If it doesn't work, I'll try a brown wooly monkey... in case they only respond to humanoid shapes... and use that pará tree to keep away from them.*

The soldier who had been guarding her took a potshot, but she banked in time to avoid it.

Zita dove at the monsters, making as if she would strike them, then used the speed gained on the dive to swoop up before their teeth could catch her.

Both of the remaining dinosaurs lifted their heads to snap at her.

As a rifle shot sounded, the creature on the left stopped when its collar snapped. Before that corpse hit the ground, another round took out the other creature's gem, and it fell.

Zita landed on top of the stack of crates and changed back to Arca, Portuguese tumbling out of her mouth as fast as she could manage. "Metahumans are going after the SNARC ball. I've got a magic healer, two fighters and me here to help you, plus someone hired mercenaries to handle the undead dinosaurs. The giant bird your helicopters are wasting missiles on is on your side. They sent me down here to tell you we're allies, so work with us here. You've stalled the invaders at the checkpoints, but they're using powers to show up on your grounds and to let those things loose." She had to shout to be audible over the now-constant sound of jet engines and helicopter propellers.

The sergeant grumbled something into his radio. It squawked back.

"This is above my pay grade, but I'll take you to an officer to discuss it," he said. "I'm sure you understand."

Once all the soldiers confirmed the creatures were dead by shooting them several more times, they turned, scanning the area for more enemies. To Zita's dismay, most of the guns were now aimed at her.

She gestured at her body and continued talking in Portuguese, her words tumbling out fast. "If you can't tell, I'm unarmed. I don't even have shoes on." She raised a foot in the air and wiggled her toes at them.

A few of the gun barrels lowered, but most stayed on her.

The sergeant put the safety on his handgun but frowned at her. "Get down here if you want us to trust you."

Zita held up both hands. "All I ask is you at least take me to someone with brains enough to be sensible and power enough to keep my friends and I from getting hurt. I'll have my flying friends land, if you can keep people from shooting them. Or me. I'm much more helpful alive."

He eyed her, then his eyes cut to the dead dinosaurs. "Empty your pockets," he said.

She blinked and tapped one pocket.

"Slowly!"

Moving her hand at turtle speed, she patted the same spot again. "My phone. You saw me make calls on it. I'd rather not toss and break it since you want me to talk to my friends."

When he nodded, she reached for her other pocket. With a wary eye on the young soldier closest to her, the one whose cheeks were flushed with color and a shadow of stubble, she pulled out a bag of homemade protein bars.

"What are those?" The twitchy guy barked out the question.

"Snacks. I get hungry." At the sergeant's gesture, she forlornly dropped it on the ground and descended from the crates.

Wyn's mental voice cut in. *Can we land yet? They're shooting machine guns at us, and I don't know how long we can stay up here before Andy gets angry.*

The eerie multi-part chorus of Andy's bird form spoke again, disapproval strong in its tones. *They are disrespectful. I will land by the plane houses.*

Correction, angrier, Wyn corrected herself.

I got faith he won't eat them. Zita cleared her throat. "Call off the air support on the big bird. He'll come down somewhere by the hangars. We don't have time for this to drag on."

Her pocket rang, but she ignored it.

With a wave of the sergeant's hand, three soldiers surrounded Zita. "The rest of you, spread out and watch for invaders or more of those things." He brought the radio up to his lips and spoke into it, moving far enough away that Zita couldn't make out the words. When he finished speaking, he waited.

Zita tried to relax, be still, and wait too, but her whole body vibrated with impatience when the radio buzzed again with an answer minutes later. Her phone had stopped ringing by then.

After a brief exchange with whomever was on the radio, the sergeant nodded and turned to her. "Do your friends need to taxi to a landing?"

After she shook her head, he said, "Tell them to land in the empty parking lot by the hospital." He made a gesture, and his men herded her to the west, toward the front of the closest hangar.

Machinery hummed, and a plane engine revved somewhere nearby.

Careful to raise her phone to her ear and repeat his words aloud, Zita sent the military's request to her friends. *Maybe they're taking me with them to check it out? The hospital is halfway between one checkpoint and the hangars, and as far away from the corporate jet as it can get and still be on the base.* When she finished, she slipped the device back into her pocket. She went along with the uniformed men, arms loose at her sides and her weight balanced in case more of the undead dinosaurs burst from cover. The only gunfire she heard, however, was distant enough to make her suspect the main fighting had not yet reached this far.

Andy did not acknowledge or reply.

After a glance upward to where her friends circled low enough for her to see the lightning tracing Andy's form, the sergeant spoke again into his radio.

The plane and helicopters overhead peeled off above, providing a welcome surcease from the relentless pounding noise of their engines, leaving only one or two audible nearby. Zita and the squad with her turned the corner.

At the sight of her and her escort, the officer waiting there bristled in an uncanny resemblance to a javelina, down to the short white hairs standing upright on his head, cranky expression, and an impressive underbite. Another eight men in dress uniforms surrounded him, though their alert appraisal, firearms at ready, and suspicious expressions resembled the professional scrutiny of bodyguards rather than a personal dislike of her. After a second, she saw an additional member of the group, a slim fellow with the face and litheness of a weasel, poke his long nose out from around the guards to survey her. She decided he had to be an aide, as his only weapons were multiple phones, a radio, and a tablet.

I think we're setting down now. Have you gotten them to agree not to shoot us? Nerves sang in Wyn's voice.

Zita huffed. *They're talking about it. Give me a break, I'm trying to be all inoffensive and non-threatening here.*

Her words seemed to placate Wyn. *That would be a challenge for you.*

The sergeant saluted. His words, as expected, were in Portuguese. "Brigadeiro Silva, sir! We brought the intruder, a bird shapeshifter. She claims her friends on the large bird are here to help against other metahumans."

I am so much more than that, but fine. Andy will be happy to know the video hasn't made it this far south yet. Zita tried for a charming smile but feared the result was a goofy teeth-baring expression.

One soldier in the squad whispered something.

With a glance at the man, the sergeant spoke, distaste in his voice. "I'm told they're Americans who star in some Internet video called the 'Vigilante Party.'" His pronunciation of the English title held the careful cadences of someone who didn't speak the language.

Or perhaps it has. Now to be awesomely polite and charming. Zita spread her arms and addressed the officer in Portuguese. "Brigadeiro Silva, my friends and I came to help. We request that your men please refrain from shooting us while we do so." She tried smiling again.

The narrow fellow with the weasel face tapped on his tablet.

When the brigadier stared at her from under his heavy brows, he said, "We do not need the aid of the United States to handle this! You can tell your keepers that if they want to send a metahuman to us, they can negotiate with our government. We'll see about allowing one or two of you."

"Oh, we're not with the American government. In fact, we spend as little time as possible with them." Her smile felt tight, as if she had glued it on.

Familiar bouncy music came from the tablet, and the aide hastily shut it off. He murmured in the brigadier's ear.

The officer purpled. "You're just attention-seeking glory hounds, not even a real agent like Caroline? Assign two men to escort her to holding until this mess is over."

Words spilled out of Zita's mouth before she could remember to be diplomatic. "What, are you stupid? You're wasting missiles and ammo trying to shoot down my friend when your actual enemies are already in the base, touching your billion-dollar stuff, and probably running off with it while we speak."

All eyes on the surrounding guards went wide, and the sergeant sighed.

"That's it, I'm done with her. Lock her up! We'll decide charges later," the brigadier said, slashing the air with his hand. His aide nodded and tapped the tablet again.

"Yes, sir," the sergeant barked. He pointed to two men, then to her.

The designated soldiers swung their guns to their backs, then each took one of her arms. They marched north, along the length of the hangar and away from the portal.

"Seriously? Are you turning down the opportunity to have the giant bird as your ally?" Zita pulled, but the men had reach on her and firm grips. While she waited for an opening to escape, she tried joking to relax them... and herself. "You know, if it weren't for all the uniformed guys standing around, the expectation of demented thugs with powers showing up, and undead dinosaurs, this'd be almost like a walk in a bad city neighborhood."

The soldiers surrounding her did not visibly appreciate her attempt at humor and dragged her forward.

She harrumphed and kept pace. *I think I convinced them we're nuisances, not menaces to shoot on sight, but you'll have to talk to them, Wyn. They think they're going to jail me until this mess is over and will probably upgrade us to enemies once I escape.*

How... reassuring and not unexpected. Wyn's mental voice sighed. *Very well. We'll be nearby and try again. Do you need help?*

Zita shrugged, making one of her captors give her an odd expression. *No, I'm fine. I just don't know where Zeus' people are or if they've already got the SNARC ball. The mercenaries tipped me off where the portal was, but they might've moved on from there.*

Party line shut off for a few seconds, then returned. Wyn's mental voice sounded steadier. *Rani's on the General Aetherics plane still with the SNARC ball, and while alarmed, she hasn't seen them yet. They're refueling to take off and go somewhere safer.*

Zita couldn't stop herself from asking the question. *Are you spying on your girlfriend or does she know about your telepathy?*

Rani doesn't know. I'm just checking on her safety, Wyn corrected.

Zita's pocket rang again as she was force-marched wherever they were going. "You guys mind if I get that?"

They ignored her.

She sighed and continued watching for an opportunity to escape without harming her guards. Percussive gunfire, punctuated by the heavy tank discharges, continued to pound in the distance. Somewhere closer, she thought she heard a familiar shout, though a plane's engines roared to life and drowned it out. *Jerome?*

A pony-sized gray form exploded from the bushes and attacked.

One man holding her whipped his M4 carbine out and fired at it, slowing the undead creature. The other shouted but kept hold of her arm as he brought his own weapon around.

Zita became the big dinosaur she'd been before, but this time gave herself neon stripes in the brilliant green, yellow, and blue of the Brazilian flag.

One soldier dangled from her arm, gaping at her and the undead. He tried to bring up his weapon.

As Zita leaned forward to let him down without hurting him, the zombie dinosaur turned and struck at the dangling man. Without thinking, she snapped at it, biting its head off. When she realized what she had in her mouth, horror and disgust shot through her, and she spat it out.

Now headless, the monster clawed at the air.

Backing away, Zita returned to Arca's form, spat again, and wiped her mouth with her arm, wishing she could get rid of the nasty, spoiled meat taste. "Shoot the necklace!" she said in Portuguese.

Both soldiers unloaded on the neck of the creature, pulping it and the ugly brown gem in the collar.

The dinosaur dropped.

While they waited to see if it would rise again, she shifted to a greyhound and raced toward the portal. Zita heard the men cry out for her to stop, but she rounded the corner and darted into the dense jungle next to the base before they could fire. When she almost stumbled over the exposed roots of a tree, she switched to a jaguar. At a glimpse of incandescence, she slunk through the jungle toward it.

Voices had her lowering her belly, so it grazed the forest floor, and she crept forward. Her nose wrinkled as the breeze brought a whiff of either manure heated by the sun or a nearby hoatzin bird, but she caught a handful of a familiar scents, including Jerome's. *I hope he's smart enough to be sneaking up too, though floundering up might be a more accurate term with his woodcraft.*

In a tight group, Tiffany, Zeus, Pretorius, and a handful of their men huddled in the jungle. To her surprise, the only visible weaponry consisted of handguns and Pretorius' giant overcompensation knife. Surrounded by the others, a sullen Janus kicked at a small metal plate on the ground. Each person had dull brown gems duct-taped to their arms, except Tiffany, who held one in her hand. Zeus and Tiffany must've been arguing given the way they faced each other, bodies stiff with anger.

Zeus scowled, his nostrils flared and gaze flinty. "If you'd done your job and kept them away until tomorrow, we wouldn't have to deal with the vigilantes, and the mercenaries wouldn't have injured Surt. He'll be pouting for months at missing a chance to burn Manaus' city center, and now we have to change my perfect plan."

Burn the city center? That's only about five miles from here, and heavily populated, Zita thought with horror.

"He should've been more careful," Tiffany snapped. "And we didn't know the gem was swapped until we got back to the compound. At least we got the dinosaurs."

Pretorius raised both hands placatingly, his voice even and measured. "We have the local cartel and the Jessup criminals as distractions too. Let's concentrate and get on with it."

Focusing on the party line, Zita sent, *I found the bad guys. They're in the jungle east of the hangar with the helicopter circles in front of it.* She licked her lips and grimaced. *If you've got breath mints, I could really use them.*

When the brown gems dissolved into dust, Tiffany sniffed. "The last of the dinosaurs are down. I'm done here." She snapped her fingers at Janus.

His movements mechanical, the teen opened a portal. Big, black and hairy, Garm sat on the other side, his ears perking. The wolf's tail shivered, as if he'd wanted to wag and repressed it, but not quite in time.

Tossing her hair over her shoulder, Tiffany said, "Don't take too long. I'll have the minions prepare cells for the technicians." She stepped through.

Janus closed the portal behind her, then retreated to molesting the sign on the ground.

A man in a military uniform pushed through the trees. After a moment, Zita recognized Brazilian Taco Thug. "Plane's taxiing to take off. They refused additional guards on board," he said in his accented English.

With an evil grin, Zeus cuffed Janus. "Now, boy, before they catch on about that care package we slipped on there."

Nearby, Brazilian Taco Thug smirked and adjusted the collar of his uniform, accepting a spare CZ-75 handgun from one of the others. He verified it was loaded and nodded to the man next to him as he holstered it. A second later, Zita recognized American Taco Thug.

After shooting a resentful glare at Zeus, Janus ripped open a new portal.

Between the incandescent lime green edges of the opening, Zita saw a narrow room filled with equipment, strapped down or bolted into place.

Keeping his gaze averted from Zeus, Pretorius gave his men their orders. "Remember, no guns, no blasting, and no big powers on the plane until the portal home opens. You've all got strength and the ability to take a punch, so go take them out. Go!" After the two taco-loving thugs and six other armed guards went through first, Pretorius brought up the rear.

As Zeus began to follow, Jerome burst from the bushes and tackled him, the force of the impact sending both men through.

One guard remained behind with Janus.

His shoulders slumping, the teen picked up the metal plate on the ground, another sign with a series of emojis on it.

Zita pounced on the guard, knocking him to the ground. As she sat on top of him, she became Arca again. Cupping her hands, she slapped both of the guard's ears, then ripped his gun out of his hands.

He howled and curled up as well as he could.

She knocked him out with the butt of his firearm, even if he couldn't hear her after her assault on his eardrums. As she emptied the weapon, scattering .40 caliber cartridges everywhere, she said, "Janus! Your family's in the Witness Protection Program! This is your chance to run for it."

His thin body jerked as if she'd hit him. "No."

"Yes. Your sister insisted on taking some stuffed toy of yours with her if that sounds right. Just let me go through before you run off. If you want, I'll tell Zeus the military shot and killed you, too." She tossed the empty firearm aside after clearing the chamber.

A smile spread across his face, and Janus let the plate drop from his hands. "Go. And yes, I'd love to die."

"Bye, dead guy." With a wink at the kid, she dove through the portal.

Chapter Twenty-Five

Right after Zita stepped through the portal, it closed behind her. The plane vibrated, and engines roared as it left the ground. At her feet was another one of the emoji plates. Before she could do any more than get a brief impression of a freight room, with shelves and racks against the walls and an open area in the middle, a man slammed the door shut to the rest of the aircraft. The sounds of fighting from the other side cut off.

After shifting to an anaconda, Zita slithered under a rack, twining herself around the base. In the enclosed space, the metallic tang of blood and the pungent chemical gunsmoke hung in the air.

As he turned and descended the short flight of steps, the guard she recognized American Taco Thug said, "Well, you took enough time, Janus. Zeus said to smack you good for taking so long, but you're to stay here with me until they kill that guy." He swore and staggered as the plane tilted upward and pressure increased, his head swiveling from side to side as he searched for Janus.

With a glance at the sealed interior door, American Taco Thug stalked toward the small metal plate. "Kid? I won't hit you that hard."

Her coils soundless on the textured floor, Zita slithered behind him and switched to a gorilla. She wrapped her beefy arms around him and held him in the same chokehold she'd used before.

Again, he struggled but fell unconscious as she counted. *It's always nice when the same trick works a second time.*

She disarmed him, dropped him, and detached the belt from a leather seat. Tying him up with that, she grabbed a fancy hand towel from a bag labeled laundry and shoved it in his mouth. After securing him to the wall using conveniently placed clamps, she took a moment to examine their surroundings.

Zita had been in planes before, but she'd never been in one like this. Part of the main body of the plane had been customized to allow an oversized freight area, although it was not packed full so much as obsessively organized. It sported racks and an extra-wide door with a lever painted in cautionary red and black. The resemblance to a normal cargo hold ended there. Every visible inch of wall had obvious armor plating, and the door to the interior appeared to be solid metal, ringed with the cushioned seals found in vacuum-sealed doors. Each item being shipped—whether unidentifiable electronics or other pieces more commonplace, like a pair of toolboxes, nestled in custom-made shelving with heavy-duty straps and webbing. An industrial jetpack took up an entire wall, turned sideways and secured with custom clamps. Even the laundry bag and first aid kit had their own niches. The velvet-lined cradle for a box the size of a microwave sat empty; she assumed that was where the SNARC balls usually went. The only section that seemed standard was a small corner shelf where a pair of suitcases had been knocked to the ground.

Half-buried under the rolling luggage, an unconscious man bled, droplets leaking out of tailored body armor and staining the cool gray fabric with red. The logo on his chest read General Aetherics, so she assumed he'd been a victim of the initial assault on the plane.

Angry growling came from behind her. With a hasty return to Arca's form, she wiggled her fingers over her shoulder at American

Taco Thug and ran to the injured man instead. A swift examination revealed a nasty gouge on his head and a bullet wound, so she did her best to remove the luggage and hastily bandage him with the limited supplies in the first aid kit.

Her prisoner snarled.

"Be good, and I won't breathe on you. My breath is all kinds of deadly nasty right now," Zita told American Taco Thug as she picked up his gun and headed for the interior door. Before she left, she opened one toolbox and took out a long, heavy wrench. After she dumped all the ammunition into the toolbox, including the cartridge in the chamber, she tossed the weapon behind a rack.

On her walk to the door, her toes bumped an object lying on the floor, a simple metal plate with the embossed emoji of two men and a globe. Zita slapped her forehead, realizing what they were. *Janus opens portals to these. He doesn't have to view the entire area if he focuses on something he knows, like uniformly made signs, and a decent idea of the flooring. I should try that trick to see if I can use it, though we'll want to remove this from the plane when we go. Good thing we took the one from the cave, so they can't get more dinosaurs if they get Janus back somehow.*

Yanking her attention away from practice scenarios, she focused on opening the interior door a crack. As she did so, Zita heard and felt the impact of the landing gear folding up. Angry voices and the sounds of combat echoed from ahead. *Jerome might need my help.*

Even with her limited view, the passenger section screamed money even more than the freight hold had. A narrow corridor led to an open area where she glimpsed leather loveseats in a creamy color and men moving around. Her filthy bare feet sank into the lush pile of a carpet in that ubiquitous industrial cream color with flecks of black, a shade meant to hide dirt by always seeming a bit dingy. The polished gray interior wall held three closed doors, and

Arca's face peeked back at her from it. She eased back until she could no longer see herself. Smudges from people bumping against the surface marred the reflective wall in several sections, including one where cracks radiated out from what must've been a powerful hit. Blood decorated the breaks in stark contrast to the subdued color scheme, a deadly spatter pattern that ended with another man in General Aetherics uniform. Unlike the one in the freight hold, he was definitely dead, his eyes staring, blank and accusing. The miasma of recent death surrounded him.

Dios be with you, hombre. With a deep breath, she swallowed her nausea and darted through the first door in the hall, wrench raised like a club.

The air tasted of leather and fear. A queen-sized bed took up almost all the floor space, but it had a creamy leather headboard, matching cabinets, and a tiny bathroom she didn't explore. When movement caught her eye, she tiptoed closer. A man in flight attendant's clothing cowered beneath the bed, his eyes wide as he stared at her. Motion in the bathroom suggested someone else hid behind the pitiful cover there as well. *Smart people to hide.*

After checking to ensure she remained unseen, she closed the bedroom behind her and slipped through the next door. Her hip bumped into a wheeled snack cart that rested just inside, and she nudged it aside as she scanned the new compartment. Four padded chairs faced each other around a glossy gray table polished to match the walls. Glassware shone under display lights in a mirrored wet bar that stood among wall-to-ceiling storage cabinets, all of which had locks. Spotting a tin of mints on the cart, she popped a couple in her mouth to remove the awful taste of the undead dinosaur from her mouth. She dropped the candy next to an array of soda cans.

With another check to ensure the hallway was clear, she snuck to the next door and found a tiny powder room. At that point, she suspected every padded surface on the plane, including the toilets in either of the lavatories, had been upholstered in the finest buttery leather she had ever touched. *How many herds of cows died to decorate this place? Marble on an airplane? Rich people are weird.*

Steeling herself, Zita exited and peeked into the last passenger area. Although more spacious than any of the other rooms, this area was only twelve feet across. It had four wide recliners in pairs, each with its own small table and television screen. Springs, padding, and small bits were all that remained of one seat.

In the aisle between the seats, Zeus and Pretorius, both bruised and disheveled, punched a strangely compliant Jerome, who spat out blood and glared. The muscles on her friend's arms stood out, as if he had tensed to free himself or strike them, but he remained still instead.

Two of Zeus' men held his shoulders. Another pair stood a few feet away, their backs to her. All but Jerome showed injuries, and as she peered around the corner, she caught sight of two other thugs, either dead or unconscious on the floor.

As Zita watched, Pretorius stepped back, stumbling over the unmoving body of one.

The reason for Jerome's acceptance of the beating became clear when a guard near Zita moved an inch. A teary-eyed Rani and an equally unhappy silver-haired man stood in a corner as far away from the combatants as possible, with a guard standing behind them, his gun out and pointed at Rani's back. Both captives wore tailored coveralls or jumpsuits with a discreet logo on the left breast, in the same gray hue that permeated the plane's decor. A microwave-sized black case sat on a loveseat nearest them. *Found Rani, her technician teacher, and the SNARC ball. They're keeping Jerome from fighting back by threatening a hostage.* At the last minute, she avoided mentioning that the person threatened was Rani.

Worry threaded Wyn's mental voice. *We've got to save them.*

Working on it. After becoming a lizard with scales the colors of the carpet, Zita darted along the floor behind the guards until she reached the toes of the man with the gun on Rani.

Exploding up into Arca, Zita knocked the man's gun aside before he could shoot Wyn's girlfriend.

The gun fired, making her ears sting, and Jerome cried out.

"Watch the guns!" Pretorius shouted.

The guard she'd attacked tried to push her away.

"Gun's off the hostage. Go, Chevalier!" Rotating her hips to increase the force of the hit, Zita drove the heel of her hand into the guard's nose before he could bring his weapon around on her. When his head snapped back with her strike, she slid behind him and grabbed his head with both hands, making him arch backward toward her. After using her leverage to pressure his body to twist until he fell, she hammered an elbow into his back.

Scuffling and groaning assured her that Jerome had taken action.

Zita felt someone behind her before she could strike again. Switching to a fluffy black cat, she scooted between the legs of her new attacker. The punch meant for her missed and made a hole in the glossy wall instead.

Changing back to Arca, she used a recliner as support and kicked with both feet at the new guy. It wasn't as effective as she'd hoped, but it sent him reeling back enough to trip over her previous victim.

Right, they're all bigger, stronger, and tougher than me. Why would this be easy? Zita vaulted over a chunk of the broken chair and slid into the hallway, retrieving the wrench. *Well, this will help with the reach issue.*

Zeus shouted, "Two of you kill that annoying rat, and the rest get this idiot under control!"

As he struck Pretorius and sent the mercenary flying across the room, breaking another chair, Jerome panted. "He must mean you, Arca. I'm too pretty to be a rodent." He had a fierce smile on his face as he slammed one of Zeus' men against a wall.

Brazilian Taco Thug, the half-healed injuries of their last fight still visible on his face, joined her second attacker and closed in on her. The new guy pulled his gun.

Her whole body tensed. Zita waggled a finger at the two men aiming at her and lied with no guilt for once. "The Brazilians shot the head off the boy who does portals, so you'll want to be very careful with those."

"Bloody—" Pretorius swore and struggled out of the ruins of the chair. "No guns!"

Direct fight? Ni madre, this place isn't big enough for two fights and the hostages. Bypassing the bathroom, Zita ran into the room with the table and chairs, hopping over the cart and spinning it to slam it into her pursuers. The one in front stumbled, but Brazilian Taco Thug kept coming. He lunged. "Well, time for some—"

She vaulted over the snacks and kicked him in the face, still hanging onto her wrench.

He grabbed for her, but she had already landed on his buddy's back, knocking the new guy down again.

Brazilian Taco Thug swung a nasty uppercut at her.

After shifting to a capuchin monkey, she scampered under him, dragging her wrench. Behind him, she changed to Arca and brought the tool up between his legs. Hard.

He let out a high-pitched keening cry, doubling over.

The other guy got up and rushed her.

Zita stepped aside at the last minute, hitting him in the back with her wrench and sending him face-first into the wet bar. Glasses shattered in crazy cacophony and crashed around them. As she came up behind him, Zita switched to a gorilla, grabbed his shirt, spun him, and threw him into Brazilian Taco Thug.

Both men collapsed in a tangle of limbs and an angry shout.

Tears streaming down his face, Brazilian Taco Thug struggled to get out from under his unconscious friend.

Reclaiming her Arca form, she kicked the side of his knee and heard a popping sound.

He screamed and crumpled.

After opening an oversized wall cabinet, Zita seized him and his buddy and stuffed them both into a compartment. She slid the lock in place. "Stay put. My foot does less damage than the wrench!"

"What's going on in there!" a man's voice demanded from outside the room. "Can't you handle one weakling?"

Skittering over to and crouching in front of the door, Zita turned into a king cobra.

Zeus yanked it open. One eye was swelling, and his lip was already puffy enough to distort his words. He held the SNARC ball case in a hand. "What the—"

Zita rose, flaring her hood and hissing.

His eyes widened. Zeus did the unexpectedly sensible thing and pulled the door shut with a bang.

With a sick feeling, Zita slithered to the side in time to avoid the barrage of bullets that came through the door where she'd been. When the gunfire fell silent, she shifted to Arca and checked for something to use. While none of the bombardment had hit her, the table slanted like a drunk cow, and the snack cart had been destroyed, scattering food all over the floor and hiding her wrench. When she heard him reloading, she grabbed a can of soda by her foot and shook it up.

He kicked open the door, his gun pointed down where a snake would be.

Aiming the drink at his face, Zita made a hissing sound as she pulled back the tab. Soda fountained out in a high-pressured rocket of sugar and artificial orange into his eyes.

"I'm blind!" he screamed, falling backward. "The cobra got me!" Panicked, he scrubbed at his face with one hand and reached out to the wall with the other.

Electricity shot out of an outlet and coiled around his fist. The plane engines hiccupped.

"Stop! You'll bring down the plane!" Zita shouted. Spotting her wrench, she seized it.

The lights went out, and the engines fell silent. Rushing wind howled outside, and the floor shivered beneath her feet as if they'd hit a series of irregularly placed speed bumps. Scorched plastic and leather scents accompanied a rhythmic thud and an angry male voice from elsewhere on the plane.

Hefting her tool, Zita whacked it against Zeus' knee, followed by his head as hard as she could.

He dropped and didn't move, the lightning in his hand sinking back into his skin.

The damage was done, however, as the aircraft tilted to the side. An ominous thrum reverberated from the SNARC ball case.

"Pinche pendejo," Zita swore at him as she ran to where she'd left Jerome and Pretorius. "J—Chevalier, we got problems!"

As he kneeled on top of Pretorius, Jerome methodically ground the mercenary's face into the carpet. "Who you calling boy now?" he panted, ripping the belt off a nearby seat with one hand. Bodies, most of which continued breathing, littered the floor. Jerome, Rani, and the silver-haired man were the only others standing.

"Can you fly a plane, Chevalier?" Zita said. "Zeus is down, though I don't know for how long. Also, I'm pretty certain Pretorius has enough carpet up his nose now."

The silver-haired man spoke before Jerome could. "I could, but you'd have to get the power back first."

Anger still marring his features, Jerome snorted. "I don't think he does," he said, but he stopped mashing the other man's face into the carpet.

"You need to turn off the SNARC ball. I think it's on," Zita told Rani and her trainer.

The older installer blanched. "If it's been activated, there's no fix for it."

Beneath Jerome, Pretorius bucked, trying to throw the large man off, but even his enhanced strength couldn't counter Jerome's weight and grip. His free arm waved in the air, making it hard for Jerome to tie him.

Swearing internally, Zita reached for the party line, relieved to feel it. *Guys, Zeus sucked the electricity out of the plane, and now it's going down! I don't know if I can save everyone, and I think the SNARC ball might be activated.*

Rani's eyes were wide, and she gulped. "I can't fix a plane engine. I mean, I could fix a loose wire, but I don't know how to repair the power to an aircraft. Or SNARC balls yet. This is my second day, and all I did yesterday was paperwork."

Oh, Goddess, no! Wyn sent.

His tone grim, Andy said only, *On my way.*

Zita heaved a relieved sigh. As she started to tell the others, out of the corner of her eye, she saw Pretorius' free hand creep to the huge blade strapped to his belt. "Watch out for his knife!" She lunged to stop him, knowing she'd be too late.

Even with the awkward grip that was all his position would allow, the mercenary sank the blade into Jerome's leg.

Jerome shouted in pain and pulled out the knife. Reversing it, he struck Pretorius in the back of the head with the hilt.

The mercenary went limp.

Once his prisoner was no longer struggling, Jerome trussed him up, and Zita found another seat belt so he could be hog-tied.

Something banged, and she and Jerome both turned to face the corridor. The door to the freight hold was ajar, and Zeus' form no longer decorated in the hall. The SNARC ball holder sat open and empty.

"Wingspan will handle the imminent death by plane crash issue." Zita waved the wrench toward the hold. "You want to see if we can stop Zeus from doing any more damage?"

Jerome cracked his knuckles. "With pleasure. Try not to get me shot this time."

"No promises," she said.

Chapter Twenty-Six

Jerome shoved open the freight hold door and entered first, Zita a few feet behind.

A large piece of equipment hit him, sending chunks of circuit board flying in a no doubt expensive cloud of debris.

"Oye, I hope that wasn't the SNARC ball," she said. The disparity in their sizes kept any of the shards from hitting her much smaller form.

The big man swore and stomped farther in.

"It wasn't." Zeus held a long rod in one hand and an ornate metal sphere in the other. Light pulsated inside the ball, snaking over the intricate green and gold surface in an uncertain rhythm and glinting through the many openings. He swung the rod at Jerome's head.

Jerome caught it and forced it backward toward Zeus.

The entire plane shuddered and leveled out with a rough jerk. Both men fell to the floor. Zeus released the SNARC ball in an attempt to stay upright. He failed when his injured knee gave out.

Zita seized a nearby rack and clung to it.

The sound of the wind was gone. Except for their breathing and the slow rumble of the SNARC ball rolling toward the front of the aircraft, the plane was now silent.

Zita ran to the window and she peered outside. Massive avian claws gripped the visible wing. "Wingspan's got the plane!" she called out to the others. "The falling to our death crisis is over."

Jerome stood.

Zeus was faster, and he snatched the SNARC ball. "Convenient for me." He jerked the lever on the outside door and leapt out.

When the unconscious General Aetherics man slid toward the opening, Zita, now an orangutan, hooked her feet around a shelf base and grabbed him with her long arms, letting the wrench go. She drew him closer until he was cradled in her arms, relieved the poor guy still breathed.

Jerome had lunged for Zeus and missed but kept himself from falling out. He slammed the door shut. "Well, shit. Now what?"

*None of my flying shapes, even the pterosaur, are strong enough to get the ball away from Zeus. My more powerful shapes can't fly...*Through the window, Zita eyed the glowing object being carried away and then stared around the freight area. She transformed to Arca. "I need to deal with that. Hold my bud and watch this."

"What?" Jerome stared at her.

"Bad joke, apparently." She shoved the unconscious man at him.

His arms full of the injured guy, Jerome must've been too surprised to argue, as she expelled them from the cargo area and shut the door behind them. For good measure, she bolted it. Turning to the rows of strapped down gear, she mumbled to herself. "With luck, General Aetherics will forgive some equipment loss for the sake of saving their precious SNARC ball from exploding over a city or being stolen by jumped-up thugs with powers." Zita eyed the thug she'd tied up earlier. "Stay put and you'll be fine."

American Taco Thug cringed in the webbing.

Zita rushed over to the construction jetpack and undid most of the clamps, her mind racing through possible animals. *I'll need to be the size of an elephant to wear it, since it's meant to lift industrial equipment, not people. Hands will be necessary to use that remote control strapped to it and to hold the SNARC ball.* Shifting to a giant sloth, she hit her head on the ceiling and hunched down to back into the jetpack, swiping open the last clamp. She aimed her body at the doorway and mashed buttons until the pack roared to life. It rose unsteadily, banging her against the ceiling again. She pounded on the controls, swerving from side to side before she found the setting she needed.

This is such a bad idea, Zita thought, adrenaline singing in her veins.

Wariness laced Wyn's mental voice. *Zita, what are you doing?*

Zita couldn't repress the sensual thrill running through her and felt her lips stretching wide in what had to be a feral grin. *I'm saving the city from an exploding SNARC ball.* Crouching on her powerful hindquarters, she jumped toward the door as the pack kicked on. Even with the massive size and weight of her prehistoric form, the pack still rose faster than she had expected.

Much faster.

Maybe I should've opened the exit first. Zita crashed into the ceiling again with a thud that jarred her whole body and slammed the pack against the roof. Mentally cursing, she contorted herself, trying to alter her angle of ascent. Just in case, she jerked her head down below the top of the pack.

This time it smashed against the closed door to the outside. Pain shot through her. Once she stabilized her precarious hold, she hung there, reaching for the door lever again.

This was much smoother in my head, she thought. After repeated small bumps against the door, she realized the best way to control it was through lower body movements. She kicked out again and again, inching toward the lever. At last, her long, dark claws hooked the handle and pulled.

With an ear-wracking screech as the edge of the door scraped the side of a fuel tank on the pack, she was out. Zita dropped through calm air for a few weightless seconds. Once she cleared the plane, wind hit her in a rush, and the pack faltered for a moment before it stabilized. Her speed rose, and the jetpack engines settled into a steady roar without walls to hold her back. A vibration so low as to be more felt than heard, the SNARC ball called to her.

From behind her, she heard a startled chirp. Without glancing back, she raised a hand and waved at Andy.

Kicking her legs in midair to circle until she could see Zeus, she found him doing a slow, graceful flight toward the bright colors of Manaus. In his hands, the SNARC ball flared irregularly.

I doubt it's supposed to pulse like it'll throw up any second. She kicked out to bring up the rear of the jetpack and zoomed toward him. A hoot escaped as her flight leveled out, the jetpack stabilizing, and the wind whistling and shoving against her face. *I realize all those people are counting on me, but this is fun.*

Although the pack seemed fast, they had almost cleared the city before she caught up with Zeus. In a stolen glance back toward the base, she spied Andy's bird form flapping to a landing. A corner of her mind relaxed, knowing the plane was safe.

Her flight was not soundless, and Zeus twisted around to see who approached. After changing to an awkward one-handed grip on the SNARC ball, he made a dramatic throwing gesture at her. Nothing happened.

Zita hooted and barreled into him, sending him spinning as she hooked her claws around him. Her fur tingled where the front of her body contacted the mesh of the SNARC ball.

He punched her with superhuman strength, but her thick hide and bulky form absorbed most of it, so it was painful, but not bone-crushing as it otherwise might have been.

Gauging the hit so she wouldn't behead him with her heavy black claws, she swiped at his arm, opening three long, deep gashes in it.

With a howl, Zeus threw a wild haymaker at her again. He hit and dented one of her fuel tanks with a sickening crack. He screamed and yanked back his hand.

Tendrils of electricity shivered over her jetpack and reached toward the man.

Zita yanked on the SNARC ball, just as Zeus got his injured hand to crackle with lightning.

She twisted to avoid the strike to her chest.

His glowing hand hit the pack again. Zeus winced and made a choked sound at the impact.

Lightning raced over the metal and into her giant form.

Pain chased through her. All of her muscles stiffened, and her curved sloth claws froze around the SNARC ball. A yelp, resembling a high-pitched quack, escaped her.

The world went dark.

Zita struggled to consciousness in a haze, aware of the increasing rush of air past her. *I'm falling. I should make sure I stick the landing this time.*

Andy called her name, and she cracked her eyes open enough to see him leap up and past her as a human.

When she forced herself to assess her situation, she realized the pack was silent, save for the occasional sputter that slowed her descent and sent her sideways. The ground rushed up toward her. Despite the few moments she'd been unconscious, her claws had remained hooked in the SNARC ball, and it throbbed in her arms. Her eyes widened. *Carajo.*

Panic on his face, Andy shot past her again, this time on the right.

Zita tried to focus her scattered thoughts enough to teleport to safety. It was harder than it should have been.

Just as she accepted the inevitability of her teleportation getting out or falling to her death and dooming Manaus, Andy fell past her, and she spotted his face hardening. His eyes filled with a silver glow. He stretched out his arms and improbably crossed the ten feet between them to catch her. His body slammed hers with the impact of hitting a wall at a full run.

"Gah," Sloth-Zita bleated.

Cradling her much-larger and unwieldy form in an awkward hold, Andy slowed and hovered in midair, then began a slow, controlled descent.

Andy landed at the Brazilian Air Force Base and set Zita and her burden down by the hangar. The General Aetherics jet was there already, along with her friends, the elderly installer, and the sergeant's squad of men. He grinned. "I flew. As a man."

By that time, her mind functioned normally again. She shifted to Arca and set down the SNARC ball. "Way to go, mano... and great save."

"Thanks." He beamed, his eyes once again their familiar warm chocolate color.

Reaching them first, Jerome clapped Zita and then Andy on the shoulder. "Glad you're alive, and nothing exploded."

As he rushed to the SNARC ball, the silver-haired installer exclaimed in English, "It's been partially activated. We need to get it into place and fast before it finishes too many cycles and roots permanently in this hangar or explodes with nowhere to put the generated energy." He wrung his hands.

Rani and Wyn trailed behind him

Zita swore, translated the installer's comments into Portuguese for the military nearby, then added her own addendum. "Who knows where this thing needs to go?"

The sergeant stepped forward. "I should arrest you, but I know where the power plant is. If you'd all consider yourself arrested while we sort this out, that'd be great."

"Fine. We'll take you, the installers, and a few men you pick to the factory. Wingspan here can have you there in less than a minute, and they'll get this thing installed. I'll ask one favor in return." Zita ran a hand over the heavy mass of her hair. Turning to her friends, she repeated the plan for the ones who didn't speak Portuguese. Wyn, of course, was following with bright eyes.

The sergeant squinted at her and tilted his head. "I can't promise not to arrest you. The brigadier was clear about that, though I'm not certain we could stop you if you broke away."

Zita held his gaze and nodded, understanding the unspoken message. "Did you guys find a boy creeping around?"

His forehead wrinkled, and the sergeant shook his head. "Not that I heard."

She relaxed. "Good. If anyone asks, you haven't seen one, or he might've been killed in the crossfire, take your pick. Zeus had a kid that he forced to work for him by holding his family hostage, and he might think the boy's dead now."

After an intense study of the floor, the sergeant's eyes softened, and he nodded. "Do what I can."

Having listened to the English translations with an intent expression, even if his gaze was glued to the SNARC ball, the silver-haired installer said, "Excuse me, but we can't do the install. The jetpack you broke was necessary to hold the containment cage in midair while connections are wired up, and the facility plans don't show space for a crane to replace it or the right kind of platform. It'll take hours to get a new pack with the right software here." He made a gesture toward the damaged pack she had dropped on the pavement.

Now that Zita no longer wore it, she could see the gouged, battered remains. It had also lost a few pieces when it had hit the ground and those littered the area surrounding it. *I don't think that's getting fixed anytime soon.* Her mind raced, and her leg jiggled as she switched to English. "Wingspan can fly, and he's more than strong enough to hold something up. Bet he can stand in for the jetpack."

Andy blinked. "I... I guess so."

The silver-haired installer stared at him and nodded. "This'll be the quick and dirty version of the install. Someone retrieve our gear from the plane. Rani, call headquarters to see if I can get a manufacturing tech on the phone to help with a tricky bit. Normally we don't ignite it until it's in place, so I want to run some shortcuts by them. Nobody put their fingers in the cage. Grip it with flat hands on the outside since it's partially active. General Aetherics takes no responsibility for anyone killed, maimed, or disappeared who puts their fingers through the mesh." He gave Zita a long glance as if he wanted to say more... but stopped.

She translated the instructions into Portuguese for the soldiers. The ones who had been about to pick up the ball blanched.

Rani nodded and dug out a satellite phone from her bag

Wyn squeezed Rani's shoulder and stepped away.

"Great, we'll get going then. We'll all stay together so the sergeant can keep an eye on us." Zita smiled brightly, then repeated herself in Portuguese.

We're ditching them as soon as the installers don't need us, right? Andy sent.

Órale, you better believe it. Zita's phone buzzed, indicating a new text. "What now?" She pulled it out and checked it.

Andy grinned, his eyes sparkling. "Let's transform... and roll out."

Jerome snickered.

The text was from Andy's stolen phone. "We're even now. No more free samples."

Zita laughed.

Epilogue

Two nights later, Zita and Andy were again in the desert, though this time she'd chosen an old picnic area for the relatively flat ground, lack of cacti, and number of interesting surfaces to use while sparring. For Andy's peace of mind, Wyn sat in a nearby folding chair, complete with an umbrella over her head, working on her tablet. All of them wore their disguises, in case Andy's bird form had been tracked.

Ducking a kick, Zita danced around Andy and struck his shoulder with an elbow before spinning away. She grinned. "Point, me!"

"By the way, Zita, I finished reviewing your resumé and the job application letter you wanted to send to your district head," Wyn said. "I emailed them back to you. You'll find I added a short paragraph to the letter noting that the sudden decrease in need for your services coincided with you having the coma illness. You'll want to leave that in. Andy, I'm starting yours next." She gave a little smile.

"You're the expert. Thanks, Wyn." Zita said, dodging an elbow strike and kicking Andy's knee. "So, you're applying for some jobs? Two points." She fell into her ginga, orbiting around him.

He exhaled as he stepped backward and turned to face her. "Yeah. Things still suck, but it's getting better."

"Since it's stopped raining over your house every day, I was hoping so. Awesome. Órale, mano. Are you thinking what I'm thinking?" She grinned and feinted back.

Wyn's answer was dry. "I really doubt it."

"I think so, Brain, but where would we find rocket ships that have already been stocked with enough Cheetos to satisfy you?" Andy said, ignoring her distraction. "Sorry, that just slipped out. Of course, you don't get the reference, or you would have used 'pondering' instead of 'thinking.'"

Despite her pleasure that he was again making jokes, even if they were incomprehensible, Zita rolled her eyes. "No, weirdo, I've been considering the whole wasting our powers thing."

Andy fell back, slipping into a more defensive stance. His face grew tight and pinched, and his shoulders hunched.

She continued to circle in a steady ginga. "I've been reacting to stuff, but not seeking trouble. It's hard to break the habits of a lifetime. But, you're right, that's a waste and not my style. I don't sit around and wait for things to come to me."

The beginning of a smile peeked out on his face. "You're going to be more active?"

"Is that possible?" Wyn said, glancing up from her screen.

Andy explained, keeping his attention on Zita. "As a superhero, instead of a private citizen only stepping in when the stakes are personal or directly in her path."

Zita grumbled. "I still think patrolling is stupid, especially since we can only cover so much on our own, but I came up with a compromise. Computers aren't my thing, but you two are good at them. If we let Jerome in on it, he'd be even better. Anyway, you guys keep your ears to the Internet—do whatever it is you've been doing to cull news on supers and stuff that needs doing—and if you find something we can fix, call me. If I hear anything any other way, I'll call you, even if it doesn't impact us directly."

A full smile burst out on her friend's face, and he crowed, lowering his hands. "You're offering to be my sidekick!"

Wyn sniffed. "No, she wanted to be my minion," she said, eyes twinkling. "Isn't that right?"

Zita snorted, but a grin escaped. "As if. I was offering to be a team, but if you insist, you can be my sidekicks. We won't replace the cops, but if they're outclassed, or if DMS or someone else abuses metahumans, we step in. Keep the power balance even. And if there's anything else we can help with, like a jackknifed semi blocking the Beltway or a natural disaster, we do it." She kept moving.

Amusement danced on Wyn's face. "I'm not the best suited for field work, so increasing our investigations prior to such misadventures suits me. I'm in."

Andy nodded. "That works for me... all of me."

"Great. Unless something else bigger comes up before then, our first task will be to find Sobek. He can't keep running around torturing people and stalking my family. The cops believe he's dead somewhere based on the blood loss, but I don't." Zita danced closer to Andy.

He spoke before a frowning Wyn could. "Agreed. That can be a longer-term project since most of it will be research."

Wyn nibbled on her lower lip, but his words seemed to mollify her. "Very well. Speaking of family, how is Quentin?"

Zita made a face. "He's talking to me, but just barely. We're driving to Mamá's for a week around Thanksgiving, and we'll patch it up on the way there. If I can't get through to him, I'll call in the big guns."

"What guns are those?" Wyn said. "Wasn't one of Miguel's complaints that you lacked firearms?"

Andy caught on faster. "She'll set her mother on him."

Zita grinned. "Absolutely. By the way, do you want to rethink the whole name thing, mano? You turn into a giant glowy bird, and it rains when you're cranky and not controlling your powers. If anyone should use the name Thunderbird, it's you."

He straightened and rubbed the back of his neck. "No, I'm Wingspan. I can handle all of him." Somehow, he seemed as if he meant more than just the name.

Zita beamed. Her eyes moistened. *Stupid desert dust.* "No hay bronca. Just asking. One more thing..."

"What?" He turned toward her, his body relaxed.

"Think fast!" She laughed, hopping into a rapid martelo de negativa kick that connected with his chin and bounced off without damaging him. She snuck in a lower kick as she catapulted away, resuming her ginga. "Three points! The soda will be mine," she called out.

He flinched and slipped back into his judo mode. "Cheater," he accused.

"We do this thing for real with the bad guys, mano, so you need to handle a little distraction," Zita said. "You want to try again? I wouldn't mind upsizing that drink."

He grinned.

"Guess the sparring's back on," Wyn said, settling down and tapping her screen.

***

Later that night, Zita shook out wings warm from the long flight and shifted to a monkey. She peered down at the lonely cairn and scanned the area.

Assured she was alone other than the wildlife, she scampered down the massive tree and stopped at the edge of the rock. It hadn't been the custom of her friend's people to indicate a gravesite with rocks, but she had refused to leave it unmarked.

Shapeshifting to her natural form, she verified again that she was alone before addressing the grave in Portuguese. "Hey. I'm sorry I couldn't save you. I still wish I could've. Now... I've got more options than before. I've got friends, too... So maybe nobody else will have to sacrifice themselves like you did. I'll do better next time. Thanks for everything."

The voices of the animals stilled.

She looked up and around. "Someone's coming, so I'm done." Zita teleported.

The only thing she left behind was a delicate orchid in the vibrant hues her long-dead friend had loved.